Sheikh's

FORBIDDEN QUEEN

Sheikh's
COLLECTION

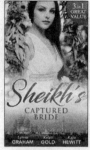

May 2017

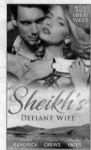

June 2017

July 2017

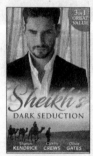

August 2017

September 2017

October 2017

Sheikh's

FORBIDDEN QUEEN

Lynne
GRAHAM

Lynn Raye
HARRIS

Carol
MARINELLI

MILLS &
BOON

Published in Great Britain 2017
By Mills & Boon, an imprint of HarperCollins*Publishers*
1 London Bridge Street, London, SE1 9GF

SHEIKH'S FORBIDDEN QUEEN © 2017 Harlequin Books S.A.

Zarif's Convenient Queen © 2014 Lynne Graham
Gambling with the Crown © 2014 Lynn Raye Harris
More Precious than a Crown © 2014 Carol Marinelli

ISBN: 978-0-263-93113-6

09-0917

Our policy is to use papers that are natural, renewable and recyclable products and made from wood grown in sustainable forests.
The logging and manufacturing processes conform to the legal environmental regulations of the country of origin.

Printed and bound in Spain
by CPI, Barcelona

ZARIF'S CONVENIENT QUEEN

LYNNE GRAHAM

Lynne Graham was born in Northern Ireland and has been a keen romance reader since her teens. She is very happily married, with an understanding husband who has learned to cook since she started to write! Her five children keep her on her toes. She has a very large dog, which knocks everything over, a very small terrier, which barks a lot, and two cats. When time allows, Lynne is a keen gardener.

CHAPTER ONE

ZARIF WAS BORED. The opulent attractions of his creamy-skinned and highly sophisticated mistress had palled. Right at that minute she was posed on the bed, entranced by her reflection in the mirror as she adjusted the glowing ruby pendant now encircling her throat. 'It's so beautiful,' she told him, wide-eyed with avid admiration. 'Thank you. You've been very generous.'

Lena was shrewd. She knew the pendant was a goodbye gift and that she would vacate his lavish Dubai apartment without argument and cruise off in search of another rich man. Sex, Zarif had discovered, was no big deal. He preferred amateurs to professionals in the bedroom but had few illusions about the morals of the women he took as lovers. He gave them the means to enjoy the good things in life while they gave him a necessary outlet for his highly charged sex drive. Such women understood the need for discretion and appreciated that approaching the media would be a seriously unwise career move.

And Zarif had more need than most men to conserve his public image. At the age of twelve he had become the King of Vashir with his uncle acting as Regent until Zarif attained his majority. He was the latest in a long line of feudal rulers to occupy the Emerald throne in the old palace. Vashir was oil-rich, but very conservative, and whenever Zarif tried to drag the country into the twenty-first century the old guard on his advisory council—composed of twelve tribal sheiks all over the age of sixty—panicked and pleaded with him to reconsider.

'Are you getting married?' Lena shot the question at him abruptly and then gave him a discomfited glance. 'Sorry, I know it's none of my business.'

'Not yet but soon,' Zarif responded flatly, straightening the tailored jacket of his business suit and turning on his heel.

'Good luck,' Lena breathed. 'She'll be a lucky woman.'

Zarif was still frowning as he entered the lift. When it came to marriage or children, luck didn't feature much in his family tree. Historically the love matches had fared as badly as the practical alliances and very few children had been born. Zarif had grown up an only child and he could no longer withstand the pressure on him at home to marry and provide an heir. He had only got to reach the age of twenty-nine single because he was, in fact, a widower, whose wife, Azel, and infant son, Firas, had died in a car crash seven years earlier.

At the time, Zarif had thought he would never recover from such an indescribable loss. Everyone had respected his right to grieve but even so he was well aware that he could not ignore his obligations indefinitely. Preserving the continuity of his bloodline to ensure stability in the country that he loved was his most basic duty. In truth, however, he didn't want a wife at all and he felt guilty about that. But he *liked* being alone; he *liked* his life just as it was.

A sleek private jet returned Zarif to Vashir. Before disembarking he donned the long white tunic, beige cloak and rope-bound headdress required for him to attend the ceremonial opening of a new museum in the city centre. Only after that appearance had been made would he be free to return to the old palace, a rambling property set in lush perfumed gardens. It had long since been surpassed by the giant shiny new palace built on the other side of the city, which now functioned as the official centre of government. Zarif, however, had grown up at the old palace and was strongly attached to the ancient building.

It was also where his beloved uncle, Halim, was spending the last months of his terminal illness and Zarif was making the most of the time the older man had left. In many ways, Halim had been the father whom Zarif had never known, a gentle, quiet man, who had taught Zarif everything he had needed to know about negotiation, self-discipline and statesmanship.

Zarif's business manager, Yaman, awaited him in the room Zarif used as an office. 'What brings you here?' Zarif asked in surprise for the older man rarely made such visits.

Unlike his brothers, Nik and Cristo, who had both made names in the financial world, Zarif had little interest in his business affairs. Vashir had become oil-rich long before he was born and he had grown up wrapped in the golden cocoon of his family's fabulous wealth. Yaman and his highly professional team presided over that fortune and conserved it.

'There is a matter which I felt I should bring to your personal attention,' Yaman informed him gravely.

'Of course. What is this matter?' Zarif asked, resting

back against the edge of his desk, his dark eyes enquiring in his lean bronzed features.

The middle-aged accountant's air of discomfiture increased. 'It relates to a personal loan you made to a friend three years ago…Jason Gilchrist.'

Disconcerted by the mention of that name, Zarif stiffened. Yet it was not his one-time friend's face that he pictured, it was that of Jason's sister, Eleonora. An image of a young woman with a honey-blonde fall of silky curls, gentian-blue eyes and the legs of a gazelle flashed in his mind's eye. Zarif froze into angry defensiveness at the speed of his own unwelcome response and the unwelcome remembrance of the staccato delivery of insults he had never forgotten:

We're both far too young to get married.

I'm British. I couldn't live in a culture where women are second-class citizens.

I'm not cut out to be a queen.

'What has happened?' he asked Yaman with his customary quietness, only the charge of sudden flaring energy lighting his dark gaze to amber belying his outer façade of cool.

Ella walked into the silent house. She was so tired that only will power was keeping her upright.

A light was burning below the living-room door: Jason was still up. She walked past quietly, unable to face another clash with her hot-tempered brother, and went into the kitchen. The room was a disaster area with abandoned plates of food still resting on the table. The chairs were still pushed back from the day before, when they had each leapt out of their seats as Jason broke his devastating news of their financial ruin during a family

meal. Straightening her shoulders and reluctant to recall that dreadful lunch, Ella began to clear up, knowing that she would only feel worse if she had to face the
mess in the morning.

The house didn't feel like home without her parents.
Distressing images of her mother lying still, frail and
newly old in her hospital bed, and her father sobbing
uncontrollably, filled Ella's mind. Hot tears stung her
eyes and she blinked them away fiercely because giving
rein to self-pity and sadness wouldn't change anything
that had happened.

The horrors of the past forty-eight hours had piled
up like a multiple-car road crash. The nightmare had
begun when Jason admitted that the family accountancy
firm was on the brink of bankruptcy and that her parents' comfortable home, where they all lived together,
was mortgaged to the hilt. Only just returned from the
Mediterranean cruise that Jason had persuaded his parents to take while he looked after the business, her father
had been irate and incredulous that matters could have
been brought to such a desperate pass in so short a time
period. Gerald Gilchrist had rushed off to the office to
check the firm's books and then consult his bank manager for advice while Jason stayed behind to explain the
situation in greater detail to their mother.

Initially, Jennifer Gilchrist had remained calm, seemingly convinced that her clever, successful son would
naturally be able to sort out whatever problems there
were and ensure his family's continuing prosperity. Unlike her husband she had not angrily condemned Jason
for his dishonesty in forging his parents' signatures on
the document used to remortgage their home. Indeed she

had forgivingly assumed that Jason had merely been trying to protect his parents from needless financial worry.

But then Jason had, from birth, been the adored centre of her parents' world, Ella conceded wryly. Excuses
had always been made when Jason lied or cheated and
forgiveness and instant understanding had been offered
to him on many occasions. Born both brainy and ath-
letic, Jason had shone in every sphere and her parents'
pride in him had known no bounds. Yet her brother had
always had a darker side to his character combined with
a disturbing lack of concern for the well-being of others. Her parents had scrimped and saved to send Jason
to an elite private school and when he had won a place
at Oxford University they had been overjoyed by his
achievement.

At university, Jason had made friends with much
wealthier students. Was that when her sibling had
begun to succumb to the kind of driving ambition and
greed that would only lead him into trouble? Or had
that change taken place only after Jason had become a
high-flying banker with a Porsche and a strong sense of
entitlement? Whatever it was, Ella thought with newly
learned bitterness, Jason had always wanted *more* and
almost inevitably that craving for easily acquired riches
had tempted him down the wrong path in life. But what
she would never be able to forgive her brother for was
dragging their parents down with him into the mire of
debt and despair.

The worst had already happened though, Ella told
herself in urgent consolation. Nothing could equal the
horror of her mother's collapse. Once the shock of their
disastrous financial situation had finally kicked in, her
mother had suffered a heart attack. Rushed into hospi-

tal the day before, Jennifer Gilchrist had had emergency surgery and was now mercifully in the recovery ward. Her father had tried hard to adjust to his sudden change in circumstances but, ultimately, it had been too much for him once he appreciated that he would not even be able to pay his staff the wages they were owed. Shock and shame had then overwhelmed him and he had broken down in the hospital waiting room and cried in his daughter's arms, while blaming himself for not keeping a closer eye on his son's activities within the firm.

A slight noise sent Ella's head whipping round. Her brother, who had the thickset build of a rugby player and the portly outline of a man who wasted little time keeping fit, stood in the kitchen doorway nursing a glass of whisky. 'How's Mother?' he asked gruffly.

'Holding her own. The prognosis is good,' Ella told him quietly and she turned back to the sink, keen to keep busy rather than dwell on the disquieting fact that her brother had neither accompanied her to the hospital nor made the effort to visit their mother since.

'It's not my fault she had the heart attack,' Jason declared in a belligerent tone.

'I didn't say it was,' Ella responded, determined not to get into an argument with her sibling, who even as a child would have argued twenty-four hours straight sooner than yield a point. 'I'm not looking to blame anyone.'

'I mean…Mother could've had an attack at any time and at least the way it happened we were here to deal with it and ensure she got to hospital quickly,' Jason pointed out glibly.

'Yes,' Ella agreed soothingly for the sake of peace and she paused before continuing, 'I wanted to ask you…

that massive loan that you said you took out three years ago…'

'What about it?' Jason prompted with a harshness that suggested that he was in no mood to answer her questions.

'Which bank was it with?'

'No bank would've given me that amount of cash without collateral,' Jason countered with a look that scorned her ignorance of such matters. 'Zarif gave me the money.'

When he spoke that name out loud, the sink brush fell from Ella's hand as her fingers lost their grip and she whirled round from the sink in shock. *'Zarif?'* she repeated in disbelief, her voice breaking on the syllables.

'After I was made redundant at the bank, Zarif offered me the cash to start up my own business. An interest-free loan, no repayments to be made for the first three years,' Jason explained grudgingly. 'Only an idiot would have refused to take advantage of such a sweet deal.'

'That was very…kind of him,' Ella remarked tightly, her lovely face pale and tight with control while she battled the far more powerful feelings struggling inside her. Reactions she had learned to suppress during three long years of fierce self-discipline, never ever allowing herself to look back to what had been the most agonising experience of her entire life. 'But you didn't start up your own business…you became Dad's partner instead.'

'Well, home's where the heart is, or so they say,' her brother quipped without shame. 'The family firm was going nowhere until I stepped in.'

Ella bit back an angry rejoinder and compressed her lips in resolute silence. She wished Jason had chosen to set up his own business. Instead he had bankrupted a stable firm that had brought in a good, if not spectacular, income. 'I can't believe you accepted money from Zarif.'

'When a billionaire flashes his cash in my direction, I'd be a fool to do otherwise,' Jason informed her in a patronising tone. 'Of course Zarif only offered the loan in the first place because he thought you were going to marry him and an unemployed brother-in-law would have been a serious embarrassment to him.'

The muscles in Ella's slender back stretched taut as her brother voiced that unsettling claim. 'If that's true, you should've given the money back to him when we broke up.'

'You didn't break up, Ella,' Jason interrupted scornfully. 'You *inexplicably* refused to marry the catch of the century. Zarif was hardly going to come back and visit us after a slap in the face like that. So, if you're looking for someone to blame for this mess, look at the part *you* played in setting us all up for this fall!'

Blue eyes flying wide with dismay, her delicate cheekbones flushed, Ella spun round again. 'Are you trying to suggest that I'm in some way responsible for what's happened?'

Bitter resentment flared in her brother's bloodshot blue eyes. 'You made an entirely selfish decision to reject Zarif, which not only offended him but also destroyed *my* friendship with him... I mean, he never contacted me again!'

Ella lowered her pounding head, loose waves of thick honey-coloured blonde hair concealing her discomfited face and deeply troubled eyes. Her brother's friendship with Zarif *had* to all intents and purposes died the same day that Ella had refused Zarif's proposal of marriage and she could not deny that fact. 'I may have turned him down but it wasn't a selfish decision—we weren't right for each other,' she declared awkwardly, staring at a hole in the tiled floor.

'When I accepted that money from Zarif, I naturally assumed you were going to marry him and I had no worries about repaying it,' Jason argued vehemently, tossing back another unappreciative slug of his father's best whisky. 'Obviously it's *your* fault that we're in trouble now. After an you've had your share of Zarif's money too!'

Ella frowned, sharply disconcerted by that sudden accusation coming at her out of nowhere. 'What money? I never touched Zarif's money.'

'Oh, yes, you did,' Jason told her with galling satisfaction. 'When you needed the cash to go into partnership with Cathy on the shop, where do you think *I* got it from?'

Ella studied her big brother in horror. 'You told me it was your money, *your* savings!' she protested strickenly. 'Are you saying that the money came from Zarif's loan?'

'Where would I have got savings from?' Jason demanded with vicious derision. 'I was in debt to my eyeballs when I was made redundant. I had car loans, bank loans, a massive mortgage on my apartment...'

Ella was stunned by that blunt admission. After finishing college, she and her friend Cathy had opened a bookshop with a coffee area in the market town where they lived. Ella had borrowed from Jason to make her share of the investment and she made heavy monthly repayments to her brother in return for that initial financing. In fact, two and a half years on she was still as poor as a church mouse and couldn't afford to move out of her parents' house or run a car on her current share of the takings from the shop. The shop was doing well though, just not well enough to put icing on Ella's cake and offer her any luxuries. Cathy, the only child of affluent parents who owned a chain of nursing homes, was in a much more comfortable position because the shop was not her only means of support.

'You deliberately misled me,' Ella condemned shakily. 'I would never have accepted that money had I known it came from Zarif and you know it.'

'Beggars can't be choosers. You were glad enough to get the money at the time.'

'If it's true that my share of the shop investment came from Zarif's loan, then obviously I'm more involved than I appreciated.' On weak legs, Ella made that grudging concession before she sank down heavily in a chair by the kitchen table. 'But you can't seriously blame me for the fact that you've spent such a huge amount of that cash on silly superficial things like new offices and the like, and now can't repay it.'

Jason sent her a withering look of pure dislike that made her pale. 'Can't I? When I first got that money, I never expected to have to pay *any* of it back!' he told her bluntly. 'Naturally I assumed you'd marry Zarif, and if you *had* married him Zarif would never have expected me to repay the loan! If you must know, I blame you for this whole bloody nightmare. If you hadn't played ducks and drakes with Zarif and thrown his proposal back in his royal teeth, we wouldn't be in this situation now!'

Her teeth gritted, Ella jumped back out of her seat in a temper. 'That's not fair. From the moment you got that loan, you have been totally dishonest and criminally extravagant. You broke the law when you forged Mum and Dad's signatures to remortgage this house, you deceived all of us about what was really happening with the firm... Don't you *dare* try and make out that any of this is my fault!' she slung back at him in angry self-defence.

'You're *so* selfish and short-sighted!' Jason condemned, his face reddening with fury and his fists clenching. 'You're the one who wrecked Zarif's friendship with this family and put us into this humiliating position, so you should be the one to go and see him now and ask him to give us the time to sort this out.'

'*See* him?' Ella repeated half an octave higher, her consternation at that suggestion unhidden. 'You want me to go and actually *see* Zarif?'

'Who better?' Jason queried with a curled lip. 'Men are always inclined to be more understanding when a beautiful woman asks them for a favour and Zarif wouldn't be human if the sight of a woman begging didn't give him a kick.'

Ella flushed to the roots of her hair and studied the surface of the table. Her heightened colour slowly receded while she contemplated the prospect of meeting Zarif again and her pallor was soon matched by a rolling tide of nauseous recoil from the image of *begging* Zarif for anything. 'I can't do it. I can't *bear* to see him again,' she framed between gritted teeth, ashamed that she was being forced to admit to such a weakness, such a lingering sensitivity towards something that had happened so long ago.

'Well, he's unlikely to want to see me in the circumstances but curiosity alone is sure to gain *you* an entry to the royal presence,' Jason forecast with soaring confidence. 'And you don't even have to go to that godforsaken country of his to do it. He's endowing some fancy science building at Oxford University and making a speech there the day after tomorrow.'

Her lovely face was pale and tight with strain. 'It hardly matters because I don't want to see or speak to Zarif again.'

'Not even to rescue Mummy and Daddy from this nightmare?' Jason chided unpleasantly. 'Let's face it— you're our only hope right now. And I can only hope that Zarif has a sentimental streak hidden somewhere behind that stiff upper lip of his.'

'I'm not responsible for the loan or the mortgaging of this house behind Mum and Dad's back,' Ella stated curtly while secretly wondering whether she *was* being selfish and feeling tortured by her brother's insistence that only she could help her parents in their current plight.

Was Jason only trying to manipulate her to save his own hide? Making a last-ditch suggestion that would mortify her pride but that would ultimately make no difference to the situation? Did he really think that Zarif would listen to her? Certainly, Zarif had liked and respected her mother and father and probably had no idea that Jason's mishandling of the loan had destroyed her parents' security as well as his own.

'Have you no idea how valuable so rich a friend can be? Have you no concept of what you did to *my* hopes and dreams when you turned him down?' Jason demanded with stinging bitterness. 'I could've been flying high again on the back of Zarif's support.'

'But not on the strength of your own efforts,' Ella muttered in disgust half under her breath.

'What did you say?' Jason shot at her accusingly, striding forward, red-faced rage ready to consume him.

Ella slid out of her seat and carefully avoided his aggressive stance on her passage to the door. 'Nothing...I said nothing,' she lied unsteadily. 'We're both too tired and stressed for this discussion. I'm going to bed.'

'You're a selfish, *stupid* little bitch, Ella!' Jason snarled furiously behind her. 'You could have had it all and instead what have you got? A half share in a bookshop the size of a cupboard!'

Her spine stiffened and she slowly turned. 'I also have my integrity,' she declared, lifting her chin while trying not to think about the source of the loan that had helped her to buy into the shop. But it was a thought she could not evade while she went through the motions of washing and getting into bed with the slow, heavy movements of a woman moving on automatic pilot. Exhaustion was finally overcoming her.

But even as her weary body lay heavy as lead on the mattress her thoughts marched on. Whether she liked it or not she was much more personally involved in her family's financial crash than she had thought she was. As she could not afford to pay the money back in its entirety, Zarif literally owned her half of the shop, not that she thought there was any imminent risk of a billionaire putting in a claim on a share of the venture.

Jason's other allegations had hit home even harder. It was unquestionably *her* fault that Zarif had withdrawn his friendship from the Gilchrist family. Ella's rejection had stunned and angered him and quite understandably he had never visited her home or her family again. For the very first time, Ella felt guilty about that reality. She was equally willing to credit that Jason had never expected to be forced to repay Zarif's loan because he had assumed that Ella would say 'yes' if Zarif proposed.

Evidently he had guessed long before Ella had that Zarif had serious intentions towards his sister and Jason had made his plans accordingly. Had her brother spent that money recklessly because he assumed he could afford to do whatever he liked with it and would never be called to account for his behaviour?

Reluctantly, Ella acknowledged that three years earlier with his expectations of advancement soaring on the idea of Zarif marrying his sister that had most likely been Jason's outlook. In the darkness she winced, shrinking from the daunting sense of responsibility now assailing her. She was not the innocent bystander she had assumed she was in the mess that her brother had created, she conceded painfully. Her relationship with Zarif had almost certainly influenced Jason's attitude to that loan and what he subsequently chose to do with the money.

She recalled that the new offices chosen for her father's accountancy firm and the hiring of extra staff had taken place while she was still dating Zarif, which meant that Jason did have some excuse for his assumption that he would never be expected to repay the money he had borrowed.

The persistent ringing of the front door bell wakened Ella from an uneasy doze. Clambering out of bed in a panic when she realised that it was after one in the morning, she dragged on her dressing gown and hurried to answer the door.

Her father's best friend, Jonathan Scarsdale, stood on the doorstep and immediately apologised for getting her out of bed. 'Your landline was constantly engaged and I thought it would be better to talk to you in person.'

Ella glanced at the phone table and noticed the handset wasn't set on the charger and sighed because it was little wonder that the phone wasn't working.

'No…no, don't worry about that,' Ella urged, for her parents' best friends, Jonathan and Marsha, were also Cathy's parents and familiar to her from childhood. 'I'm glad to see you. Come in.'

'Perhaps I'd better,' the older man said heavily. 'Although I hate bringing you more bad news than you've already had.'

'Mum?' Ella gasped, jumping to conclusions and wide-eyed with apprehension.

'No, Ella. Your mother's fine,' Jonathan reassured her quietly. 'But your father called me from the hospital. He was so upset, I drove over to join him although there's little enough I can do to help in the current circumstances.'

Ella was pale with strain as she led the way into the lounge, switching on lights as she went. 'I'm sure Dad was grateful for you being there.'

'I'm here to talk to you about your father,' the older man told her heavily. 'I'm afraid he's having a breakdown, Ella. Jason's betrayal of his trust, your mother's heart attack, the whole situation… Unfortunately he's not able to cope with it all right now. I phoned Marsha and she came out to the hospital to speak to your father and make a professional diagnosis. She suggested that Gerald should stay in our nursing home here for a few days until he's calmed down and come to terms with things…'

'Dad…a *breakdown*?' Ella repeated sickly. 'But he's not the type.'

'There *is* no type, Ella. Anyone can have an emotional breakdown and at the moment your father simply can't handle the stress he's under. He's in the best place for the present with trained staff able to offer the support he needs,' he pointed out soothingly. 'I'm sorry though that this leaves you alone.'

'I'm not alone…I have Jason,' she pointed out, avoiding the older man's compassionate look out of embarrassment while struggling to absorb the news of her father's predicament.

Ella was shell shocked as she thanked Cathy's father for his help and she got back into bed in a daze, gooseflesh prickling at the disturbing realisation that *both* her parents had collapsed from the trauma of Jason's revelations. There was no room for manoeuvre or protest now, she acknowledged dully. If she could do anything at all to alleviate the crisis in her parents' lives, she needed to make the attempt to do so: she had no choice but to ask Zarif for a meeting.

CHAPTER TWO

ELLA PARKED HER mother's car with the extreme care of someone strung up tight with nerves and terrified of making a mistake at the wheel.

Earlier that morning she had visited both her parents and that had proved a disorientating experience. On medication her father was now much calmer but he had seemed utterly divorced from the events that had led to his breakdown in the first place, not once even referring to them. In any case she had been warned before her visit not to touch on any subject that might cause him distress. Luckily Gerald's overriding source of concern had been his wife's recovery and he had lamented his inability to be with her. At least Ella had been able to tell her father that her mother was out of Intensive Care and receiving visits from her friends. Jennifer Gilchrest, however, had been equally reluctant to discuss the events that had preceded her heart attack.

As a result, Ella had been left feeling totally bereft of support and she was still guiltily reproaching herself for being so selfish. After all, neither of her parents was well enough to assist her. At the same time, Ella remained horribly aware of the huge burden of expectation resting on her shoulders while bankruptcy and repos-

session threatened her parents' business and home. She
had already fielded several excusably angry phone calls
from staff members who hadn't received their salary and
who were struggling to pay their bills. In the midst of
catastrophe, and in spite of being their father's partner
in the firm, Jason had done absolutely nothing beyond
contacting another former student friend to establish
where Zarif was staying prior to delivering his speech
at the university. Jason had then contacted the hotel on
the evening of Zarif's arrival, had spoken to his chief
aide and had been granted an appointment.

Jason had then made some wildly opportunistic and
slick forecasts about the likely result of his sister speaking to Zarif in person.

'Zarif's really hot on family values, so he'll be very
sympathetic when he appreciates how devastating all
this has been for us,' Jason had opined optimistically.
'I'm tremendously relieved that you've decided to see
sense about this.'

'Don't you think that you should be coming with me?'
Ella had asked in surprise for she had certainly originally assumed that her brother would, at least, be accompanying her to the meeting. 'I mean, Zarif made the
loan to you, not to me, and I won't be able to answer any
business queries he has.'

'Take it from me. You're the best messenger the family could have,' Jason had insisted.

Only, unhappily, Ella did not feel equal to that challenge. She was painfully aware that any slight regard
Zarif might have cherished for her three years earlier had
died the same day she refused to marry him. Determined
not to reveal her true feelings after he put her on the spot
and demanded an explanation for her refusal, she had

employed lame excuses, which had not only offended him but which still made her cringe in remembrance. Could she really blame him for his anger that day?

Zarif al-Rastani was born of royalty and was scarcely the average male. She might often have overlooked that reality when he was visiting them in the UK and displaying few of the trappings of his true status, but the day she had said 'no' Zarif had regarded her with stunned disbelief and his extremely healthy ego had visibly recoiled from the affront of her rejection.

Of course, he had said and done nothing that could be remotely termed *emotional* that day. Evidently Zarif didn't *do* emotion and she would have been far too emotional a being to make him a good wife, she reflected wryly. She had been sadly mistaken when she once naively assumed that Zarif's icy reserve and self-discipline masked powerful inner feelings that he preferred to keep to himself.

While she had fallen madly in love with Zarif and had craved him with every fibre of her being, she had recognised the very last time that she saw him that he was virtually indifferent to her and was not in love, merely in *lust* and in need of a male heir. Had Jason only realised how shallow her former relationship with Zarif had ultimately proved to be, he would not have been so hopeful that by some miracle his sister would somehow be able to save her family from the consequences of his extravagance. Indeed Ella suspected that Zarif was more likely to be annoyed than appreciative at her daring to request another meeting with him. Women were gentle nurturing motherly creatures in Zarif's world and that kind of woman was his ideal, as Ella knew to her cost.

She walked into the imposing country house hotel.

Jason had told her that Zarif and his entourage were occupying the entire top floor of the building.

'Miss Gilchrist?' A slim Arab man with a goatee beard was on the lookout for her before she even got to engage with the reception staff. 'I am Hamid, the King's chief aide. I spoke to your brother on the phone. His Majesty will see you upstairs.'

While Hamid talked valiantly about the weather, his efforts undimmed by her monosyllabic replies, Ella smoothed damp palms down over her long skirt, wishing she had had a smart business suit to don in place of her usual more casual clothing but she didn't own any formal outfits. She had teamed the skirt with a pristine white layered blouse and camisole. At least, she wasn't wearing jeans, she told herself in consolation, desperate to think about anything other than the approaching challenge of an interview with Zarif. Her heart started to beat very, very fast, a chill of nervous tension shivering through her slender frame and making her tummy flip. She breathed in, slow and deep, striving to calm herself.

'Miss Gilchrist...' Hamid announced, pushing wide the door.

Ella walked a few steps into the room and then saw *him* and her courage failed her and she came to a sudden halt. Six feet two inches tall with a lean, powerful build, Zarif was a stunningly beautiful male and, in her opinion, far and away the most handsome of the three half-brothers. He was also the youngest of the trio, the other two of whom she had met briefly.

Zarif had the tawny eyes of a lion framed between lush black lashes and set deep below straight ebony brows. An arrogant, slim-bridged nose dissected exotically high cheekbones and his stunning features were completed by a strong masculine jaw line and a perfectly modelled mouth, the very thought of which had once kept Ella lying awake at night. She had craved his touch like a life-giving drug.

The memory sent chagrined heat surging through her tense body as she remembered all too well how frustrated she had become with his hands-off courtship. She had been a virgin but she would have surrendered her innocence any time he asked and if she was *still* a virgin, she conceded with undeniable resentment, it was only because she was determined not to settle for anything less than the intense hunger that Zarif had once inspired in her.

'Eleonora…' Zarif murmured, his rich as dark chocolate deep drawl dancing down her spine like the brush of ghostly fingers from the past. He did not have a definable accent because he had learned English from his British grandmother.

Her throat convulsed. 'Zarif…' she responded, struggling to push his name past her lips.

Zarif surveyed her with razor-edged intensity, luxuriant black lashes covertly veiling his acute gaze. He'd had an antique storybook as a child, which featured a lovely pale-haired princess imprisoned in a tower, and had once idly wondered if that had been the mysterious source of his one-time obsession with Ella Gilchrist. She was a beauty of the pure English Rose type with her translucent porcelain skin, bright blue eyes and long waving hair that had the depth and gloss of rich golden honey. Slim and of medium height, she had surprisingly lush curves for her slight frame and she moved as gracefully as a dancer. He scrutinised her soft bee-stung pink mouth and his body betrayed him with an immediate reaction. Anger stirred along with the indignity of the prickling heaviness of arousal at his groin.

She had always contrived to look natural, unadorned, *untouched*. His even white teeth ground together at that improbability. It had probably only ever been part of the demure fawn act she had staged for his benefit in the days when he had been that credulous and impressionable with the female sex, he reflected with angry resentment.

Time would have moved on for her in any case, just as it had done for him, and he refused to think further along that line because it would cross the bitter defensive boundaries he had raised inside his mind. After all, it was purely due to Ella Gilchrist's power over him that Zarif had later betrayed every principle he had once respected, and he still reeled from any recollection of the mistakes he had made and the very large dent inflicted on his once stainless sense of honour. She had embarked on a dangerous power game with him. She had played him like a fish on a line, vainly determined to get the ego boost of having royalty propose marriage to her without ever considering acceptance as a viable possibility.

He had considered the matter many times and believed that was the only practical explanation for her behaviour.

'Won't you sit down?' Zarif invited smoothly, his outer assurance absolute. 'Then you can tell me how I may be of assistance.'

So, Zarif was going to play dumb, Ella reckoned uncomfortably and then wondered if she was being unjust. Was it possible that he hadn't a clue about the situation her family was in?

She settled into a high-backed, opulently upholstered

armchair and went straight to the heart of the subject. 'Until this week, I had no idea that three years ago you gave Jason a very large loan.'

'It was not your concern,' Zarif fielded without skipping a beat.

Ella stiffened defensively. 'But I wish it had been,' she fenced back, refusing to be intimidated by his powerful presence. 'Giving Jason a million pounds without any form of supervision was the equivalent of putting a fox in charge of a hen coop.'

Zarif compressed his handsome mouth. 'You are not very loyal to your brother.'

'I wonder how loyal you would feel towards one of your brothers if his wheeling and dealing had plunged your father's firm into bankruptcy and left your parents facing homelessness. Right now, I'm worried about them, *not* about my brother,' Ella spelt out combatively.

A gleam of surprise lightened Zarif's spectacular eyes for it had been a very long time since anyone had addressed him with such a pronounced lack of respect. Indeed the last to do so had probably been her and he was both aggravated and yet strangely entertained by her boldness. It was a complete novelty in his world, where almost every word addressed to him was wrapped in flattery and a desire to ingratiate and please. His jaw line squared. 'I was not aware that your parents were involved in this debacle.'

'They were very much involved the moment Jason became a partner in Dad's firm. My father was so proud that his son was joining the family business that he gave Jason a completely free hand,' Ella explained heavily.

'My business manager has already presented me with

a file covering his investigation into how the loan was utilised,' Zarif revealed gently.

'So, really it wasn't very nice of you to ask *how* you might be of assistance when I arrived!' Ella shot back at him with spirit. 'You were being facetious at my expense.'

'Was I?' Zarif quipped, scanning the animated expressiveness of her exquisite face, which openly brandished every emotion she experienced. He was convinced he could now read her like a children's book and recognise her angry resentment and mortification that she should be put in the position of pleading her unworthy brother's cause.

Zarif, in point of fact, had very few illusions about his former friend's character. Long ago, Zarif had slowly been repelled by the traits he saw in Jason and would have dropped the friendship much sooner had it not been for the draw of Ella's presence in the same house. His dark gaze hardened when he thought of the day it had all ended and the persistent bite of his indignation and dissatisfaction stung his ferocious pride afresh, tensing his spectacular bone structure and settling the charismatic curve of his mouth into a hard stubborn line. She had humiliated him, insulted his country and his people and outraged him beyond forgiveness but torture would not have persuaded him to admit that reality.

'I think so,' Ella told him squarely, noting the way his long dark lashes shadowed his cheekbones when he glanced down at her, seeing his handsome dark head take on a familiar angle, recalling how he had once listened to her with just that attitude. Unnerved by the memory and the overpowering urge to stare and eat up his heartbreaking gorgeousness without restraint, Ella glanced furiously in the direction of the window like someone calculating the chances of her escape.

Unbelievable as it now seemed, she had once loved Zarif with her whole heart and soul, she recalled painfully. She would have done absolutely anything for him and in return he had *hurt* her very badly, inflicting a wound and an insecurity that even the passage of three long years had failed to eradicate. Even so, it had been a novel experience to discover that a marriage proposal could actually be wielded like an offensive weapon.

'When I gave that loan to Jason, it was in the true spirit of generosity,' Zarif countered with quiet assurance. 'He was devastated by the loss of his employment and your parents were equally upset on his behalf. I genuinely wanted to help your family.'

'That may be so,' Ella conceded uncomfortably, because he seemed sincere, 'but nothing is ever that simple. Jason needed another job more than he needed that cash. The loan just tempted him into dangerous fantasies about building his own business empire.'

'As well as the settling of his personal debts, which was dishonest and in direct conflict with the terms on which the loan was made,' Zarif sliced in calmly, cold censure of such behaviour etched in his lean bronzed features. 'Your brother squandered the bulk of the money on frivolous purchases, which included a new Porsche and a personalised Range Rover. I will not write off the debt and forgive it. It would be against my principles to overlook what amounts to fraudulent behaviour.'

'That is all very well, but what about my parents' position in all this?' Ella demanded emotively. 'Do they deserve to suffer for Jason's mistakes?'

'That is not for me to answer,' Zarif responded without expression. 'They raised Jason, taught him their values. They must know their son best.'

'No.' Ella challenged that view with vehement force. 'They only know the man they *wanted* him to be, not the man he actually is! At this moment, my mother and father are distraught at what Jason's done.'

An untimely knock on the door at that instant of high tension heralded the appearance of a waiter with a tray. Ella closed her lips and breathed in deep to master her tumultuous emotions. Coffee was served in fine china cups, cakes proffered. Any appetite Ella might have had following her scratch meals in recent days had been killed stone dead by her ever-growing sense of dread of what the future might yet visit on her parents. In the lingering silence while the waiter walked to the door to leave, she searched Zarif's extravagantly handsome features, cursing his inscrutability, desperate to see some sign of a softer response to her appeal on her parents' behalf.

'I'm afraid I don't understand what you want from me,' Zarif murmured half under his breath, his temperature rising as she sat forward, inadvertently revealing the shadowy valley between her full rounded breasts. There was a bitter irony to his response for he knew in that moment of fierce driving desire that what he wanted from her was exactly what he was convinced he could have had for the asking three years earlier.

Back then he had been no sophisticate, having never slept with anyone other than the wife he had married at the age of eighteen. He had wanted Ella and she had wanted him but he had believed it would be dishonourable to become intimate with her before he married her. Thanks to Ella's rejection, he was no longer that innocent, he reflected with a bitterness that was laced with regret for past mistakes. His wide sensual mouth narrowed and compressed while he wondered if she was deliberately playing the temptress as women so often did with him in an effort to divert and attract him.

'No, you are not that stupid,' Ella flung back at him feelingly, pushing her slender hands down on the arms of the chair to rise upright and confront him. 'You know very well I'm asking you to show some compassion for my parents' predicament.'

The swishing luxuriance of her golden hair as it swung round her shoulders engaged his scrutiny, which lingered to take in the rosy colour warming her delicate features, serving only to accentuate the sapphire brilliance of her eyes. 'In what way? And what are you offering me in return?' Zarif murmured very drily. 'Do you not think that in the complete loss of that loan, I have already paid dearly for my act of generosity towards your family?'

Confronted with that blunt question, Ella felt her face burn as though he had slapped it hard because that was not an angle she could take into account when she was asking him for yet another favour. 'Yes, you have paid dearly…we all have, but I do genuinely believe that you should have thought about what you were doing when you offered Jason that loan in the first place.'

'Before you start blaming me for your brother's dishonesty and awakening my anger,' Zarif purred like a jungle cat, shimmering dark golden eyes settling on her with predatory force and shocking her into sudden silence, 'think about what you are saying and what you are asking me for. Some form of forgiveness which, as I have already stated, is out of the question in this case?

Or are you asking me to throw away more money on your family?'

Standing there, Ella turned very pale, shame and anxiety combining to stir nausea in her tummy. Her tongue was glued to the roof of her mouth. She absolutely got his point and she could not bring herself to outright *ask* him for money to aid her parents because that seemed so very wrong, indeed quite outrageous in the circumstances. For the first time she questioned why she had approached him in the first place and why she had allowed Jason to influence her attitude. Surely, had she taken the time to think things through, she would have recognised that to ask Zarif for further financial help would be indefensible?

'I'm just asking you to show some compassion, not for Jason or me but for my parents,' she completed limply, too mortified to even make an attempt to meet his slashing gaze, knowing that it would only intensify her awareness of the weak and humiliating role she had allowed her brother to browbeat her into accepting. For an instant, she almost burst into speech about her parents' current health problems, but compressed her lips on the conviction that playing a thousand violins to invite Zarif's pity would only shame her and her family more.

'Nicely put,' Zarif countered with sardonic bite, his dark eyes glittering like jet knives, so shrewd was the stab of his incisive gaze. 'You know how wealthy I am and like many other people I have met you expect me to come to the rescue. And I would have to ask you, especially when you have the audacity to ask me to go against my principles, what am I to receive in payment?'

The suffocating tension was convulsing Ella's dry throat. She turned away, dropped down into her seat again and lifted her coffee cup like a tiny shield. 'In payment? Anything I can offer,' she muttered unevenly, knowing she had nothing to offer but gratitude and seriously embarrassed by that reality.

'Are you offering me sex?' Zarif enquired lazily.

And for a split second in receipt of that shocking question Ella wondered if she would agree to such a belittling act of intimacy if it could magically return her parents' lives to normal. The answer came fast and forthright in her mind. And colour surged across her cheeks and ran up in a tide of pink to her hairline while her coffee cup rattled on the saucer as her hand trembled.

'I can get sex anywhere whenever I want,' Zarif derided.

'I wasn't going to offer it,' Ella told him with as much dignity as she could muster, her teeth gritting on his arrogant self-assurance. Nevertheless, she suspected that he was simply stating the situation as it was. He was exceptionally good-looking and shockingly rich even without considering the kick it would give some women to bed a reigning king. She was quite sure that willing women formed queues for the privilege of getting him into bed and her staunch conviction that he was a virtually irresistible package only incensed her more.

Surprisingly for a male so well aware of the high currency value of sex, Zarif believed Ella because he couldn't credit that a truly sophisticated woman would still blush the way she did. But the imagery in his mind was far from sophisticated and he knew from the intensely male burn of his rapidly awakening libido that if she *had* offered, he would have said yes and to hell with whether or not such ignoble behaviour would be beneath him!

That discovery shook him because while sex was easily available to Zarif and an appetite he could not ignore, he had never viewed it as a special or even greatly prized pleasure. But for some reason when he looked at Ella Gilchrist his body hummed with the expectation of *extraordinary* pleasure because it was the passion in her volatile nature that had drawn him to her from the first. He crushed that exciting fantasy at source, reminding himself that he needed a wife and a child much more than he needed a passionate mistress.

On that thought, he stiffened, unable to overlook the reality that had she said yes when he asked her to marry him he most likely would have been a father again by now. All the old dark anger and bitterness he had buried stirred deep inside him once more, razor-edged thoughts of his unresolved desire for her taunting his ferocious pride.

He had never wanted a woman as much as he had once wanted Ella Gilchrist and she was the only woman he had ever desired whom he had not enjoyed. Perhaps that was the secret of her persistent attraction, he reasoned with inherent self-loathing at the concept of such a personal weakness, and it would naturally follow that familiarity would soon breed contempt. That conviction soothed him, offering as it did the promise that in the future he would forget about her and the way she had once adversely affected him. Life was too short for regrets and 'what ifs'. He would get bored with her. He *always* got bored in the end because women could be very predictable. She would be his very last rebellion against the staid and respectable married future that awaited him. He would have some fun and *then* he would do his duty by settling down again with a wife and having children, he swore to himself.

'That's unfortunate,' Zarif responded in reply to her proud declaration that she had not been offering him sex. 'Because what you say you would not offer is the only thing that I want from you.'

Extreme disconcertion slithered through Ella while she mentally unpicked his words several times to persuade herself that she had not misunderstood his meaning. He was telling her that he still found her attractive and that the only thing he wanted from her was sex? How dared he admit that with such smooth and utterly shameless cool? Heat warmed her cheeks afresh and speared down between her breasts as she bit back furious words of reproach and fought to breathe normally.

'I can't believe you can say that to me.'

'Duplicity would be of little use to you at this point,' Zarif countered quietly. 'Whatever else I may be guilty of, you can trust me to always tell you the truth.'

For an instant, Ella froze, recalling the last unforgettable occasion when he had told her the truth that he did not love her and would *never* love her: a hauntingly savage moment that had coloured her every memory of him with pain and a deep sense of humiliation. She had often thought that lies would have been kinder, only then she would have married him and ultimately would have ended up being very unhappy.

'I want you in my bed,' Zarif admitted with unblemished cool. 'In return I would ensure that your parents' financial status is restored to what it was before Jason's mismanagement ruined their security.'

I want you in my bed. A tingling sensation curled like a tongue of flame low in her pelvis and Ella shifted uneasily on her seat, trying not to imagine what it would be like to share Zarif's bed. Wide-eyed and hot inside skin that suddenly felt tight over her bones, she focused on the undoubtedly handmade leather shoes on his feet and kept her ready tongue clamped firmly between her teeth. She was fighting her own natural instincts harder with every second that passed. She could have asked him if he was joking and instantly rejected such a shocking proposition. She could have made a scene and stormed out in an impressive temper. But Ella had a strong streak of caution and practicality and she was all too well aware that Zarif al-Rastani was the only possible individual in a position to help her family.

'That's immoral,' she declared half under her breath, unable to resist making that accusation. 'You're inviting me to sell myself to you.'

'I'm offering you the only rescue bid you're likely to receive. It is for you to choose whether or not you will accept my proposition,' Zarif contradicted, shutting out every protest emanating from his clean-living conservative soul and refusing to listen. One final act of rebellion, he reminded himself doggedly. And didn't she deserve it for the games she had played three years back when she had lured him in with the promise of her passion and her beautiful body and falsely encouraged him to believe that she genuinely cared for him?

'How long would you envisage this…arrangement lasting for?' Ella prompted, her voice high and tight with strain for she could barely credit that after three years apart she could even be having such a conversation with him.

'A year…' Zarif murmured, disconcerted by the speed with which that time period had suggested itself to him and wondering where that idea had come from. After all, he had never kept a single mistress for as long as a year. His interest in a woman faded within the first few weeks of bedding her even though he saw comparatively little of his lovers. At the same time he tried and failed to picture Ella in the Dubai apartment while wondering if word of an Englishwoman's presence there would be more likely to be leaked to the press. Just as quickly, he realised that the Dubai option would be a very bad idea. And that indeed he had a much better idea in the offing and one indeed that would make the punishment fit the crime.

'For the sake of appearances, we will get married,' Zarif decreed without hesitation.

'Married?' Ella exclaimed with stark incredulity.

'I don't want a scandal and if I marry you, even when it ends in divorce after a year, it will be a safer and more acceptable option to my people. Marriage would also have the advantage of allowing me to see as much of you as I want to,' Zarif completed smoothly, his mind made up, the stirrings of his conscience magically washed away. If he married her, after all, he wouldn't be breaking any rules or taking advantage of her. It was wonderful, he thought with a rare lightness of heart, what a little thinking outside the box could achieve.

Feeling rather as though she had gone ten rounds with a champion boxer, Ella stood up and set down her coffee cup. Marry Zarif? Embrace all that she had rejected three years earlier? Her entire being shrank from such a challenge. 'I couldn't do it…I *couldn't* marry you.'

Raw anger roared like a hurricane through Zarif's lean powerful frame and gleamed pure, startlingly bright gold in his tawny eyes. 'You have twelve hours in which to consider that position,' he breathed in a raw-edged undertone. 'If you don't phone me within that period, I will assume that the negative answer stands.'

Ella's feet were locked to the carpet, her eyes flying wide on his hard, darkly handsome features. Dismay was piercing her with little warning stabs and reminding her that rejecting her parents' only rescue option was not a good idea. 'Twelve hours is ridiculous,' she said none-theless, playing for time.

'It is more than generous,' Zarif contradicted.

Ella was pale as a white sheet. 'Even when you know you've already won?' she whispered, because all the pros and cons were piling up like an avalanche inside her brain and she could not evade the obvious answer.

Zarif could turn the clock back for her parents, re-turning their lives to the safe cosy routine that had been theirs before Jason's interference. Zarif was the only per-son with the power to do that. Her father's staff would also be protected from unemployment. How could she possibly turn her back on such important results and walk away, leaving her parents and everybody else con-cerned to sink or swim? All the cons, after all, would be on *her* side of the fence, making the payment one of personal sacrifice.

Zarif stalked closer with all the grace of a prowling black panther. *'Have I won?'*

'How could I turn down an offer like that?' Ella asked shakily. 'My parents don't deserve what they're going through right now. It's bad enough for them to be forced to face the kind of person Jason really is without facing financial ruin at the same time.'

Zarif stretched out a slim tanned hand and closed it round hers to tug her closer. 'So, you *will* marry me?'

'But it won't work…even for only a year,' Ella protested weakly. 'I won't fit in.'

Eyes golden as the heart of a fire flamed over her troubled face. 'You will fit in my bed to perfection,' Zarif assured her and as panic and sexual awareness clenched her every muscle with raw tension Ella registered that that was really the *only* thought in his mind.

She stared up at him, almost mesmerised by his stunning gaze, and he lowered his head. His wide sensual mouth nuzzled against the corner of hers and she shivered, suddenly hot and cold inside her skin while little tingles of sexual awareness snaked through the lower part of her body. The scent of him was in her nostrils, a hint of some exotic spice overlaid with clean, husky male that was both familiar and dangerously welcome. His wide mobile mouth drifted across hers, his tongue breaking the seal of her lips and darting within, plunging deep in a single measured stab of eroticism before he pressed his hard mouth urgently to hers. That kiss was like being hit with white lightning, desire exploding within her like a fire ball, fiery tendrils of heat reaching low in her belly, and her knees trembled, her breasts swelling and nipples pinching tight.

Zarif lifted his handsome dark head and slowly drew in a deep breath to look down at her with hot possessive appreciation blazing in his golden eyes. 'Yes, you will fit into my bed as though you were born to be there.'

In the aftermath, rage gripped Ella and she wanted to smack him across the face. For a split second she had lost control, indeed lost sight of everything because he had thrown her straight into that disturbing world of exciting sensation that she had almost forgotten. And she could have wept at that knowledge for she had diligently dated more than one attractive man over the past three years and not one of them had made her heart leap and her body tremble with a single kiss. At the same time she had no doubt that that brief embrace had affected Zarif on a much less high-flown level.

'No, I wasn't born to be in your bed... Azel was,' Ella murmured flatly.

Disconcerted by the mere mention of Azel's name, Zarif froze and shot an icy look of censure down at her. 'You will not mention the name of my late wife or that of our child ever again,' he warned her forbiddingly.

Well, at least she didn't need to have any doubts about exactly where she stood in her future husband's affections, Ella reflected grimly. But then that had been exactly why she *didn't* marry the man she had once loved. Even seven years after her passing, Azel still ruled Zarif's heart.

CHAPTER THREE

'No,' ELLA TOLD her brother with quiet determination. 'If you want to ask Zarif anything, *you* go and see him.'

'And what use is that going to be? For goodness' sake, you're *marrying* the guy!' Jason reminded her angrily. 'Obviously you've got more sway with him than anyone else. Mum and Dad are over the moon and everything in everybody's garden but mine is coming up roses. What about *me*?'

Ella studiously averted her gaze from her sibling's furious face. Over the past three weeks everything had changed within the family circle. Once her father had heard his daughter's news, he had made a steady recovery and had gratefully accepted Zarif's contention that he could hardly let his future wife's family either go bankrupt or lose their home. Zarif's business manager, Yaman, had booked into a local hotel and the two men had worked out a viable rescue plan for the ailing firm. But right from that first day, all financial assistance on offer had been subject to the assurance that Jason would resign from the partnership and that her father would promise not to hire him again in any capacity. Gerald Gilchrist had duly given those guarantees and Jason had now officially left the firm. Her father had also insisted that Zarif's aid be given in the form of a loan, which he intended to start repaying as soon as he could.

'I'm sorry, Jason,' Ella breathed uncomfortably. 'Zarif isn't a forgiving person.'

'I'm out of a job and Dad thinks it would be easier all round if I move out of this house before your bloody ridiculous wedding!' Jason snapped out resentfully. 'What am I supposed to do?'

'Look for a career that suits you. Something that isn't financially orientated,' Ella suggested ruefully.

Her brother stomped off. Ella's mother, Jennifer, emerged from the kitchen and winced at the slam of a door overhead. 'Thank you for taking the heat off me and your father. I don't have the patience to listen to Jason's bitter rants right now and I don't want him making your father feel guilty again,' she confided.

The older woman had lost weight since her heart attack, which was hardly surprising if one considered her mother's new walking regime and healthier diet, Ella acknowledged fondly, relieved and proud of the way her mother had adapted to the challenge of changing her lifestyle.

'I'm *so* looking forward to the wedding,' Jennifer admitted happily. 'It's wonderful to have something to smile about again.'

And that was her parents' attitude to her nuptials in a nutshell, Ella conceded wryly. They thought it was wonderful news that she was marrying Zarif. She had lied to them and they hadn't suspected a thing was amiss. She had told them that she had turned down Zarif's first proposal because she didn't feel up to the challenge of the public role he was offering her and they had completely understood and accepted that explanation. In the same way it had been quite easy to persuade the older couple that once Zarif and their daughter had met again, they had recognised that their feelings were unchanged and had reconciled while deciding to waste no further time in getting married.

Ella's personal feelings were exactly that: *strictly* personal. Jason, of course, who thought everybody thought the way he did, assumed she was marrying Zarif for his money. And, of course, in a twisted way, she *was* marrying him for his money, Ella acknowledged shamefacedly. Marriage was the price of protecting her parents from a nasty wake-up call at an age when they no longer had the time and strength to deal with such a colossal challenge. Ella was, however, willing and able to pay that price for the mother and father who had surrounded her with love from the day of her birth. As a boy, Jason might have been the favourite but Ella had never been short-changed when it came to parental care and attention.

The phone rang and her mother, still mistily smiling at the prospect of her daughter's wedding, which was only three days away, answered it. 'The wedding planner,' she said, passing the receiver straight over to Ella.

Ella breathed in deep. Zarif had instructed his aide, Hamid, to put all the wedding arrangements in the hands of a top-flight professional, able to work to a very tight schedule and stage the wedding within weeks. A fixed smile tightening her tense lips, Ella listened to the planner's dilemma on whether the napkins should be purple or plum in colour before admitting that she didn't care which colour was chosen.

'You're the most easy-going bride I've ever worked for,' the planner told her and not for the first time.

No, Ella was simply an unwilling bride, who, while

prepared to play along with appearances for the sake of
her parents, refused to pretend otherwise when it came
to all the bridal decisions. A woman in love would want
everything perfect and would have her own ideas. But
Ella was not in love and no longer the dreaming romantic
girl she had been at the age of twenty-one when she had
fantasised about walking down the aisle clad in blind-
ing white to greet Zarif.

She had taken the phone into the drawing room,
which her parents only used when they entertained. As
she hovered there she remembered her twenty-first birthday and the night when Zarif had first deigned to notice
that she was alive and female. To her surprise, he had
come to her party and he had given her a very pretty
contemporary silver necklace and matching bracelet. Her
heart had been hammering fit to burst while he stood
there chatting to her and when he had invited her out
for a meal the following evening, virtually announcing
his new interest in her, it had been like her every dream
coming true at once.

It was ironic, she had often thought, that Azel had
been Zarif's first love and that Zarif had then become
Ella's. Nobody knew better than Ella how desperately
hard it was to shake free of the trappings of adolescent
fantasy. Zarif had first come into her life when she was
only seventeen and she had taken one dazed look at him
and fallen like a ton of bricks. At that time, he had given
her not the smallest encouragement. His eyes hadn't lingered on her, he hadn't flirted with her and he had never
been alone with her but Ella had still lived for the week-
ends that Jason brought Zarif home with him. The boys
her own age who paid attention to her had seemed like
immature kids in comparison to Zarif, who had spent

five years in his country's army as a soldier before he came to the UK to study for a physics degree. His spectacular good looks, wonderful manners and exotic background had enthralled her.

On their first date he had kissed her and a whole other level of attraction had surged through her in response. She had felt things she had never felt before; she had felt her whole body light up like a blazing torch in his arms and afterwards that had become the bar other men had had to reach to impress her. Only none of them ever had, she conceded reluctantly. And that last kiss, the one in his hotel suite, had proved that Zarif still had the power to make her want to rip his clothes off. Uneasy with that reality, Ella paced the floor.

She had only spoken to Zarif a handful of times on the phone since she had agreed to marry him. He had returned to Vashir while she had been busy running after her parents, dealing with the wedding planner and persuading Cathy to hire someone to take her place rather than asking Ella to sell her share of the business to her. At least she would still have the shop to come home to in a year's time, she reflected ruefully.

Would it even take a year for Zarif to decide that he had had his revenge and was now bored with it and her? What else could possibly be motivating him? She was the woman who had said no and evidently her value in his estimation had leapt sky-high at the same moment. She was convinced that had he slept with her three years earlier, he would no longer have wanted her. But what drove him hardest? Sexual hunger or a need for revenge?

Three years earlier he had been icily outraged by her gauche foot-in-the-mouth refusal of his proposal. He hadn't been prepared for it, hadn't foreseen that even though she was in love with him she had had doubts about whether she could successfully live in his world. So, although she had worded her misgivings clumsily and insulted him, her concerns had been genuine, and layered over the disappointment of learning that he had buried any ability to become emotionally attached to a woman in the grave with his first wife and child.

It totally amazed her that Zarif's desire for her body could act as such a powerful incentive on him. How would he react when she proved inexperienced in his precious bed? Was sex really that important to him? And to offer her marriage on such a score? That was crazy, she thought ruefully, particularly as he presumably had no intention of working to establish a normal marital relationship with her. After all, in a year at most it would be over and she would be a divorcee back at home with her disappointed parents, probably using the excuse that her marriage had broken down because it had just been too difficult to surmount the differences between them in background and culture.

A year was such a short time, she told herself, surely it would pass quickly. Though a split second later she conceded that time never passed quickly though when you were unhappy. She would just have to hope that Zarif was prepared to put more effort into being married to her than his approach had so far suggested...

'You need to get up,' Cathy urged Ella, shaking her awake from a deep dreamless sleep.

Ella looked up drowsily at her best friend, a blonde with a spiky short haircut and bright brown eyes that were currently frowning. She was bemused by her tone of urgency. Cathy had stayed over and they had sat up late relaxing and talking. 'What time is it?'

'Only seven,' Cathy confided ruefully. 'My father came over with the morning papers and then the phone started ringing and that four-letter word has really hit the fan.'

Ella sat up and grabbed her dressing gown. 'What are you talking about? It *is* my wedding day…isn't it?' she queried in a daze.

'You should go downstairs. I'll be tactful and stay up here,' her friend told her uncomfortably. 'My dad's already gone home. There's an utterly preposterous story about you in the newspaper and your parents are upset. There's also a pack of photographers standing out on the drive and I think one of them has his finger stuck in the doorbell. I don't know how you've slept through it all.'

'Blame the large glasses of wine we shared. A story about me? *Photographers?* What on earth?' Ella exclaimed, blundering into the bathroom to steal a moment in which to freshen up before starting down the stairs, noting that the curtains were still pulled in the lounge and also over the glass-panelled front door, cocooning the house in dimness. The phone was off the hook and the doorbell was ringing but seemingly being ignored.

There was a deathly hush inside the kitchen where a newspaper was spread open on the table. Her mother was mopping tears from her reddened eyes and her father was tense and flushed with annoyance.

'What on earth has happened?' Ella whispered.

'Read that,' her father told her, directing a look of angry revulsion at the newspaper.

It was a double-page spread in the *Daily Shout*, the most downmarket tabloid sold in the UK, and generally full of celebrity exposés of cheating married men and women. Scandals sold newspapers but Ella could think of absolutely nothing in her own life, aside of her upwardly mobile wedding plans, which could possibly have attracted such salacious media attention. She froze by the table, recognising the photos scattered at random across the article.

'Where did they get those photos?' she demanded in consternation, because they were *family* photos. There was one of her aged eighteen wearing a bikini on a Spanish beach holiday, another of her as a fair-haired toddler in her mother's arms, yet another of her aged about ten in school uniform.

'Jason must've taken them from the albums in the trunk in our bedroom,' Jennifer Gilchrist opined heavily, ignoring her husband's instant vocal denial of such a possibility. 'It's the *only* possible explanation for this. Nobody else would have known where to find those photos or had access to them.'

'Why the devil would Jason launch a vicious character assassination on his sister on the very day of her wedding?' Gerald Gilchrist demanded.

'Because he's very bitter and selling a sleazy story like that would have got him a lot of money,' Ella's mother breathed in a pained undertone. 'Of course, he told a lot of lies to spice it up—it probably got him a bigger pay-out.'

'Let's not judge without proof,' her father urged uneasily.

'How much proof do you need, Gerald? He's moved out into a flat we didn't know he owned and he texted you to tell you he'd gone skiing yesterday.' Jennifer Gilchrist sighed. 'Where did he get the money to pay for an expensive holiday when he told us he was broke?'

In growing dismay, Ella was studying a more colourful image of herself, racily dressed in a short black leather skirt and a low-necked lace top with fake black wings attached. It had been taken at a Halloween fancy-dress party the previous year. Cathy by her side, the two girls were giggling and slightly the worse for wear. As well as a large photo of Zarif looking very forbidding there was one of a man she didn't recognise and that snapshot was labelled 'Ex-boyfriend, Matt Barton'. Who on earth was Matt Barton? Ella finally took in the headline: THE SEX EXPLOITS OF A FUTURE QUEEN.

Exploits? *What exploits?* Her tummy executing a sick somersault, Ella thrust back a chair and began to read. The salacious content of the article sent shock reeling through her in waves. This Matt Barton claimed she had attended sex parties with him and he called her 'an adventurous woman with a voracious appetite for sex and new experiences.' She was gobsmacked.

'Is it *all* lies?' her father queried darkly. 'I mean, who's this Matt Barton chap? Why have we never heard of him before?'

'Probably because I've never heard of him either… in fact I've never seen him before and I've certainly never gone out with him,' Ella declared between compressed lips as she read. 'Apparently he owns some London nightclub that's just closed down… I do hope Zarif doesn't take this newspaper,' she concluded weakly.

But that was a hope destined to end in instant disappointment when a large dark man in a suit knocked loudly on the back door for entry. As her father lurched forward to deal angrily with what he assumed to be an-

other reporter Ella glanced out, only to be totally transfixed by the sight of Zarif poised squarely in the middle
of their large back lawn, clearly having used the back
entrance to avoid the photographers on the doorstep.
'It's Zarif,' she framed warningly.

'Oh, well, the more the merrier…but the bridegroom
is not supposed to see the bride before the wedding.' Her
mother twittered in consternation while she unlocked
the back door.

Five men as big and bulky as army tanks and clearly
bodyguards ringed Zarif. Immaculate in an exquisitely
tailored grey pinstripe suit cut to enhance every line of
his tall, broad-shouldered, lean-hipped body, he settled
grim dark golden eyes on her. He still looked unutter-
ably gorgeous. She had realised that his mood made little impression on his heartbreaking good looks the day
he first proposed and stood there silently seething at
her rejection without losing a single ounce of his charismatic attraction. He stalked into the kitchen, uttering
a strained but polite acknowledgement of her parents'
presence while her father noisily bundled up the offending newspaper and thrust it into the bin. His real attention, however, was locked to Ella.

Ella reddened, caught barefoot in her comfy tartan
pyjamas and ancient fleece dressing gown without a
scrap of make-up to hide behind. Damn him for not
phoning first, she thought initially, because though the
landline might be off the hook he had her cell number
and he had chosen not to make use of it. Had he deliberately chosen that element of surprise? *Sex parties?*
After reading that ludicrous claim, Ella was convinced
that nothing in life would ever surprise her again. She
had not the slightest doubt that Zarif had read the same

newspaper. Was he now planning to call off the wedding? Consternation filled her, teaching her that, without even knowing it, she had become accustomed to the idea of becoming his wife.

'Ella…may we talk?' Zarif breathed grittily, running eyes as bright as polished black jet over her somewhat bedraggled appearance. Her golden mane fell untidily round her shoulders, framing the luminous oval of her face and somehow magically highlighting her beautiful eyes.

Sex parties, he thought with a rage beyond anything he had ever experienced—a rage that was only held in restraint by a lifetime of iron discipline. The very thought of other men seeing her naked, not to mention the image of her lying beneath another man, sent an energising charge of pure violence roaring through Zarif's tall powerful frame. He wanted to beat someone up, shoot something, smash his fists into walls and shed blood. The idea that there could have been a whole legion of men already well acquainted with the leggy perfection of her slender, curvaceous body sent Zarif into a towering rage.

Ella rose from her seat and led the way into the little-used dining room, turning only when she reached the head of the table to look back at him, her chin set at a mutinous angle as he thrust the door firmly shut behind him. He was going to do it; she knew he was going to do it. He *was* going to ask the one unforgivable question.

Zarif released his breath on a slow hiss. 'Is it true?'

There he was, bang on target, she thought crazily, almost drunk with the sudden rush of anger and disappointment that he could, for even one moment, credit such wild and fantastic stories about her. 'Which bit?

The insatiable desire for sex and the latest kink? Or the sex parties?' she questioned tightly. 'Choose your answer…it's all the same to me.'

Taken aback by her boldness, Zarif shot her an incredulous appraisal, his strong jawline hardening. 'Don't take that attitude with me. I have the right to ask.'

'No, you don't have any rights over me. I'm not married to you yet. You didn't question my past when you had the opportunity and I didn't question you about *yours* either… It's a little late in the day to start changing your mind now.'

His ridiculously long black lashes screened his gaze and a dark flush rose to accentuate the exotic line of his high cheekbones. Something she had said had really hit home hard with him but unfortunately she didn't know which part of her brave speech had struck him like an arrow hitting a bullseye. Indeed she only grasped that she had, for once, inexplicably achieved the feat of putting Zarif out of countenance.

'Unhappily I do not have the freedom to overlook a wife's colourful past. I have too many other considerations to take into account, not least the royal status I would be granting you,' Zarif bit out, lean tanned hands clenching into fists by his side. He could give her up; of course he could give her up if he had to. He could revisit the idea of putting her in the Dubai apartment though, couldn't he? The choking tightness banding his chest receded just a little, comforted by that reflection.

What was she playing at? What the heck was she playing at? Ella asked herself in sudden disconcertion because with a few defiant, well-chosen words she could easily blow her parents' rescue plan right out of the water and she had no wish to do that. But Zarif had disappointed her expectations, demeaning and offending her by asking her that inexcusable question.

Is it true?

But she could see his point; she could *really* see and understand his point. Vashir was a conservative country and a scandal-besmirched queen would be about as welcome there as snow in the desert. Jason had played a blinder, she thought painfully, for how could she possibly defend herself against such accusations? Didn't mud always cling to such victims? But, hell roast it, she was nobody's victim and certainly not her greedy brother's!

'Surely you had my lifestyle checked out before you proposed?' Ella prompted, because it would have struck her as incredibly reckless of him to have proposed without first assuring himself of her continuing suitability and she refused to believe that Zarif had a single reckless bone in his body. 'Surely you already know the answer to your own question?'

'Regrettably not. I had no thought of marriage in mind when we met at the hotel,' Zarif admitted stonily, furious that she wasn't giving him a straight answer.

'My goodness, that was very irresponsible and quite unlike you,' Ella told him in dulcet surprise, her golden head tilting to one side as if she was taking special note of that fact.

His dark-as-molasses eyes flamed tawny gold, his outrage at her mockery unconcealed. *'Answer me!'* he instructed her rawly, his tone cracking like a whip in the smouldering silence.

'Exactly what sort of a past did you think I might have?' Ella enquired in a brittle voice, striving not to yield an inch at the intimidating mien of granite-hard purpose and authority that had hardened his darkly handsome face. He could be tough but she could be tough too when it came to self-defence.

'Nothing out of the ordinary. Obviously I'm not expecting you to be a virgin. I assume you've had the usual adult experiences and I have no desire to pry any more intimately than that into your past. But *that*,' Zarif breathed with harsh emphasis, 'would be my personal outlook. In my public role I have to take into account my people and what they expect from their royal family. We are an old-fashioned people and my family is expected to set high standards. I would also like to know how all this got into the hands of the press.'

'Family photos appeared in that article... Mum and I think that Jason sold the story.'

Zarif frowned in disbelief. '*Jason* has done this to you?'

'You seem surprised. But Jason is burning with resentment and bitterness right now. He's not going to profit in any way from our marriage and that has enraged him.'

'I had assumed he would take the benefits to your parents into account.'

Ella rolled her eyes at that principled view. 'My brother has a vengeful streak. Since you're cut from the same cloth, you should understand that.'

Fresh outrage roared through Zarif. 'In no way can you compare me to your brother!'

'Blackmailing me into marrying you to get me into bed is revenge,' Ella informed him shortly. 'Maybe you still think it's a big thrill and an honour for me but I don't feel the same way.'

'You still haven't answered my question about the veracity of that newspaper story,' Zarif reminded her with stubborn grit, furious that she had labelled his generosity as blackmail when he saw it as something else entirely.

'Because…really, you don't deserve an answer,' Ella condemned with an angry bitterness she couldn't hide. 'And you should be ashamed that you even asked. You knew me three years ago. Can you really credit that I've changed that much?'

A forbidding edge hardened Zarif's jawline. 'I have lived long enough to accept that people *do* change in unexpected ways. Events can make people act out of character,' he pointed out flatly, refusing to yield an inch on that score for he himself had once behaved in such a way.

'I bow to your superior knowledge, but choosing not to marry you three years ago didn't push me into trying out the lifestyle of a porn queen,' Ella declared with licking scorn, blue eyes mutinously bright. 'I've never heard of Matt Barton before, never even met him. I suspect he's someone Jason paid to malign me as, being my brother, it would be odd for Jason to have made sexual allegations against me and it would also have meant exposing the fact that he sold me down the river in the first place.'

A small tithe of the tension holding Zarif rigid eased. 'You've never even met the man who is referred to as your ex-boyfriend?' he pressed. 'You're saying the whole story is a lie? Don't tell me that just to impress me because I will investigate this matter further.'

'Right at this moment,' Ella proclaimed, tossing back her head so that rumpled golden hair tumbled in glossy disarray round her shoulders, 'I haven't the *smallest* desire to impress you.'

'But you *do* need to ensure that our wedding goes ahead,' Zarif reminded her in a roughened undertone because he was noticing that the well-washed cotton of her pyjama jacket was snagging on her pointed nipples, vaguely delineating the firm, full curves of the breasts he longed to explore. He swallowed back a curse, infuriated by his loss of focus and the suspicion that he was behaving like a sex-starved teenage boy.

Zarif's reminder was unnecessary because Ella was painfully aware that her parents' future security was reliant on what she did next. He had gravely offended her but he was the one in the position of power, not she, and, while she refused to grovel, she also saw that she had to fully defend herself to clear her name. 'I'm telling you the truth. I'm not guilty of any of it. I would never *go* to a sex party. I've been set up for a fall and horribly slandered in newsprint.'

'If you are certain that this is the case, I will sue,' Zarif asserted, dark golden eyes welded to her flushed and indignant face with satisfaction. 'But be warned, if I do sue any intimate secrets you have in that line will inevitably be exposed by the proceedings.'

'I have no such secrets,' Ella parried curtly, sucking in a deep sustaining breath. 'My conscience is clean as a whistle. You go ahead and sue.'

'Should I be prepared for genuine disclosures to emerge from any of your former lovers?' Zarif enquired between visibly gritted teeth.

CHAPTER FOUR

ELLA'S EYES GLINTED. Of course she could have told Zarif the truth that she had yet to have a lover but he didn't *deserve* that revelation. Her eyelids lowered secretively while a smile that was amused, but came across as saucy, unexpectedly curved her lips. 'No. In that line you're safe. I've always been cautious about who I choose to date.'

Zarif's gaze burned gold when he saw that smile because he was convinced that she was fondly recalling one of her lovers. He breathed in slow and deep. He was not the jealous, possessive type—what was the matter with him? Other men had slept with her, discovered the secrets of that slim, curvaceous body, listened to her cries of pleasure... Get over it, he told himself impatiently, fighting the tide of destructive X-rated imagery threatening to engulf him. 'This has been a most unlucky start to our wedding day.'

'Yes—' Ella shrugged a careless shoulder '—but let's not pretend it's a real wedding day or that we're people who care about each other like a normal bride and groom.'

His nostrils flared. 'I can assure you that it will be a *real* wedding and that I *do* care about your well-being.'

'Not convinced…sorry about that.' Beneath his disconcerted gaze, Ella lifted a slender hand and screened an uninterested yawn in a disdainful gesture as she moved towards him, keen to show him out of the house. 'If you'd cared, you would have offered me support and felt angry on my behalf.'

Even less accustomed to censure than he was to scorn, Zarif squared his sculpted jaw. 'That is unjust. How would I know whether it was the truth or not when I haven't had any contact with you for years?'

Unimpressed, Ella raised a delicate honey-coloured brow. 'Do you think you could leave now so that I can have breakfast and go do the bridal stuff?' she asked sweetly.

Zarif shot out a lean brown hand and closed it round her wrist to stop her in her tracks. 'You will not speak to me like that or try to dismiss me like a servant,' he told her angrily.

'Does that really matter as long as I go to bed with you?' Ella asked in a brittle voice. 'Do you honestly also expect me to be servile like some sort of medieval sex slave?'

Zarif glowered down at her in seething frustration. She was being childish, her immaturity spelt out in cheap gibes and he was tempted to shake her. *'Stop it.'*

He towered over her, so close that she could smell the faint spicy tang of designer cologne that was achingly familiar to her. Suddenly tears stung the backs of her eyelids as a tide of almost forgotten memories threatened to drown her: deceptively romantic moments three years earlier when he had held her hand, given her thoughtful little gifts, listened carefully to her concerns, acted in a way that was protective and caring. And *it had all been a lie*, she reminded herself bitterly, because his true feelings for her had gone no deeper than a lusty desire to take her to bed and ensure that she became conveniently pregnant with the required son and heir.

'Eleonora…' Zarif chided huskily, running his finger down her cheek to trace the path of an escaped tear. 'You're upset, angry.'

Ella looked up at him, involuntarily enthralled by the beauty of his dark fallen-angel features, the sheer richness of his stunning amber-gold gaze framed by luxuriant ebony lashes. She shivered, inordinately aware of the brush of his finger across her cheek. 'Don't—'

'I *must*,' Zarif growled hoarsely, his hand dropping to her chin to push it up to enable his mouth to come down with hungry driving dominance on hers. Taken by surprise, Ella reeled dizzily, mouth opening to receive the erotic plunge of his tongue. He tasted so wonderfully good, a knot tightened in her pelvis and she gasped, feeling the scandalous dampness of desire surge between her taut thighs in treacherous contrast to her anger with him. The comparison shocked her and broke through the mesmeric power of his mouth on hers.

'No, don't,' Ella protested, squirming against his lean, powerful frame in a manner that only stretched his control thinner than ever.

'Tonight you'll be mine,' Zarif pronounced with unashamed satisfaction, lifting her up against him as though she were a doll and planting her on the edge of the table, pushing her knees apart to stand between them, leaning forward to thrust his aroused body into the apex of her thighs.

Tingling awareness bubbled like a volcano low in her body. Her bright blue eyes widened, pupils dilated as she stared back at him because for once they were on a level. He had sinfully sexy eyes. Her top felt scratchy and uncomfortable against her tender breasts and her breath was catching in her throat. A voice was screaming in the back of her mind, telling her to get a grip, but what kept her still was the warm liquid melting sensation steadily spreading through her lower limbs and most pressing of all, at its pinnacle, a downright unbearable physical ache for the fulfilment she had never known. 'And you'll love every moment of what I do to you,' Zarif forecast hoarsely.

Ella heard his voice through the wall of sensation caused by the outrageous stroke of the long, lean fingers encircling her hips just below her top, the touch of his fingertips across her skin alerting her to an innate sensuality she had not had the chance to experience with him before. She could feel his erection through the fine barrier of his pants and the knowledge that she aroused him even in her pjs and without make-up was ridiculously empowering. She struggled to draw another breath past her tight throat as he pressed his mouth hungrily against the tender skin between her neck and her shoulder and her head fell back without her volition, a tiny gasp escaping her parted lips.

His hands slid up beneath her top and cupped the full globes of her breasts and excitement sent her heart racing so fast she felt light-headed. The surge of heat and wetness between her thighs as he tugged at her straining nipples sent shockwaves through her as his mouth found hers again with a raw passion that thrilled her. Her hands clutched at his arms, nails biting into his sleeves, frustration hurtling through her that she couldn't touch him the way he was touching her.

'Oh, I'm so sorry...!' The sound of her mother's voice and the door opening and closing again in fast succession roused Ella from her sexual stupor as nothing else could have done. She opened her eyes, not even recalling when she had closed them.

Infuriatingly, Zarif had regained control first and had already stepped back from her. She clashed with burning golden eyes and snatched in a shuddering breath, her face crimson as she acknowledged what she had allowed to happen between them. And when she was furious with him too? That was the most galling admission of all: that Zarif could touch her and every other consideration could simply melt away.

'I will see you later, *habibti*,' Zarif murmured tautly, a flush lining his hard cheekbones.

Ella slid off the table like an electrified eel and hauled open the door. Her mother beamed at her from the hall. 'The beautician's here and you haven't had breakfast yet,' she fussed. 'Will Zarif be staying?'

'No...' From behind her, Zarif took over the conversation with effortless ease and not the smallest hint of discomfiture.

Zarif watched his bride exchanging greetings with the children of some of the guests. She was good with little ones, he recognised, watching her animated face and her sparkling eyes as she laughed and chatted, displaying the first warmth she had shown since he saw her at the church. She was so naturally beautiful in her simple elegant gown he had found it a challenge to look away. She had played the bridal role with a shuttered look in her gaze though, polite and smiling but with all true feeling edited out of the show. *His* wife. The designation still felt like a shock—almost as much of a shock as it had been to his uncle Halim when he phoned him three weeks earlier to break the news.

'Of course, it is past time for you to take a wife,' Halim has declared valiantly, holding back on the word, '*again*', diplomatic and generous to the end. 'And British like your grandmother? She will be a popular choice with those who wish us to look West rather than East as we move into the future. I shall look forward to meeting her.'

And for an instant Zarif had felt a piercing shame that he was about to foist such a sham on the old man, who had watched his only child, Azel, become Zarif's first wife, queen and mother before the heart-rending car crash took both her life and that of their son. Devastated, Halim had taken refuge in his academic books, finally requesting permission to leave palace politics and return to his professorship at the university where lectures and students had, at least, distracted him from his grief.

Times without number, Zarif had crushed the futile wish that he too could find such an outlet to escape his memories because the only change in his daily life had been a constant shadow of indescribable loss. Even so, Zarif was well aware that his remarriage, his doing what *had* to be done and before Halim died, would be a comfort to the older man. After all, Halim had raised his nephew to believe that the stability of Vashir came first and last, before personal feelings, *before* everything else. And now, for the first time in his life, Zarif was suddenly shockingly conscious that he was guilty of betraying his duty because he had allowed his desire to possess Ella Gilchrist to suppress every other consideration.

Across the room, a little girl was examining Ella's

shiny new platinum wedding band and complaining mournfully that it didn't sparkle and Ella was explaining the difference between wedding and engagement rings, a clarification that ran out of steam when she was asked why *she* didn't have an engagement ring.

Rising to her feet with a rather stilted laugh, Ella abandoned the challenge, her attention roaming to Zarif, tall, dark and extraordinarily handsome in a tailored morning suit teamed with a grey striped silk cravat, where he was chatting to her parents. He was so damned smooth and polished in his every move that she wanted to scream. Nobody would ever have guessed that the wedding was a charade that cast a respectable veil over the most basic transaction possible between a man and a woman. Inside herself she shrank, thinking there could be little difference between her and any other woman who sold her body for money, for wasn't that exactly what she was doing?

And worst of all, with a male who felt absolutely nothing for her, she reflected wretchedly, for while Zarif's outer façade of cool might have convinced their small select band of guests that he was a joyful bridegroom, it had not fooled Ella. That rare flashing smile of his had not been in evidence once. She just *knew* he was thinking about Azel because she could feel the distance and reserve in him, see the haunting darkness in his eyes. The one and only time he had discussed his first wife with her had been the day he proposed marriage to Ella three years earlier and his words then were still branded into her soul like unhealed wounds.

He had referred to Azel as *irreplaceable* while assuring Ella that he was not asking her to supplant his first wife in her role as that would, apparently, have been an impossible task.

And when she had asked Zarif if he loved her in surely the most poignant question a young woman in love could ask?

'I will always hold Azel in my heart. I cannot pretend otherwise.'

And yet after that little speech, the living proof that some men wouldn't understand or recognise emotion unless it was tipped over their heads like boiling oil, Zarif had been stunned when Ella turned his proposal down. Even madly in love and at only twenty-one years of age, Ella had foreseen what a disaster it would have been for her to have even *tried* to follow in Azel's perfect footsteps. Zarif, whether he had known it or not, hadn't been ready or able to put another woman in Azel's place. Ella, heartbroken, had backed off from such an impossible and thankless challenge.

Accordingly, there Zarif was now mere hours after marrying Ella, no doubt looking back with regret to his first wedding day when he had had the joy of wedding a woman he loved with all his heart and his soul. The very thought hurt, just as it had hurt like an acid burn all those years ago when Ella had been forced to accept that, although she adored Zarif and longed for him with every cell in her body, he would have sacrificed her in a moment if, by some miracle, he could have brought Azel back to life.

He wouldn't have wanted Azel purely for sex, Ella acknowledged unhappily. He had loved and respected Azel and Ella was challenged to understand what she herself had done to rouse such hostility in Zarif that would incur such a devastating revenge. Three years ago, she had said no and her excuses had gone down like a brick on glass but even though she had been in an agony of pain at his virtual rejection of her she had certainly not intended to cause offence.

Of course, rejection had to have been something entirely new to Zarif, she acknowledged ruefully. All women noticed his stunning dark good looks, automatically turning to take a second glance when he was nearby. Those brief weeks she had dated him it had been like going out with a movie star, for everywhere they went women had watched, giggled flirtatiously and tried to catch his eye. He had seemed sublimely unconscious of the effect he had on her sex. He seemed not to have an ounce of vanity but how reliable a character witness was she?

After all, it would never have occurred to Ella three years ago that Zarif would sink to the level of literally *paying* her to share his bed. As soon as she thought that, Ella frowned, reminding herself that she had agreed to his terms for the sake of the parents she loved. *Her* choice, then, and even if she couldn't quite manage to be grateful that he had given her that choice, she knew it would be unjust to blame Zarif for how she felt now that she had accepted the role of mistress within marriage from him. Unhappily, the 'sex and nothing but sex' label made her feel worthless and degraded.

There could be no denying that Zarif had changed and much more than she could ever have expected. The man she remembered had been so upright and so straight in every way and it was ironic that only now when she no longer loved him was she learning that he had a much darker, more complex side to his character and that could only make her fear for her future.

* * *

Ella stared wide-eyed at the opulence of the private jet with its cream leather sofas and luxurious fittings, not to mention the four uniformed cabin staff bowing and scraping respectfully in their presence. She finally sat down, nerves bubbling in her tummy at the knowledge that once the craft was airborne she was leaving home and everything familiar behind. Who knew when she might return?

Already it felt as if the day, which had begun with such drama, was turning into the longest day in existence. They were flying to Vashir and tomorrow would undergo a second wedding ceremony in the presence of Zarif's ailing uncle Halim and the local VIPs. Just then it felt as if she were facing another endurance test in how to please everyone other than herself.

Zarif studied his bride with barely repressed hunger burning in his veiled gaze. Her delicate profile was as taut as her slender body and his attention lingered on the flutter of her lashes, the slim, elegant hand resting on her lap and, more potently, on the thrust of the luscious breasts he had stroked. The hem of her royal-blue dress exposed long shapely legs and he breathed in slow and deep, disturbed by the force of desire gripping him and unaccustomed to such a challenge to his self-control.

No other woman did this to him. He didn't know what it was about Ella but he had barely to look at her to get hard and he shifted in his seat because the tight heaviness at his groin was uncomfortable. Temptation lurked in the existence of the sleeping compartment at the back of the main cabin but it was cramped and time would be short. He didn't want a quick snack, he wanted a feast, a consummation worthy of the time he had waited for her. *His, at last,* he savoured, in name if not yet in action.

Ella leafed through a glossy fashion magazine with blank eyes, her tension rising in the silence rather than abating. 'I was surprised your brothers weren't on the guest list today,' she said abruptly.

'They will be attending our wedding tomorrow,' Zarif proffered. 'I imagine you will be glad of Betsy and Belle's company.'

'I hardly know them, but I suppose so,' Ella conceded in such a limp voice that Zarif wanted to shake her.

Anyone could be forgiven for thinking that marrying him and becoming a queen was a cruel and unusual punishment, Zarif reflected in exasperation. Of course, it was only for a year, he recalled absently, wondering why he hadn't demanded two years or even three until he remembered that sooner rather than later he had to marry for real and reproduce and he marvelled that he could even have momentarily forgotten that salient fact.

'Why didn't you tell me that your mother had had a heart attack and your father a breakdown?' Zarif demanded without warning. 'Your father's friend, Jonathan, spoke to me at the reception and clearly assumed that I already knew.'

Ella compressed her lips. 'I didn't think that plucking a thousand violin strings would cut any ice with you.'

'Telling me would not have been plucking strings,' Zarif censured. 'It would have been giving me relevant facts and it would have changed my outlook.'

Ella shot him a dark look. 'I doubt that very much. I didn't sense any compassion in the room.'

Zarif gritted his teeth, exasperated that she could think him that cruel. Her parents were good, decent people, who had been kind and welcoming to him for several years without any hope of reward or profit. 'You have a seven-hour flight during which I expect you to get over your sulk and accept your new status,' he delivered grimly once the jet was in the air.

'I do *not* sulk!' Ella exclaimed furiously, her blonde head swivelling to deal a fiery glance at his lean, dark, beautiful face.

'Oh, I can assure you that you do,' Zarif drawled, smooth as glass. 'But I am impervious to such moods.'

Ella undid her seat-belt fastening and shot upright as though jet-propelled. 'I will say it once more only...*I am not in a mood!*' She launched the declaration furiously down at him. 'You're as insensitive as a rock. Have you no concept of how difficult it is for me to leave my home to live in a foreign country with a different culture and a man who doesn't even have the saving grace of loving me? Have you any idea how I felt today *lying* and putting on a fake happy-bride act for all my family and friends?'

Zarif stayed where he was and contemplated her with an immense sense of satisfaction for the Ella he knew best was back on display. Her volatile emotions and innate spirit never failed to entertain him while other women displaying similar tendencies had swiftly been dismissed from his life, he acknowledged dimly. But in a rage, Ella was magnificent, sapphire-blue eyes splintering defiance, lovely face angrily flushed, lush bee-stung lips prominent and offering pure pink invitation.

'Are you just going to sit there saying nothing?' Ella positively snarled, nonplussed by his stillness and lack of reaction.

'When you get all steamed up,' Zarif murmured huskily, 'you look incredibly hot and sexy.'

Ella did what any sane woman would have done, because it was clear that he had not paid heed to a single word she had said. She lifted her glass of water and emptied it over his arrogant dark head. 'Then it's time you cooled off…'

Totally taken aback by that liquid assault, Zarif sprang upright, tawny eyes ablaze with anger and no small amount of disbelief as he flicked dripping black hair off his wide, intelligent brow. 'You are behaving like a madwoman!'

'No, a madwoman would have used a knife, not water,' Ella told him succinctly. 'Now I will say it again. I was not sulking. I'm simply nervous about the challenge of embracing a new lifestyle.'

'And so you should be because I am no pushover when I lose my temper!' Zarif grated as he snatched her off her feet without the smallest warning and stalked stormily down the cabin to thrust open the door at the foot.

'Put me down!' Ella yelled at him.

Zarif dropped her from a height down onto a bed without a great deal of bounce and she fell back against the pillows, bright honey-coloured hair rioting round her flushed features. She surveyed him in shock as he began to wrench off his jacket and haul at his tie. 'What are you doing?' she demanded.

'You soaked my clothing,' he reminded her grittily as he ripped open the buttons on the white silk shirt plastered to his muscular chest. 'And if we're about to have a row, we will stage it in here where it is more private.'

Ella sat up, more than a little embarrassed at the water she had thrown over him. 'I shouldn't have drenched you…but when you go all stony-faced and unemotional, I *hate* it!'

'I *am* unemotional by nature,' Zarif shot back at her as he stripped off the shirt. 'I'm afraid you'll just have to learn to deal with that. Assaulting me isn't an option I'm prepared to tolerate.'

Ella's tummy somersaulted and a slow heavy heat spread in her pelvis as she looked at him because he, undoubtedly, had the most beautiful male body she had ever seen. Roped muscle defined his broad bronzed torso. Dark whorls of hair adorned his impressive pecs, arrowing down over a flat washboard stomach to disappear below the belt encircling his lean hips. For a split second, he simply took her breath away.

'Particularly when there are so many more entertaining possibilities on offer now,' Zarif completed softly as he came down on his knees on the bed beside her, still bare chested, his tailored trousers pulling taut across his lean, powerful thighs.

Unnerved, Ella froze like a stone pillar. 'I don't know what you mean.'

'Of course you do,' Zarif contradicted, running a mocking fingertip along the compressed line of her mouth. 'Freezing into stillness like an animal being hunted isn't going to save you. You're my wife. I can touch you, *hunt* you any time I like…'

That awareness had taunted Ella from the moment he whipped off his shirt without a shade of self-consciousness to expose his glowing bronzed skin and whipcord muscles. But then why would Zarif be self-conscious in any intimate situation? Ella mocked her own naivety, all too painfully aware of the many highly experienced lovers he had evidently enjoyed. He was so close now that she could have reached out and touched him and her fingers braced harder to the mattress as if she feared being tempted. And she *did* fear it because he had always tempted her and it would destroy her self-respect if she gave him anything more than passive compliance.

Zarif lowered his head and used his lips to pluck teasingly at the taut line of hers. Oxygen feathered in her tight throat and with a faint gasp she opened her mouth. But he continued to play games with her, suckling at her lower lip and then darting the tip of his tongue along the underside of her lip, setting off an astonishing flurry of reaction that slithered through her like a sweet piercing dart that went deep. She trembled, astonishingly aware of the prickling tightness of her nipples, and then all of a sudden, literally between one breath and the next, she wanted his mouth hard on hers with a ferocity that shook her. Her hands wanted to claw into his hair to drag his head down to hers.

Her head fell back on her shoulders even as she felt the faint brush of his fingers against her spine. Cooler air washed her backbone and surprise gripped her as she registered that he had unzipped her dress without her even noticing. Her lashes flew up, her gaze connecting with scorching gold fringed with lush black lashes. He had such beautiful eyes, she acknowledged, and every other thought in her head evaporated simultaneously.

Zarif tugged the perfumed weight of her honey-blonde hair forward as he eased the dress down her arms. 'I always loved your hair… It's the most amazing colour when the sun catches it.'

'No sun here,' she framed nervously, feeling alarmingly shy at being stripped down to her bra and panties. He was coolly undressing her without a hint of passion and she was so unnerved by the experience that she could not even contemplate the much greater intimacy that surely still lay ahead of her.

Hard as a rock, Zarif studied the ripe mounds of her full breasts and swiftly removed the bra to cup the lush heavy globes in his appreciative hands. He stroked the quivering tips to aching sensitivity and only then did he kiss her.

Ella quivered, her whole body alight and tingling. Her hands dug into his shoulders as he took her rosy nipples between his fingers while claiming her mouth in a long drugging kiss. He skated his tongue across the sensitive roof of her mouth and she gasped, starting to moan as he let his tongue plunge deep in a much more primitive demand. The ache in her pelvis tightened like a knot being snapped tight, every atom of control wrested from her as mindless hunger took her in a shocking surge.

Zarif tugged her down flat on the bed, deft hands releasing her from the confines of the dress creased round her hips. He kept on kissing her and, oh, he was *so* good at it that she was on fire, pushing closer to his lean, hard body, wanting more, her entire body stimulated to a painful degree by responses more powerful than any she had previously experienced.

Zarif lifted his head to gaze down at her while he trailed his fingers through the damp tangle of curls at the apex of her thighs. 'I want to watch you writhe and come, *habibti*,' he husked. 'I want to hear you scream with the pleasure I give you.'

'Don't want to scream,' Ella framed with the greatest of difficulty, so hard was it for her to control her breathing and her voice enough to speak.

A fingertip found the swollen bud of her clitoris and

dallied. He knew exactly what he was doing. He touched and she burned with every delicate caress. Her hips rose off the mattress in a movement as old and unstoppable as time. She struggled to breathe, actually sobbed out loud as he lowered his proud dark head and captured an engorged pink nipple between his lips and teased with his teeth. As he divided his attention between her straining, unbearably sensitive breasts and the tormentingly tender bud between her thighs, the twin assault became too much for her to bear. The hollow sensation at the heart of her was getting stronger while rhythmic waves were washing through her womb until suddenly the knot of tension there sprang free, plunging her into the grip of writhing convulsions of almost intolerable pleasure.

That shattering climax and the flood of ecstasy that followed took her by storm.

Zarif stared down at her, glittering tawny eyes alight with a new knowledge that made Ella cringe. She closed her eyes in self-protection, shamed by her complete loss of control. He pulled a sheet over her.

'Get some rest,' he advised smoothly. 'Tomorrow's festivities will last even longer than today's and tonight I would prefer you wide awake.'

Hot with mortification and with her body still liquid as melting honey from his sensual attentions, Ella lay there long after the cabin door had closed behind him. It was only Zarif she could not resist, she tried to tell herself in consolation. Other men had tried and failed to seduce her into going further than she wanted to but Zarif did not even have to try. Why was that? How would she ever look him in the face again? At least, however, he would know what he was doing even she did not, she told herself soothingly, nervous tension pinching at her as she considered the night that still lay ahead.

CHAPTER FIVE

THE AIRPORT LAY just outside the city of Qurzah. The jet landed to be greeted by a formal welcome in the form of a military band, a crowd of officials and a very cute little girl in a fancy frock, who curtsied and presented Ella with a bouquet. Ella was relieved that she had followed her mother's advice and chosen a classy outfit to travel in because her mostly vintage wardrobe would not have met conservative expectations. Her blue shift dress, jacket and high heels, however, exactly fitted the bill.

Zarif watched his bride respond with beaming charm to the greetings and would have been more impressed had she once aimed those sparkling eyes and smiles in his direction. She was stubborn, capricious and paraded her moods too easily.

He marvelled that he had asked her to marry him *for real* only three years earlier. What *had* he been thinking of? Had he become obsessed by his overwhelming desire to make her his? Unlike him she had not been raised to respect the concept of duty or the rules and the restraint that went hand in hand with the exalted and privileged status of the al-Rastani dynasty. When the time came, he would be practical and he would seek a wife from one of the other Gulf royal families, one who knew exactly what he needed from her, he reflected grimly, wondering why the very prospect of that day should make his heart sink like a stone.

The limo wafted them through the crowded streets of Qurzah and he watched Ella look surprised when she saw the modern layout of the city as well as the shopping malls and the many parks adorned with fountains and sculptures. 'It's just like any city,' she remarked in evident relief. 'But rather more attractive than many I've visited.'

'We are not a backward or primitive country,' Zarif countered drily. 'The oil wealth of decades and an education system and health service second to none have naturally made their mark.'

'I didn't think Vashir was backward…although you don't let women drive here,' Ella commented in a small aside redolent of her incredulity at such an embargo.

Zarif breathed in deep and slow and tried not to grit his teeth. He sometimes thought that his country was more famous for that restriction than for anything else and he would be changing that perverse law as soon as his uncle was no more. To do so beforehand had struck him as needlessly distressing for the old man, rousing as it would grievous memories that were better left buried.

The limo purred between lofty gates into a property surrounded by tall walls and turrets. Ella gazed in wonderment at the vast ancient building stretched out before her because with its Moorish arches, weathered and elaborate stonework and the glorious greenery softening the frontage it was very redolent of an Arabian nights fantasy dwelling. 'I thought the palace was brand new.'

'The new one is on the other side of the city and used for government council meetings, conferences and all official functions. This is where I grew up and I prefer to live here, certainly while my uncle is ill,' Zarif proffered, his beautiful wilful mouth tightening as if he was waiting for her to argue.

Ella said nothing although she had pinned her confidence on staying at the new palace where she could be secure in the awareness that Zarif's first wife could never have lived there. So much for that hope! And why should she be so oversensitive anyway? It was not as if she were in love with Zarif or jealous, she reasoned, exasperated by her odd thought train.

She slid from the car. Darkness was falling and the heat was already less oppressive than it had been at the airport where within minutes of being deprived of air-conditioning cool her dress had literally felt as though it were plastered to her damp, perspiring skin. 'It looks like a fascinating building.'

'Hamid will show you round.' Zarif referred to his chief aide. 'His father used to be in charge of running the old palace and he, too, grew up here. He knows everything about the palace's history.'

Ella would have been more impressed had Zarif offered to conduct such a tour personally and kept her expressive eyes veiled as she reasoned that she had been shown her true importance in the grand scheme of things again. Not that she wasn't already well aware of her lowly status. Regardless of the fleeting intimacy they had shared, Zarif remained ultra-cool and detached. Her body might still hum at the very thought of his fingers trailing across her sensitive skin but he was still as remote as the Andes.

A small crowd of women in distinctly elaborate clothing waited two steps inside the giant front doors of an echoing stone hall ornamented by a long parade of pillars.

'I am Hanya,' a very pretty dark-eyed brunette informed Ella in perfect English. 'I will look after you until tomorrow.'

Zarif froze on the threshold, ebony brows pleating and rising in a frown. 'Where are you taking my wife, Hanya?' he demanded abruptly.

'According to the imam Miss Ella Gilchrist will not be your legal wife or our queen until tomorrow, cousin,' Hanya announced in a soft, deeply apologetic tone, her head bowing low as if she hated to break such news. 'Our uncle discussed his regard for the old ways with me and I'm afraid this is what he expects.'

Zarif almost looked heavenward to pray for patience but restrained the urge. Hanya had been cousin to Azel and insisted on maintaining the bond between them created by marriage. But Hanya was right. Halim was an old-fashioned man, always eager to venerate the proprieties. Clearly, Zarif had another day to wait before he was able to claim his bride. He threw back his shoulders, ready to lay down the law and refuse to part with her to a separate bed. After all, Ella was still his wife even if she hadn't yet married him according to Vashiri law and the concept of restraining his already very unruly libido for still longer had no appeal whatsoever.

A year, his more honourable and tolerant self reminded him staunchly, to take the edge off his temper. Ella would be his for an entire year…surely he could wait another day? He did not want to disappoint or alarm his uncle and with a brief jerk of his arrogant dark head he strode past, pausing only to say to Ella, 'I will see you tomorrow, then.'

'Thank you, Your Majesty.' Hanya, who had an extremely irritating laugh, giggled like a little girl and
clutched Ella's sleeve with a dainty, perfectly manicured
hand. 'I will show you to your suite…come this way.'

The following morning Ella winced and cringed through
what had amounted to a public bathing experience in
which she was surrounded by a flock of strange women
wanting to bath her, wax her and anoint her body and
her hair with exotic scented oils. After that ordeal, being
wrapped in a modern towelling robe felt refreshingly
normal, and it was almost relaxing to have to sit down
and patiently wait while a pair of henna artists knelt on
the floor beside her to draw intricate swirling patterns
onto her hands and her feet.

Indeed Ella was feeling remarkably tolerant and relieved that she was getting through the trial of the wedding preparations without losing her temper or showing
irritation because she did not want to spoil the day by in-
sulting Vashiri bridal traditions or rejecting them. After
all, there was no doubt whatsoever that her female companions, virtually none of whom spoke English, were
overjoyed that their king was getting married again.
That she was a foreigner did not appear to be a stum-
bling block in any way.

'Ella!' A female voice carolled from the doorway
and Ella glanced up to see Cristo Ravelli's vibrant wife,
Belle, with her mane of wild Titian hair, surging towards
her and she grinned because it was quite impossible to
do anything else. Although she had met Zarif's brothers and their wives on only one previous occasion she
had not forgotten Belle with her warm Irish friendliness,
or the quieter but no less sociable Betsy, because at the

time she had met them—*before* Zarif's proposal—she had been fantasising that some day she would become a part of their close-knit family circle as well.

'I thought we were never going to get through all the obstacles being put up to us joining you up here!' Belle exclaimed, settling a heap of gift-wrapped packages and an enormous tote bag down carelessly on the floor. 'This is my first visit to this palace. I had no idea it was still running at about five hundred years behind the times.'

'Belle…' Tiny blonde Betsy emerged from behind Belle and bent down to kiss Ella's cheek in greeting. 'How are you bearing up?'

'Oh, don't waste time asking her that!' Belle exclaimed. 'No, we're more interested in hearing why you said no three years ago and are now suddenly saying yes to our Desert King.'

Ella froze at that blunt question, which was, nonetheless, perfectly understandable in the circumstances. 'That would be a…er…challenging story to tell. Hanya,' she murmured, seeing the pretty brunette hovering with a suspiciously stiff look on her face as if she resented the intrusion of the two Western women. 'Could we have some drinks and snacks for Zarif's family, please?'

'I thought the whole palace was dry,' Belle commented out of the corner of her mouth. 'Not that Zarif doesn't take the occasional alcoholic drink, but the old boy who's ill never touches a drop of the evil stuff.'

'If you put your foot in your mouth one more time I'm not going to fish you out of it!' Betsy warned her companion on the back of a groan. 'Ella, we're here to provide support.'

'We're here to celebrate!' Belle contradicted. '*Why* would Ella need support? She's marrying a gorgeous billionaire who's also a reigning king and obviously he's madly in love with her because I'm shocked he's forgiven her for rejecting him the first time around!'

'No, he's not madly in love with me and I'm not sure he's forgiven me either,' Ella heard herself admit flatly as glasses of pomegranate juice and a tray of little appetisers were handed round. Belle wrinkled her nose at the lack of stronger spirit in her beverage.

'Cheers,' Belle pronounced nonetheless, knocking her glass noisily against Ella's. 'Cristo wasn't in love with me when we got married either, so don't worry about it. That came afterwards and surprised us both. I married him to get a name and security for our half-siblings and he married me to stop me going to court to fight for their rights. But I know Zarif…he *has* to be in love.'

'Why?' Ella asked baldly before tucking into a tiny delicious appetiser consisting of a mini pastry case and a mousse filling.

'Because all this is happening so fast. It's just *not* Zarif. He's usually so cool and right now he's acting all hot-headed and spontaneous.'

'That is true.' Betsy too was looking thoughtful.

Hanya intervened to tell Ella that it was time for her to get dressed. An elaborate kaftan was displayed to her along with a silk chemise composed of several voluminous layers while Hanya added that underwear was not traditionally worn.

Belle frowned when she saw Ella's expression of dismay and stooped down to her collection of parcels to retrieve one and present it to Ella with a flourish. 'One of my gifts is some pretty lingerie. The bride has to wear something new, Hanya. It's one of *our* traditions and going naked beneath a petticoat isn't.'

Ella vanished into the giant Victorian bathroom with the gift box and wrenched it open to pull out a handful of pristine white lace, the sort of fancy underpinnings she had never worn in her life but the prospect of wearing them was infinitely preferable to going bare, with large breasts that felt uncomfortable without support. She put them on in a rush, fearful that at any moment the door, which did not have a lock, would open because her tribe of watchful Vashiri companions did not seem to have much idea that a woman might want privacy from an audience. Pulling the robe back on, she returned to the huge bedroom.

Within the space of a minute the heavy kaftan was being swiftly dropped over her head, the hooks fastened and the satin ribbon ties tightened to fit. The elaborate hand-done embroidery on the sky-blue fabric was truly magnificent.

'That doesn't look half bad,' Belle began in evident surprise.

'It's beautiful…especially with your colouring,' Betsy cut in with an admiring smile.

Ella sat down in a chair while her hair was brushed. 'I'll do my own make-up,' she told Hanya firmly when extravagant compacts of very brightly coloured eye shadows were unfurled threateningly in front of her. 'Zarif doesn't like a lot of make-up.'

And then she thought, Why am I thinking like that, as though I *want* to make myself more attractive for him? Where did that weird thought come from? Had it been born in the moment when with only a little elementary foreplay Zarif had sent her careening into an explosive climax, giving her more pleasure than she had ever dreamt was possible? Her cheeks burned with mortification.

Belle thrust a glass into her hand. *'Enjoy,'* she urged. 'Don't let Hanya bully you.'

'I'm not timid. I'm just very reluctant to do or say anything that might offend anyone,' Ella confided wryly as she sipped and munched on another appetiser. 'And she *has* to know the right way to do everything here because she was Azel's cousin.'

'And unless I'm very much mistaken, she was exceedingly hopeful that Zarif would marry her, *not* you. I sense a generous helping of the old green monster envy every time she looks at you,' Belle spelt out in her ear.

Ella's eyes rounded as she did her make-up. 'But I won't ever measure up to Azel,' she muttered in rueful acceptance.

'First wife still casting a big shadow in the present, is she?' Betsy murmured. 'You shouldn't let that bother you. I mean, it's not as if Zarif *chose* to marry her. He was *told* he would be marrying her when he was only a kid. It was set in stone, an arranged marriage—no romance there or any room to act on his own feelings in such a rigid set-up. You were the very *first* woman he went on a date with and *he chose you...*'

He chose you. It was a different take on Zarif's history, which Ella had not previously considered, and she was grateful for it. Her shadowed eyes suddenly brightened and she laughed, unable to kill the smile creeping across her formerly tense mouth. 'Are you serious?'

'Very. Zarif was married at eighteen and he was a virgin when he got married. Nik and Cristo tried to persuade him to wait longer before tying the knot but Zarif followed his grandfather's dictates and he always puts his duty to his country first. Let's face it, all Zarif's advisors were mad keen to marry him off to a suitable woman asap, particularly once he began connecting with his half-brothers from the West. When he met you three years ago, we were all really happy for him.'

Ella stiffened and wielded her mascara brush with great care. 'It didn't work out.'

'None of us understand why. It was *so* obvious you were mad about him when we first met,' Belle told her bluntly. 'You couldn't take your eyes off him. It was kind of sweet.'

In chagrined silence, Ella swallowed more of her drink and Belle topped it up with a tall bottle that had come out of nowhere. 'What's that?' she asked.

'Vodka. I had it in my bag. I'm not swearing off drink at a wedding,' Belle declared defiantly.

'I shouldn't have too much… I haven't much of a head for alcohol,' Ella admitted.

Her make-up done, Ella stayed still while an elaborate coin-hung headdress was anchored to her brow. Then it was time to gaze in a full-length mirror at the vision of exotic splendour she had become in her opulent royal regalia.

'Now we go and view some ceremonial sword dance,' Belle announced cheerfully, having had a discussion with a very disapproving Hanya while urging Ella towards the door and slotting her glass back in her hand. 'Drink up. I haven't yet given up hope that I can transform you into a *happy* bride.'

Guilt assailed Ella as she realised she had not been putting on a good enough show to make the expected impression. *A happy bride?* No indeed. But, these women were members of Zarif's family and she should've been trying harder. 'I'm sorry, I'm—'

'No worries,' tiny Betsy whispered, squeezing her arm comfortingly. 'Weddings are ninety-nine per cent stress even without cultural differences involved.'

'But thanks to our objections you're not going to be sentenced to a female-only reception,' Belle broke in with satisfaction. 'For the first time ever, a palace wedding will be a mixed gathering. We talked Zarif into it last night and he admitted that many of his subjects have long since abandoned all this dated separating-the-sexes-stuff. If you ask me, you can blame his uncle for all the old-fashioned stuff around here. Nobody wants to tread on *his* toes.'

'Hush…' Ella urged, skimming concerned eyes at the forthright redhead while she rubbed her aching brow with a fleeting brush of her fingers because she was starting to get what she assumed to be a tension headache. 'Zarif is very attached to his uncle Halim and he's seriously ill.'

'If you can't say something nice, say nothing,' Betsy advised. 'Ella's not used to you yet.'

'But I do like and respect honesty,' Ella admitted, following Hanya out onto a large stone balcony. A large group of men wielding swords and clad in white traditional robes were lined up in the courtyard below. Towards the rear she could see Nik and Cristo, Zarif's brothers, standing in the shade to watch. Zarif was easiest of all to pick out of the crowd. He wore magnificent gold-coloured robes that glimmered in the brilliant sunshine. A belt with an ornate golden dagger thrust through it accentuated his narrow waist. His white *kaffiyeh* was bound with a double gold cord and, framed by that pale backdrop, his hard bronzed features were shockingly handsome. It was all very solemn and serious. A drum beat sounded and the lines of men shifted their feet at a rhythmic pace, roared something incomprehensible and lunged forward with their swords.

'Could we have just five minutes alone with our sister?' Belle asked Hanya pleadingly.

With a look of deep resentment, the young Vashiri woman backed into the corridor and Belle shut the door on her while heaving a sigh of relief. 'Of course you can't talk with her listening in!'

Ella drank from her glass. She felt incredibly thirsty, her mouth very dry as she watched Zarif leap across the central fire pit with astonishing athleticism and grace, his lean, muscular body soaring high above the flames. At that moment he simply took her breath away.

'He's so fit and he's probably been doing that stuff since he was about five years old,' Betsy commented admiringly. 'Nik said he had a very traditional upbringing with his grandparents and his uncle.'

Belle was scanning Ella's expressive face as she watched her handsome bridegroom bring down his sword with a metallic clash to meet the other men's weapons in the inner circle. 'Why on earth did you reject him three years ago?'

'None of our business,' Betsy slotted in uneasily.

'He told me he would always love Azel and that she was irreplaceable,' Ella heard herself admit before she could think better of it.

'You're kidding me,' Belle breathed, her face stunned. 'I can't believe he was that stu—'

'At least he was honest,' Ella countered defensively.

'It wasn't what I wanted to hear but I was better off knowing.'

'Men!' Belle exclaimed in a tone of lingering disbelief as Ella opened the door to invite Hanya back in to join them. Ella was annoyed with herself for speaking so freely and reckoned that Hanya's deflating presence would, at least, make her guard her tongue.

When the dance was finished, Ella's mind was stuffed with exotic imagery of Zarif as she had never seen him before. Hanya led them downstairs into an ornately tiled room where Zarif was waiting with his brothers, the imam and an older man in a wheelchair with a nurse hovering over him. Halim al-Rastani's poor state of health was obvious in his sunken dark eyes and pallor but he smiled warmly at Ella and he lifted a frail hand to urge her to come closer.

Lean, strong face grave, Zarif moved forward to join her and perform a formal introduction.

'You are indeed very beautiful,' Zarif's uncle told her kindly. 'It is a joy for me to meet you at last. May you and my nephew be blessed with many children and a long life.'

Momentarily colliding with Zarif's warning golden gaze and feeling rather as though she had run into a brick wall, Ella swallowed hard and lowered her lashes. Quite ridiculously she felt guilty about the reality that she had no intention of having any children with Zarif and indeed was currently taking medication that should prevent pregnancy. Her head was also beginning to swim a little. It had to be the heat getting to her, she thought ruefully, perspiration dampening her upper lip. The palace had ceiling fans everywhere but no proper air conditioning and she was sweltering in the heavy kaftan layered with petticoats.

The imam stepped forward and began to speak while Betsy's husband, Nik, stationed himself to Ella's left side and quietly and smoothly translated every word of the Arabic ceremony for her benefit. A guiding hand resting in the shallow indentation of her spine, Zarif led her over to the table where a document awaited their signatures.

'The marriage contract,' Zarif explained as the witnesses followed suit. He lifted a large and ornate wooden box from the table and extended it to Ella.

'What's this?' she whispered, leaning slightly sideways at the sheer weight of the box.

'It's the *mahr*...your dowry,' Nik translated with some amusement.

Hamid darted forward to remove the box from Ella's hold and bestow it on Hanya, who was waiting outside the door.

'I have a *dowry*?' Ella muttered to Zarif, her disbelief at the explanation unconcealed.

One hand cupping her elbow, Zarif drew her into an alcove off the corridor. His lean, extravagantly handsome face was forbidding in its uninformative stillness. 'It is traditional that I give my bride the royal jewel collection.'

'But you've already given my family so much,' Ella muttered in growing discomfiture.

'That is our private business. I sincerely doubt that you want that fact spread round my entire family,' Zarif spelt out very drily. 'I'm sure I need not add that you must surrender the jewels when we part.'

Her face flamed hotter than a fire in embarrassment and she tore her discomfited gaze from his lean, darkly handsome features, embarrassment and resentment creating a heady tempest of reaction inside her. 'I'm not stupid,' she declared, wrenching her arm free of his and leaving the alcove to join Hanya where she waited with the box several feet away.

'Your Majesty.' Hanya curtsied to her for the first time and ushered Ella into another room. 'You will want to put on some jewellery before you meet your guests.'

In actuality there was nothing Ella wanted to do less than don any piece of jewellery that was only on loan to her until Zarif took a *real* wife and which had previously been worn by Azel. How dared he assume that she would have the cheek to try and retain valuables that did not belong to her after their fake marriage ended? Pride brought her chin up but she thought better of protest and compressed her lips, leaving Hanya to the task of selecting items from the overflowing casket of glittering gold-encased gems.

Decked out, in her own opinion, like a Christmas tree, Ella followed Hanya slowly into the vast reception room where all the guests were gathered. Hanya left her hovering just inside the doorway and approached Zarif. Ella watched the dainty brunette speak to her tall, powerfully built husband and wondered what Azel's cousin was saying to stamp such a look of brooding dissatisfaction on Zarif's lean, strong face. Ella joined Belle, who admired the collar of flawless sapphires encircling Ella's elegant neck and the superb matching pendant earrings reaching almost to her shoulder.

'Wow,' Belle breathed in reverent admiration. 'I've seen loads of jewels but in all my life I've never seen anything to equal the size and clarity of those.'

Zarif studied his bride, whose gait was almost imperceptibly unsteady. His expressive mouth tightened. While the famous sapphires certainly enhanced the breathtaking gentian blue of her eyes, the feverish colour highlighting her cheekbones and the pallor of her porcelain skin beyond it were equally obvious to him. Most probably the large amount of alcohol she had consumed was having an effect, he thought derisively, furious that she could have been so foolish as to indulge in such a dangerous practice when their behaviour was the focus of every person present.

One hand on her elbow as guidance, he escorted her round the room to introduce her to local dignitaries and then he took her through to the banqueting room where the wedding meal was being staged.

Ella was feeling very hot, literally as though she were burning up below the kaftan. There was a sensation of tightness across her chest and her breath was wheezing and catching a little in her throat. The jewellery was as heavy as the dress and she felt dizzy and slightly nauseous. 'I think I need to sit down,' she told Zarif before he could make her talk to any more strangers.

A pair of throne-like chairs sat below a canopy and he settled her down in one with great care. 'Food will be brought to us,' he informed her, taking a seat by her side.

Ella had never felt less hungry in her life. Indeed the prospect of food turned her stomach. There was a metallic taste in her mouth and her throat felt funny. Strong black coffee was served to her by a kneeling servant.

'Coffee will sober you up,' Zarif pronounced with lethal derision.

'I'm not drunk…I only had *one* drink,' Ella whispered back at him, staring at him in consternation and surprise. 'And I don't feel like coffee.'

'Drink it,' Zarif instructed in a raw aside.

Ella felt more like throwing it at him but, conscious that they were the cynosure of attention, she sipped doggedly at the bitter brew, hoping it would ease her tight throat. Unfortunately the coffee seemed to exacerbate her nausea and before very long she flew upright without a word to Zarif and headed off in urgent search of the nearest cloakroom.

'Where are you going?' he demanded, catching her hand in his to still her in her tracks.

'Cloakroom...*sick*!' she gasped in desperation.

He urged her out through a side door with a scantily leashed curse. 'In there...' he told her grimly.

In merciful privacy, Ella lost the meagre contents of her stomach and then hung on the edge of the vanity unit to stay upright while she tried to freshen her mouth. Cramping pains continued to course across her abdomen. She was feeling really ill and she staggered slightly as she reeled dizzily back to Zarif's side. 'I'm not well,' she muttered shakily, feeling hot and cold and dreadful, black spots appearing in her vision.

'You will have to control it,' Zarif informed her unsympathetically.

Her head swimming, her legs hollow and weak, Ella gave him an incredulous glance from heavily lidded eyes and then she dropped like a stone to the tiled floor at his feet.

CHAPTER SIX

Zarif studied his bride, his stern gaze welded to the still slight figure in the big bed. Recent events had made certain facts painfully clear: Ella was his wife and his to protect. *His* responsibility alone. And he had almost lost her, indeed come within minutes of doing so and he was still in shock from the experience.

Had he known what he was doing when he married her? Had he really believed he could shrug off all sense of obligation and sidestep the commitment? So what if, once, she had played games with him and hurt his pride? She had only been a girl, a fickle, lively girl playing with fire without knowing she could get burned. And yet he *had* intended to burn her, had intended to punish her.

His wide sensual mouth compressed on the acknowledgement that everything had changed in the space of a moment, the same moment in which Ella had collapsed at his feet. He had made a grievous error of judgement and it could have cost Ella her life. He did not want to picture a world in which Ella no longer walked. His bitterness was not so deep, his pride not so high. He still wanted her more than he had ever wanted a woman and he could not let her go, he *would* not let her go until he was free of his craving for her. Only then could he move on and remarry, awarding his next wife the full unquestioning commitment that was her due.

Ella's eyelashes fluttered and then lifted on a dimly lit room.

An ornate canopy hung over the bed. The edges of the fabric were fringed and tasselled and swinging a little in the breeze. She identified the source of the breeze as the whirring fan in the background and put a hand up to discover what was covering her nose.

'Don't touch the oxygen mask!' Zarif warned her, suddenly appearing by the side of the bed and giving her a fright.

Ella blinked up at him as though he were a mirage. Muddled and confusing images of the sword dance, the wedding and the guests were racing through her mind faster than the speed of light until she recalled the last ignominious moment in the cloakroom, after which everything became a complete blank.

'What happened?' she whispered limply, focusing on his lean, darkly handsome face, paying special notice to the black spiky lashes that heightened the effect of his stunning dark golden eyes. Evidently, his mood hadn't improved because he still looked bleak and forbidding as hell.

Disconcertingly, Zarif sank down with confusing informality on the side of the bed and closed an imprisoning hand over hers as it crept inexorably towards the irritating oxygen mask again. 'You almost died.'

'That's not possible,' Ella told him, shifting her arm and only then noticing the IV attached.

'We believe you are allergic to shellfish.'

'I'm not allergic to shellfish. I'm not allergic to anything,' Ella proclaimed.

'You may not have been until today but you *are* allergic now. The shellfish pastries you ate before the wedding are the most likely explanation and when you are better you will undergo tests so that we can discover what it is safe for you to eat. You went into anaphylactic shock. I thought you were drunk…and all the time you were *ill*,' Zarif breathed in a hoarse undertone of remorse, dark eyes blazing gold over her flushed face, his lean hand tightening over hers. 'If Halim's doctor had not been present and able to administer an immediate shot of adrenalin, you could have gone into cardiac arrest.'

Ella breathed in slow and deep. 'But I didn't. I'm fine,' she told him quietly. 'What a thing to happen in public—you must've been very embarrassed.'

'Embarrassment was the least of my concerns,' Zarif admitted. 'I wronged you. I made an unjust assumption and you suffered for it. Hanya told me you'd drunk a lot of alcohol.'

Ella stiffened. 'That *is* a lie. Belle gave me one drink. It may have been a large drink but there was only one and I didn't finish it.'

'It is immaterial. I should naturally have given you the benefit of the doubt. It is my duty to look after you and I failed and it could have cost you your life,' he breathed harshly.

'How on earth could you have known that I was going to suffer a severe allergic reaction to something I ate?' Ella asked ruefully. 'It's not your fault. It's not anyone's fault. It was just bad luck.'

'Nonetheless, we will be very, very careful about what you eat in the future,' Zarif decreed. 'Dr Mansour warned me that another attack could be fatal. He asked me to call him as soon as you wake up.'

In a daze, Ella watched Zarif unfurl his cell phone and within minutes the middle-aged doctor put in an appearance. He confirmed that it was possible to suddenly become allergic to a substance that one might have eaten for years without ill effects but while urging her to exercise caution he was considerably less dramatic about her prospects than Zarif had been. Zarif, Ella registered, was in still in shock at her collapse and blaming himself for it. The oxygen mask removed because she was breathing easily and the IV removed because she faithfully promised to drink lots of water, she levered herself up against the pillows once they were alone again.

'I'm sorry about all this,' she murmured awkwardly. 'I suppose it's no use telling you that I'm usually as healthy as a horse.'

'I owe you an apology,' Zarif murmured tautly. 'I misjudged you. I should have realised that you were genuinely ill.'

'How could you have?' Ella parried uneasily. 'I didn't realise what was wrong with me either.'

'You need to rest now,' Zarif told her simply. 'Could you eat something first? You've had very little today.'

Ella identified the hollow sensation inside her as hunger and smiled ruefully. 'Yes, I am hungry.'

Servants brought food while Ella watched Zarif from below her lashes. He had removed his headdress and his luxuriant black hair was tousled as though he had run his fingers through it several times. He needed a shave as well, black stubble cloaking his stubborn jawline and somehow highlighting the effect of his beautifully modelled mouth. In truth, still clad in the gold robes that glimmered richly even in the lamp light, he looked utterly amazing and beautiful and she simply couldn't take her eyes off him.

'You should've stayed with your guests,' Ella remarked uncomfortably, struggling to rein in her overpowering reaction to his lean, lithe, dark good looks.

'I'm your husband. You should always be my first priority,' Zarif fielded in surprise. 'What sort of husband would behave otherwise?'

Ella was silenced while she mulled over that response. He certainly seemed to feel a lot more married than he had the day before. Was that a good thing or a bad thing? She wasn't sure. She picked pieces from the various dishes spread on trays around her on the bed and ate with an appetite that surprised her. When Belle and Betsy arrived to visit her, she greeted them with an apologetic wince.

'I'm a real party pooper, aren't I?' she sighed.

'I should never have given you that vodka,' Belle commented guiltily. 'It's my fault that Zarif initially assumed that you were tipsy.'

'I'd blame Hanya,' Betsy said, disconcerting Ella with that frank opinion. 'I think she convinced Zarif that you had drunk enough to be dancing on tables. She quite deliberately misled him to make you look bad.'

'But those stupid prawn appetisers would have wrecked your wedding night anyway,' Belle pointed out sympathetically. 'And at least Zarif knows the truth now.'

It was only then that it actually occurred to Ella that it *was* her wedding night and she flushed, amazed that she had so easily forgotten what had earlier dominated her every thought. She exchanged fond goodbyes with her new sisters-in-law and promised to visit them when she was next in London—whenever that might be. As they departed she slid out of the high bed, keen to go for a shower and freshen up. That was when Zarif chose to reappear.

'I'm going for a shower,' she told him tightly, murderously conscious of the horribly old-fashioned and shapeless white nightdress that she had been put in after her collapse and hoping very much that Zarif had not been involved in undressing her.

Zarif scanned her tense figure and anxious face. Sheathed in a white cotton gown that could only have belonged to someone either very old or very modest, she looked like an angel with her wealth of blonde hair tumbling round her shoulders and her blue eyes big and bright above her pink cheeks. Doubtless she was worried that he might be selfish enough to try and claim his marital rights regardless of her weakened condition and he straightened his broad shoulders.

'I'll sleep elsewhere tonight,' he told her flatly.

Ella added two and two and made four. 'This is *your* room?'

Zarif nodded, brilliant dark golden eyes veiled as if he was reluctant to remind her that she was his wife and that this was their wedding night.

'I wouldn't dream of putting you out of your room,' Ella declared, tense with discomfiture and determined not to prove any more of a nuisance than she had already been. 'Stay—we're grown-ups, surely we can share the bed?'

Without another word, she vanished into the bathroom, which she was relieved to discover was infinitely more modern than the one she had used at the start of the day. Indeed the jets from the power shower stung her out of her lethargy and soon had her reaching for a towel. She had no choice other than to don the same old-fashioned nightie when she was dry. The bedroom was empty when she emerged and she wasted no time in climbing into the bed.

About ten minutes later, Zarif returned to the bedroom, naked but for the towel knotted round his narrow hips. Water droplets still clung to the dark curls of hair scattered across his virile pecs and his hair was still damp, spiked up by a rough towelling. Her attention roamed to the muscled planes of his strong brown back and lean hips before straying without her volition to his heavily muscled torso and the hard, corrugated slab of his flat stomach.

Her mouth ran dry as he extracted something from a drawer and let the towel drop carelessly to the floor, exposing taut brown buttocks. Muscles rippling, he yanked on a pair of black boxers and she suddenly closed her eyes tight, embarrassed that she had been spying on him, ashamed that she could be twenty-four years old and still that naively curious about the male body.

Wouldn't everything have been easier had she been more experienced? Sleeping with Zarif would then have been no big deal, she told herself. Only to change her mind as she lifted her lashes half a sneaky inch and watched him stroll towards the bed with the predatory grace of a prowling panther, almost stopping her heart dead with excitement in the process. She swallowed hard as he doused the lights and the bed gave beneath his weight.

'You know if you want to, you can... I'm feeling fine now,' she told him with startling abruptness, utterly fed up with the ridiculous level of nervous tension he inspired in her and ready to do virtually anything to put it to flight.

Perplexed by that unexpected offer, Zarif flipped over on his side to peer at her, his dark eyes gleaming in the moonlight. 'I can wait until you're back to full strength. After the day we've had, you must be tired. I know I am.'

Heat surged up from Ella's throat to her hairline and mortification almost choked her. She gritted her teeth. So, he was too tired to be tempted by her. Well, she had offered and he had turned her down. Let it not be said that she could not take rejection on the chin. Punching the pillow beneath her head, she turned her back on him and curled up, eyes wide and stinging like mad.

When Ella wakened she was alone in the big bed. Rising, she went through the closets and drawers until she found her own clothing. Leaving out lingerie and a sundress, she went into the bathroom to freshen up. When she emerged wrapped in a towel, a maid was changing the bed and as soon as she saw Ella the young woman curtsied and swept open a communicating door to indicate the table laden with dishes in the room next door.

'Good morning, *habibti*,' Zarif drawled, springing upright from the table.

Ella hovered. 'Good morning. I'd better get dressed.'

'There is no need. We won't be disturbed and I would assume that you don't want *cold* hot chocolate.'

Taste buds watering, Ella took a step forward. 'You have hot chocolate?'

A wolfish grin slashed Zarif's darkly handsome features and his tawny eyes gleamed. 'I have hot chocolate and croissants for you…'

Ella gave him a huge natural smile and closed the

door behind her, tucking in the towel knotted above her breasts and sinking down into a chair. 'When did you get up?'

'I go into the office about six and answer my emails while it's quiet. I like to enjoy a leisurely breakfast.' He poured the hot chocolate and the rich aroma of it made her sniff in appreciation as she reached for a croissant.

Ella was disconcerted that he had remembered two of her favourite things. The past beckoned and she struggled to fend off memories of their bittersweet time together three years earlier. Back then she had been utterly convinced that he was a romantic and she had been so much in love that even the feel of his hand enclosing hers had lit her up inside like a firework display. She blinked, pushing away the unproductive memories and all recollection of the dreaming, trusting girl she had been. Then as now, she told herself, it had *all* been about sex and she had better not forget that for a moment.

Zarif withdrew the ring box from his pocket and set it in front of her. 'I intended to give this to you yesterday but there was no opportunity.'

Ella opened the box to stare down at the magnificent sapphire and diamond ring. 'What's it for?'

'I heard the child at our English wedding ask why you had no engagement ring. I bought it for you three years ago,' Zarif admitted ruefully.

'And you don't mind me wearing it?' Ella had flushed. He had very much disconcerted her.

'I want you to wear it, *habibti*. It was always meant to be yours.'

Ella slid on the ring. It was a perfect fit. He had kept it for three years, maybe even forgotten he still had it until a child's chatter had reminded him. He was being practical, that was all. He would hardly want to give the ring he had chosen for her to another woman in the future. 'It's gorgeous. Thank you,' she said quietly.

Zarif liked looking at the two wedding rings and the engagement ring on her slender finger. She was his at last, a surprisingly soothing thought. He watched her eat the croissant, crumbs scattering while a look of delight slowly wakened on her lovely face. Within seconds he was hot and hard and when she sipped the chocolate, just a hint of the sweet drink coating her full, soft lower lip as she emitted a soft moan of pleasure, he was ready to rip her out of the chair and carry her to bed. Suddenly all he could think about was seeing that expression on her face while he pleasured her.

'I want you…' he husked.

Ella froze like a cornered kitten, blue eyes flying wide as she stared back at him, a tiny pulse beating like crazy just above her collarbone.

'I meant to wait…I intended to wait,' Zarif confided thickly as he sprang gracefully upright. 'But when I look at you, I *can't.*'

Her mouth ran dry while the blood in her veins ran hotter than lava. He towered over her, all male, decidedly exotic and stunningly sexy in his pristine robes. Her gaze locked tight to him, her heartbeat quickening, her breath feathering in her throat while her lungs laboured to fill again. That stillness, that primal sexual awareness that engulfed her was exactly what had made mincemeat of her principles when she had first met him. It shocked her that that could happen to her again, cutting through her new maturity, her bitterness and distrust to leave only the mindless yearning she had once suppressed.

As Ella began to rise from her seat Zarif bent his

head and claimed a long, intense kiss. His tongue skated across hers and a piercing dart of such primitive long-ing slithered through her that it was a challenge to stay upright. A strong arm slid to her spine to support her slender frame and he lifted her off her feet with breath-taking ease to carry her back into the bedroom.

CHAPTER SEVEN

ELLA SURFACED TO find herself lying on the bed. After that burning kiss she felt a little as if she had been hit with a brick because her brain no longer felt as if it were functioning. Zarif was poised several feet away, stripping off his robes and letting them fall on the rug, his proud dark head already bare. Ella breathed in slow and deep.

It was time, she told her quailing nerves firmly. They were married. This was the deal she had made. Neither love nor liking came into the arrangement. Sex was on the menu, nothing else, and she had to learn to be practical about the fact.

Naked but for his boxers, Zarif was an intimidating sight, a literal power-house of whipcord muscle overlaid with smooth bronzed skin. Her intent gaze skated down over the steely muscles of his formidable chest, down over the little furrow of soft dark hair disappearing below the waistband of his boxers, and screeched to a sudden halt. The bulge of his straining masculinity was larger than she had expected and she tensed, telling herself not to be silly, not to get all worked up about something that other women took in their stride. She wasn't a child. She might not have had sex before but she was an educated adult and none of her friends had been swept off to paradise by their first-time ex-perience. Once it was done, though, it was done, she bargained with herself, desperate to establish a calmer outlook. Afterwards she would know what all the fuss was about and she would be able to treat such intimacy as a mundane event.

'I've wanted you for so long,' Zarif admitted, run-ning long supple fingers through the swirling spill of her honey-coloured hair across the pillows. 'You're so beautiful...'

Ella very nearly laughed. She could see herself as pretty on a good day but only when she was all done up and her hair absolutely perfect. Certainly she did not compare well to the true beauties she had seen him pic-tured with in newspapers three years earlier. Zarif was the truly beautiful one, an outstandingly gorgeous male, who had stolen her heart the first time she saw him and broken it the day he proposed, sending her plunging from the heights of happiness straight down into the darkness of despair. In the aftermath she had picked herself up and gone on but the trust he had broken remained bro-ken and she was a much more anxious, suspicious per-son than she had once been.

His thick silky hair nudged her cheek and then his mouth, velvet and warm, claimed hers again, closing out the rest of the world as though it had never been. There was nothing then but the racing beat of her heart and the tightening at her secret core. Without warning the towel she wore was gone and he cupped her full breasts, his thumbs strumming her engorged nipples to send currents of fire shooting down into her pelvis. Her hips shifted, rose without her volition and at the heart of her she felt tight as a drum and desperate for more.

Zarif drew back, lean, strong features taut. 'If you truly don't want this, I will stop. I don't want anything from you that you don't want to give, *habibti.*'

Taken aback, Ella stared up at him, still partially lost in the stirring responses shimmying through her lethargic body.

Luxuriant black lashes dipped low over his tawny eyes. 'You didn't want this,' he extended. 'You agreed because you had no other choice but I find that I no longer want a sacrifice in my bed.'

Disconcerted, Ella stiffened. 'I'm *not* a sacrifice.'

His mouth dipped to her delicate collarbone and the tip of his tongue flicked the pulse beating there below her pale fine skin and she tingled in reaction from her head to her toes. 'I will have you willing or not at all. To say no is your right and I promise that there will be no reprisals,' he asserted thickly.

In shock at that startling offer coming when she least expected it, Ella opened her eyes to their fullest extent and stared up at him, almost mesmerised by the stunning amber gold of his steady gaze. 'But I agreed and you—'

'You agreed under the duress of your concern for your vulnerable parents,' Zarif reminded her. 'And I am man enough to only want what is offered freely.'

His hands rested on her ribcage and she wanted so badly for him to lift his hands and touch her breasts again. The strength of that craving took her aback for nothing in her experience had ever equalled it. She shut her eyes, shutting him out but the craving, the sheer hunger mushroomed up inside her without abating. And why was she surprised? She wanted him; she had *always* wanted him.

Her lashes lifted, her decision easily made. 'It's free...

I mean, it's only sex…let's not make a production out of it,' she framed awkwardly.

Zarif frowned in disagreement, automatically writing off her quip about sex as a clumsy careless joke. 'I very much want it to be a production with you, *habibti*.'

Ella lay back, pliant and melting with helpless anticipation. She had come to an understanding with herself and the past and present were melding into a seamless whole. She wanted Zarif to become her first lover because she had never wanted another man the way she wanted him and sharing her body with him made perfect sense to her. He nipped at her lower lip and then blew softly over a rosy straining nipple before suckling erotically at the tender peak. Ribbons of hot desire pulled taut between her breasts and her thighs.

Zarif slid down the bed, tugging away the towel still partially wrapped round her and skimming off the boxers he still wore with impatient hands. Lying there naked, Ella reddened, fighting off the urge to yank the sheet over her exposed body. He parted her thighs and before she could react moved down the bed towards her on his knees with the predatory grace of a stalking cat. Ella lay still, eyes rounding when she glimpsed the long thick length of his erection hung low between his muscular hair-roughened thighs. A spasm of something she didn't recognise pulled taut in her pelvis.

Zarif dropped a kiss on her gently rounded stomach and tension leapt high inside her as he stroked the soft skin of her inner thighs, moving ever closer to the heart of her desire. 'I want to taste you,' he told her hungrily. 'I want to drive you crazy with need and then I want to make love to you until you are senseless…'

'A lot of wants,' she pronounced shakily, shy of that

new side of him and the raw sexual self-assurance she had never seen him display before.

'And all the time in the world in which to enjoy them,' Zarif murmured, pushing her slender thighs back at almost the same time as he lowered his head and swiped his tongue across her clitoris.

The sensation was so powerful that she almost shot off the bed in shock. 'No…no, you *can't* do that!' she told him when she had found her breath again.

'You'll discover that I am naturally domineering in the bedroom,' Zarif confessed without apology, his strong hands clamping to her hips to hold her in place for his attentions.

'I've…I've just never quite…' Ella mumbled unevenly.

'But your body loves it and so do I,' Zarif countered hungrily, marvelling that an experienced woman could have such an inhibition while he ran long fingers soothingly down the outside of her slender thighs to relax her tense muscles. 'Close your eyes…I promise only pleasure, *habibti*.'

Afraid of making a fool of herself and entering into an undignified tussle, Ella shut her eyes tight, mentally willing herself to play it cool. She really didn't want Zarif to know that she hadn't done any of these things before. If he realised she was still a virgin he might then appreciate what a catastrophic effect he had had on her life three years earlier and her pride was too great to reveal the massive hurt he had unwittingly inflicted.

He teased the entrance to her body with gentle fingertips and she jerked, insanely conscious of where she needed to be touched and cringingly aware of how wet she was. He eased a finger into her and then lowered his

head to tease her with his sensual mouth. Almost unbearable sensation engulfed Ella in a never-ending cascade. She no longer controlled herself; *he* controlled her.
Her body hummed and jerked with constrained power
like a race car at the starting line, raring to go. Excitement roared through every cell in her body, drowning
all thought, closing out everything but what he was making her feel. The ripples of growing sensation soared to
a peak and her back arched and she cried out while ripples of pleasure spread outward, making the pleasure
last and draining every ounce of energy from her body.

'I have no condoms here,' Zarif groaned in frustration and he levered himself off the bed.

Ella blinked as she struggled to emerge from that
frighteningly intense climax and suddenly reached out
to close a hand over his before he could move out of
reach. 'I'm on the pill…it's safe,' she muttered, assuming it would be safe, then certain it was because she had,
after all, been taking the mini pill for years to regulate
her periods and surely all those years had to count for
something.

For a split second, Zarif hesitated and then he came
back to her with alacrity. 'It's a very long time since I
had sex without a condom,' he confided, pulling her
close to his warm, musky male length, his erection pressing against her lower stomach. In that instant her hunger for him rose to such a height that she felt weak and
dizzy with it.

'You can be assured that I am clean and healthy,' he
murmured, studying her with scorching dark golden
eyes fringed by quite ridiculously long black lashes.
'And you?'

'I've never had sex without a condom,' Ella replied,

trying not to laugh because, of course, she had never had sex at all but she was convinced he would not be able to tell the difference between her untried body and a more practised woman's.

He captured her lips in a soul-shattering kiss and deep down inside her the tingling and the prickle of awakening heat and the awful aching emptiness began to fire her up afresh. He was so hot, she reflected helplessly, so hot that he made her crave him like a sunburn victim craved ice. She quivered below the hard, warm weight of his lean, powerful body, entranced by the intimacy but nervous of what the next step entailed, regardless of how much her body seemed to yearn for it.

He tilted her up to facilitate his entry and nudged at her entrance before pushing in, filling her completely and stilling to give her time to adjust.

'You're very small,' Zarif husked, his black hair brushing her cheek. 'I don't want to hurt you.'

Ella was all bound up in the alien sensation of his intrusion in that wildly sensitive place and in the same moment he pulled back and then drove forward, thrusting into her with primal force. A strangled shriek of shocked pain escaped her and he froze over her.

'What the hell?' he breathed rawly, frowning down at her in consternation.

Ella gulped and regrouped. 'It's been a while for me,' she told him weakly.

Ebony brows pleated, Zarif began to withdraw and her hands whipped up instinctively to close over his muscular forearms even as her hips lifted to contain him. 'No, don't stop,' she protested, incredulous at the idea that he could go so far and then stop without letting her experience what she had ached to share only with him for so long.

That would be another rejection and just then she couldn't face that prospect; no, not to be left with the suspicion that she was so much less than other women and so useless that she could not retain his interest even until the act was finished. She could not bear that her only sexual experience should end in failure and shame.

The muscles in his arms strained and Zarif groaned, fighting for control until the shift of her hips embraced him and sent him beyond the point of return. He sank deep and she was tight and hot and wet and he knew nothing else because much more basic instincts had taken over by then. His hands gripping her hips, he plunged right into the heated core of her with a shout of shuddering satisfaction. The slap of his flesh against hers joined with the sound of her sobbing breaths and helpless cries. He pushed her legs over his shoulders and drove hard into her tight sheath. She shuddered, feeling the gathering surge of excitement coalesce inside her again as he upped his tempo. It was all too much for her and as he slammed into her one last time she felt the hot blast of his release. Bucking wildly under him, her hips writhed as he thrust her into an indescribably powerful orgasm.

Afterwards the silence was so intense that the sound of her own breathing felt like a roar in her ears. Zarif settled her back down on the bed with care, resisting the urge to hold her close, and sprang off the bed at speed. He was feeling far too much all at once, too many thoughts screaming through his mind. He was shocked, appalled, drowning in guilt and regret. Snatching up his clothing, he began to get dressed.

'So…that's it, is it?' Ella heard herself say limply, hurt winging through her in an enervating surge. 'No cuddling afterwards?'

'It would not alter what we just did,' Zarif breathed curtly, brushing straight his robes with unsteady hands and heading for the doors that opened out onto the stairs down to the courtyard beyond, desperate for some fresh air and clarity of thought.

Ella's body ached: she was sore. Strange how she had never suspected that the first occasion might hurt so much, she acknowledged numbly. So, of course, Zarif had guessed her deepest darkest secret. She had let the cat out of the bag herself. He was shocked. And he wasn't pleased, of course he wasn't. Clearly he had wanted an experienced lover to entertain him for a year, not a first-timer unfit for a repeat encounter or more carnal games.

Zarif came to an abrupt halt by the central fountain, which played its water in the shade of a clump of palm trees. A virgin. Ella had been a virgin and he had taken her with all the finesse of a rutting beast and naturally he had hurt her. He recalled how careful he had been as a newly married teenager with Azel in spite of his co-lossal ignorance and he recoiled in disgust at his lack of control with Ella. He had hurt her, wronged her… Was there to be no end to the mistakes he made with her?

In public life, Zarif had made very few mistakes. He was highly intelligent and naturally cautious and he had learned early how to think ahead and protect himself from missteps. A king couldn't expect second chances, a king needed the support of his subjects and had to stay in touch with their prevailing mood to retain the right to rule. He knew for a fact in that instant that he was a better king than he was a husband.

But then, in truth, he had not been fit to touch an innocent woman in the first place and that inescapable awareness tormented him. She had stayed pure in a much more liberal culture than his own, setting a standard he had strikingly failed to follow. For so long he had blamed her for that reality because it had been her rejection that had sent him careening off the rails of restraint. Unbearable as it was to acknowledge, he had been weak where she had been strong. Shame drenched him like perspiration in the heat. He had tried to bring her down to his level by treating her like a sex object and he had failed. But why had she refused to take advantage of the escape clause he had offered her?

Ironically, he had never understood Ella and was indeed beginning to suspect that she was a complete and utter mystery to him. Yet he had often assumed that he *did* understand her and just as often read her entirely wrong, only to discover too late that he had made yet another miscalculation.

She seemed so deceptively open, he acknowledged broodingly. He had believed she was playing games with him three years earlier when she said no to his proposal. He had believed she wanted him to propose purely to relish the narcissistic charge of her power over him. Now he doubted that hypothesis and found it quite a challenge to fit an innocent young woman into such a scenario. Perhaps she had said no to marrying him for the very reasons she had stated…the same reasons he had arrogantly dismissed as offensive red herrings. Perhaps she had genuinely *feared* having to adapt to a culture and royal expectations so far removed from her own experience and he had said and done nothing to soothe her concerns.

But why was he looking back to the past when he had created so many more problems here in the present? He had essentially forced her to marry him and forced her into his bed because, loving her parents as she did, she had not had a choice. Possibly that was also why she had urged him to continue in bed, believing as she must have done that sooner or later she *had* to surrender her body to his to meet the terms he had demanded.

Zarif swore below his breath, recognising how complicated everything had become and knowing he had brought it down on himself with no help from anyone else. But then guilt had, for so long, been Zarif's constant companion in life that he almost welcomed it back like an old friend. He was in the wrong. Once again he was in the wrong.

A hundred years ago, one of his ancestors would have dealt much more easily with such a situation, he reflected with sardonic humour. He would have kidnapped her, offered her family handsome compensation for the loss of her and hidden her in the harem, eventually offering her marriage as a reward for her acceptance. It would not have been considered dishonourable. That approach would have dealt practically with a man's need for a woman he could not otherwise have. Zarif knew that his contemporary solution had crashed and burned at spectacular speed, particularly when all he could think about *in spite* of all that had gone wrong was climbing back into that bed with Ella again and proving that in some fields he *could* get it right.

* * *

Ella lowered her body into the bath of warm water and hugged her knees. Well, it was done, she had met the conditions of their agreement and he had no reasonable grounds for complaint now. Seemingly he had not enjoyed the sex as much as he had thought he would, but that was the essential flaw in male fantasy, Ella thought grimly. Fantasy wasn't *real*. He'd had a fantasy about what she would be like and she had failed to live up to it, which wasn't really surprising when one considered that she was simply an ordinary young woman and neither stunningly beautiful nor amazingly sexy.

The bedroom was filled with flowers when she finally emerged from a long soothing bath, wrapped in a towelling robe. Innumerable baskets of white roses sat on every surface and she frowned. Someone knocked on the door and she opened it. An envelope and a gift box were extended to her by a maid.

The envelope contained a plain white card. 'Forgive me,' it said and she compressed her lips into a rigid line. She would have been more inclined towards forgiveness had Zarif stayed around in the flesh to *be* forgiven. She unwrapped the jewellery box and flipped it open on a breathtaking bracelet shaped like a glittering white river of diamonds. She detached it, fastened it round her wrist and rolled her eyes at the extravagance of his apology. She was very much aware that everything Zarif and she herself did was the focus of all too many watchful eyes and wagging tongues amongst the palace staff. People would know he had given her a gift and she had to wear it.

The maid reappeared and opened the closets in the dressing room to withdraw a selection of outfits. Ella stared in surprise at the unfamiliar and obviously brand-new items sheathed in garment bags. Clearly they were for her. She pulled out her phone and called Zarif.

'Did you buy me clothes?' she asked bluntly.

'Ella…how are you?' Zarif enquired smoothly.

'The clothes?' she prompted impatiently.

'Yes. I asked my mother, who is very much involved with the fashion world, to choose a new wardrobe for you.'

'Your mother?' Ella repeated, disconcerted, for the older woman had not even been present at their wedding the day before.

'I assure you that she was happy to be of assistance.'

'But I don't need anything. I have my own clothes.'

'I doubt very much that your present wardrobe will meet the standard of quality and formality which will now be required from you as my queen,' Zarif informed her wryly.

Wandering round the spacious suite of rooms as she talked on the phone, Ella stiffened. 'Is that so?'

'I did not intend to offend you. I merely spoke the truth.'

Ella's vexed gaze fell on a silver-framed photo sited on a corner table in the dining room where they had had breakfast at the start of the day. She stared in dismay at the photo of an attractive brunette with beautiful almond-shaped dark eyes smiling into the camera as she held her equally dark-eyed son.

'Thank you for the flowers, the clothes and the bracelet,' Ella said woodenly, still gaping at the photo of what could only be her predecessor.

'I should have stayed to speak to you.'

'No, saying it with flowers was better,' Ella broke in. 'We really don't have much to say to each other.'

Not giving him the chance to respond, she tossed the phone down and lifted the photo of Azel and her infant son, Firas. Of course he kept a picture of his late wife and child in his private suite and why wouldn't he? It was a perfectly normal thing to do. He wouldn't want to forget them and he would want to show respect: of course, he had retained a photograph and she couldn't begrudge him that. But she knew the image would very likely haunt her. Zarif's first wife, and cousin, had been an undeniable beauty and the baby was downright adorable but rather too young to be showing any resemblance to his parents in his indeterminate features. Ella returned the portrait to its place, deciding there and then that she didn't want to share living space with Zarif in what was still Azel's place.

There was no reason why she and Zarif should share a bedroom, she reasoned feverishly. Good grief, had he taken her to the very same bed he had once shared with Azel? She swallowed hard, scanning the decoration of the rooms suspiciously and feeling very much like an intruder. Naturally she would neither ask nor expect him to put the photo away. At the same time, though it possibly wasn't very nice or sympathetic, she worried immediately why she was so determined not to live daily with that reminder of Azel or inhabit the same rooms.

Smartly garbed in a tailored cotton dress, Ella went off to explore and soon discovered that there were so many rooms available that she could probably choose a different one for every night of the year she was to spend in Vashir. She picked a set of interconnecting rooms on the other side of the corridor and was engaged in removing her new clothes from the dressing room when Hanya joined her.

'You are packing to go somewhere?' the tiny brunette asked in surprise.

Ella studied Hanya for a split second, recalling the misunderstanding about how much vodka she had drunk and she still forced a smile. In the future she would watch out for Hanya but for as long as she was forced to consult the other woman as an interpreter and for advice, it would be wiser not to make an enemy of her. 'Just across the corridor. I like my own space and Zarif likes his,' she said lightly.

Hanya called for two maids and, without Ella having to say a word more, she and her belongings, old and new, were resettled across the corridor.

'Queen Azel planned to turn this suite into a nursery because it had more space,' Hanya confided. 'So sad. I expect had my cousin survived she would have been the mother of several children by now.'

'Yes.' Ella refused to let the gloss be stolen from her new accommodation by the news that Azel had hoped to site a nursery there.

'My uncle and the King were inconsolable.' Hanya sighed. 'I wept most for the baby. He was so little and cute.'

'Yes,' Ella responded a little gruffly, finding her own vocal cords tightening when she thought of that tiny face in the photo, a life taken before it even got properly going.

'Azel was much older than I was and because of that we weren't close,' the other woman admitted honestly. 'But we all knew how much she adored the King. For a long time he was lost without her.'

'It was a huge loss,' Ella conceded and then she quite deliberately busied herself putting away her toiletries in the cupboard in the spacious bathroom. In the same bag she came on her contraceptive pills and realised that she had missed one the day before. She took another and hoped that her having missed one would make no difference. She vaguely recalled being told something about having to try and take it at the same time every day and she shook her head ruefully. Two weddings in forty-eight hours and an apparent allergy to shellfish had destroyed her usual routine.

Around ten, Ella went to bed. She had dined with Hanya after Zarif phoned her to tell her that he wouldn't be back until late. She wondered if newly marrieds usually went straight back to work after the wedding in Vashir. Certainly, Zarif did not seem to be acknowledging any need to change his schedule to accommodate a wife. But then why would he? she asked herself irritably. Zarif was well aware that she wasn't a proper wife and that within a year she would be gone, so, even if it was boring and lonely for Ella, it made sense that he should see no point in altering his usual habits.

Just as Ella was contemplating reaching out to douse the bedside light her bedroom door swung open without warning. Startled, she sat up.

Zarif stood poised in the doorway, breathing heavily, his spectacular cheekbones scored with colour. 'What are you doing in here?' he demanded.

'Is there some reason why I shouldn't sleep in another room?' Ella asked shortly, colliding with the fiery golden eyes pinned to her and challenging that look.

'You're my wife. I want you in my bed.'

Ella was astonished by his attitude. 'Surely you can visit me here?'

'But I do not want to *visit*,' Zarif derided with savage distaste, stalking to the bed, thrusting the sheet back with impatient hands and snatching her up off the mattress without ceremony. 'I want you where I know I can find you twenty-four-seven.'

CHAPTER EIGHT

ZARIF TUMBLED HER down on his four-poster bed like a stolen parcel he had forcibly retrieved. Ella sat up, honey-blonde hair fanning round her flushed face, sapphire eyes very bright. 'What are you playing at?'

'This is not a game,' Zarif told her sternly. 'Why did you move out of here?'

Ella stilled. 'I saw Azel's photo in the dining room—at least I assume it was her—and suddenly being here didn't feel comfortable. This is where you lived with her.'

Zarif was rigid with tension, as he always seemed to be when she made any reference to his first wife or child. 'No, it wasn't. We didn't live together in the Western sense.'

Her brow furrowed. 'I don't understand.'

'My grandparents lived together, sharing the same rooms and mealtimes. That was *their* way. My uncle Halim and his wife, Azel's parents, were more traditional and preferred separate accommodation. Azel was accustomed to that lifestyle and this building has so much unused space that it was not a problem,' he explained flatly. 'Try to remember that we were only teenagers when we married and Azel wanted her own suite where she could entertain her friends and occasionally forget that she was a queen. I doubt if she ever set foot in here.'

Ella was very much surprised by that snapshot of a marriage she had blithely assumed to be a love's young dream of constant togetherness and suddenly she was unable to meet his direct gaze. Had she simply fled from the threat of a photograph? Was she still that over-sensitive about Azel's unassailable position in his heart? And why was that, when she no longer loved him? She didn't love him, had no excuse to feel jealous or possessive about a part of his past that had been written long before she even met him. What was the matter with her?

'The presence of the photo offended you?' Zarif pressed.

'No, of course not.' Ella studied her linked hands with fixed attention. Offended did not describe her feelings. She had felt irrationally *threatened* and *hurt* but that was not for sharing.

'You're still wearing the bracelet,' he said in surprise.

Ella clamped a rueful hand over the glittering diamonds and went pink. 'I couldn't get the clasp undone.'

'Let me…' His dark head lowered, his luxuriant black hair almost brushing her cheek and the exotic scent of sultry spice and earthy male assailed her nostrils. Deft fingers unfastened the tricky clasp and set the bracelet onto the cabinet by the bed. 'I was with my uncle all evening. I didn't intend to leave you alone for so long.'

'That's OK,' Ella said breathlessly as a cell phone buzzed in the tense silence.

Zarif stepped back from the bed to answer his phone. 'I'm sorry, I must take this…'

Talking in Arabic and already, she sensed, mental miles from her, Zarif wandered fluidly across the room and eventually into the room next door. Ella slumped back against the pillows to await his return. It shouldn't matter to him where she chose to sleep. Why was he suddenly bent on always reminding her that she was his wife? Their marriage was fake, and a temporary fake at that, and to her way of thinking she was not *really* his wife, so why did he feel the need to pretend otherwise? As she listened to Zarif's call continuing and the undeniably soothing sound of his calm, well-modulated drawl she smothered a yawn and finally slid out of bed, closed the interconnecting door quietly and switched out the lights.

She had no idea what time it was when she was wakened by an arm tugging her back into contact with a hot, damp, very masculine body. 'Oh!' she gasped, flinching.

'I'm sorry...I didn't intend to wake you,' Zarif breathed.

'Then you shouldn't have put your arm round me... *and* you're damp!' Ella complained loudly before she could think better of it because he immediately whipped his arm off her and shifted away from her.

'Fresh from the shower. I'm not used to sharing a bed,' Zarif sighed. 'I kept on bumping into you and I thought that if I held you close, it would be less unsettling.'

Ella felt oddly abandoned by his retreat and she shimmied backwards until their bodies had made contact again. 'There, now you know where I am.'

Zarif's core temperature was so much hotter than her own that her spine felt burned by the connection, or possibly the real problem was the overheated tingles of awareness that immediately coursed through her when she felt the hard thrust of his erection against her hip.

She tensed, insanely aware of the swelling of her breasts and the melting liquid sensation in her pelvis.

'Ignore it…it's just the normal male reaction to being close to a beautiful woman,' Zarif informed her deflatingly.

'I do know that much about men!' Ella shot back, her cheeks warm in the moonlight filtering through the drapes.

'And of course, I've thought of little else all day but the sheer joy of being inside you, *habibti*,' Zarif confessed in a roughened undertone. 'That doesn't help. Even the knowledge that you did not experience the same pleasure doesn't cool my enthusiasm.'

'But I did…at the end,' Ella whispered back, cheeks hotter than ever.

'If only you had told me beforehand that I would be the first,' Zarif groaned into her hair, his arm closing round her to pull her even closer, long finger smoothing across her shoulder. 'Had I known, I would have been much more patient and infinitely more careful to prepare you. It might still have hurt but probably not as much.'

'I didn't *want* you to know,' Ella admitted.

'But why not? It was a gift I never thought to have from you. You should've been proud of your innocence,' he countered in a tone of rebuke. 'But then I should never have just assumed that you had had other lovers.'

'But wasn't that part of your fantasy? That I would be an experienced partner?' Ella prompted tight-mouthed.

'There *was* no fantasy,' Zarif protested heatedly. 'I wanted you so much I didn't care whether you had a past or not. I am not a narrow-minded man.'

'I'm not sure I can believe you…' Ella hesitated but then she *had* to ask, 'Was it really sheer joy for you?'

'It was amazing for me but the fact that it wasn't for you only made me feel worse,' he growled with grudging honesty.

'It wasn't only the end I enjoyed,' Ella confided.

'No?' Zarif eased his hands below the hem of her camisole top and cupped her breasts, catching the swelling sensitive nipples between his fingers and tugging gently to send curls of molten lust travelling straight to her core. Her hips squirmed, a small explosion of air dragged from between her lips.

'It was only that few s-seconds I didn't enjoy,' she stammered as he began to pull the camisole up and over her head, baring her breasts for his caresses.

'Will you give me another chance to prove myself?' Zarif murmured hungrily in her ear, pausing to nip at the tender slope of skin between her neck and her shoulder with his strong white teeth.

Jerking with a stifled gasp, Ella laughed. 'Now would be a good time.'

Zarif tugged up her legs to extract her from her shorts. 'If you had said no, go to sleep, I do believe I would have killed you,' he confided with raw amusement. 'I ache for you, *habibti*.'

Ella was aching too and there was an overflowing sensation inside her in the region of her chest, emotions rolling about in wild disarray and, although she couldn't distinguish them, she knew she was on a high and vulnerable. It was just sex, *only* sex, she bargained wildly with herself; there was no need to make it more than it was and little point in punishing herself for meeting the terms of a bargain she had agreed to make. He flipped her round in his arms to kiss her before she could get any further with the sensible talking-to she was giving herself and that single kiss sent every rational thought flying into nothingness. Her hand came up and speared into his thick black hair to hold him to her and the flicker of his tongue inside her mouth filled her with wild hunger.

She twisted against him, squirming, needing, in a way she had never known before. The swollen petals of flesh between her quivering thighs throbbed and when he came over her, she was more than ready for the long hard glide of his sex into hers. Delicious ripples of response fluttered within her. As he rose over her she had a vision of him soaring above the flames during the sword dance and her heart thumped out a wild tattoo.

He shifted his hips, finding another angle, and thrust into her receptive flesh. Plunged into raw excitement, she sobbed with pleasure. Every skin cell was primed to want more as she arched up to him like a cat and locked her legs round his lean hips. Need exploded in her, voracious and impatient, driving her on as she rose to meet his every thrust, helplessly reaching for the climax and revelling in the great starburst of release when it swept over her, raining down a cascade of intense pleasure that relaxed every bone in her body.

'You are delicious, *habibti*,' Zarif husked into the coconut-scented depths of her hair as he eased her onto her side to release her from his weight and kissed her shoulder. 'Utterly delicious.'

Ella roused herself from her slump, surprised that she was still in the circle of his arms. 'You're holding me.'

'Yes…' Zarif breathed without any expression at all.

'This morning you said it would be inappropriate.'

'This morning I felt very much in the wrong for taking advantage of an innocent.'

'But that's not how it was,' Ella countered squarely. 'I knew what I was doing.'

'What is done is done. But on reflection, I see no reason why we should not be together as long as we treat each other with respect and honesty,' Zarif framed stubbornly, ramming down every misgiving, long fingers smoothing the impossibly soft skin of her slender waist while he drank in the scent of her. It was so many years since he had spent an entire night in bed with a woman. He had never slept with his lovers and even Azel had only been an occasional overnight visitor but the idea of returning to find Ella in his bed every night was amazingly appealing...although he could never afford to forget that she was a supreme indulgence that came with time limits.

'So you show respect and apologise by giving me clothes, flowers and a diamond bracelet,' Ella remarked gingerly. 'Don't you know any other way to show care or concern with a woman? Do you always just *buy* things?'

Zarif was stunned by the question, which cut right to the heart of his previous dealings with women. Yes, sadly he *did* just buy things. To say sorry for a cancellation, to express sympathy for a loss or dismissal, to say thank you for an especially good night.

In the silence, Ella gulped. 'It just makes a girl feel a little cheap...that's all,' she told him abstractedly, her voice dwindling because she did not want to start an argument.

'I have had very few...what you might term relationships,' Zarif admitted grittily. 'I am not trying to buy you. Why would I when I have already bought you?'

Stinging tears of painful surprise washed the backs of Ella's eyes. She pulled away from him and turned defensively onto her side. She had spoken without thinking, foolishly forgetting how she had ended up married to him. But how could she have forgotten? How could she have forgotten for one moment how big a part his fabulous wealth had played in their relationship? Without that wealth, without her parents' need for security, she would not be with him now.

'You didn't buy me outright,' she contradicted in a small, tight voice. 'You bought a year-long lease. That's not the same.'

In the dimness, Zarif suddenly grinned with sheer appreciation. He loved that distinction that she brandished like a weapon, refusing to grant him full ownership. *A year-long lease?* Only Ella could have come up with that qualifier.

'And of course we both know that you won't be extending the lease at any stage,' Ella completed thinly, and swallowed hard before adding, 'You know, if this is us being respectful and honest with each other, Zarif, you can keep it! We're just tearing everything apart.'

Involuntarily, Zarif reached for her. They had both spoken the truth, although admittedly not in a productive manner, but he did, however, have a great reverence for the truth, regardless of how tactless or wounding it might be. Yet a tiny, tiny hint of a sniff from the far side of the bed sent him flying across it before he could think better of his behaviour and he tugged her small rigid body back across the divide into his arms.

'Nothing has been torn apart. You are still the same woman. You gave up your freedom for your parents' benefit. How can I not respect such strength and loyalty?' he demanded.

Ella breathed in so deep she was surprised she didn't

swell up like a balloon and float away. Some of her rigidity eased and she allowed her body to bend into the heat and solidity of his. 'You really mean that?' she checked.

'I do.'

'By the way, if you decide you want to buy me something…you could make it something small and cheap,' she told him impulsively. 'You know, like the silver pendant and bracelet you bought me for my twenty-first birthday?'

Zarif almost laughed out loud but he held it back. Presumably she had never had that first gift of his valued nor had she studied its marks. The pendant and the bracelet were *not* silver, they were platinum and designed by one of the most famous jewellery designers alive. Although at the time he had not wanted to give her a gift that attracted attention by being too excessive, his desire for her had been so powerful that a small, cheap gift could never have matched what he then believed she was worth. 'Do you still have it?' he asked curiously.

'Yes, that set is still one of my favourite pieces,' she muttered sleepily.

Ella wakened still wrapped in Zarif's arms. 'What time is it?' she whispered.

'Almost six. I have to get up soon but you can lie as long as you like,' he breathed lazily, sliding against her, the hard thrust of his intentions obvious to her even in her drowsy state.

Heat burned low in her body and she couldn't believe it after the night they had shared. 'I need a shower,' she told him uncomfortably.

'No, you smell of me and a long adventurous night of loving and you wouldn't believe how hot I find that, *habibti,'* he husked, long fingers rubbing at her engorged nipples and sliding lower to tease the most sensitive spot on her entire body. 'You make me insatiable.'

But if that was his flaw, it was one she shared with him, her head falling back against a broad shoulder as he lifted her thigh and eased into her in a long, slow, gentle glide that left her bereft of breath and protest. Her body stretched to hold him and a piercing sweetness gripped her racing heart at how natural and right it felt to lie with him like that. With subtle erotic movements, he stroked her inner depths with fluid insistence and the pleasure rose and rose and rose until she couldn't contain it any more and it spilled over into bliss as she gasped her excitement into the pillow beneath her.

When she wakened the second time she was alone and hot and she got straight out of bed to stand directly below the whirling fan on the ceiling and flinch at the tenderness that motion wrenched from the long night of loving, as he had called it. Only it wasn't love, she reminded herself, it was just sex. Incredibly good and satisfying sex, she was willing to admit, but love had nothing to do with it. She showered and breakfasted and dressed, determined to go out and at least see the city rather than pass the day in aimless pursuits. Zarif had a purpose in life and she needed one as well, even if it was only the role of acting tourist for a year, she reflected ruefully.

Hamid phoned while she was eating to offer her a tour of the palace. She played for time. 'When will Zarif be back?' she asked.

'He will be in meetings with the council most of the day,' his chief aide informed her.

A germ of an idea occurred to Ella. 'And those are

like parliament...held in public? I'd like to attend today,' she told Hamid cheerfully. 'Perhaps someone could translate the proceedings for me.'

There was a lengthy period of quiet at the other end of the phone and then Hamid said that he would call her back. Frowning while she wondered if her every move had to be run past Zarif first, Ella ate another piece of croissant.

Zarif was having coffee with his personal staff at the new palace when Hamid phoned him to tell him what his wife wanted to do.

'No woman has crossed the threshold of the council chamber before,' his chief aide pointed out.

'I hope you didn't tell her *that*,' Zarif retorted, thinking of how he had proudly declared that Vashir was not backward. 'There is no actual rule against female attendance.'

'But it still hasn't happened.'

Lean, darkly handsome features furiously tense, Zarif took his phone into a private room. 'I don't care if you grab women in off the street to attend,' he admitted tautly. 'My wife will attend but I don't want her to be the *only* female present. And I very definitely do *not* want her to realise that, until now, only men have come to observe how the ruling council works. She will think we are very old-fashioned and that our women are not politically aware.'

Hamid thought of his wife, who was a radical with equally radical friends, and knew exactly who to call. He came off the phone, stunned by his royal employer's assent to breaking a tradition that had held firm for at least two hundred years.

'This queen is going to make a difference!' his wife

carolled jubilantly. 'Just like the King's British grand-mother—she's going to be an innovator and drag this wretched country out of the ark.'

Gloriously unaware of the hopes she was raising with her simple request, Ella selected a dark-coloured outfit with a jacket from her new wardrobe, reasoning that such a visit was formal. Hanya came hurrying down into the palace foyer to join her as she awaited the limo drawing up outside.

'I had no idea you had such plans. My cousin, Azel, would never have dreamt of entering the council cham-bers,' she exclaimed, giving Hamid a look of reproof as if Ella's wilfulness and unwomanly interest were to be laid at his door. 'Azel said it was the men's place.'

Ella gave the excitable brunette a tranquil smile. 'The machinery of government is not wholly the province of men where I come from. I'm simply interested to see how the council works.'

The new palace was a massive domed building sur-rounded by a park composed of trees, fountains and walkways and it was extremely busy. Ella only became aware of the half-dozen palace guards accompanying her when they climbed out of the cars that had travelled in front of and behind the limo. Feeling uncomfortably conspicuous and colouring from the intensity of the at-tention she was attracting, she was even more embar-rassed when two of the soldiers stationed at the front entrance insisted on leading the way and clearing every other unfortunate out of her path. The buzz of comment around her grew louder and many phones were used to take photos.

'Why's there such a fuss about me coming here?' she asked Hamid.

'I have no idea, Your Majesty,' Hamid lied dutifully for his royal boss. 'But you must remember that apart from the official photo taken at the airport and published in the evening paper very few people have actually seen you and naturally they are curious.'

It was a relief for Ella to leave the busy halls and corridors to ascend the stairs into the main council chamber. A gaggle of chattering women sat to the far left and she naturally moved in that direction as the men present craned their necks and then suddenly shot up and began to bow. An absolute hush fell and seconds later Ella was silenced as the dozen or so old men seated round the large table in the centre of the room also rose to their feet and ceremoniously bowed in her direction. Her colour high, she was trying to spot Zarif but couldn't see him.

Thirty seconds later, he arrived through another door and the whole bowing and scraping thing happened again for his benefit. Ella would have followed suit had not Hamid rested an apologetic hand on her arm as he stood and told her, 'You are the only person in the room who need not rise. It was a courtesy extended by the King's grandfather to his British wife and will also be extended to you. Before the King's grandfather married, Vashiri subjects used to kneel and touch their forehead to the floor in the royal presence, so bowing was also a big step forward...'

Taken aback by the information of how servile the response to royalty had once been, Ella nodded while abstractedly watching Zarif and smiling. He was the only man at the table wearing a business suit and he wore it to perfection. A man so old and wizened he bore a definite resemblance to an Egyptian mummy began to speak about a boundary dispute with a neighbouring country and recommended a heavily armed squad of Vashiri troops be sent to the area. Hamid translated fluently. Zarif spoke well and suggested that diplomacy be employed before the army became involved.

'The sheikhs will not argue with the King when it comes to military matters because he was once a soldier and the army would follow him into hell, so there's no point in them interfering,' Hamid assured her. 'But only in that field does your husband get a free pass.'

And so it transpired as Ella watched and listened to the discussion of various questions on the agenda, ranging from how best to deal with drunken tourists in Qurzah to the troublesome matter of the royal museum in the new palace, which was still not officially open after months of preparation. Zarif's patience was astounding. There were several petty objections from the council, several of whom appeared to be of the opinion that allowing any private information about the royal family into the public domain even in the educational guise of a museum was unwise. Ella guiltily swallowed back a yawn because she was finding it very tiring to concentrate on the flow of constant translation in her ear.

'Your husband takes a break in a private room for lunch,' Hamid informed her. 'He has asked that you join him there.'

Ella nodded and quietly stood up. Hamid asked if he might introduce his wife, Soraya, to her and signalled with his hand towards the group of women on the other side of the room. An elegant brunette with upswept hair and a bright smile moved forward and introductions were performed. Soraya was on the PR committee for the royal museum and, while frustrated by the fact that the project was moving so slowly, she was very much a working woman, plainspoken and direct in her manner, unlike Hanya. They chatted for a couple of minutes before Hamid intervened and swept Ella off.

'This is a surprise, *habibti*,' Zarif murmured with a slow-burning smile when Ella entered the room.

It had been so long since Zarif looked at her like that that Ella was momentarily thrown back in time. The forbidding aspect of his lean, strong features was washed away by the warmth and welcome of that smile and it flipped her heart inside her chest and shortened her breathing.

'You suit dark blue,' he remarked while the meal was being brought to the table, his attention ranging over the contrast of the honey-coloured skeins of her hair against the backdrop of the comparatively dismal colour. He had once thought blue eyes were dull and ordinary but the brilliant blueness of Ella's gaze against her smooth pale skin never failed to attract his attention.

'You can thank your mother's wonderful taste,' Ella said, and paused before she decided to just come right out and ask what politeness had urged her to suppress since the wedding. 'Why didn't your mother return to Vashir for our wedding or even come over for the UK one?'

Zarif's mouth took on a sardonic twist. 'Mariyah has lived abroad since my birth and has never played a role in my life.'

Ella was taken aback by that admission. 'Why not?'

'What are the two most important facts you need to know about the al-Rastani dynasty? One, we have always been a family with very few male heirs and, two, it has always been the ruler's right to *choose* his successor,' Zarif explained wryly. 'My grandfather, Karim, had one son, Halim, and my mother was his only other child. When my uncle Halim was still quite young, his father decided that he was not suited to being a ruler—Halim does not perform well in a crisis.'

'That must have been a devastating blow for Halim,' Ella remarked with sympathy.

'My uncle very much prefers his books and considered the life he led while Regent during my minority unpleasant and stressful,' Zarif advanced ruefully.

'You were telling me about your mother before I interrupted you.'

'Halim's wife gave birth only to daughters and, consequently, the lack of a male heir to the throne became a crisis. That was when my grandfather asked my mother to marry and provide the remedy.'

Ella pulled a face as she casually picked at her lamb and rice casserole with a fork. 'And you were the remedy,' she guessed.

'But not an easy remedy from my unfortunate mother's point of view,' Zarif declared grimly. 'She married an obnoxious playboy with a proven history of fathering male sons purely because she knew that all he was interested in was her money and that he would never seek to interfere with her life or mine.'

'You're referring to Gaetano Ravelli, who's Nik and Cristo's father as well?' Ella prompted. '*Was* he obnoxious?'

'Without a doubt, he was a very selfish, dissolute man. I actually never met him. He had no interest in his children.'

'I know that Belle and Cristo are raising his children by Belle's mother, who was his mistress for years,' Ella admitted. 'But I really know nothing else about him.

Did your mother hold your genes against you? Are you estranged because you remind her of Gaetano?'

'We're not estranged, but we are basically still strangers,' Zarif admitted, his dark golden eyes unusually sombre. 'She handed me over at birth to her parents to raise and when my grandparents died, Halim took over. Mariyah knew that I would never fully be *her* child because my grandfather planned to make me his heir and would insist on overseeing every aspect of my upbringing. Karim ensured that I attended a military school, went straight into the army and that I married Azel. After my mother divorced Gaetano she asked my grandfather's permission to live abroad. She has lived in Italy ever since and the only visits she has ever made back to Vashir were to honour my grandparents' passing and to see Halim, shortly after his terminal illness was diagnosed.'

'Have you ever actually *tried* to connect with her?' Ella prompted.

'Not in the sense that you mean. Although when I approached Mariyah for help with your wardrobe it was because I knew she would enjoy the challenge...and perhaps I wanted to make her feel a part of my life, even if it was only in a small way.' Zarif shrugged broad shoulders and sighed in frustration, spelling out the reality that he hated to talk about emotional things. 'But as people, what would my mother and I have in common now? Although my mother was born royal she hated the restrictions and sacrifices that being royal forced on her. She refuses to even use her title. She forged a successful career as a fashion stylist in the film world and enjoys the freedom of her anonymity.'

'I still think it's sad that you have no contact.' Ella

was thinking unhappily of him growing up without a mother while wondering if his grandparents had been loving replacements or more concerned about guaranteeing that they raised the most suitable possible royal heir to the throne. Military school, the army and a very youthful marriage to a chosen bride, the cousin he had grown up with. Such a rigidly conformist background did not suggest to her that Zarif had been allowed much licence to develop as an individual in his own right. From an early age, he had been denied the freedom to choose that which other people took for granted. She believed that the presence of a protective mother might have ensured he had more fair and liberal choices.

'My life is what it is and my mother and I inhabit different worlds,' Zarif retorted wryly.

Her cell phone pinged with a message and she pulled it out because her mother had been seeing her heart specialist that morning and had promised to relay her latest test results. But the name that popped up on the screen was Jason's and she put the phone back in her bag because she was in no hurry to read what her brother might have to say. Doubtless it would be another boastful text about wildly entertaining drunken parties or the ludicrously dangerous ski runs that he loved to do.

'I'm afraid I have to get back to work again,' Zarif revealed. 'Are you staying on for the second session?'

'No, I think I'll go and do a bit of shopping this afternoon.' Ella drained her glass of water and slowly stood. 'So, you're going back to deal with the old fossils, are you?'

Zarif's brilliant dark gaze glittered with wicked appreciation. 'I try to be a democrat.' He reached for her hands and pulled her close, his thumbs massaging her fragile wrist bones. 'I'm dining with you tonight.'

Her pink-tinted mouth pouted as she looked up at him. 'To what do I owe the honour?'

'You want an honest answer?' As she nodded, Zarif laughed. 'Your show of interest in government. Until today no woman had ever set foot in the council chamber and my uncle is so shocked by news of your interest that he suggested I am leaving you alone too much!'

Her eyes widened and then glimmered with matching amusement. 'And you said Vashir wasn't backward?' she teased.

'I lied. I wanted you to love it here as much as I do and I didn't want to line up all the flaws for your edification at your very first viewing.'

His mouth settled down over hers and her lush lips clung to his with a sudden fervour she could not restrain, hunger winging through her slender body in a wave she could not suppress. Zarif yanked his proud dark head back up, studying her with raw heat in his burning gaze. 'Later,' he husked sexily.

'Hold on a minute!' Ella exclaimed, digging into her bag with a tissue and stretching up on tiptoe to wipe the stain of pink from his wide, sensual mouth. 'The King can't be seen in public smeared with lipstick.'

Ella was still smiling without knowing what she was smiling about when she climbed into the limousine. She thrust the stained tissue back in her bag and then remembered Jason's text. With a rueful look in her eyes, she dug out her phone to read her brother's message.

RUNNING OUT OF MONEY. NEED A CASH INJECTION... 100,000 WOULD TIDE ME OVER.

Ella studied Jason's demand with wide, discomfited eyes and her mouth tightened. Jason really did have no shame. She texted back in haste.

I WILL NOT ASK ZARIF FOR MONEY FOR YOU.

HE'D BETTER PAY UP IF HE DOESN'T WANT HIS MISTRESSES IN DUBAI REVEALED TO THE MEDIA.

Hollow with shock and horror, Ella sat transfixed, staring at the screen of her phone. They were driving through the city centre by the time she got a grip on her roiling emotions. She lifted the phone to communicate with Hamid, who was seated beside the driver. 'I want to return to the old palace. I'm too tired to go shopping this afternoon,' she announced.

Mistresses? In Dubai? Her tummy dropped to the soles of her feet and her facial bones were clenched so tightly that her face felt frozen. Was it true? Was Zarif entertaining multiple women in his bed, just as his ancestors had done in the days of the harem?

CHAPTER NINE

ELLA AGONISED FOR what remained of the afternoon over the thorny question of whether or not she had the right to ask Zarif awkward questions.

It was a matter of decency, she told herself. She wasn't prepared to have sex with a male who might still intend to engage in encounters with other women at the first opportunity. The sick feeling in her stomach was disgust at that suspicion, nothing more personal. She was not hurt or jealous. To experience either reaction, she would have to be in love with Zarif and only the most stupid woman in the world would have fallen in love with a man who only wanted her body in his bed for a year. And she was, most assuredly, not stupid. Zarif had never had deeper feelings for her and what you didn't have, you could hardly miss. In fact, a sexual affair conducted on the lines of the utmost practicality and honesty was much less dangerous than one wrapped in honeyed lies and pretences.

Thus bolstered by a fine head of superior steam interlaced with deep abiding shame at her brother's threats, Ella sat down to dinner with Zarif and simply placed her phone in front of him, opened up so that Jason's texts could easily be read. 'You said we should be honest with each other, so I thought you should see this.'

In smouldering silence, Zarif studied the screen, beautiful wilful mouth twisting with derision, but Ella also noticed the hint of pallor that had paled his golden skin and the tension that steadily entered his big powerful frame.

'I will deal with this. Don't respond,' he instructed smoothly. 'But I think Jason will find it a great challenge to sell another story about either of us. My legal team has already demonstrated my zeal with regard to protecting your reputation in the British courts this week. The tabloid that printed that sleazy article on our wedding day will be printing a retraction and I am suing them for millions.'

Ella stuffed a lettuce leaf into her dry mouth and waited but that, it seemed, was that. Zarif mentioned how unexpectedly well Halim was doing on his new drug treatment and informed her that he had decided to extend their current accommodation into the suites on either side to give them more space. He then told her with a warm smile of amusement that her appearance in the council chambers that morning had made the headlines in the evening paper.

Indeed they had reached the dessert course of fresh fruit and cheese when Ella mastered her growing incredulity at his shocking ability to avoid the obvious and said dulcetly, 'And that's it? You've said all you intend to say about Jason's allegations?'

Dark golden eyes set with stunning effect below winged ebony brows and a lush cloak of blacker than black lashes gazed in serene challenge back at her. 'I answer to no one on the score of my private life,' he declared smooth as velvet.

Temper bubbled up through Ella's stiffening frame. 'You answer to me!' she contradicted without hesitation.

'And why would you assume that?' Zarif enquired in the mildest of tones, his handsome features taut with proud assurance and steadfast cool.

Ella thrust back her chair and stood up, her eyes electric blue with steadily mounting rage. 'Because you married me.'

'But it is not a conventional marriage. It is more one of convenience for both of us.'

Ella whirled round to face him so fast that her hair slapped against her cheeks. 'I will not sleep with a man who is planning to sleep with other women!'

Zarif left the table at an infuriatingly leisurely pace and strolled forward. 'Then you have no possible cause for concern. You are presently the only woman in my life or my bed.'

'Couldn't you just have told me that upfront?' Ella almost screeched at him in vexation. 'And ditched the macho need to tell me that I have no right to question your behaviour?'

'My past is none of your business,' Zarif stated on a note of distinct challenge. 'You go beyond your boundaries when you try to question me.'

'Do I indeed?' Ella hurled back, trembling with rage. 'Then maybe you should've spelt out those boundaries *before* we got married!'

'A clear oversight for which I apologise,' Zarif murmured as smoothly as ever.

'There are times when I *hate* you!' Ella launched at

him full volume, her hands clenching into fists of frustration by her side.

'I will not stand here while you shout at me,' Zarif told her grimly, lean, strong face hard as iron as he strode towards the door.

'If you run away sooner than answer my perfectly reasonable questions, I will see it as an act of *extreme* masculine cowardice,' Ella informed him with fiery vehemence.

Temperamentally incapable of ignoring a charge of that magnitude, Zarif froze two steps from the door before swinging almost violently back round to survey her with glittering golden eyes of sheer fury. 'How dare you?'

'I dare because I want answers,' Ella admitted grittily.

'Even if you're not entitled to them?'

'The way I see it, I was entitled to answers the instant we shared a bed,' Ella replied with a toss of her head. 'Do you have an apartment in Dubai?'

Zarif considered the question for several burning seconds and compressed his lips. 'I do. Have I kept women there? I have but it is presently empty,' he concluded curtly.

'And is it going to stay empty for the duration of our marriage?' Ella prompted, more than a little relieved that he had chosen to respond.

'For as long as you are with me,' Zarif confirmed in a low-pitched growl, his brooding rancour over her persistence unhidden in the stubborn set of his jaw line and the angled-back height of his proud dark head.

A touch mollified, Ella nodded. 'But you *did* keep women there?' she could not resist asking, her curiosity thrusting to the fore naked and embarrassing in its strength.

'One at a time,' Zarif divulged, lean, strong face set hard. 'I have needs like any other man. I will not apologise for that.'

Ella studied him with a sinking heart, suddenly feeling very vulnerable. 'Tell me, how did I escape an invite to occupy the apartment in Dubai?'

Zarif vented a harsh laugh. 'I wanted to see more of you—an ambition that is presently ebbing fast.'

Ella felt the bite of that derisive dismissal like a knife piercing her breast. This was her lover talking down to her as if she was nothing, nobody, virtual mud below his royal feet. This was not the respect he had promised her. 'On *both* sides,' she stressed tightly. 'But it's perfectly obvious to me that all I am is your mistress within marriage.'

'If that is true,' Zarif countered with a raw edge to his deep dark drawl, 'then go and wait for me in bed and put on something sexy before you go there because I am in the mood to play and dispel the memory of this distasteful scene.'

'You can go take a running jump into the nearest sand dune!' Ella launched back at him in outraged disbelief.

The door opened on the servants entering to clear the table. Zarif was rigid and the silence smouldered and crackled like an invisible fire. His stunning eyes were a ferocious golden blaze of unashamed fury.

'Or not,' Ella framed, just a little unnerved by the unholy temper she could see him restraining for she had never, ever seen him lose it.

'A word?' With an imperious signal of one lean brown hand, Zarif virtually ordered her out into the corridor where he lowered his arrogant dark head to say, 'Three years ago I asked you to marry me and you said no. Do not expect to enjoy the same privileges that I would have offered you then,' he advised grimly. 'That time is past.'

He was a bad loser, Ella translated, a little shiver of foreboding travelling down her taut spine. 'I think I liked you better back then.'

'But not enough to marry me.'

You stupid, stupid man, I *loved* you! she almost screamed after him as he strode off, shoulders back, military carriage obvious in every angle of his bearing. She went out to the gardens to walk at a fast pace. She had to do something to expel the billows of rage still shrieking around inside her in need of an exit. The two guards following her down every path taxed her patience as she could not imagine that any possible ill could befall her in a literal fortress surrounded by high walls and enough armed men to fight a war. Her temper under control again, she opted for a long bath and an early night.

She could not stop thinking about the apartment in Dubai where Zarif had clearly been entertained by a steady procession of women. Sexually sophisticated women, who would think nothing of putting on adventurous lingerie to titillate him. Women who probably did exactly what he told them every time because they were eager to please and be rewarded for their obedience. Shallow, superficial affairs, she decided heavily. Yet Zarif, as proven by his deep attachment to his first wife, was capable of so much more.

Only he didn't want *more*, particularly not with Ella, who had once turned him down. He wanted only convenient sex, and her wedding ring simply put a stamp of respectability on the arrangement. In reality, however, she was as much of a whore as the women he had kept in the Dubai apartment, she reflected wretchedly. She might think that she did not have a submissive bone in her body but she had pretty much done exactly as she was told from the minute she agreed to marry him. And why had she agreed? For the cold, hard cash that had put her parents' lives back on the rails. Consequently, she had no right to feel superior in any way to Zarif's mistresses. He had recognised that at heart she was just the same as his other sexual partners and willing to do whatever it took if the reward was great enough, so how could she ask for respect?

Zarif came to bed late and stayed on his own side of the bed while Ella pretended to be asleep. She was ashamed of the facts he had forced her to face and deeply unhappy at the position she had put herself in because she could see no escape hatch. In the morning Zarif was gone and that was the start of a very lonely three weeks during which Ella scarcely saw him. He breakfasted before she got out of bed, which relieved her as during the third week she realised that she seemed to be suffering from a lingering tummy bug, which she blamed on her new diet. She was nauseous several mornings and actually sick on a couple of occasions but was fine the rest of the time.

Unaware of those early morning travails, Zarif occasionally appeared for lunch, during which time he would make perfectly polite conversation, which chilled her. He went back to dining nightly with Halim. One morning he announced without any self-consciousness that he was flying out to a meeting in Dubai. She lay sleepless in bed that night, wondering if he had betrayed her trust because, while he was not sleeping with her, she did not think she could afford to assume that he would not seek relief with someone else. She kept busy during the days, reading and bathing in the giant deserted swimming pool in the basement that had once housed the harem. She also embarked on lessons in Arabic and wandered aimlessly round the shopping malls, rarely buying anything but frequently photographed.

During the second week, Zarif's uncle came unexpectedly to her rescue by asking her through the medium of Hamid if she would like to preside over the official opening of a new school. Realising that a positive response would be expected of her, she agreed and then fretted about what to say and do at the event until Hamid offered her his wife, Soraya, as an advisor.

Soraya gave her invaluable help. The other woman helped her write a short speech, taught her to say it word perfect in Arabic and even advised her on what to wear. Ella made the visit, inwardly quaking with nerves, but soon relaxed at the friendly response she received and she loved chatting with the children, who wanted to practise their English on her. She managed to smile for the photographers and was feeling both proud and defiant by the time she returned to the old palace.

'You did well today at the school,' Zarif startled her by saying when he was undressing for bed. 'Everyone was impressed.'

The sudden break of his icy reserve disconcerted her. 'I didn't know you were aware of it.'

'Who do you think suggested it to Halim?'

Ella flushed and felt foolish. She watched his silhouette, which was starkly apparent in the moonlight piercing the drapes. As he dropped the towel he wore round his hips she glimpsed the long thick length of his erec-

tion and stared before hastily shutting her eyes tight.
Perhaps he hadn't had his needs met in Dubai, after
all. But then she hadn't had her needs met either, she
thought impatiently, pressing the swollen tenderness of
her breasts into the mattress and clamping her thighs
tight shut on the ache stirring there.

It was all his wretched fault, Ella decided angrily. She
had managed fine without sex until Zarif appeared on
her horizon like a battleship bent on a seek-and-destroy
mission. Now the scent of his cologne, the memory of
their lovemaking or even the sounds he made getting
ready for bed lit a fire of treacherous longing in her pelvis. She told herself that it was good to know that he was
suffering too and that his self-control was little better
than her own. But she still cursed the fact that he had
refused to let her occupy a room of her own. And then
she thought, Why should he have it all his own way?

In a movement that startled Zarif she flung back
the sheet and flipped over to study him. His long, lean,
aroused body lay extended for her perusal and the fire
inside her leapt higher, a surge of wetness moistening
her feminine core. Before she could even think about
what she was doing she pressed her mouth to the smooth,
muscular expanse of his bronzed stomach. The salty
taste of his skin went to her head like wine and the way
he jerked in surprise sent a wicked smile of amusement
across her mouth.

One hand resting on a hair-roughened thigh, she
trailed the tip of her tongue along the length of his bold
shaft and felt every muscle in his body snap taut. She
traced his hard, velvet-smooth contours with lingering enjoyment, a sense of power flooding her when he
laced his fingers into her hair and arched his hips up to

her in ready acquiescence. As she sucked him deep he groaned out loud and she wanted to punch the air at finally smashing through the icy deadlock barrier of his reserve. Long fingers caressed her scalp.

Zarif was in shock but incredibly turned on by her unexpected sensual assault. Once or twice he winced when she grazed him with her teeth and then suddenly he smiled triumphantly at her down-bent head, guessing that he was very probably the first man in her life to benefit from her attention. As the intensity rose he gently tugged at her hair. 'No more, *habibti*,' he husked. 'I want to finish inside you...'

A little uncertainly, Ella lifted her head and he sat up so fast and claimed her mouth in a searing kiss that she felt dizzy but unbelievably eager for him to continue.

'I've been such a fool,' Zarif groaned, flattening her to the mattress with more haste than finesse and sliding between her slender thighs with barely contained eagerness. 'I'm too proud, too used to winning every argument. Azel never argued with me, never confronted me.'

'That was bad for you,' Ella breathed on the back of a long dragged-out gasp as he pushed up her hips and plunged into her with a stirring groan of appreciative hunger that she felt down to her toes.

'You're good for me,' Zarif intoned hoarsely, circling his hips to longer enjoy the hot, tight, wet depth of her welcome. He shifted into a series of fast, deep thrusts that drove all prospect of dialogue from her head.

Every mad skip of her heartbeat and every impelling plunge of his possession was breathlessly, insanely exciting. He laboured long and hard over her yearning body and she came in a great pulsating surge of release, his name breaking from her lips as he shuddered over her.

They lay still, wrapped tightly together, both of them struggling for breath.

'You had a right to ask those questions,' he conceded wryly. 'But although I should stop the tasteless comparisons, Azel never asked and I'm not accustomed to full and frank discussions of that nature.'

Stunned by his sudden loquaciousness on the forbidden topic of Azel, Ella lay as still as a mouse facing up to a cat. 'She never asked you if you were faithful to her?'

'She was probably aware that I had been told I didn't have to be faithful when I agreed to marry her. Her parents would have prepared her for that eventuality. They left nothing to chance. We were pawns in a much bigger game. Halim might not have got the throne but his consolation was that his daughter would become my queen.' Zarif sighed.

'Was she ambitious for that status?' Ella whispered.

'No. She genuinely loved me,' Zarif conceded, rolling back from her to throw himself into a cooler spot on the bed. He stretched out a hand though and enclosed hers. Suddenly the future no longer seemed so threatening and uncertain. The silence stretched and it was a strangely soothing silence. Ella slid slowly into a deep sleep, more relaxed and happier than she had been in weeks.

'You mean, this is not the *first* time?' Zarif exclaimed, unfurling his cell phone to contact Halim's doctor and furious that he had been left out of the loop. 'Why didn't you tell me?'

'Oh, do go away and stop fussing, Zarif,' Ella groaned as she endeavoured to freshen up at the sink after a bout of sickness had sent her careening out of bed straight into the bathroom where the very last thing she had wanted was an audience. 'It's only a little tummy upset…probably the change of diet. I'm eating so much spice.'

'I will hire a British cook if this is the result. How often has this happened?' Zarif demanded, directing a stream of Arabic at the two hovering maids, nodding, compressing his wide sensual mouth as the answers came and confirmed his worst suspicions. His lean, devastatingly handsome face darkened along with his mood.

'You're going back to bed,' Zarif informed Ella, scooping her up and carrying her back into the bedroom where he laid her down with great care.

Ella felt too dizzy and sweaty to argue. Dr Mansour arrived with a nurse, his voice a deep soothing rumble that eventually contrived to make Zarif simmer down. Anyone would be forgiven for thinking that a minor bout of sickness was an emergency, Ella thought ruefully. Some tests were done with her assistance and were quickly followed by an examination.

At the end of it all, Dr Mansour asked the nurse to wait in the other room. A big beaming smile had transformed his guarded expression and the look he spread between Zarif and Ella was warm with appreciation. 'I am deeply honoured to offer my congratulations on this happy event, which will mean so much both to you and to our country…'

'H-happy event?' Ella stammered in bewilderment.

'You have conceived, Your Majesty. You must've conceived almost immediately after your marriage,' the older man informed her cheerfully. 'Hardly a surprising development for a young and healthy couple but a very welcome one.'

In shock, Ella focused on Zarif, who appeared to be frozen in the centre of the room. She could see the pallor spreading below his bronzed complexion, the skin tightening over his spectacular bone structure. *Pregnant?* How on earth could she be pregnant?

'But I've been taking the contraceptive pill,' Ella protested and named the brand.

'We wanted to wait a few months,' Zarif breathed stiltedly, clearly already engaged in a cover-up because the older man had not been able to hide his surprise that in their circumstances they could have chosen to use contraception rather than try immediately to provide the very much wanted heir to the throne.

The older man smiled wryly. 'Of course but that particular brand, I'm afraid, was not a good choice. It is usually prescribed to regulate a woman's system.'

'Which is what I was taking it for...' Ella's voice was dwindling away while the great tide of sheer astonishment was rolling over her. A baby... She was going to have a baby, Zarif's baby? Even in that first piercing moment of disbelief, she was aware of the warm tide of acceptance and happiness rising inside her. She might not be able to have him but he couldn't stop her from having his child, she thought helplessly.

'Unfortunately that type of pill has to be taken strictly at the same time every day and it is not reliable if pills are missed or there is an episode of illness, such as you had on your wedding day,' Dr Mansour explained. 'Other precautions would have had to be taken for the rest of that month.'

Ella nodded with all the animation of a marionette and dared not look at Zarif to see how he was reacting to the news that her ignorance of the efficacy of her contraception had contributed to their current predicament. 'Thank you for clarifying that, Doctor.'

The older man lingered to advise her on how best to cope with the morning sickness and recommended an obstetrician in the city, while adding ruefully that it would be unwise to consider conducting the allergy tests he had advised until after she had given birth.

A baby? Zarif was in a daze. He studied Ella's flat stomach and thought of his child growing there and he wanted to touch her so badly at that moment that his hands knotted into fists by his side. Ella had conceived. Had she planned it that way? There could be no surer way of holding onto her status as his wife than by giving him a child.

'You said it was safe,' Zarif reminded her tautly as soon as they were alone.

Ella stared up fixedly at the canopy of the bed above her, guilt slashing through her at the simplicity of that reminder that really said all that needed to be said. He felt he had been deceived. He felt trapped by a development he would actively have guarded against had he known it was possible.

'I honestly *did* think it was safe. When I began taking that pill, it wasn't for contraception and I probably didn't pay a lot of heed to any warnings that were in the instructions. That first day…we were together,' she framed awkwardly, 'I assumed it would be safe because I've been taking it for a couple of years and one's always reading about how very long it can take for a woman to fall pregnant. I mean, I really didn't think it *could* be that easy.'

'Obviously you're very fertile,' Zarif pointed out flatly.

'I couldn't help the fact that I was sick the night before we slept together!' Ella argued, feeling that she had to defend herself. 'It didn't occur to me that I was probably no longer protected because of that. I was convinced that I was telling you the truth when I said it was safe.'

'Were you really?' Zarif queried in a tone she had never heard him use before, a tone of doubt and mistrust. 'Or did you work out for yourself that this is the one development that will ensure I do *not* divorce you and set you aside after a year?'

Ella dealt him an appalled appraisal, shaken that he could think her capable of such manipulative behaviour. 'That's a filthy thing to say. How can you even suspect that?'

'Naturally I'm suspicious…particularly after you threw yourself at me last night. Presumably you didn't yet realise that you were already pregnant and we had not been having sex. Obviously you had to ensure sex took place to have any hope of conceiving.'

'I did not *throw* myself at you!' Ella launched, rearing up in the bed in a positive fury.

Zarif knew he was burning boats but he couldn't stop himself from working up a firestorm in which resentment, incredulity and suspicion dominated. Just at that moment it was too deeply painful for him to think about the baby on the way and the savage irony that for him and Ella conception had happened so very easily. All that he would allow himself to think was that once again he was being forced into a path he had not freely chosen. There were very few things in his life that he was free to choose for himself but this time around, at least, he had had the freedom to choose his own wife. And now that was gone and his little piece of self-indulgence had become a life sentence.

His stormy departure left a terrible silence stretching in its wake. Slowly, carefully, Ella got up, standing only when she was convinced that the sick dizziness had faded. She sat down at the breakfast table and sipped at the special ginger tea Dr Mansour had said he would order from the kitchens for her. She supposed she would have to start thinking of all sorts of things that she had never had to consider before. In fact her every action would have to be tailored to whatever would best suit the baby she carried. A baby, Ella thought, splaying a hand across her flat tummy with quiet and loving satisfaction. Zarif's baby. Yet how could she want the child of a man she hated?

Of course hatred was a little over the top as a description of her feelings, she conceded. Events had suddenly got wildly out of control and Zarif was a dot every 'i' and cross every 't' man, who liked to plan everything. The conception of a child with the wrong woman was a shockingly unexpected development and he hadn't reacted well. Had she supposed he would? Presumably being male he was not being bombarded by the warm, positively fluffy pictures of a cuddly baby currently consuming her thoughts.

CHAPTER TEN

ZARIF SHARED THE news with Halim and Halim was over-joyed and hailed Ella as the most wonderful woman ever. 'So soon…already a little mother-to-be,' he kept on saying, patting his nephew's arm in fond emphasis. 'A gift is in order, a gift to express my great joy and gratitude.'

'It could be a girl,' Zarif pointed out, disconcerted by his uncle's gushing effusions and suddenly painfully aware that his own reaction should have been similar.

'Then the next will be a male.' Halim would not allow anyone to rain on his parade. 'Are you happy, my boy? Or does all this only bring back unhappy memories?'

'A little of both,' Zarif admitted truthfully. 'You will forgive me if I return to Ella now?'

'This is a new beginning for you and our family, Zarif,' the old man told him quietly. 'Don't allow the sadness of the past to shadow the present.'

But the past had made Zarif who he was, honing him down to the essentials of duty and honour and making him a very tough judge of his own behaviour. And now without the smallest warning he was aware of all the many things that he had *not* said to Ella and, desert robes swishing in accompaniment to his long, forceful stride, he sped back to the quarters he shared with his wife.

When Zarif strode into the dining room, Ella spared him a careless glance of acknowledgement. 'Oh, it's you,' she said in the same voice with which she might have greeted an unappetising serving of cold porridge.

'I said some things I should not have said,' Zarif announced.

'How's that new?' Ella asked waspishly, watching his long, beautifully shaped fingers flex across the chair back in angry response and getting a mean kick from that tiny display of human frailty. 'Apparently you think I am calculating and mercenary, and someone who wants to stay a queen and spend loads and loads of your money.'

'Instead of which you are the heartbreak of the Qurzah shopkeepers because you browse and never buy. I know that material things are not important to you,' Zarif told her tautly, 'but from this moment on we are truly man and wife with all that that entails and it is permanent.'

Ella stared stonily at the jug of hot chocolate whose fumes now made her tummy roll as though she were on the deck of a storm-tossed ship. *'Permanent?'* she queried half an octave higher. 'No, thanks. I still want the divorce I was promised.'

Zarif stared back at her in stark disbelief, darkly fringed tawny eyes full of condemnation. 'You can't have a divorce now…you're *pregnant.*'

'And yet you are *not* a happy camper about that,' Ella slotted in drily, ramming back her sense of pained rejection as she made that observation. 'So, please don't think for one moment that I intend to ruin both our lives, and our child's for that matter, by staying with you as your wife *for ever*. On those terms for ever sounds like a death sentence.'

Zarif straightened to his full imposing height. 'Even if I have to lock you up and throw away the key, understand one thing now...' he advised harshly. 'I will not lose *another* child.'

Jolted out of self-pitying sarcasm by that very real statement of loss, Ella pushed herself up out of her seat with a troubled frown. 'Zarif?'

'My son died as a stranger to me,' Zarif bit out not quite steadily, shocking her where she stood from the pain he made no attempt to hide, lean, dark features stamped with lines of grief and regret he had never allowed her to see before. 'I held him only once and briefly after his birth. Then he was kept away from me because men were not welcome in the nursery. It wasn't thought proper or normal for me to take too much of an interest in him while he was still a baby. I was told I could get to know my son later when he was older...but there *was* no later and he never *did* get any older...'

And Ella's heart cracked right down the middle inside her, tears on his behalf stinging her eyes and clogging her throat. She hurt so much for him at that moment that she almost crossed the room to wrap her arms round him in a desperate effort to comfort him. 'I'm so sorry, Zarif,' she said weakly instead.

'That is why I will not let you leave me or take my child away from me. Boy or girl, it is immaterial. I will *be* here for this child at every stage of his or her life,' he completed hoarsely.

'I completely understand how you feel,' she whispered and she honestly did. He had lost his infant son and her talk of divorce had made him feel threatened and, of course, if she were to take their child back to the UK, he would see little of him or her, so his concern and fear on that score were perfectly understandable.

'Then understand that I will not let you go,' Zarif repeated doggedly. 'We will stay married and, if need be, we will *work* at staying married.'

Ella lost colour, wondering if he would need to work that hard to live with her as his wife. Would he be constantly wishing she were Azel? Wishing she were a woman from his own culture? Longing for a break from her? Wishing he could occasionally ring the changes by taking another woman to his bed?

Exactly how would it feel to be granted the status of being a for-ever wife purely and simply because she had given birth to his baby? She believed that the burden of being essentially unwanted would crush her spirit. She wanted him to want her, didn't she? She always had. She thought of her clumsy seduction attempt the night before when she had been thrilled by his response and her face burned hot. Sadly, Zarif was not saying anything she wanted to hear and he never would, would he?

He hadn't wanted or planned a child with her. He hadn't chosen her as the mother of his child. He had chosen her to share his bed, to provide light entertainment and sexual satisfaction within the respectable guise of marriage. But he hadn't ever wanted a *real* marriage with her, had he? And why did that hurt so much? Why did all her emotions feel raw-edged? Why did she feel so desperate and despairing?

Because she wanted more from him, had always wanted *more* from the instant she looked at him at the tender age of seventeen and fell head over heels in love for the one and only time in her life. And now she was looking at Zarif afresh and with much greater maturity and the sudden sinking acknowledgement that she still loved Zarif al-Rastani with all her heart and her soul. No other man had ever stirred her brain or her body the way he did, no other man could hurt her so easily. Pride had made her tell herself that she had got over him but she had been lying to herself all along. Unrequited love could have tremendous sticking power.

'What I don't understand,' Ella admitted thinly, 'is that three years ago you wanted to marry me and yet now you're behaving like you've been trapped by some designing hussy! What changed?'

'You said no,' Zarif growled like a grizzly bear.

A great storm of fiery emotion engulfed Ella, who was thoroughly sick of his inability to work out the obvious. 'Of course I said no. I was madly in love with you and then you told me you still loved Azel and that she was irreplaceable—'

His brilliant dark eyes narrowed as he stared back at her in evident bewilderment. 'I'm sure I did not say that.'

'You *did* say it. You said she would always be in your heart and only a total madwoman would have married you after being told that!'

'You said you were madly in love with me...' he breathed uncertainly.

'Three years ago...before I wised up and realised that you were a lost cause better left lost in the past!' Ella parried with hot cheeks and acid bite as she stalked past him.

Zarif was frozen in the centre of the room trying to recall saying what she had flung at him. Had his guilty conscience stirred him into making that claim? Could he really have been that crass that day? Was it possible

that Ella had loved him then? A flicker of gold burned
in his abstracted gaze as he mulled that idea over until
it burst like a rainbow on a sunny day over his every
thought. *Inshallah*, he had been blessed by the gift of another child and the perfect excuse to keep the woman of
his dreams. Did he really need that excuse? What had he
been agonising about? And why had he driven her away?

Even his uncle had urged him to move on and recognise that this was a fresh start. But he hadn't moved
on, had he? He had allowed his guilt and regret from the
past to wall him off from the infinitely more promis-
ing present. It was time to tell her the truth even if that
threatened to change her view of him in a way that he
dreaded. Swallowing hard, Zarif headed to his office
safe. Pride was all very well but his marriage was on
the line and he did not think he was in a strong enough
position to keep secrets.

CHAPTER ELEVEN

ELLA WAS SO angry and wounded that she wanted to scream her hurt to the rooftops. Zarif wanted the baby but he didn't want her.

Ella would only be tolerated and accepted as a wife because she was the baby's mother. Zarif would continue to view Azel as the perfect matchless partner even while Ella lay in his bed and gave birth to his child. It wasn't fair, it simply wasn't fair, she thought with ferocious resentment even though she knew that life was frequently unfair. She could not face leading such a life with Zarif even for the sake of their unborn child. Such a marriage could not possibly be happy and their child would be damaged by the strife between them. He *had* to divorce her. Somehow she had to persuade him that a divorce that would grant him liberal access to their child was the best solution for all of them.

Of course, she could do something scandalous, which would make it much easier for him to accede to a divorce, she conceded, her brain roving off on a tangent as she descended a rear set of stairs in search of fresh air. She was desperate to escape the palace and leave behind the hothouse tension of her row with Zarif. It was running away and she knew it was running away but she couldn't face another session with Zarif, particularly not after having exposed herself to the extent that she had. Why had she told him that she had been madly in love with him three years earlier? What had she hoped to achieve with that admission? In retrospect she felt humiliated but knew she had brought it on herself.

As the heat engulfed her in an area not cooled by fans, Ella longed for a breeze and thought nostalgically back to the occasion when her father had taken her mother and her out for a drive in an open-topped sports car. Of course, if she wanted to scandalise the populace she could go for a drive now, she thought suddenly, thinking of the vast basement of high-performance cars she had viewed only the week before when she was exploring the palace. Zarif might rarely drive himself anywhere but he had a fabulous collection of vehicles. Her chin rising at a combative angle, Ella crossed the courtyard to the garage block.

It was the work of a moment to indicate which car she wanted brought out to the two men engaged in lovingly polishing one. Naturally they didn't question the command: she was Zarif's queen and they undoubtedly assumed that he or someone else would be driving her.

Within minutes, the fire-engine-red Ferrari was parked out on the forecourt, paintwork gleaming in the hot sunlight. Ella breathed in deep and slow and got behind the wheel. It was a very powerful car. As she drove towards the gates she travelled slowly while she familiarised herself with the steering and the controls. There was no way she would take it into the city centre, she conceded, shrinking from the prospect of all that traffic, but she could certainly take it for a spin on the desert highway that encircled the walls of the old city.

The gate guards made no attempt to hide their shock when they saw her seated behind the wheel driving and without a team of bodyguards in tow. Obedience, however, was engrained in the royal staff and they opened the gates, although she had not the smallest doubt that the minute she drove out the guards would be on the phone informing the powers-that-be that she had left the grounds and, even worse, was breaking the law by driving herself. Indeed she had only travelled a couple of hundred yards before she glanced in her rear-view mirror and saw two army vehicles hurtling out onto the road behind her. The sight made her foot press down on the accelerator.

'Your wife has just driven out of the gates in your Ferrari!' Hamid informed Zarif, huffing and puffing and red-faced from the speed with which he had mounted the stairs to deliver that explosive news.

Cold sweat drenched Zarif at the thought of Ella behind the wheel of so powerful a car. He closed his eyes and for a split second he prayed, warding off the images of the aftermath of Azel's fatal crash, the wreckage scattered across the road, the poignant sight of his son's tiny jacket lying by the roadside covered in sand.

'I must follow her.'

'I have put the army in pursuit.'

Zarif spun in disbelief. 'Are you crazy? I don't want anyone chasing her, panicking her into crashing!' he exclaimed in horror. 'Tell them to keep their distance from her and not to try to stop her because I don't want her speeding up to escape them.'

Hamid was already on the phone muttering fervent

apologies, regretful eyes locked to Zarif, who was already racing for the stairs and the fastest means of transport he possessed.

Ella was relieved that the army escort stayed well back from her. Two cars loaded with teenagers, however, overtook the Ferrari. They waved and honked horns noisily, poked their heads through their sun roofs to take photos of her and, even though she was deliberately driving slowly to be safe, Ella was childishly affronted at being overtaken in Zarif's high-performance car.

On her first loop of the city walls, she glimpsed a police car parked at the entrance to the old city with its roof light flashing and it was at that point that two other cars fell in behind her. She peered in the rear-view mirror, registering that the nearest car definitely had a female driver at the wheel, and she grinned. Without warning, the police car appeared on the road behind her, travelling at great speed to overtake her, and she was about to pull off the road feeling that she had made her point when the police car simply moved into the lane in front of her, slowing her down but taking up pole position.

Hamid was on the phone to Zarif, who was airborne. 'Women are pouring out of the shops and the offices and getting behind car wheels all over the city to follow the Queen's car. It's turning into a mass demonstration on the desert highway and the police and the army say there is a danger of public disorder and they want to arrest everybody involved.'

'No woman is to be stopped or arrested,' Zarif decreed. 'Interference would only raise the risk of an accident occurring.'

'My wife is out there in a car too,' Hamid confided in a small voice.

'We married gutsy women, Hamid. They have a good side and a bad side, or should I call it an exciting side?' Zarif sighed, trying to work out how best to get Ella off the road safely.

He could not phone her. He would not *risk* phoning her. Azel had been on the phone when she crashed.

The noise of hundreds of car horns blaring made Ella look in the rear-view mirror and she almost jumped on the brakes because there was a whole procession of cars following her. Overhead she could hear more than one helicopter hovering. Swallowing hard, she drove on behind the leading police car, wishing they would step on it a bit. She was ready to head back to the palace. She had made her statement but she had not intended to cause traffic chaos or involve other women in her protest.

It was a stupid sexist law and it ought to be changed but she didn't want to get anyone else into trouble. She looked on in disbelief as a pickup truck with a large film camera mounted on the back overtook the police and what she assumed to be the news crew proceeded to film the parade of cars. It was a very dangerous manoeuvre, which convinced Ella that it was time for her to wind down the tension by quietly bowing out.

Ella pulled off the road onto the stony, sandy desert plain. Her army escort followed. Before she could even climb out of the Ferrari a ring of soldiers surrounded the vehicle and there was the truly deafening noise of a helicopter landing nearby. The car horns were still going like mad. Barely a minute later, the ring of soldiers parted and Zarif strode towards her, his lean, breathtakingly beautiful face taut and informative.

Anxiety exploded inside Ella. She had done what she had done. It was a senseless law and she had made a mockery of it but she had not realised that she might inspire other women into staging a massive demonstration alongside her. That made her feel guilty. That was more of a lesson than she had intended to teach and, although she had known her protest would embarrass Zarif, she was suddenly not proud of what she had evidently achieved. In fact the huge fuss and the pull on resources that her simple drive had created suddenly made her feel ashamed and about one inch tall.

'Zarif…' she began hesitantly.

Without a word he bent down and scooped her bodily up into his strong arms and carted her back to the helicopter he had evidently landed in. He settled her into the passenger seat and did up the safety belt in a series of silent determined movements.

'You're furious with me,' she breathed shakily.

'No, I was more afraid for your safety in the mood you were in,' Zarif contradicted. 'I'm a natural worrier… Azel and my son died on that same stretch of road.'

Ella turned pale. 'I'm so sorry…I didn't think.'

His strong jaw line clenched. 'She was a new driver. I told her that she needed more practice before she took to the road but she was determined to meet me at the airport. She was on the phone, something may have distracted her…possibly the baby. We'll never know. She crashed head-on into a truck. And because of a tragedy that could have been foreseen, Halim drew up an unjust law forbidding women from driving. It was the only law he put forward in all his years as Regent and, in the light of what had happened to his daughter and grandson, nobody had the heart to say no to him,' he proffered heavily as he vaulted back out of the helicopter and stood by the door talking to her. 'But *I* should've had the strength to oppose him. When I saw all those women driving behind you, determined to show solidarity with you, I finally realised what a huge source of resentment that law has become. Regardless of how Halim feels about it, the law will be removed from the statute books as soon as possible. The taxi drivers will be furious but there are always losers in every scenario.'

Slamming the door on her, Zarif strode round the nose of the helicopter and climbed into the pilot's seat.

'You're flying us?' she prompted in surprise.

'I've been flying for many years,' Zarif told her gently.

'I didn't know,' she said as he fiddled with the controls and spoke into the radio.

'Changing the law is the right thing to do,' she told him as the whine of the whirling rotor blades began. 'But it wasn't fair for me to do something like that in public to embarrass you.'

'I wasn't embarrassed. I was surprisingly proud of you for standing up for what you believed in,' Zarif admitted with a sidelong glance at her from black-fringed dark eyes. 'Why did you pull off the road and stop it?'

'When that film crew thrust their vehicle in front of us, I realised it was getting dangerous and I didn't want anyone to get hurt. How the heck did people find out about what I was doing so fast?'

'It was plastered all over Facebook and Twitter within minutes of you leaving the palace. You're a heroine now. Why did you do it?' he shot at her loudly and abruptly when they were airborne.

'I thought it would make you divorce me and that that would be for the best.'

'*Never!*' he rebutted succinctly and that was the last word exchanged for some time.

They landed in the desert, the *real* desert, which she had only seen in pictures, a place of deep rolling golden dunes and grey rocky outcrops, and it was like stepping out into a cocoon of unbelievable heat. 'Where on earth are we?' she asked as Zarif lifted her out of the passenger seat.

'Honeymoon Central,' Zarif quipped as he tucked something that might have been a book under one arm.

'I beg your pardon?' Ella gasped, her head whipping round as she stared in disconcertion at the great steepwalled and turreted grey fortress built on top of the stony hill that lay directly ahead of them.

'The Old Fort, once used as a hunting lodge, latterly as my grandparents' holiday home. It was a special place for them,' Zarif told her. 'There's a long route in by road and our luggage will be coming in that way tonight.'

'We're going to *stay* here?' Ella queried in bewilderment, worry stirring that this could be the first step in his threat to lock her up and throw away the key. Would he really maroon her in this remote place on her own?

'Yes, until we get everything ironed out between us. It's peaceful here and there are no distractions,' Zarif pointed out smoothly as he stood back for her to precede him up the flight of steps carved out of the rock face. 'You go first and take your time because it's a long climb. We're not in a hurry.'

She was so out of breath that he had to carry her up the last flight of steps. At the top she found herself in a surprisingly pretty cobbled courtyard. Urns overflowed with colourful flowers in the shade below the arches. An old gardener was watering the plants in a corner bed and he greeted Zarif with a toothless smile and a very low bow.

The solid wooden doors of the entrance already stood open on a wonderfully cool blue and white tiled hallway. 'This is very pretty and not at all what I expected from the outside of this place,' Ella confided.

'My grandmother renovated it. I'm afraid it's a little old-fashioned now,' Zarif warned, urging her into an elegant salon furnished very much in the British style. The curtains and the paintings and the wallpaper all looked sadly faded but a gracious atmospheric charm remained.

'You never told me how your grandmother met and married your grandfather,' she remarked, perching on a window seat to catch her breath.

'She and her father were hired to conserve the library at the old palace where we used to store many very old and valuable documents. Now they're in the latest temperature-controlled environment in the new palace. For my grandfather, Karim, it was a case of love at first sight. Her name was Violet,' Zarif divulged. 'But Violet refused to have anything to do with him because he kept a harem full of concubines.'

'Oh, my word, even I didn't have an excuse to say no that was that good!' Ella could not resist gasping.

'He offered to reduce the harem by half.'

'Whoopy-do!' Ella carolled, unimpressed.

'Then he endowed all his concubines with dowries and found them husbands and thought that Violet would finally agree to be his.'

'And she didn't?'

'No, she wanted the assurance that she would be his one and only wife because, of course, the Qu'ran allows a Muslim four. The council were very much against him giving such an undertaking before there was proof that Violet could give him children but Karim rebelled and went ahead and married her.'

'And were they happy?' Ella prompted.

'Very much so and that, you must understand, is the example that I grew up with. A happy loving marriage conducted very much in the Western style. Violet was a daredevil. She jumped out of aeroplanes, raced camels and deep-sea dived. She would have driven that car today just like you did. And she would have stopped for the same reason.' Zarif's lean dark face shadowed. 'Yet she and Karim, who had such a caring relationship, thrust me into an arranged marriage as a teenager. It was a done deal to unite the two different factions in Vashir. Those who preferred Halim's conservatism to the risk of the unknown rule of a young man, who was the son of an absentee Vashiri princess and an Italian playboy.'

Ella was tense and afraid of saying something that might offend but she was finally beginning to suspect that Zarif's marriage had not been as idyllic a match as he had led her to assume. 'But your marriage worked, didn't it?'

'After a fashion,' Zarif conceded uncomfortably. 'It was far from ideal.'

'But you *loved* her,' Ella reminded him staunchly, not wanting him to try and deny that truth for the sake of soothing her feelings of jealousy.

'Not in the way Azel wanted me to love her. I loved her as a childhood playmate, a cousin.' His expressive mouth curled and he lifted his hands in a sudden violent gesture of frustration. 'How can I tell you the truth *without* betraying her memory?' Zarif spun away from her before continuing harshly. 'To me, she felt more like a sister than a wife because we spent too many years being raised together in her father's home. There was no chemistry, no romance. I didn't *want* to marry her but I did my duty to the best of my ability.'

Ella was so shocked by that admission that she literally stared at him with wide incredulous eyes. 'I thought you adored her...'

'She was my best friend and very supportive,' Zarif hastened to assure her. 'But I could not return her idealised feelings for me and that made me feel very guilty. I felt as though I was taking all the time while she did all the giving.'

'But if she gave that was *her* choice,' Ella whispered. 'And if she loved you she may well have been content.'

'She was content but I was not happy with her,' Zarif confessed in a ragged and reluctant confession. 'I hid it as best I could. I would have done anything rather than hurt her. But I was always aware that there was a big empty pit of nothingness at the centre of our marriage and the one thing we could have shared...our son, she preferred to keep to herself.'

Ella stared steadily back at him. 'So, if you weren't that happy with her, why did you go out of your way to stress how much you loved her three years ago?'

'Blame my guilty conscience for that piece of foolishness. I *was* sincerely devastated when she died. That was the main reason why I left Vashir to study abroad. I needed a change of scene and the chance to occupy my brain, but that is not what I ultimately found there,' Zarif told her flatly.

'I don't think I want to talk about the past any more,' Ella admitted ruefully. 'I think our current troubles are very much of the present.'

'I should have told you how happy I am about the baby,' Zarif replied instantly, resting tawny eyes on her with extraordinary intensity. 'Yes, I was shocked but I do very much want our child.'

Ella sighed. 'I never doubted that, Zarif.'

'But you *do* doubt that I want to retain you as my wife. And yet I have *always* wanted you, *habibti*.' Zarif withdrew the object she had assumed was a book from below his arm and set it on the coffee table where she could see that it was a leather-bound photo album. 'It shames me to show you this but I hope that revealing one of my biggest secrets to you will persuade you that I am telling you the truth.'

Ella was frowning. 'What secret?' she questioned.

Zarif bent down and flipped open the photo album at random and she stood up to approach, recognising even from a distance of several feet that she was looking at a photograph of her younger self. She was wearing jeans and a sweater, walking along the street beside Cathy. 'Who took that and when?' she demanded in bewilderment.

'I paid someone to take a collection of discreet photos of you when you were eighteen. It was…my secret stash. I could not have you—you were too young for me. I needed something and the photos were the only consolation I dared to take,' he framed with a ragged edge to his deep drawl. 'The first time I saw you was the first weekend Jason brought me to your home with him. You were seventeen and in the garden with your mother. You were wearing shorts and a pink top and you were laughing and you were literally the most beautiful sight I had ever seen. I was obsessed from that moment on…'

Ella was stunned by that speech. 'I don't believe you,'

she told him bluntly even though she remembered that same first meeting. He might have said she was a beautiful sight but her memory was different. She had been mortified that a very hot and fanciable male should see her in shorts that she was convinced showed far too much of her chubby thighs and bottom. She reached for the album and flicked through it, finding photo after photo taken without her awareness. She was shocked, disbelieving.

'Let's face it—I behaved like a stalker,' Zarif breathed, dark blood lining his spectacular cheekbones. 'I have no excuse.'

'But you *never* showed the slightest interest in me!' Ella reminded him helplessly.

'I couldn't. You were still at school when we first met. I had to wait for you to grow up and exist on very occasional glimpses of you,' Zarif countered grimly. 'It was an obsession that didn't fade. I didn't want any other woman. I waited for you.'

Ella viewed him wide-eyed. 'You waited *four* blasted years for me to grow up?' she prompted. 'Were you crazy? I wanted you too! Eighteen would have been fine!'

'No. I wanted a woman, not a child, which is why I waited. I didn't want to take advantage of your inexperience. I didn't want hero worship. I didn't want to turn your head with my money. I just wanted you,' Zarif breathed emotively. 'But what I didn't appreciate then, because I had never felt that way before, was that I was not simply attracted you, I was in love with you.'

'Oh, no, please don't tell me that now three years *too late*!' Ella suddenly framed in anguished reproach. 'If you loved me when you proposed and I turned you down it will break my heart because I loved you too.'

'But it was my fault. I screwed up back then. And even after demanding this second chance with you I screwed up again so badly that I honestly didn't know how to convince you of the duration and strength of my feelings for you without showing you that embarrassing album of stolen photos,' Zarif told her in a hoarse undertone. 'I felt such guilt that I was unable to love Azel. How could I admit that within two years of her death I took one look at a seventeen-year-old girl and fell in love with her?'

'You loved me and you *lied* about it, you idiot!' the woman of Zarif's dreams hurled at him in a tone of tragedy.

'Yes, *habibti*...when it comes to the love stuff, I'm pretty useless,' Zarif was willing to admit because it gave him the chance to sweep her up into his arms and hold her so close that she could barely breathe. 'But I *do* love you. I love you so much that I don't think I could live without you now.'

'But *you* said—' Ella began.

'No, don't remind me. We both said lots of things that day—like you telling me that women in Vashir are treated like second-class citizens.'

Ella reddened. 'It was the driving-ban thing. I didn't know what it was really like until I lived here. I didn't mean to insult you. I was just trying to think up excuses. I couldn't tell you the truth and you seemed to feel nothing at all for me—you were so cold, so emotional.'

'I was very upset. I was genuinely expecting you to say yes. That was arrogant of me. But then I didn't know how I really felt about you until you told me about the baby and suddenly I realised that I was glad of *any* excuse to keep you.'

'An excuse?' she gasped.

'And then I asked myself why I needed an excuse to do what I wanted to do, which was keep you for ever,' Zarif extended abstractedly, studying her lovely face with warm dark golden eyes of appreciation. 'And that's what I intend to do if you'll let me...keep you for ever.'

'I can't believe that you've loved me all this time,' Ella admitted apologetically.

'I will teach you to believe it, *habibti*,' Zarif swore as he carried her up the narrow staircase and across a wide landing into a shaded bedroom. 'But first, since there should be no more secrets between us, there are some other things I must talk about.'

He loved her? Could she believe that? She could certainly understand his guilt over his inability to love the first wife who had patently loved him. She could understand why he had been unable to admit that and why it would have been much easier for him to credit that his reaction to Ella was simple lust. 'Am I the only person you've ever been in love with?'

'Yes, *habibti*.'

'That's unusual,' she pronounced, trying to take a sensible attitude as he set her down on a bed made up with snowy white linen. 'Although you're the only person I've ever been in love with as well.'

'As my grandmother would have said were she here now, we're a match made in heaven, *habibti*,' Zarif declared with tender amusement. 'You came back into my life to save me from a lifetime of regret, and loneliness.'

'No,' Ella corrected. 'I came back into your life to ask you for a favour—'

'And I was a total bastard,' Zarif said softly, carrying her hand to his lips and pressing a kiss to her palm in mute apology for that meeting at the hotel. 'I was very bitter when you turned me down three years ago. I thought you had deliberately lured me into proposing just for the ego boost of blowing me off.'

Ella was shaken. 'But I wouldn't have done that to anyone!'

'I was bitter,' Zarif repeated doggedly. 'Angry, desperately unhappy. I wanted you so much, believed you were about to become my wife and then, suddenly, I couldn't have you.'

'You'd have got me with bells on if you'd told me you loved me then. Of course you didn't appreciate that what you were feeling was love or you wouldn't have wittered on about Azel,' she worked out for herself, her lovely face reflective. 'But maybe on some level after your first marriage you just weren't ready to make such a major commitment to me and maybe I was still too immature.'

'I'm trying to make excuses for the way I behaved after you turned me down,' Zarif confessed grittily. 'I went off the rails for a while…sex, alcohol.'

Ella quirked a fair brow. 'Loose women?'

As she studied Zarif he flinched and reddened with embarrassment. 'All blonde, all blue-eyed. I tried to fantasise every one of them into being you,' he groaned. 'My brothers thought it was good for me to live like that for a while and that it would have been foolish of me to get married again so soon and tie myself down.'

'But what did *you* think?' Ella pressed, pained by what he was telling her, although it really wasn't anything she hadn't expected when she had seen photos of him in clubs and at parties with glamorous women.

'I would have exchanged all of the partying for one day married to you. It was sleazy and I'm ashamed of it but for a long time afterwards I blamed you for having set me off on that path by…hurting me.' He found it so difficult to get that confession of vulnerability past his lips that he almost choked on that word.

Ella hated to think that she had hurt him but then he had hurt her as well and that was what happened when two people didn't understand each other or their feelings. Slowly she laced her small fingers with his long tense ones, recognising what it had cost his pride to speak as freely as he had done about both the duration of his love and his mistakes, and loving him all the more for that sacrifice. 'We're all good at blaming others for our mistakes, and at least I know you've satisfied any curiosity you had about that kind of lifestyle. As for the apartment in Dubai—'

Zarif tensed. 'I'll sell it. I could never take you there.'

'So, we draw a line under it and put it *all* behind us, no more recriminations, no more shame or regrets. Stop beating yourself up about your blunders. It's the past,' she emphasised with quiet assurance. 'We'll make a wonderful future together for our child.'

'A future in which you occasionally throw yourself at me again?' Zarif whispered wickedly.

Ella pushed him flat on the bed. 'For the last time, I did not *throw* myself at you!'

'I loved every second of it,' her husband admitted shamelessly, shooting her an irreverent grin that lit up his lean, darkly devastating features and made her heart leap inside her chest.

'When's your birthday?' she asked him.

'That's months away!' Zarif groaned as he drew her

down and extracted a very long and passionate kiss from her lush mouth.

Supporting herself on one hand, Ella traced teasing fingers along the line of a long, powerful thigh and watched him jerk taut. 'I'm not sure I could wait that long either. I love you so much, Zarif, but from now on you have to tell me that you love me at least once every day.'

He sat up and peeled off his robe and the shirt beneath in one potent and impatient movement, revealing his golden muscular torso. 'I love you, *habibti.*'

Ella felt incredibly powerful when he looked at her with his heart in his beautiful eyes. 'I love you too.'

Ella twisted and turned to get a good view of her outfit. Brought as a gift from her mother-in-law, Mariyah, the sleek sapphire-blue evening gown oozed Italian chic.

'It looks amazing,' Cathy told her cheerfully.

Ella turned to smile at her childhood friend. 'Fine feathers make fine birds.'

'No, it's the jaw-dropping sapphire jewels, not the dress, that knocks the eyes out first,' Soraya teased. 'But even when you're in jeans, you look great, Ella. You've kept your figure so well.'

But the baby weight had been an uphill challenge to shed, Ella reflected wryly. She had managed it twice, however, and now, and quite unexpectedly, she was going to have to do it again, but that was still a secret. 'There's still lumps and bumps in places there didn't used to be,' she lamented.

Five years of marriage and two children, Ella mused in wonder, because the time had flown and seemed to speed up with every passing month. Halim had only passed away eighteen months ago and Zarif still missed the older man a great deal. His mother, Mariyah, had gradually become a more frequent visitor, who took great pleasure in her grandchildren.

Given the opportunity, she had talked frankly to Zarif about why she had handed him over so completely to his grandparents. Mariyah had known that she had no father figure to offer her son and had deemed her own father preferable to the risks of Gaetano Ravelli's potential influence. She had called herself selfish for wanting to pursue a career, which she could never have had in those days had she returned to Vashir, but she had believed it would be even more selfish to deprive Zarif of his heritage and very probably the chance to become King. Mother and son had made their peace and, although they might never be especially close, they were becoming friends and Zarif valued the connection.

Ella's parents were frequent visitors in common with Zarif's brothers. Ella and Zarif had seen Jason occasionally when they visited her home but contact had been minimal. Jason had narrowly escaped a jail sentence two years earlier and had been put on probation when he became marginally involved with a pyramid selling scheme that broke the law. Since then Jason had been working in a sales role for a national company and Ella suspected that Zarif had somehow fixed that job for her brother behind the scenes, either because he felt sorry for him or because he felt sorry for the worry and distress Jason caused their parents. In recent times, however, her brother had not been a cause for concern and Ella was starting to dare to hope that he had learned his lesson and was prepared to turn his life around.

As for Ella, she was still head over heels happy in her

marriage. When she and Zarif wanted alone time, they flew out to the Old Fort for a few days. Now it was their fifth anniversary and they were having a giant weekend party at the old palace attended by all their family and friends.

Cathy was now a mother as well with a toddler and she ran the thriving bookshop with her husband, since Ella had surrendered her share of the business. Soraya had had twin girls the previous year and had barely paused in her hectic career schedule. Ella and Soraya had become close friends while working together on the opening of the royal museum. Although the exhibits closely followed the rise of the al-Rastani dynasty, the central focus had become the history and civilisation of Vashir, which Ella had come to love almost as much as she loved her husband. But then she didn't think she could ever love anything or anybody as much as she loved Zarif and their children.

Her ears pricked up as she heard a distant roar from the courtyard.

'Your husband is home,' Soraya remarked with a grin.

Through the doors open onto the stone balcony beyond the window, Ella could hear Zarif laying down the law to their sons, Hatim and Murad. Hatim was a boisterous and daring little boy and his little brother, a scant eighteen months his junior, tended to follow him slavishly into mischief. 'A little military-style discipline keeps the boys in order,' she confided.

She heard Zarif's steps on the stairs and her face lit up as she instinctively looked towards the doorway.

'It's like *Romeo and Juliet* round here *every* day,' Cathy muttered appreciatively as she caught that look.

Zarif strode in and lowered the two little boys clinging to him like monkeys to the floor. Evidently the military discipline had not been too tough this time around. 'They were teasing the guards again, playing hide and seek round them, which is very dangerous,' their father said sternly. 'But they have apologised and now they are going to their rooms.'

'Oh, but…right, OK.' Ella bit back what she had been going to say about how overexcited the boys were waiting for their band of cousins to arrive. She had learned the hard way that two very lively boys were a handful and a staff who adored the little princes and could not do enough to please them didn't help.

'*Mum?*' Hatim said pleadingly, a miniature Zarif with flashing tawny eyes and a killer smile.

'Do as your father says,' Ella told him coolly, hardening herself, knowing that Hatim had to learn about self-control and safety, young though he was. If he wanted to follow in his father's footsteps he had to learn about consequences.

Murad simply burst into floods of inconsolable tears and she could see even Zarif tense against the urge to offer comfort because Murad, cheerful and loving, was that kind of child. But it was Hatim who bent down and took his little brother's hand and patted his back and led him off and Ella was proud of that.

'We'll go downstairs and see how the dinner arrangements are progressing,' Soraya suggested tactfully to Cathy and, with a polite curtsy to Zarif, the two women left the royal couple alone.

'Thanks for not caving in. I could see Murad pushed you close to the edge,' Zarif told his wife with a gleam of appreciation in his beautiful dark golden eyes as he closed the bedroom door. 'They need half an hour to think about what they did and cool off and then they can come out. My brothers and their families have just landed. By the way, is it too late to tell you that you look *amazing*?'

Ella smiled widely at him. 'No.'

'You look amazing but the dress has to come off,' Zarif told her, hauling her close without the smallest warning and kissing her with passionate hunger.

'Be careful with the zip. It's a tight fit,' Ella told him helpfully without a single word of protest. Yes, she would have to redo her make-up and get dressed again but one of the aspects she most loved about Zarif was the strength of his passion for her, his *need* for her.

'I won't have you to myself again until the early hours of the morning...if even then,' Zarif lamented. 'You and Belle and Betsy get talking and sit up half the night.'

'You know you do the same with your brothers... that last holiday we had with Nik and Betsy, you came to bed the first night at dawn.' Skimming off her lingerie with careless hands, Ella lay back naked on the bed but for the famous sapphires and watched her husband strip at even greater speed, enjoying every lithe bronzed and muscular inch of him that emerged from beneath his clothing. Five years hadn't made him any less hot, she thought gratefully.

'And you were in a temper and you got straight back out of bed and now I know what not to do,' Zarif husked, his stunning eyes locked to her lush pale curves with hungry appreciation. 'You're so beautiful, *habibti*.'

'But I'm going to get fat again,' she countered, deciding that it was as good a time as any to break her news.

'Fat?' Zarif repeated blankly.

'Cast your mind back to the shower at the Old Fort...

no condoms,' Ella reminded him ruefully. 'We thought we'd take the risk—'

'We're pregnant again?' Zarif exclaimed with a huge grin of satisfaction. 'I love it when you're pregnant! That's not fat, that's lush, curvy, *sexy*,' he asserted with rich vocal approval.

Zarif came down on the bed with an even greater hunger for the woman who had transformed his life. He studied her with immense pride and tenderness. 'Maybe this super fertility is a Ravelli thing and we have my father to thank for that one gift.'

'And the "absolutely insatiable for sex" gift? Do we thank him for that too?' Ella asked with a comic roll of her eyes, because she loved the fact that he still couldn't keep his hands off her.

'No, only you do that to me,' Zarif told her, lowering his lithe, aroused length down over her prone body and lowering his head to lick at a perky rosy nipple. 'I could eat you alive at any time of day or night—'

'And frequently *do*.'

'Can't help it…I love you so much, *habibti*,' he murmured with raw sincerity.

And she ran her hands through his luxuriant black hair, framed his spectacular movie-star cheekbones and told him that she loved him too. They were both fully dressed and respectable by the time their guests arrived. Hatim and Murad were released from captivity to mingle with their equally excited cousins and the noise of their games and the rising tide of chatter from their parents rang round the ancient palace walls, giving it more life than it had enjoyed in centuries.

* * * * *

GAMBLING WITH THE CROWN

LYNN RAYE HARRIS

To my editor, Flo Nicoll, who always pushes
me—very politely—to do my best.
I complained and moaned and dragged
my feet on this one, but you were right.

USA TODAY bestselling author **Lynn Raye Harris** burst onto the scene when she won a writing contest held by Mills & Boon. The prize was an editor for a year – but only six months later, Lynn sold her first novel. A former finalist for the Romance Writers of America's Golden Heart Award, Lynn lives in Alabama with her handsome husband and two crazy cats. Her stories have been called "exceptional and emotional," "intense," and "sizzling." You can visit her at www.lynnrayeharris.com

PROLOGUE

THE KING OF Kyr was dying. He sat in his chair on the balcony, wrapped in a blanket—though the desert sun had not yet sunk behind the horizon and brought cooler temperatures with it—and contemplated his life.

He'd had a long reign, a good reign, but it was time to name his successor and make sure Kyr continued to thrive when he was gone. He could no longer put off calling his wayward sons home and determining which of them would be the next king.

He pushed to a standing position, unwilling to give up even a tiny bit of independence while he still had strength in his body. The cancer would win, but not today. He moved slowly but surely, making his way toward the desk in his study while a hovering servant shadowed his every move. Waiting to pick him up should he collapse.

Well, he was not collapsing. Not yet.

He had one last task to finish. And it began with two phone calls.

CHAPTER ONE

EMILY BRYANT STRAIGHTENED the severe black skirt she wore, patted the French twist she'd wedged her hair into and steadied the coffee in her hand as she faced the double doors that led to the bedroom of His Most Exalted Highness, Prince Kadir bin Zaid al-Hassan.

Outside, the sky was that special blend of salmon and purple that indicated dawn's approach. Despite the early hour, Paris was awake and rumbling on the city streets below. Soon, Kadir would be awake, too.

Just as soon as Emily knocked on the carved wooden door. She frowned and dragged in a fortifying breath. The man was impossible—and probably not alone. If this morning was anything like other mornings, she'd be stepping over lacy underwear, rumpled stockings and a couture dress lying in a heap on the floor. On one memorable occasion, a bra had dangled from the priceless Venetian glass chandelier. What city was that in?

Ah, yes, Milan.

Emily firmed her lips in what she knew was a distasteful frown—she couldn't abide messes, especially from people who should know better—and lifted her hand. Then she rapped three times.

"Prince Kadir? It's time to get up."

No matter the hour he came in the night before,

Kadir always wanted to be awakened before the sun rose in the sky. Sometimes he went back to sleep, but not before peppering her with orders and instructions about the day. And not before he drank the coffee she always brought.

More often than not, he got up. Emily had learned to relax her expression into an impassive and unimpressed mask of cool professionalism when the covers whipped back to reveal sleek tanned skin and acres of lean muscle. She'd also learned to turn her head discreetly to the side on the rare occasions when he'd failed to add clothing to his lower half before he leaped up and shrugged into his robe.

If he were any other man—if this were any other job—she'd probably be horrified. But this was Prince Kadir, and she knew what the job entailed. He'd warned her as much when he'd hired her. When he'd expressed that a man might be better suited for the job of his personal assistant, she'd assured him she was up for the task.

Therefore, she endured his quirks and his singlemindedness. If he weren't brilliant, if he didn't pay her extremely well—*extremely*—she might not have stayed as long as she had. Not to mention that getting this job straight out of college had been a coup. She still believed that if Kadir hadn't been so desperate to find someone who could put up with his shenanigans, he would never have agreed to interview her, no matter how impeccable her references.

"Come." His voice was dark and raspy with sleep on the other side of the door.

Emily opened it up and walked across the darkened room in her sensible heels. There was a time when she'd loved platforms and flash as much as the next girl, but these shoes were a whole lot more comfortable. She opened the thick damask curtains to let in the light and took his coffee over and set it on the antique bed-side table.

A quick perusal of the room indicated he was alone. She breathed a sigh of relief. She did not like the woman he'd been dating recently. Lenore Bradford, fashion's latest runway darling, was not nice in general and evil to Emily in particular.

It was as if the woman was jealous, which was insane, since Kadir had never once looked at Emily as anything more than the person who ran his life and kept his calendar up-to-date. But that did not stop Lenore from shooting Emily angry looks or demanding outrageous things from her.

Like the morning Lenore had wanted chocolate croissants from a *boulangerie* halfway across Paris. Croissants she knew damn well she would barely sniff before turning to the egg-white omelet instead. Emily had fumed the whole way. Fortunately, she'd not had to do that again, because Kadir had been rather angry when he found out.

Yet another thing Lenore blamed her for. But Kadir wasn't a stupid man and he could read the address on the bag, which apparently Lenore did not try to hide when she tossed them aside as predicted.

Kadir sat up against the headboard and picked up the coffee. His dark hair was tousled and he needed to shave, but he was still one of the most attractive men she'd ever seen. Not that she was attracted to him. Of course not. He was an arrogant, entitled, brilliant jack-ass and she did not like men like that.

Heck, she probably wouldn't like him at all if he didn't pay her so much.

Except, dammit, that wasn't quite true. He drove her crazy with his cool confidence and certainty he was always right, but he remembered her birthday and the anniversary of the date she'd started working for him. She liked to think that meant he cared about people in his own fashion, though it was probably just that mind of his, which never forgot a fact.

But she chose to believe the former; therefore, she couldn't dislike him.

Much.

Emily flipped open the notebook she'd tucked under one arm and steadfastly ignored the sheet as it slipped down and revealed a hard, muscled chest and that damn arrow of dark hair that marched down the center of his abdomen and disappeared beneath the fabric.

"You have a seven-thirty meeting with the chairman of RAC Steel, and a phone call after that with Andrakos Shipping. There is also the real estate agent to meet with on the specs for the property and a site inspection this afternoon."

Kadir sipped the coffee and peered up at her from beneath those impossibly long lashes of his. His eyes were a clear, dark gray that snapped with intelligence.

Really, did a man so beautiful also have to be so smart?

"You are a model of efficiency as always, Miss Bryant. *Shukran jazeelan.*"

She glanced at her watch and tried to ignore the flush of pleasure rolling over her. "Breakfast is on the way up, Your Highness. And I have told the driver to be here at seven sharp."

Kadir's gaze slid over her. He was assessing her, the way he assessed everyone, but she always felt that strange little prickle that started at the back of her neck and continued down her spine like electricity dripping through a conduit.

She didn't like it. She licked her suddenly dry lips and closed the notebook. Kadir's eyes narrowed.

"If that is all, Your Highness?"

"It is."

She turned to go when a racket sounded outside the doors to the bedroom. She wasn't particularly alarmed, as Kadir traveled nowhere without armed guards, but it was unusual in the extreme. She started toward the door when Lenore Bradford burst in.

Emily drew up short. When she realized she clutched the notebook to her chest, she lowered it. Her heart thudded alarmingly. Behind Lenore, a man in a dark suit stood there like a mountain. An angry mountain, she realized.

He would have let Lenore into the suite, because she'd been here before, but he would have expected her to wait while he announced her.

Clearly, she had not done so.

"Lenore." Kadir's voice would have sounded lazy to anyone listening. But to someone who knew him, who'd worked beside him for four years, the note of danger was distinct.

Oh, Lenore. You've done it now.

Emily closed her eyes briefly and waited for the coming storm. Behind her, the blankets stirred and she knew that Kadir had risen and put on his robe. He must have flicked a hand in dismissal because the guard melted away.

"You walked out on me last night," Lenore shrilled. "It was *my* party, and you walked out."

"Perhaps I would not have done so had you not invited six reporters and a camera crew. I am not bait for your ambition, Lenore."

Lenore's pretty hands fluttered and her eyes widened. She was blonde, tall and thin, perfectly coiffed from head to foot, even at this early hour. A real looker, as Emily's dad would have said. But she wasn't very bright where Kadir was concerned. He was not the sort of man to be handled or manipulated.

Emily started for the door again, intent on getting out of the room before the fight blew into the stratosphere. Not that Kadir would tolerate much of that, but Emily didn't need to be here for it. It was personal, and while she might like to snatch Lenore bald-headed for being such a bitch, it was none of her concern.

"Stay where you are, Miss Bryant." Kadir's voice was commanding, as always, and Emily froze. "Lenore was just leaving."

The other woman's skin flushed pink. "I won't leave without discussing this, Kadir. If we are to have a relationship, we have to talk about these things. Perhaps I was wrong, but—"

"It is Prince Kadir or Your Highness," he said coolly. "And there is no relationship. There will be no relationship. Now, get out."

Every word was measured and mild, as if he could hardly be bothered to get angry. Emily almost felt a pinprick of sympathy for the other woman. Almost, but not quite.

Kadir moved past Emily until he was between her and the door. Facing Lenore. He was clad in a navy silk robe and his hair was still tousled, but he looked every inch a prince. It was hard not to admire him in these moments. Her heart swelled with a strange kind of pride that confused her.

Lenore had gone purple. "That's it? You are not even going to talk about it with me?" Kadir didn't answer as he stood there with his arms folded and gave her his best imperious stare. Emily couldn't see his face, but she knew the look. And she could see its effect on Lenore's expression.

Lenore suddenly pointed a manicured finger at Emily. "You think I don't know what's going on here? You think I don't know about your *assistant*—" she somehow made the word sound dirty, as if she'd said *whore* instead "—about how she's tried to come between us from the beginning? She wants you for herself!"

Emily opened her mouth to utter a protest, but Kadir was there first. "I don't particularly care what Miss Bryant thinks of you. It is what I think that matters. And I am finished."

He strode to her side, took her by the elbow and marched her toward the front door of his suite while she screamed at him. Then she was thrust through the door, and it closed again with a thud. Kadir turned, his face black with fury. Emily dropped her gaze and studied her shoes while her heart thrummed hard.

She had never witnessed the breakup scene before, but she knew it had played out again and again over the past four years she'd worked for him. She could almost feel sorry for the women who committed the mistake of thinking there was a future with him. He was rich, titled, wealthy and successful in his own right. Every woman he dated wanted to tame him. None of them had managed it yet.

"I am sorry you had to hear that."

Emily's head snapped up to meet his hot gaze. He'd moved closer to her and her pulse skidded with unwelcome heat. "I don't want you for myself," she blurted. Her cheeks blazed.

Great.

Kadir quirked an eyebrow. "Really? I am told I am quite delightful. How stunning to encounter a woman who does not want me."

For a moment she didn't know what to say. And then she realized he was teasing her. Emily dropped her gaze again. She needed this job and she wasn't going to do anything to jeopardize it. He might be humored this time, but she could not let it pass. "Forgive my outburst, Your Highness."

"There is nothing to forgive. Lenore was incredibly rude to you."

"It won't happen again, I assure you."

He laughed. "Oh, I think it will."

Emily could only stare at him, her pulse a drumbeat in her throat, her fingers. And then she realized he meant the scene with Lenore.

"Don't look so worried, Miss Bryant," he continued, his voice smooth as silk, hard as steel. "Lenore will not be back. But there will no doubt be others."

Emily wanted to roll her eyes. She resisted the urge. Kadir's eyebrow quirked again.

"You wish to say something?"

"Your breakfast will be here any moment."

"That is not it." His voice was a knowing murmur as his gaze dropped to her lips, back up again. Shockingly, she felt as if he'd touched her. As if he'd taken one of his golden fingers and slid it across the pad of her lips. He grinned, and her insides turned to liquid. She was not happy about it either. "Come, Emily. We've known each other for nearly four years now. You know more about my life than anyone besides me."

He'd called her Emily a handful of times. It always rattled her the way his accent slid over the syllables of her name. Like a caress. Like the touch of a lover.

As if she would know what that was like these days. It had been so long since she'd last had sex she couldn't even remember when it was. She traveled too much, moving with Kadir as he trotted the globe and built his skyscrapers. It left little time for a personal life.

Except for when they were in Chicago. Then she took time to go see her dad, to make sure he had everything he needed. Dating was hardly a blip on her radar compared to that.

"You pay me to keep your life in order, not to advise you on it."

"And yet you wanted to say something. I could see it in your expression. The way your lips pursed ever so slightly. The downward tilt of your eyebrows, the flare of your nostrils. The green fire in your eyes. I would like to know what it was."

"I prefer to keep my job." Her voice contained an edge of tartness that she couldn't quite control. *The green fire in her eyes?*

"And you shall. I give you leave to say what you wish. I'd rather not have you pop from holding it in, Miss Bryant."

Emily sighed. He wasn't going to give up until she'd spoken. If she knew anything about this man, she knew that. She'd watched him in negotiations, watched the way he closed in on his prey like a hawk, circling ever closer, until the moment he snatched them up and got precisely what he wanted, whether it was a bargain on steel, a commitment to sell only to him, incentives on a piece of land or a premium from someone who desperately wanted his company to build their new skyscraper.

"I was going to say that it was ridiculous to expect more of the same. That perhaps if you conducted your, er, affairs a little differently, they might not get to this stage."

He looked amused. Heat flared in her belly.

"And how should I conduct my affairs? I would imagine that swearing off women for good would do it. But so far as I like women—and I certainly do—there will always be some who think I am going to make them my princess. They never take it kindly when they find out it is not going to happen."

"Then perhaps you should choose women based on their intellect and not their bra size."

He burst out laughing and a prickle of something ran up her spine. It wasn't fear. It wasn't even embarrassment. Perhaps it was relief. Relief that she'd said the words after all.

"I will take your charming suggestion under advisement, I assure you."

"You did ask."

"Indeed I did." He raised his arms, stretching like a supple, sleek cat. The robe fell open to reveal the tight muscles of his abdomen—along with that damn arrow of hair again. Thankfully, he was wearing a pair of black silk boxers that were perfectly decent. Emily averted her gaze as her heart rate picked up once more. Fresh fire licked across her skin, shortened her breath.

She forced it down again, buried it beneath the mountain of decorum and duty she always lived by. She was not the sort of person to be ruled by urges. She was not the sort of person to *have* urges—not anymore. She'd worked very hard to make sure of that.

So what on earth was the matter with her today? He was devilishly attractive, but that was nothing new. She'd thought herself inoculated a long time ago. Apparently, he could still rev up her pulse under the right circumstances.

Perhaps she should make an appointment with her doctor. Her hormones were surely out of whack or something. It was the only explanation.

Kadir moved with liquid grace, sauntering back into his bedroom while Emily stood and gulped in air. He didn't close the door and she soon heard the sound of the shower. She imagined him dropping the robe, sliding the silk boxers down his lean, hard thighs—

Emily gripped her notebook hard enough to make her fingers ache. Then she smoothed her hair, straightened her clothing even though it was perfectly straight already, and went to check on Kadir's breakfast.

The day had been long and productive. Kadir sat in the limo as it moved through the brightly lit streets of Paris and rubbed a hand over the back of his neck, easing the kinks of sitting at a desk for the past few hours. He'd been going over the projections for his newest project. This office building in Paris's business district was simply the latest in a series of buildings he'd constructed over the past couple of years.

But he loved the process, loved watching the steel skeleton rise high above the city and take on a life of its own. This building wasn't as tall as some he'd built, but it was modern and sleek and efficient. The company that had hired him would be very pleased when he was finished. He prided himself upon it.

Beside him, his assistant typed away on her laptop. He slanted a glance toward her. Miss Emily Bryant was quite possibly the best assistant he'd ever had. She was eager to work, professional, and she'd taken over his life with the kind of efficiency he valued.

Nothing escaped her notice. Nothing remained undone. In spite of this morning's episode, a thousand Lenores could not ruffle her calm for long.

He'd come to look forward to her marching into his room, in whatever city they might be staying in, and standing over him in her crisp black-and-white—or sometimes navy-blue or gray—business suits and ugly shoes as she told him about his day.

Emily was blessedly uncomplicated. The only female in his life who was. Thank goodness he wasn't attracted to her, or he would no doubt ruin what was the longest relationship with a woman—unrelated to him—that he'd ever had.

He thought of her this morning, telling him to choose women based on intellect rather than bra size, and wanted to laugh again. She'd shocked and amused him at the same time. He'd asked her opinion, but that was not the answer he'd expected. Emily was always so circumspect that it hadn't crossed his mind she had anything remotely sarcastic to say.

He'd loved it because it was so unexpected from his proper assistant. That was something he almost never got in his relationships with anyone: honesty. No one wanted to disagree with a prince.

His mobile phone began to buzz. He took it from his pocket and handed it to Emily. He was too tired to deal with anyone just now. She answered with that voice of hers that sounded so young and fresh, as though she was still sixteen instead of twenty-five. Kadir closed his eyes and leaned his head back against the seat. Tonight, he would sleep the sleep of the dead. No parties, no manipulative fashion models, no distractions.

"Your Highness." Emily sounded a touch breathless. Her pale green eyes were wide as she held out the phone. "It's your father."

CHAPTER TWO

KADIR GRIPPED THE balcony's iron railing with both hands as he stared at Paris spread out below. The Eiffel Tower glowed ocher against the skyline as cars slid through the streets. He could hear laughter coming from somewhere in the hotel where he'd booked an entire floor, and a soft breeze slid across his skin, cooling him.

His father was dying. The phone call tonight played again and again in his head, filling him with so many emotions that he could hardly sort them all. He remembered a lion of a man when he was a child, a man who had both frightened and awed him. He remembered wanting to be important to that man, wanting his attention and doing nearly anything to get it.

If his father had had a favorite son, he was it. Not that that was saying much, since he'd often felt his father's belt against his skin. But Rashid had felt it more. And Kadir had been so convinced as a child that if his father was angry with Rashid, then he might be pleased with Kadir—not to mention, if his father's attention were on Rashid, Kadir would escape the harsh punishments his father meted out. So he'd encouraged his father to be angry with Rashid in any way he could.

Kadir raked a hand through his hair and thought about ordering a glass of some type of strong liquor.

But he did not drink when he was alone, so that was out of the question. It was a matter of self-discipline and he would not violate his own rule.

He picked up his phone from where he'd set it on the table and willed it to ring. He knew Rashid would call him. Because Rashid would know that Kadir had been told the news first.

When he and Rashid had been children, he'd taken shameless advantage of his father's apparently strong dislike of Rashid. When Kadir let the horses out of the stables, his father blamed Rashid. When he released his father's prized hawk, Rashid got blamed. When he accidentally poisoned his father's favorite hound—who thankfully recovered—their father had blamed Rashid for that as well.

Rashid always took the punishment stoically and without complaint. He never cried during the beatings, but he would return to their shared quarters red faced and angry. Kadir shuddered with the memories of what he'd caused Rashid to endure.

It was a wonder Rashid did not hate him. He always felt such a dark and abiding shame in his brother's presence, though Rashid did not ever speak about anything that had happened in their father's palace. It was as if, for Rashid, it did not exist.

Kadir wished it were the same for him.

He stood there for another hour in the dark, waiting and brooding. And then his phone rang and an odd combination of regret and relief surged inside him.

"I've been waiting for you," he said by way of greeting.

There was a long pause on the other end. "It is good to talk to you, too, brother."

"Rashid." He sighed. He could never say everything

he wished to say to his brother. His throat closed up whenever he thought about it.

I'm sorry I caused you so much trouble. I'm sorry for everything. And then, *Why don't you hate me?*

Instead, he said the one thing he could say. "You know I don't want the throne. I've never wanted it."

In Kyr, the throne usually passed to the eldest—but it didn't have to. The king could choose his successor from among his sons, and that was precisely what their father was proposing to do. Kadir couldn't begin to express how much this angered him.

Or worried him. He was not, in his opinion, suited to be a king. Because he did not want it. For one thing, to be king would mean being trapped for the rest of his life. For another, it would feel like the ultimate dirty trick to be played against Rashid.

"You are as qualified as I," Rashid said with that icy-cool voice of his, his emotions wrapped tight as always. To talk to Rashid was to think you were talking to an iceberg. It was only when you saw him that you realized he blazed like the desert.

"Yes, but I have a business to run. Being king means living in Kyr year-round. I am not willing."

That was the reason he could voice. The other reasons went deeper.

"And what makes you think I am?" There was a flash of heat that time. "I left Kyr years ago. And I, too, have a business."

"Oil is your business. It is also the business of Kyr."

Rashid made a noise. "He only wants the appearance of fairness, Kadir. We already know his choice."

Kadir's throat was tight. He feared the same. And yet he could not accept the throne without a fight for what he knew was right.

"He's dying. Do you really plan not to go, not to see him one last time?"

If anger had substance, then Kadir could feel the weight of his brother's anger across the distance separating them. "So he can express his disappointment in me yet again? So he can hold out the promise of Kyr and then have the satisfaction of giving it to you while I can do nothing?"

Kadir felt his brother's words like a blow. He'd done nothing to deserve Kyr and everything to drive a wedge between his father and his brother while protecting his own skin, though he had not really known the gravity of his actions at the time. Still, being a child did not excuse him.

"You don't know this is his plan."

Rashid blew out a breath and Kadir could almost hear the derision. "It has been this way since we were children. He hasn't changed. You are the one he prefers."

As if being the preferred one had made life as one of King Zaid's sons any easier. Their father did not possess a warm bone in his body.

"I am not the best man to be king. You are." He could say that without regret or shame. His particular gift was in building structures, in turning steel and glass into something beautiful and functional. He loved the challenge of it, of figuring out the math and science to support what he wanted to do.

He enjoyed his life, enjoyed being always on the move, always in demand. If he were the king of Kyr, he would not be able to do this any longer.

Oh, he could build skyscrapers in Kyr—but Kyr was not the world. And a king had many other things to tend to. He loved his country. But he felt its responsibility like a yoke, not a gift.

Rashid, however, wanted to rule. Had wanted to do so since they were boys. He'd always thought he would be the one to inherit the throne by virtue of his position as eldest—everyone had—until their father announced one day that he had not yet chosen a successor. And would not until the time came.

If King Zaid had died without choosing, the governing council would have made the choice. There had been no danger of Kyr being leaderless.

But it had always been a carrot to dangle over Rashid's head, to make him jump to the tune King Zaid wanted.

Rashid had not jumped. He'd walked out. To Kadir's knowledge, his father and Rashid had not spoken in at least ten years. Kadir maintained a distantly cordial relationship with his father, but it was not always easy to do.

"Be the better man, Rashid. Go and see a dying old man one last time. Give him what he wants and Kyr will be yours."

Rashid didn't speak for a long moment. "I will go, Kadir. But for you. Not for him. And when it turns out as I said, when you are crowned king of Kyr, do not blame me for your fate. It is not I who will have caused it."

Emily nearly jumped out of her skin when there was a knock on her door. She'd fallen asleep on the couch of her small suite. A sheaf of papers fell to the floor as she bolted to a sitting position, her heart hammering with adrenaline.

She grabbed her phone where it lay on the coffee

table. It was a few minutes after midnight. The knock sounded again and she scrambled upright, looked askance at the papers—there was no time to straighten them—and then whipped the long tangle of her hair out of her face and shoved it over her shoulders.

She'd changed into her usual sleep set—a tank top and pajama pants—which wasn't in the least presentable. But the knock was insistent and she moved toward the door once her brain kicked into gear. Something must have happened to Kadir or no one would be outside her door at this hour. If Kadir wanted her, he would call.

She whipped the door back, unconcerned about criminals—since Kadir's security had locked down the entire floor they were on—though she was careful to keep the bulk of her body behind the door.

Kadir stood on the other side, looking handsome and moody, and a wash of heat and confusion flooded her at once. Her stomach knotted even as her brain tried to work out a logical reason for his appearance at her door.

"Your Highness? Is there a problem?"

"There is indeed. I need to talk to you."

"I—I will come to your suite. Give me a few minutes to get dressed and—"

"No. There is no time for that." His hand was on her door, his big masculine body poised to enter her room. She'd worked for him for four years. She knew he was strong and big and not in the least bit soft, but she'd never quite felt the intensity of his body until this moment.

A rush of flame slid through her at the thought of facing her boss in her pajamas, but she pulled the door back and let him in. She'd seen him in less, after all. To him, meetings in various stages of undress were completely acceptable.

He came inside, all darkness and intensity and coiled strength as he paced across her floor. She could only watch as he moved like a trapped panther in her small space, her heart thrumming at his nearness and beauty.

Emily tried to smooth her hair. And then she crossed her arms when she realized she wasn't wearing a bra. Not that she was in any danger of wowing Kadir al-Hassan with her B cups, but she'd be more comfortable if she was wearing one of her suits. Fully bra-ed and covered from neck to knee.

He stopped pacing and turned to face her. If she hadn't been watching him, she wouldn't have believed the look of surprise that crossed his face. Her cheeks flamed even more and she wrapped her arms tighter around herself.

"Did you need me to draft a letter for you? Make a call to the States? It's still early there, and—"

"No."

Emily shifted from foot to foot. The papers scattered across the floor irritated her sense of order. And Kadir, a prince, standing before her in trousers and a custom-fit shirt while she was a disheveled mess in her pajamas, did not bear thinking about.

His pewter gaze slipped over her and his expression grew tight. "I have disturbed you."

"I fell asleep on the couch." God, could she be any more inane?

He moved closer to her, and she felt his presence like a wave. A giant, engulfing wave of heat and sharp masculinity. This was not her urbane, sophisticated boss standing before her. This man was a prince of the desert, a man who stood on the edge of a precipice between civilization and the wild, untamed dunes.

She gave herself a mental shake. She knew better than that. He might be an Arab male, but that didn't make him uncivilized. That was as ridiculous as saying all Americans wore cowboy hats and said yee-haw.

Kadir was a man. Just a man.

Her pulse raced even while she had the oddest sensation of her blood beating heavily in her veins. And her brain whispered back to her that Kadir al-Hassan was *not* just a man by anyone's definition.

"You are…rumpled, Miss Bryant." He said it almost wonderingly, and a flash of irritation rolled through her.

"Well, I was asleep. And you usually phone if you want something."

He shoved a hand through his hair then, and she saw that he was not quite himself. Not the cool thinker she was accustomed to dealing with.

"We are going to Kyr."

She felt the force of those words deep in her gut. In four years, he had never once gone to Kyr. If she hadn't looked it up on a map, she'd have almost thought it didn't exist. But it was there, a slice of sand on the Persian Gulf. It was oil rich, as were so many of the countries in that region, and ruled by a king. By Kadir's father.

She had never spoken to the king until today. Until he'd phoned his son while they'd been riding across Paris and Kadir had handed her his phone, as he so often did when he didn't want to deal with anyone. She could still hear that raspy voice, the note of command as he'd told her he wished to speak to his son. He had been imperious and polite all at once, though she had not fooled herself that politeness would win out should she attempt to take a message.

Kyr. My God.

It was perhaps the most foreign of any location he had ever taken her to, with the exception of Singapore and Hong Kong.

"When?"

Kadir blinked, and she wished she had her notebook. She felt professional with her notebook and pen. She also had a tablet computer, of course, but she liked the feel of the pen scratching over the paper as she made quick notes—and then she transferred them later so that she could access everything on the tablet. His calendar was there, too, but not until she'd jotted it out on paper first.

"In the morning."

Emily bit her lip. Kadir didn't take his eyes off her and she started to worry that he'd had a shock of some sort. He was not behaving like himself, that was certain.

"I will be sure to have everything ready. What time would you like me to request wheels up?"

"I have done this already." He shoved his hands into his pockets and looked around her room as if he'd never seen it before. Which, she supposed, he hadn't. "Do you perhaps have a bottle of wine? Some scotch?"

"I—um, there might be wine. Just a moment."

She went to the small refrigerator tucked beneath the cabinets on one side of the room and pulled out a bottle of white she'd been nursing. Then she took down a glass and poured some in it. But when she turned, he was behind her. He'd moved so silently she'd not heard a thing.

Or perhaps it was the way her blood beat in her ears that prevented her from hearing something so basic as a person walking across the floor. He loomed over her, so tall and vital and surprising. It jarred her to realize that without her heels, she really was much shorter than he.

She thrust the glass at him without a word.

"Please have a drink with me."

Emily turned and poured wine into another glass, thankful to have something to do that did not involve looking at Kadir. But when she pivoted again, he was still there. Still in her space, still big and dark and intense.

She thought he might move, might go over and sit on her couch, but he didn't. He simply stood there, staring at the liquid in his glass. And then he raised his gaze to hers, and she felt the blow of those eyes like a twist in her heart.

She recognized pain when she saw it. His seemed to swallow him whole, turning those clear gray eyes to the darkest slate. She had an urge to lift her palm to his cheek, to tell him it would be okay.

But that was a line she could not cross. He was her boss, though she was having a very hard time remembering it just now.

"What is the matter, Your Highness?" The words were tight in her throat, but she forced them out anyway.

His brow furrowed. And then he lifted the glass and took a deep swallow of the golden liquid. Once more, his eyes were on hers. As if she were an anchor. As if it were her alone keeping him tethered to the earth, keeping the pain from engulfing him.

"My father is dying." The words were simple, stark, and her heart squeezed into a tight ball in her chest. She knew the pain of those words, knew how they opened chasms in your soul. How they could change you.

But she also knew the bittersweet joy of finding out there was a way to save the person you loved. The worry over if there would be enough money to pay for the procedure—not that this last was a worry a king would have.

She reached for him automatically, gripped his forearm. She had never dared to touch him before, not deliberately. Not like this. The jolt of sensation buzzing through her should not have been so unexpected. But it was. Like touching a live wire and then being unable to let go.

She had to push past it, had to speak. Had to get beyond the awkwardness and confusion when he needed so much more from her than this giddy schoolgirl behavior.

"Is there nothing they can do?" Her voice came out a whisper, but he heard it. He'd been staring at her hand, at her pale fingers clasped over his golden skin, and he raised his gaze again.

Once more, the blow of those eyes threatened to steal her breath away. Her sense. For a moment, she wished she were someone else. Someone beautiful and dynamic. Someone who could interest a man like this.

But no, that was silly. She wasn't a sensual creature. She was sensible. There was no room in her life for the kind of heat and exhilaration that went along with a man like Kadir. She'd seen how women burned for him, and how they burned out too soon. That kind of heat wasn't worth the price.

She'd almost been that sort of woman once, but she'd learned that it was far better to be sensible and staid. And if she ever doubted it, she had only to think of her mother's tragic example of what could happen to a woman who followed her hedonistic tendencies too far.

"No, it's too late now. They've done everything."

He sounded almost detached and cool, but she knew

it must affect him deeply. She squeezed his arm. "I'm so sorry."

He put his hand over hers and lightning sizzled into her deepest core. In four years' time, their hands had brushed on occasion. It would have been impossible if they hadn't.

But this. This was too much, like walking out into full sunlight after having spent a year in a cave. The feelings swirling through her were too hot, too bright.

Too confusing.

Kadir was an attractive man, but she was not attracted to him. She liked lean blond men who weren't quite so tall. Quiet men. Men who didn't make her feel jumpy and achy just by touching her.

She had to force herself to meet his eyes, because to continue to stare at his hand over hers would certainly be odd. The pain was still there, but there was something else, too. Something that flared bright for a moment and was extinguished.

She'd always known that Kadir was a complicated man. But this felt as if someone had lifted the curtain to show her the gears and pulleys that ran the show.

She'd seen beneath the veneer. Beneath the walls. But only for a moment.

A moment she was not likely to forget any time soon.

"I am angry, Emily."

"I believe that is normal." She remembered being angry herself when they'd first learned that her father needed a new heart if he were going to survive. It had seemed impossible at the time—and she'd been so furious with fate—but then a heart had become available and he'd gotten his second chance.

But every moment had been agonizing. The feelings, the fear. Not everyone in her family had handled it well. Her father had survived—but the family had not.

Kadir's gaze was searching. She had to remind herself, strongly, that he was still her boss, that this breach of their usual formal relationship was a temporary thing. If she handled this wrongly, if she did what she wanted to do—which was put her arms around him and pull his head down to her shoulder while she stroked the thick softness of his hair—she would be crossing a line that could never be redrawn.

"I need something from you, Emily."

His voice was soft and mesmerizing and her stomach tied itself into a knot as she imagined what he might ask for. But then she told herself he was simply hurting and this change in their usual relationship was a temporary by-product of that. He needed someone to talk to and there was no reason why she couldn't be that someone.

"Anything I can do, Your Highness."

One corner of his sensual mouth lifted in a smile. She'd never spent a lot of time gazing at him—she was far too busy taking care of business—but she could certainly see why the women he dated seemed to melt so quickly beneath the power of his raw male beauty. His mouth begged a woman to press her own there. His hair needed a woman's fingers in it. His shoulders needed someone's arms around them. His waist needed to be surrounded by a woman's legs—

Oh, my. Emily clamped down hard on her wayward thoughts and tried to look like her usual professional self.

Which would be far easier to accomplish if she were not standing here in her pajamas with her hair a dark tangle down her back.

He put a hand on her shoulder, his fingers touching

bare flesh. She couldn't quite contain the gasp that escaped her as an arrow of flame shot through her belly, down into her deepest core. Oh, she was so going to the doctor the instant they returned to Chicago. There had to be a pill that would fix her raging hormones. She was entirely too young for this kind of wild fluctuation.

Kadir's brows drew down, his gaze searching hers. His eyes were dark, glittering slate, and she had to force herself not to shrink from the fire in them.

"First, you are going to need to call me Kadir."

Her stomach flipped. "I—I don't think that's a very good idea. You're my boss, and I prefer to keep that straight in my head. First names invite familiarity, and—"

His finger over her mouth silenced her. And burned into her. Confusion set up a drumbeat in her brain, her blood. She had no idea what was going on here, or where it would lead if she let it.

"Emily."

He said her name simply, but it had the effect of sending a wave of calm over her. She drew in a breath and waited. Whatever he was going to say, she could handle it.

His next words shattered that illusion. "I need you to marry me."

CHAPTER THREE

SHE WAS LOOKING at him as though he'd grown two extra heads. He didn't blame her, really. What he was proposing was perfectly outrageous. But after that phone call with Rashid, he couldn't stop thinking about how he wasn't going to be forced to take his brother's birthright.

He wasn't the next king of Kyr. Rashid was. And he wasn't going to allow his father to use him as a bludgeon in his personal war with Rashid. Not any longer. When he was ten, he hadn't understood. He understood now.

He was returning to Kyr because his father was dying and he believed it was important to be there. But Kadir wasn't going to make it easy for the old man to do what Rashid believed he was going to do.

And for that, Kadir needed a very unsuitable bride. A woman who would horrify his father enough that he would believe Kadir's judgment so poor he would not, under any circumstances, give the kingdom of Kyr into his keeping.

An American woman with no connections or pedigree would fit the bill nicely. If he could persuade her to act a little more like Lenore—spoiled, entitled and manipulative—it would work even better, though it was not strictly necessary. Her origins would be enough for his father and the staunchly traditional governing council.

King Zaid would turn to Rashid, regardless of their differences, and choose the son who was the only sensible choice. He would not risk his kingdom with a son who was blinded by the charms of a most unsuitable woman.

Kadir knew it was an insane plan, born of desperation, but he was determined to carry it out. Nothing else would work. His father might be petty, but he was much too proud to allow Kyr to pass into the hands of a son who showed such a decided lack of judgment.

"I…I…" Emily raised a hand to push a stray lock of hair from her face and he was once more confronted with a fact he had somehow managed to ignore for the past four years.

Emily Bryant was not quite the unattractive automaton he'd believed her to be. Her brown hair was long, thick and shiny—and very tumbled. He'd never seen it down before. She either wore it scraped up on her head or pulled back in a severe ponytail.

And now her mouth had somehow become enticing, with all that hair to frame her face.

He'd known she was not shapeless. Indeed, her suits were well-fitted and crisp, if stark in color—it was only her shoes that were ugly. Sensible shoes, he believed they were called.

She was almost boyish, with narrow shoulders and hips. But she had a waist, and her small breasts were shapelier than he'd realized beneath her suit jackets. That surprised him in ways he hadn't expected. He knew it now because he'd had a devil of a time keeping his gaze from straying to where they jutted against the thin fabric of her top.

Still, she was Emily, his PA. Not some woman he could take to his bed and discard. He needed her in his life, and at this moment he very much needed her to agree to his plan.

"I don't know what to say." The words tumbled out of her in a breathless rush. Her green eyes, usually the color of polished jade, had darkened in what he supposed was confusion. Or horror. There was always that possibility, he decided.

"Say yes."

She did the one thing he did not expect. She took a step backward, out of his space, and wrapped her arms around her body. The wineglass was still clutched in one hand and tilted precariously to the side.

Her chin dropped and he got the distinct impression she was meditating. When she looked at him again, her gaze was clear.

"Why are you asking me this? Do you need to be married for a business deal? Is there some piece of property you cannot do without and a wife would ease the way with the owner?"

He could only stare at her. She was so close to the truth it astounded him. And yet not quite.

"I need to take a wife home to Kyr."

Her brows drew down. "I don't understand."

He blew out a breath. "It is very complicated. But suffice it to say that a wife is necessary. Think of this as a promotion."

She blinked. And then she laughed. He was almost insulted.

"This is the strangest promotion I have ever heard of." She drew in air, straightened her spine. "And it's impossible, Your Highness. I cannot do what you ask."

He felt the sting of her rejection as if it were a blow. It stunned him, if he was truthful with himself. Women did not typically refuse him.

"And why is that? This is a job, Emily. The same as always."

"You will forgive me, Your Highness—"

"Kadir." He spoke sharply, but he could not seem to help it. For once, he wanted her to call him by his name. For once, he needed to know that he was more to her than a paycheck. It was beyond insane, and yet he'd not felt quite right since he'd spoken with his father earlier.

It was as if everything he'd known had flipped upside down. As if his life had started out one way this morning—a lifetime ago now—and ended up in a completely different place. He was at the bottom of a pit, trying to find a handhold to pull himself back up again before the walls caved in and crushed him.

She swallowed. He didn't think she would say it, but then she did. "Kadir." Her voice was so small, so quiet, as if she feared that saying his name would call down a bolt of lightning.

"Was that so difficult then?"

Her eyes glinted in the dimly lit room. "No."

"Good." He retreated a few steps, gave her space. He sank onto her couch, ignoring the scattered papers. "Do I pay you well, Emily?"

She moved to one of the chairs set around a small table several feet away and sank down on it as if she feared she would break it. "Yes."

"Then you can hardly object if I give you an extra year's salary once you complete the task. All you need do is pretend to be my wife."

Her eyes were wide. "Pretend? We wouldn't actually be married?"

"We would, but it won't be a real marriage. I don't want you to think I expect anything other than the pretense of devotion." Because they would need to appear ridiculously besotted with each other for this to work.

She looked doubtful. "Won't someone figure it out?"

"How? We will act our parts."

She shook her head. "No one will believe it. Just yesterday, you were with Lenore Bradford. You were probably photographed with her. And now you are marrying me—when, tonight? After you were with Lenore at her party last night?"

He felt the noose tightening around his neck. "I did not say it was a perfect plan. But we will sell it, Emily." He twisted the stem of the wineglass in his fingers. "Besides, Kyr isn't precisely connected to the outside world. Not in the way you would think. It is modern, certainly. But gossip and tabloids are hardly my father's daily reading material. If I arrive with a wife, a wife who I am clearly crazy about, that will suffice for him."

He could see her throat work. "You want to deceive your family?"

"Yes."

"I don't understand."

He sighed and leaned his head back, staring up at the ceiling. She would never understand. And yet he had to make her do so if this were to work. It went against his nature to explain himself, but he had to acknowledge that she could just as easily turn him down if he did not. "It's about the throne, Emily. I don't want it."

She blinked. "Why not?"

A riot of emotion twisted through him. He wanted to lash out. To tell her it was none of her business. And yet, if he was asking her to do this thing, it surely was her business. He could tell her the truth without delving into his personal reasons. His guilt. That was private.

"Because a king cannot travel the world and erect

buildings. My business will be finished. And you will be out of a job."

He didn't like pointing it out so cruelly, but what choice did he have? Because that was, ultimately, what was at stake for her. If he became king, he couldn't keep her in Kyr. He'd have an entire legion of assistants and she would not be needed. Even if he wanted her there.

There was a hierarchy in serving the royal family in Kyr, and Emily Bryant did not fit into it.

She put her forehead in her palm and slanted her gaze toward him. It was an unconsciously attractive look. A twinge of heat flared to life in his belly. He tamped it down ruthlessly. His life was upside-down, he reminded himself. He was not attracted to his very ordinary assistant. If he had been, he would never have hired her. Besides, if he hadn't found her sexually appealing in four years thus far, he wasn't going to start today.

In spite of the awareness that slid through him when she'd put her hand on his arm. In spite of the urge he'd had to bend his head and fit his mouth to hers, just to see if the sparks would continue or if it was simply the incongruity of her touching him so deliberately.

An anomaly. Stress.

"I don't like the idea of deceiving your family. Besides, I'm a terrible actress. No one would ever believe I was your wife."

Kadir allowed himself a smile. It was the kind of smile he knew usually had an effect on the women he turned it upon. "I have no doubt they will believe it. You've never yet failed at a task I've set for you. And you won't fail at this one." He leaned forward then, elbows on knees, and delivered what he hoped would be the coup de grâce. "You are the only person I can trust, Emily. The only one who will not fail me. I need you."

* * *

Emily's insides were spinning and churning as though she'd taken a ride on a merry-go-round. It didn't help that Kadir looked at her so seriously. Or that he was specifically asking for her help. How could she refuse him?

And how could she go through with it? No one would ever believe that she—plain, ordinary Emily—was Kadir's chosen bride. The whole world would see through the deception.

And she'd be mortified when they did. People would laugh and point fingers. She would be noticed, and not in a good way.

It was impossible.

Yet, he looked at her with those gorgeous dark eyes and serious expression and she wanted to do whatever he asked. She closed her eyes, swallowed. It was more than that, though.

One year's salary.

With that kind of money, she could finish paying her father's hospital bills and start to put money in the bank for his long-term care. He still lived in the house she'd grown up in, but it was an older house that always needed repairs of one type or another. He tried to do things himself, but it was too much for one frail man.

Anger scoured through her then. Her mother should have been there with him. *Would* have been there with him if she weren't selfish and self-serving. If her focus on herself hadn't led her down a self-destructive path and ended in a twist of steel on a dark highway.

When Emily's father had needed his wife the most, when he'd gotten too sick to work and couldn't keep buying her clothes and vacations and cars, she'd said she was too young to be someone's caretaker. And then she'd run off with another man.

Emily experienced the same cold wash of helpless fury and despair she always did when she thought of her mother. Emily had been heading down the same path, in some ways. She'd loved flashy clothes, loved dressing up and being the center of attention. She'd spent hours at the salon, hours shopping with her girlfriends and hours discussing men. She'd had boyfriends, more than one at a time, because they lavished her with attention and gifts. And that had made her feel special.

But everything changed when her mother deserted them. Emily had realized what a self-destructive road she was traveling when there was no one left to take care of her father except for her. And now Kadir was handing her an opportunity to finally pay off her father's bills, maybe move him to a retirement community in Florida. He'd always wanted to go to where it was warm. Maybe live in a golfing community and play a few rounds.

If she could do that, it would mean the world to him. And to her, because then she wouldn't worry so much about him living in the windy, bitterly cold Chicago winters.

"How would this work?" Her voice sounded rusty, as if she hadn't used it in ages and her vocal cords didn't want to let the words go.

Kadir sighed and bowed his head for a brief moment. She wanted to tell him that she had not yet agreed, so he shouldn't get all relieved and everything—but they both knew she was going to. It was simply too good an opportunity to pass up.

No matter how it terrified her.

"My attorneys will draw up the paperwork. We will sign it. That is all that is required in Kyr—a legal marriage document, with both signatures affixed. We can have a ceremony in Kyr, if you like, but the documents will suffice."

She couldn't imagine standing at an altar—or wherever one did these things in Kyr—and pledging everlasting love to this man. To her boss.

No matter how fake it would be.

"I don't need a ceremony."

He tipped his head, as if he'd known she would say that. "Then there will not be one."

She clasped her hands in her lap, twisted them together. It was incongruous to be discussing marriage with her boss while in her pajamas in Paris, but that's precisely what she was doing. How surreal.

"Will there be other paperwork? A prenuptial agreement? A contract detailing the terms of our arrangement?"

"Do you require either of those things?"

She could only blink at him. "It seems prudent, don't you think? What if I decide I like being a princess so much that I refuse to divorce you and then ask for half your assets when you insist? Or what if you become unhappy with my performance and decide not to pay me?"

He laughed and she let the sound drip down her spine, warming her though she did not want it to.

"You are delightful, Emily. If I don't tell you that enough, I am remiss." He got to his feet then and she stood, too, more out of habit than anything. "I will have those documents done as well, if it makes you feel better."

She sucked in a fortifying breath. "I haven't said yes yet."

"But you will."

Heat rolled through her. She would, but she didn't like how easily he could read her. Or maybe it wasn't that at all. Maybe he just expected her to obey. Because she always had before.

"How can you be so certain? This is far different than ordering me to make phone calls or type up a new proposal."

He came closer to her and she forced herself to remain where she was. She would not duck away like a frightened kitten. Then he put his warm hands on her shoulders and she felt as if she'd been struck by lightning again.

"I need you, Emily. More than I've ever needed you before. And I think you will say yes because you've worked for me for four years now and you are good at what you do. You won't want to walk away when I need you. It's a challenge, and you like challenges."

She could only stare up at him, her insides clenching and rolling as his touch made things jump inside her. Things that hadn't jumped in a good long while.

"I—I have conditions," she managed.

His brows drew down, but he didn't look angry. "Conditions?"

She swallowed. *It's for the money. For my dad.* "For this to work, you can't order me to do things. The moment we sign the documents, I am no longer your employee."

His gaze slipped to her mouth, and she thought her knees might refuse to hold her a moment longer. But then he looked at her again, an expression of curiosity and bemusement on his handsome face. "Do you want to be more, Emily? Oddly, I find I might enjoy such a notion—"

"No." She cut him off, and immediately wanted to gasp. She had never done such a thing before. He was gazing at her steadily so she hurried on. "Partners. We will be business partners."

It was the only way she could do this. If she continued to think of herself as his employee, she would never manage the deception. Because she knew what happened when bosses and employees crossed the line. And she was too professional to do so, even if it was only an arrangement. For her own peace of mind, she had to separate those parts of her life.

"Fine." He didn't seem angry in the least.

Her heart throbbed painfully at what she was about to say. "Then I'll do it. I'll marry you."

Kadir seemed to relax slightly, as if he'd believed for a moment she might actually refuse him. His hands slid almost sensuously down her arms, left a trail of flame in their wake. Her skin prickled and tingled. She wanted to shrug away, to get out of his grasp—and she wanted to move closer at the same time.

"There are only two things left to do in order to seal this deal." His voice was like silk and she shivered in response.

His hands dropped away then, but before she could breathe a sigh of relief, he reached up to cup her neck. Then he drew her forward as her heart hammered. Her feet moved as if he was the one in control of them rather than her.

"Wh-what?" She cursed herself for sounding nervous—but he was touching her, and apparently that made her light-headed.

"First I have to fire you," he murmured, his gaze focusing on her mouth as she came in contact with the broad wall of his chest. Her hands went up automatically, rested on the soft cotton of his shirt. He was hard and warm beneath the fabric. She knew he went to the gym, and she knew what his body looked like beneath the cotton. Firm, tanned, beautiful.

No, she told herself. *You don't care. You haven't cared in four years.*

She had to focus, had to concentrate on what he was saying rather than on what he was doing. She could not lose her perspective here. "What's the other thing?"

His eyes glittered and one corner of his mouth lifted in what could only be termed a self-satisfied smile. "I have to kiss you, Emily."

CHAPTER FOUR

SHOCK RIPPLED THROUGH her like a wave. It was quickly followed by a pang of heat and longing that nearly took her breath away. Kadir pulled her more firmly against his body, and then his head dipped toward hers. She closed her eyes automatically, her heart hammering so hard she was going to be dizzy.

Kadir was going to kiss her. Her boss for the past four years, the man she'd served across continents and time zones without one single moment of inappropriateness, was about to kiss her.

Just like he'd kissed Lenore Bradford yesterday and a million other women before her. Emily had watched the revolving door of his life for far too long. She'd seen the women come and go. She'd walked many of them to the door herself as they clutched their handbags. Half the time with their wadded-up panty hose trailing from their purses as they took the walk of shame.

She'd witnessed it and, if she was honest with herself, she'd been utterly judgmental. What kind of idiot woman got herself involved with a playboy sheikh? Oh, she knew what they all thought. What they hoped. That they were *the* one. The one he would marry and make into his princess.

Sure, some of them just wanted sex, the same as he

did. And that was fine. She didn't pity those women, the ones who knew what they wanted and what they were getting.

The majority, however, were the other kind. The dreamers and schemers and hopefuls.

And she was not about to become one of them.

Emily shoved against his chest. His grip immediately eased and she stepped backward, out of his grasp. Her chest rose and fell as if she'd run a marathon. She wrapped her arms around herself, embarrassed at the effect he was having, and moved farther away.

Her wineglass was waiting on the table, so she picked it up and took a gulp. Then she faced him again. He looked oddly on edge, like a tiger waiting to pounce.

"No kissing," she said hoarsely.

"I'm afraid that is a condition I cannot accept." He sounded so cool, so calm, as if touching her hadn't meant a thing to him. Which, of course, it hadn't. His pulse wasn't racing like hers. His breath wasn't a struggle. She was simply another female to him.

"You have to."

He shook his head, his eyes glittering dangerously. "Impossible, Emily. I can hardly be besotted with a wife I never kiss, now can I? Besides, you have already agreed. You cannot change the terms of the agreement afterward. That is bad business."

She clutched the wineglass like a lifeline. She knew he was right, but dammit, why hadn't she thought of it before? Why hadn't she made it a condition?

Because it's stupid, that's why. Because he's paying you to be his wife, and husbands kiss their wives.

"Fine, you can kiss me. But only in public. Only when it's necessary for the illusion. No touching in private. No kissing either."

His eyebrow quirked. "Are you that afraid of me, Emily? Worried about what kissing me will do to you?"

Heat flared beneath her skin. "With all due respect, Your Highness, you really need to get over yourself. It's not professional, is all I mean. I'm your partner, not your lover."

"So no mixing business and pleasure, I take it?" He sounded amused, and it irritated her. Was there really nothing she could say that bothered this man? That got to him the way he was getting to her?

Maybe she should have been more blunt with him much sooner. But she'd always tried to be cool and professional and detached. She hadn't wanted camaraderie with him. She'd wanted nothing but her job and her paycheck and the satisfaction of performing her duties better than anyone he'd ever employed before.

She'd wanted to be indispensable to him—and she'd wanted to be the one he trusted with his business life. She hadn't wanted to kiss him or touch him or, heaven forbid, lie naked in a bed with him.

To do that would be like picking up a treasure map, pointing right to the place that said "Here Be Dragons," and saying, "This is where I want to go."

No, not going there. Not ever.

"Precisely." She tried to sound like her usual cool self, but there was a hint of hot color in her voice. She could hear it vibrating. She didn't like it.

He shoved his hands into his pockets. It was such a casual move, and yet he looked no less intense—or delicious—than a moment ago.

Stop.

"All right, we'll do it your way. For now. No touching unless necessary for public consumption. Which, by the way, includes my staff and anyone in the palace in Kyr. I expect this to work, Emily."

The tightness in her chest seemed to ease a bit now that she knew he wasn't going to try and tug her into his arms again. "I know that. And I will do my best."

"You better do more than that." He moved toward her with an easy grace that made her think of leopards slinking across the savannah. He stopped before her, hands still in pockets, intense gray eyes roving over her face. "Because if you don't, Miss Bryant, everything is going to change. And then you will be out of a job for real."

When dawn came, Emily didn't know what to do with herself. She started to get up and get dressed as usual, prepared to go to Kadir's suite and wake him as always—but then she remembered that he'd fired her. That she was no longer his employee.

Temporarily, of course. But as much as she wanted to adhere to her usual routines because they gave her comfort, she had to play a different role in his life right now. She'd spent the last several years learning to be sensible and efficient and now she was at loose ends. It was strange.

So, instead, she lay in bed and tried to go back to sleep. It didn't work, in spite of the way she'd tossed and turned last night. She hadn't slept because she'd been remembering Kadir standing in her room, looking so lost and alone and handsome, and asking her to marry him. And then he'd taken her in his arms and tried to kiss her.

Her heart did a little skip-and-slip thing every time she thought of that moment when she'd closed her eyes and felt him dipping down to press his mouth against hers.

But she'd panicked and pushed him away and now she couldn't stop wondering what she'd missed. If she'd made a mistake.

No. She had not made a mistake. Kissing him would have been a mistake. Allowing him to sweep her off her feet the way he'd done to countless women over the past four years would have been a mistake.

Asserting herself, asserting her independence and setting up parameters was not a mistake. It was good business. Kadir would respect her for it. And in the end, if this worked the way he hoped and he did not inherit the throne of Kyr, she would slide back into her role as his PA. So long as this arrangement stayed strictly business between them—including any touching or kissing that was required for the role—there would be no awkwardness later on.

Still, her stomach twisted in such a way that belied her thoughts. But she refused to let her fears get the upper hand. This was a business arrangement, albeit an uncharacteristic one. And she would do her part without fear or complaint.

Still, she worried about the way he'd been last night. He'd proposed this crazy idea, and she'd agreed, but what must he truly be feeling inside? His father was dying. She remembered that moment when he'd told her. He'd said he was angry and her heart had gone out to him. She'd known him for too long to be unaffected by his pain.

And yes, she'd agreed to help him. For the money. But also for him.

Emily threw back the covers and launched herself out of bed. She took a shower and dressed in her usual business attire—because it was all she had besides a few pairs of jeans and casual shirts—and slipped on her low heels. And then, because she wasn't quite sure what else to do with her hair when she felt as though she was dressed for work, she pulled it back in a severe ponytail.

Her cell phone rang just as she finished putting on lip gloss. One glance at the screen and her stomach started doing backflips. Emily took a deep breath and willed the butterflies away. It was ridiculous to get worked up, especially since Kadir called her often and it had never bothered her before.

"Yes," she said, hoping she sounded cool and calm.

"I need you to come to my suite, Emily. The lawyers are here."

She swallowed. Part of her had begun to hope it had all been a dream. "All right. I'll be there in just a few minutes."

She ended the call and took another look at herself in the mirror. All the color had drained from her face until she looked pale and ghostly. God, she was really going to do this. She was going to walk into Kadir's suite and marry him.

For the first time, a little stab of distress caught her by surprise. She should have worn something different from her usual attire. Something a bride would be happy to say she'd gotten wed in. Something special.

Emily closed her eyes. Except this was merely an arrangement and it wasn't supposed to be special. What was the matter with her? Why did she care what she wore when all she was going to do was sign some papers?

Papers that would change her life, albeit for a short time. She really, really hoped that Kadir knew what he was doing. It was a crazy plan, but she'd agreed to it. Too late to back out now.

She took one last look in the mirror, smoothed her ponytail and went to meet her fate.

Kadir waited impatiently for Emily to arrive. He paced back and forth in the living room of his suite while the lawyers arranged the documents on a nearby table. The sun had glided above the horizon an hour ago now, and the Paris sky was clear and blue, with wisps of feathery clouds sailing across it.

A perfect day to get married.

He tried not to shudder at the notion. Marriage was not something he'd ever intended to enter into lightly, yet here he was. It wasn't that he didn't believe in marriage, or didn't believe in falling in love—it's just that he'd never actually seen it work in his own life. His father had many wives and he didn't seem emotionally attached to any of them.

Kadir's mother had been the favorite wife before she died, but she had been desperately unhappy. Something Kadir hadn't realized until he'd gotten older.

The door to his suite opened and Emily sailed inside, looking as cool and businesslike as ever. For some reason, that irritated him. Her hair was scraped back from her face, as always, and she wore a navy-blue suit with a coral shirt—the only bright spot of color on her—and those same damn ugly shoes as always. Low heel, boxy toe, matte black.

He'd never cared one way or the other before, but now he found that he despised those shoes. Utterly. She needed new ones, and soon.

"Are you coming to take notes or to get married?"

Her green gaze snapped to him and he had the sudden thought that she wasn't quite as cool as she'd like to appear. That knowledge made him relax, though only marginally.

She ran a hand over her jacket, as if smoothing an imaginary wrinkle. One thing he knew about Emily Bryant was that she didn't dare to allow wrinkles. She was always crisp and organized, and she looked just as if she was marching in for a day's work rather than about to sign the documents that would make her his wife.

He was almost insulted she'd not made more effort. But then he chided himself. What did he care? This was about presenting his father with an unsuitable bride and declaring himself unfit for the throne, not about her current clothing or enthusiasm. So long as she appeared enthused in Kyr, he could care less what she did here.

Or so he told himself.

"I'm not carrying a notebook." Her words were pointed. And completely unnecessary since he could quite clearly see she was not holding her characteristic pad and pen.

He swept a hand toward the table where the lawyers sat. "Then if you will come this way, Miss Bryant, we shall take care of business."

She nodded once, firmly, but he didn't miss the way she bit her lip or the tremor in her fingers as she tugged her jacket hem. His buttoned-up PA wasn't as calm as she pretended to be.

Good, because he wasn't very calm either. His entire future depended on this performance. Not for the first time, he wondered if he should have gone after Lenore, made up with her and asked her to do it instead. She would have agreed for the notoriety, and she would have horrified his father into naming Rashid his successor within hours of her arrival in Kyr.

And then Kadir would have divorced her. In spite of Emily's remark last night about what happened if she didn't want to divorce him, that truly wasn't possible in Kyr. All he had to do was have the decree drawn up, sign it, and it was done. He had no fear that any woman could trap him permanently.

Emily took a seat at the table and Kadir sat beside her. He was far more aware of her than he wanted to be, but that was because she fairly vibrated with energy. One foot bounced against the other as she sat with her ankles crossed, tapping it impatiently.

Or nervously.

He had a sudden urge to reach over and pull the elastic from her hair, to see it fall down over her shoulders in a silky cloud of rich chocolate. He blinked and stiffened. Really, that was not in the least bit like him. He liked a certain type of woman, and Emily Bryant was not it. She wasn't beautiful. She didn't have blade-thin cheekbones or the kind of face a camera loved. She was ordinary.

And yet his blood hummed at her nearness. He told himself it was everything to do with his plan and nothing to do with her. Once this was done, his father would choose the correct son for the throne. That was certainly enough to make his blood buzz with excitement.

He should feel guilty for dragging Emily into this, knowing what it would be like for her in Kyr, but he was desperate. And he would compensate her handsomely for the trouble.

Kadir reached for the documents and slid them toward her. "It is all fairly straightforward. Here is the paper you required, which spells out the task you are performing and your payment." He lifted a paper. "And here is the prenuptial agreement. It states that you will get nothing of my estate or business beyond what we've agreed to in the contract."

She took them both and read them over. They were both very plain documents, as he had only had them drawn up because she'd insisted, and did not consist of pages and pages of legalese.

She picked up the pen lying near her right hand and quickly signed first one and then the other. Kadir did the same and one of the lawyers took the documents and slid them into a briefcase. The other lawyer handed the next set of documents to Kadir and he set them on the table between him and Emily.

"This is the marriage contract. We have only to sign it, and we are legally wed under the laws of Kyr."

She let out a small sigh and he slanted a look her way. She was chewing the end of the pen and she slipped it out of her mouth almost guiltily.

"It seems so sterile," she said. "Almost unreal."

"I assure you it is very real. The moment we both sign and Daoud here affixes the seal, we are married."

"It's not very romantic, is it?"

He frowned at her. "I was not aware you wanted romantic."

Her head snapped up, her green gaze colliding with his. "Oh, no, of course not. That's not what I mean. I just think of the couples who get married this way and how disappointing it must be."

"Most of them hold a ceremony after, if they are doing it for romantic reasons. When you are raised this way, it is not a disappointment. You're thinking of American girls and their white weddings, with all the flowers and pomp." He frowned. "Which seem to go disastrously wrong fairly often, if the television is to be believed."

Her lips fell open as she stared at him, and he found himself wanting to slide his fingers across them, to see if they were as soft as they looked. But then she laughed. And she kept laughing, until a tear slid from one eye and she clutched her stomach.

Kadir couldn't help but laugh with her, though he wasn't quite sure why. She wasn't taking this seriously, and he should be stern with her.

But he couldn't be. He liked the sound of her laugh. He didn't know that he'd ever heard it before. It was light and soft and yet so very, very infectious at the same time. Even the lawyers were laughing, though not as much. And none of them, save Emily, knew what they were laughing at.

"Emily," he finally said, trying to be stern. She looked at him and then dissolved into another fit of giggles. Her mascara was ruined, but he didn't think she'd like him to point that out.

Instead, he jerked his chin at the man nearest the box of tissues. A second later, he thrust the box at Emily. She took several.

"I'm so sorry," she said, gulping between giggles. "Really. I'll be fine in a minute. Honestly."

"I'm afraid I don't know what is so funny. Do you care to share it with us?"

She sucked in several deep breaths and wiped her eyes with the tissues. Finally, she seemed to have it under control. "I'm so sorry. But, well, it's you." She clutched her arm around her belly, as if willing herself not to laugh again. But the corners of her mouth lifted in a smile she couldn't quite control. A smile that quavered at the corners.

Kadir thought that he ought to be insulted, but he was having a hard time figuring out precisely why. Not to mention seeing her this way—lit up from the inside instead of calm and controlled and professional—was somehow addictive in a way he hadn't expected.

"And what have I done to amuse you so much, *habibti?*"

She sucked in another breath, let out a giggle, swallowed hard. "You. *Bridezillas.*" She waved the tissue back and forth, as if fanning herself. It was a very inadequate fan. "I never knew that a prince such as you would—" She took a deep breath, let it out again. Closed her eyes. He could tell she was biting her lip. When she spoke again, her voice shook. With laughter, he realized. "Watch a show about insane brides wreaking havoc on their grooms and everyone connected with their wedding. It's just so, so…"

"Amusing?"

She closed her eyes. "Oh, God, yes." She waved a hand at him without looking at him. "Because you're so, well, you. And I just can't picture you with the remote and a bag of potato chips, settling in for the latest episode."

"Emily."

She cracked open one eye. "Yes?"

"I think you are blowing this out of proportion. I may have seen something while in a hotel room once. I also read the newspapers. The American fascination with the perfect wedding has not escaped my notice. And what I am saying is that couples in my country don't feel that same need. They have ceremonies. They throw parties—or their families throw them—but this is how it begins. At a table, with marriage documents."

She focused on the papers. "Yes, of course. I didn't

mean to insult anyone. It's just not what I expected I would do someday."

"I am not insulted. Daoud is not insulted. Philippe is French—and he is most certainly not insulted."

Her eyes were warmer than he'd ever seen them. So green, like fresh fields in summer. She made him think of sunshine and long afternoons with a book and a bottle of wine—things he'd not done in a very long time. Since he'd started Hassan Construction, he'd had no time for anything but work and the kind of erotic play that happened with the opposite sex.

He did not mind that so much, usually.

"Good." She put her hand on the marriage documents and took a deep breath. "Do I sign first, or do you?"

"The bride signs first." The words were tight in his throat for some reason.

Emily picked up her pen and wrote her name quickly. Then she sighed and pushed the papers toward him. Kadir signed and handed everything to Daoud, who affixed the official seal of Kyr. Then both lawyers stood and bowed to Kadir and Emily both before taking their leave.

Soon, the room was empty but for the two of them.

Kadir had stood to see the lawyers out, but Emily was still sitting in her chair and looking somewhat shell-shocked. He sat down beside her, took her hand in his. She gasped softly and stared down at their clasped hands. A current of warmth slid through him.

"They bowed to me," she said. "I didn't expect that."

"You are a princess of Kyr now. Emily al-Hassan, Her Royal Highness and Beloved of the Eagle of Kyr."

She blinked. "Eagle?"

He rubbed his thumb inside her palm. Her skin was

soft, warm. And he enjoyed the slight tremors vibrating through her. As a man, he knew it was not a fear response. It was a response to him, to his skin against hers.

It was a response he understood. A response he could work with. If necessary, he would seduce her into perfect compliance with his plan. A real performance instead of a fake one. A part of him rather liked that idea.

"I am the Eagle of Kyr." He shrugged. "My brother is the Lion of Kyr, and my father is the Great Protector. This is tradition. Perhaps you find it silly, like the wedding documents."

For the first time, he was aware of how foreign this must all seem to her. How very strange. He could tell her that her culture was just as strange to him sometimes, but he didn't think that would help matters at all.

She looked stricken, and he wanted to kick himself. "I don't think that at all. I really don't."

He squeezed her hand. "I know. This is all a bit overwhelming, I imagine. Yesterday you were my PA. Today you are my wife."

Her head dropped, her gaze falling to her lap. "It is somewhat stunning, I have to admit."

He tipped her chin up with a finger, forced her to look at him. She seemed younger than her twenty-five years at that moment. A bit lost, maybe. He didn't like the guilt that pierced him at that look on her face.

"It will be fine, Emily. We'll get through these next few days and then everything will go back to normal."

"Yes, of course we will. I won't disappoint you, Your Highness. You can count on me."

"I know that. And it's Kadir, Emily. It's important you call me by my name from now on."

She pulled in a breath. "Kadir."

He smiled to reassure her. "That was not so difficult, was it?"

"It will take some getting used to."

He let his fingers glide down the column of her neck, more out of curiosity than anything. Her eyes widened—and then she pushed her chair back, out of his reach.

"We're alone." She sounded almost scandalized.

There was a stirring deep inside him, a primal urge to capture and claim. He would not act upon it, however. It was simply a reaction to her moving away. Her flight response triggered his male desire to pursue.

"I am well aware of this, Emily."

"Our agreement was no touching in private."

Anger flared inside him. "And yet there is the danger you will call me something other than Kadir, or that you will flinch when I dare to caress your cheek. If you do this in Kyr, we will fail."

"I won't, Your—Kadir." He didn't miss the way she ground her jaw at her near miss. Determination shone from her pretty eyes as she lifted her chin and met his gaze almost defiantly. "You can count on me. Like always."

He stood and ranged toward her, watched the glide of her throat as she swallowed. But she didn't move again, didn't try to escape, and he felt a hot burst of admiration for her. There was his fearless PA. That was the woman he could count on, with his very life if necessary.

She tilted her head back to meet his gaze when he stopped in front of her. Close enough to feel her heat, to smell her perfume. Closer than he would have done had she still been merely his PA.

She did not flinch as he let his gaze wander over

her face, did not speak as she waited. Finally, he met her eyes again. His voice, when he spoke, was soft and contemplative.

"I hope so, *habibti*. For both our sakes."

CHAPTER FIVE

"Are you ready for this?"

Emily swung her head toward Kadir. They were in the back of a limousine that had taken them from the airport in Milan to the fashion district in the city's center. She was still reeling over the short plane ride when, for the first time ever, she'd been the object of countless bows and *Your Highness*es. It was a far cry from how she usually traveled with Kadir. Then, she would sit in her own section of the plane and work on whatever needed working on. Sometimes, if he needed her for something, she joined him.

This time, she'd sat down right next to him and been served by the same people she used to joke with on their usual flights. Everyone had looked at her as though she'd forgotten to put on clothes or something. It had been far more uncomfortable than she'd expected it to be and she was still processing it.

"I doubt it," she said. She'd argued at first, when Kadir had told her they were stopping over in Milan in order to buy her a wardrobe, but she'd lost. Spectacularly.

She could still see his handsome face creased in a frown as he'd told her that her clothing was simply not suitable for a princess. Her shoes, he'd informed her, were the ugliest things he'd ever seen.

She'd been angry more than anything, but also a little embarrassed. So she'd informed him that walking around behind him on job sites and in the various offices he traveled to was not conducive to wearing six-inch heels.

"Yes, but my wife will wear them," he'd told her imperiously.

And now they were here, in Milan, for a shopping trip that she dreaded. It wasn't that she didn't like pretty clothes. She did. But she'd put away that side of herself a long time ago. And she'd never been tempted to bring it out again. She'd seen the damage that kind of life did.

She'd been a magpie like her mother, seeking beautiful things, beautiful experiences. She'd never realized how selfish she'd become until her father got sick and she'd wanted to run away, too. It had horrified her so much that she'd vowed to change her ways.

Her mother had run away, but Emily had not. She would not. She'd put away the glitz and glam and gotten serious. And now here she was, working for Kadir and dressing like a professional. She was happier. Calmer. Settled.

Safe.

Kadir was frowning at her. "It's important that you look the part, Emily."

It wasn't the first time he'd told her this. "I know."

"I need you to be more like Lenore."

A hot wave of anger flooded her. She would never look like Lenore Bradford in a million years. "Perhaps you should have asked Lenore then," she snapped.

His eyes widened only marginally. And then they narrowed again while her heart beat hotly. Well, dammit, she was tired of hearing about Lenore and how gorgeous she was and how Emily needed to be more like her.

"I did not ask Lenore." His voice was icy. "I asked you. And you agreed, I might add. So stop pouting and start doing your part."

"I'm not pouting, Kadir." At least it was getting easier to say his name, probably because she was so furious with him half the time. "I know what you want and I'll do my best to make it happen. Though I still don't understand *why* you don't just tell your father you don't want to be king. Surely he would understand that. It's not like you're his only choice."

His teeth ground together. His gray eyes flashed hot and sharp, but she wasn't intimidated. Not this time. What was he going to do? Fire her for good?

Maybe later, but not before he got what he wanted. She suppressed a shiver and refused to look away from that mesmerizing stare.

"It does not work that way."

"Why not? Is there a law against saying you don't want to be king?"

"Emily." His voice was a growl. "This is not something I wish to talk about. Leave it."

She folded her arms over her chest and turned to look at the window. "Fine. But stop harassing me. I'm sure Lenore would have been perfect for what you want, but then you'd be stuck with a woman who wanted you as a husband for real. And no matter what agreement she signed, she'd probably try to talk you out of it. Or screw you out of it, I imagine."

He muttered something in Arabic that she thought might be a curse.

"What?" she demanded. "Am I wrong?"

There was a wild, hot current swimming in her veins. A feeling that made her bold, made her fling herself against the forbidden gates of Kadir's life in utter fury. She realized with a start that it must be four long years of pent-up frustration with this man finally gaining a voice. Four years in which she'd done her job, kept her mouth shut and watched him be a complete ass to the women who rotated through his life.

Well, he'd freed her now, and she wasn't going to waste a moment of it.

Which, a small part of her tried to say, was career suicide. How would they ever go back to the way things were before? They'd been married for less than six hours, and already she was forgetting how to behave like his PA.

"You are not wrong."

The air between them grew thick, so thick she wanted to roll down the window and gulp in the Milanese air. But she was frozen in place while he speared her with those intense eyes. The Eagle of Kyr. *My God.*

Something was happening, something she couldn't quite figure out. But then he took a deep breath and shifted in his seat, his hot gaze facing front again, his jaw set in a hard line.

"Your opinion of me is showing, *habibti.* Make sure it doesn't happen in public."

"I don't know what you're talking about. I'm simply pointing out the truth."

His eyes were bright as he swung around to look at her. "That I am shallow? That I date women for, what was it, their bra sizes?"

"I didn't say that." She closed her eyes briefly. "This time, I mean. I was only pointing out what you already know to be true. Lenore would have been a perfectly unsuitable wife, but she wouldn't have given up the position so easily. Not when it made her a princess and gave her something she could lord over everyone else in her life."

"But what you really want to know is what I saw in her in the first place. What I saw in any of them." His voice was low and intense.

"That is none of my business." She knew she sounded prim, and her cheeks flamed. Because he was right, she did want to know. The women he dated were beautiful, but most of them were schemers and, well, groupies of one sort or another. None of them had wanted to see beneath his masks. They'd wanted the prince, the billionaire, the sheikh. They had not wanted the man. Didn't that bother him? At least a little?

"Mostly, it was sex." He went on as if she'd not spoken. "Sometimes, it was companionship. I am not a robot, Emily. I like the warmth of another person next to me. I get lonely, like anyone."

Her heart was beating hard now, throbbing in her throat. She'd never thought of him as lonely. Never. He always had people around him. He had friends in every city they visited, and he had women he took to his bed. How could he be lonely?

But she knew how. She knew because she'd been lonely, too. The loneliest she'd ever felt was in a crowded room. Emptiness was not filled by crowds of people. She was pretty sure it wasn't filled by sex either, though it had been a long time since she'd experimented with that.

"I'm sorry." Her voice was paper-thin. How had this conversation taken a turn like this? It had started out being one thing and ended up as something else entirely. Something that made her heart ache and tears press hard against the backs of her eyes.

How did he do this to her? How did he take her from murderously angry to aching in the space of only a few moments?

"And what about you, Emily? Do you get lonely? You cannot have much of a personal life working for me."

Her blood felt thick in her veins. Like syrup on a winter's day. Except she was hot with embarrassment as well. Why had she not seen this coming? Had she really thought she could snap and push him and come away unscathed?

"My life is fine."

He leaned back in the seat then, draped an arm on the armrest between them. His fingers dangled off the end, tapped some imaginary beat in the air. A slow, lazy beat. When she lifted her eyes to his, he was watching her with a hooded expression. Then he picked up that hand and slid his index finger across his lower lip, as if he was thinking.

Didn't matter why, since the effect of the gesture was currently what had her beginning to panic. Something bloomed deep inside her, in her core. Some hot, dark feeling that wanted very much to be allowed to blossom into a fuller, darker emotion.

Emily bit the inside of her lip. After all these years, after how ruthless she'd been with herself, her mother was beginning to creep out. That carnal, needy woman who wanted fun and adventure and licentious couplings with incredibly hot men.

She put her hands in her lap and clasped them together. She'd worked too hard. Too long. She was nothing like her mother. Sensuality might lurk within her, but she would not give in to that side of her nature ever again. It was under her control. Kadir al-Hassan was *not* going to reduce her to the kind of woman who would do absolutely anything for one night in his bed. Not ever.

"Is it?" he finally asked.

"Of course. I'm perfectly happy." And yet she did miss human connection sometimes. Not that she would admit that to him. She would not give him fuel for the fire he was building.

His expression grew sultry. "All those nights when I sent you away, when another woman joined me in my bed—did you think of me, Emily?"

She gasped. "Of course not—"

"Did you want to be the one beneath me?"

"No!"

He leaned toward her then, his eyes intense. "Did you lie in your lonely bed, touching yourself, pretending it was me?"

She couldn't speak as pain bloomed deep in her soul. Not because she'd done what he said—but a dark part of her had wanted to. And he knew it. Somehow, he knew it. The pain spread through her in waves, knotted her belly, clenched her throat tight. She was choking, choking on rage and hate and—and longing, damn him.

Tears gathered in the corners of her eyes then. She turned her head and dashed them away. She'd known he was ruthless in business. She'd known he always won. She hadn't known he was cruel. She hadn't known the depths to which he could make her sink in despair, or the fathoms-deep hatred she could feel for him.

She wanted to speak, wanted to metaphorically slap him down. Wanted to deflate his ego—and, yes, his penis—all in one well-timed verbal blow. She wanted to decimate him.

And she couldn't find the words. Nothing would

dredge itself up from the recesses of her brain. Nothing happened. Nothing except a long, taut silence that seemed to stretch forever but was in reality only a few moments.

The car came to a stop. Emily didn't care if they'd reached their destination or if they were only stopped at a traffic light. She yanked the handle and the door swung open, spilling in light and hot air and the sounds of Milan.

Kadir reached for her, but she slipped his grip and stumbled onto the street. Then she ran. She could hear Kadir shout at her, but she kept going, losing herself in the crowd, running blindly as the tears she'd been holding in finally spilled over and rushed down her cheeks.

CHAPTER SIX

KADIR CURSED HIMSELF as he ran down the crowded street after her. What the hell had he been thinking? Why had he been so needlessly vicious? Emily was his assistant, the closest thing he had to a friend in some respects, and she was doing him a favor.

And he had ripped into her as though she was just another gold-digging social climber. Worse, as though he hated her. He'd shredded her as if it was nothing, and that shamed him. What kind of man was he? What kind of man attacked those weaker than himself?

He couldn't say why he'd done it, except that he'd been irritated when she'd asked him so plainly why he didn't just tell his father what he wanted. As if it was that easy. He wasn't accustomed to explaining himself to anyone, and here she was, making what she thought was a simple suggestion when it was far more difficult than anything she could imagine.

And then she'd thrown Lenore in his face. All right, so he'd mentioned Lenore first—but then she'd kept on going, her contempt so evident. He'd simply had too much. He'd told her something personal, admitted his loneliness to her—and then he'd felt the need to lash out, to make her pay in kind.

He should have stopped much sooner than he did.

He should have stopped when she'd gotten the point. But of course he hadn't. Driven by his need to win, to crush, to control, he'd kept going until he'd hurt her.

And now he was chasing her down the street, angry with himself, and wondering how in the hell such a simple idea had gotten so complicated. She was supposed to be his wife, the woman he couldn't live without, the woman he would not give up for a throne. It was supposed to be simple.

But it wasn't.

He thought he might have lost her, but then he saw her as the crowd parted in front of him. She was walking now, her body hunched over as she hugged herself. Her ponytail bounced as she hurried along. She was moving fast, but he was faster. He closed the distance between them until he was right behind her.

She kept walking—and then she seemed to stiffen, as if she sensed a change in the air, before she halted abruptly. He took a step back as she swung around to face him. Her brows were drawn down in a furious expression. Her mascara had run again, and tears streaked her cheeks.

Something twisted inside him.

"Forgive me," he said simply. It was odd to be apologizing, and yet here he was, doing just that. It wasn't something he did often and the words were rusty.

She drew in a deep breath and straightened even more. Then she moved into his space. Poked him in the chest. It was not what he expected and he stepped back in surprise.

She closed the distance, poked him again. "Listen to me, you Neanderthal, and listen good. I do not want you. I have never wanted you. You're a handsome man, and you damn well know it. And you're used to being irresistible to women. Well, not to me." She sucked in a breath, her voice quavering as she continued. "I will not be talked to like I'm some kind of whore you pay to grace your bed. I'm your business partner, you hear me? Nothing more, nothing less. You might frighten a CEO into doing things your way, but you would never cross a personal line to do it."

He felt as if she'd slapped him across the face. Several times. Which, no doubt, he deserved.

"No, I would not. You are correct."

Her face scrunched up even more. She was, for some reason, attractive as hell when she was angry. He'd never seen Miss Emily Bryant in a fit of temper before. Well, not before today. And not like this.

He was oddly stimulated by her anger. He could feel the air crackle between them and he wondered how it had never happened before. How he'd never felt that subtle shift of electricity, that hum and buzz of ozone. Had she really kept all this under wraps for four years? Or had he never paid attention before?

"I want the money, Kadir. Nothing more. I agreed because of that. Not because of you."

It was always the money, with any woman in his life. That was a language he understood. Still, he felt a prick of anger in his gut. "The money. Of course."

She stood there, trembling—and then her hands dropped to her sides and her expression, while still angry, softened into something a notch below cyclone level.

"You really are too full of yourself," she said. "Not every woman wants a ride on your magic mattress."

He felt his eyebrows climb his forehead. "Magic mattress?"

She shrugged. A soft flush stained her cheeks. "Whatever you call your love nest, Kadir. Not every woman on this planet wants a turn. It would be healthier for you if you'd stop thinking so."

He suddenly wanted to laugh. And tug her into his arms so he could feel that bright fire radiating from her as it sizzled into his pores. It was a shock to realize that he wanted her. That he actually wanted to see what her mouth felt like beneath his. To peel away her staid suit and bare her lithe body for his eyes only. He wanted to run his fingers over her skin, wanted to see if she was as soft as he thought. As responsive.

He stood there in the hot sunshine and stared down at his former PA, now his wife, and felt the shift of his axis.

In the space of a few hours, he'd become utterly intrigued. For four years, he'd never noticed her as a woman—well, not often, anyway—but now he couldn't seem to shove her back into the box she belonged in. It didn't matter that she was wearing her conservative suit and ugly shoes, that her hair was pulled back or that tiny black rivulets stained her cheeks.

There was a commotion in the crowd and Kadir turned. His bodyguards were making their way toward him. Irritation flashed into him, not because they were doing their jobs, but because they were drawing attention to him and Emily.

People stopped to look—and then someone whipped out a cell phone and began to snap photos.

"We need to go," he told Emily. "We are being noticed."

She started to turn, but he grabbed her hand and tugged her into the curve of his body. She didn't pull away when he put his arm around her and started down the sidewalk in the direction they had come. She was so small in his grip, so warm. It was a shock to feel so much of her against him. Heat surged into him.

And confusion.

He hurried her toward a shop as his bodyguards took care of crowd control. Another moment and they were inside the couture house he'd been bringing her to in the first place.

"Your Highness," a man said as he came forward. "We are so glad you have come to us. Everything is ready."

"She must be glamorous and insanely beautiful," Kadir said, dragging his attention back to the matter at hand. He could not afford to feel softness for her right now. "Make her clothing tasteful but sexy."

Emily gasped. "I will not—"

"It is not up for discussion, Emily. You have agreed to it."

Her jaw worked and her eyes flashed cold fury. "You have no idea how much I'm beginning to regret that."

He only stared at her. "Too late, *habibti*. You are mine now."

He whirled and stalked out of the shop before she could say another word. And before he could drag her into his arms and silence her rebellious mouth with his own.

Emily could have chewed nails and spit fire. She was horribly, incredibly angry. With Kadir. With herself. But she had agreed to this insane scheme and now she had no choice but to endure the transformation currently taking place.

She looked at herself in the mirror, at her sleek hair, cut and styled and looking like mahogany silk. Her eyes were rimmed in dark eyeliner and there was a smudge of shadow in the crease. Her lashes had been curled and lengthened with mascara, her lips were a sultry red pout, and her dress was the most gorgeous shade of purple jersey that clung to all her curves. On her feet were tall snakeskin Louboutins with the signature red heel.

She'd endured endless fittings, the mechanical snick-snick-snick of sewing machines as seamstresses worked frantically to tailor the clothing and the ministrations of a makeup artist and hairstylist until finally Guido stood back and pronounced her fit for public viewing.

"His Most Exalted Highness is waiting in the outer room," Guido said.

"Wonderful." Emily gritted her teeth. She was going to have to practice being happy with her arrogant boss-turned-temporary-husband. No better time than the present.

Just thinking of Kadir caused her insides to clench. He made her so angry. He also made her itch to slide her palms over his chest while arching her body into his. That was a new development and one she did not appreciate whatsoever.

"You are a perfect princess, Your Highness," Guido said, smiling and bowing as she picked up the buttery-soft leather handbag he'd selected to go with her outfit. Emily wanted to tell him not to bow, but she stopped herself. This was a performance, and she most definitely was a princess. For now.

She glanced at herself again and swallowed. Her mother stared back at her from beneath the sultry makeup and curve-hugging clothing and Emily wanted to scream. She'd worked too hard to bury that sensual creature that lurked inside her and now it was staring back at her, mocking her.

Just because I look like you, she wanted to say, *doesn't mean I am you.*

Guido escorted Emily to the outer room, where Kadir was waiting. He looked up when she entered. His eyes seemed to widen and she told herself not to be pleased at that. The flare of feminine vanity she felt was not welcome. Oh, how she used to preen when a man looked at her with appreciation. She would not do so now.

Kadir's gaze skimmed over her slowly. And then his mouth curved in a smile that made her heart skip a beat. "You look amazing, Emily."

Heat seared into her. "Thank you." Because what else did you say to something like that?

She felt self-conscious more than anything, because now everyone was looking at her in ways they never had before. She'd found it easier to blend into the background, to be unobtrusive. Her job required that of her.

Guido snapped his fingers and a pair of smartly dressed saleswomen appeared with boxes and bags.

"These will see her through the first couple of days," he told Kadir. "The rest will be delivered to Kyr immediately upon completion."

"Grazie," Kadir said. "As always, you have pleased me greatly."

A sharp feeling sliced into her then. She remembered now why Guido's name was familiar to her. She'd been so distracted by everything today that she hadn't dwelled too much on why. But she had seen his name on bills. For shoes, clothing, jewels, handbags and silk scarves.

Of course she had. She wanted to put her hand to her temple and rub, but she didn't. What did she care if Kadir was buying her clothing at the same place he had bought things for his lovers?

Kadir might be a player of the worst sort, but one of the things he had never done was make Emily buy gifts for his ladies. He took care of that himself—and now she knew how. He picked up the phone and called Guido.

Emily smiled and thanked Guido and his staff personally, and then Kadir ushered her out the door and into the waiting limousine while a man in a dark suit and headset stood beside the car door, looking quietly lethal.

Once they were inside, the bodyguards seated in this car and the one following, the driver pulled into traffic and began the return trip to the airport.

Emily fixed her gaze on the passing city and tried not to look at Kadir. But she knew he was looking at her. In fact, he hadn't stopped since they'd gotten into the car. Her skin prickled with awareness that she tried to squash down again.

She did not need to be aware of Kadir. Not like that.

Finally, when her nerves were stretched to the breaking point, she whipped her gaze to his. "Is something wrong? Am I not being unsuitable enough for you?"

Kadir looked all dark and handsome and broody in his corner. He somehow managed to appear supremely relaxed and completely tense all at once. The tension was in his eyes rather than in his body.

"You are perfectly unsuitable. I am quite pleased thus far."

She ran her fingers over the fabric of her dress and stomped on the tendril of panic unwinding in her belly. "Well, that's a relief."

She couldn't help the bite of temper in her voice. Or the sarcasm.

"You have changed, Emily."

"You aren't used to seeing me with my hair down." She waved a hand over her body. "Or dressed like this."

"That is not what I'm talking about."

She looked at him, her pulse thrumming, her ears growing warm. "Isn't it?"

He shook his head slowly. "Not at all." His eyes narrowed. "I am not quite accustomed to this side of you. The side that—how do you say it?—sasses me."

She sniffed. "You wanted a wife, not an employee. A wife would not, I hope, take your pronouncements as law. She would state her opinions, even were they contrary to yours."

"And you have done a fine job of this. Even when there were no witnesses and therefore no need."

"No need? Kadir, you'd mow a girl down if she didn't let you know she wasn't going to take it."

One eyebrow lifted imperiously. "Surely I am not so callous as all that."

Emily leaned back on the seat and tried to appear casual. Was he really that clueless about his tendencies to overwhelm?

"You're intense, Kadir. You take over a room when you walk into it. You pull people to you, and you get what you want from them. I've seen it again and again. And the women you seduce? They don't stand a chance."

"Are you certain? You are speaking from observation, not experience."

Her mouth went dry. She licked her lips nervously. It was as if he were offering to show her, though he had not said any such thing. "I don't see how that changes anything."

His gaze was hooded and her heart performed a slow *thump-thump-thump*.

"Perhaps it does. Perhaps, if I were to seduce you, you would get what *you* want, Emily. Perhaps it would be a mutually beneficial arrangement instead of the one-sided venture you envision it to be."

Heat blossomed in her belly, slid into her bones, turned her into rubber. He wasn't actually offering, she told herself. He was simply trying to control her. Still, she couldn't move without wobbling. She didn't dare to move.

"And yet we will never know." She had to force the words out, but she was proud they didn't quaver. "Because that is not part of our deal."

"Yet deals can be amended."

Emily swallowed. The air in the car was suddenly thick and hot, and she wanted desperately to bend over and stick her face right in the air-conditioning vent. To pull some cold air into her lungs while she tried to find her equilibrium again.

She knew how to handle herself with Prince Kadir al-Hassan, her boss. She had no real clue how to deal with Kadir the man. With him, she was completely out of her element. It was as though she'd been riding a pony tied to a lead line and now someone had stuck her on top of a racehorse and told her she was about to ride in the Kentucky Derby.

The only defense she had was the truth. "If you want me to be at my best, you really need to stop. We aren't at war, Kadir. There doesn't need to be a victor."

He snorted. "And what I am trying to tell you is that you have a rather warped idea about seduction. It's not a win-or-lose game."

Yet it was for her. At least where he was concerned.

Because if she ever crossed that line, if she ever slept with him, then her career at Hassan Construction was over. She couldn't slip back into her role as his PA if that happened. Not only that, but sleeping with him would make her the sort of woman she was determined not to be. Giving in to the sensual side of her nature with a man like Kadir? Utterly destructive.

Emily drew in a breath, tried to instill herself with calm energy rather than the chaotic emotions whipping through her. And then she figured out what was happening between them. The answer popped into her head with such clarity that she was surprised she hadn't realized it before.

Kadir wasn't serious. He was prodding her because she'd argued with him. He was taking the conversation as far as he could with the goal of shutting down her protests. She'd seen him do it in negotiations a hundred times. She'd seen him take the most unwilling land-owner and turn them into an enthusiastic seller by the end of the day.

He conquered people. And he was intent on conquering her, simply to prove he could. Not with sex or seduction, but with words.

Relieved, Emily smiled at him. "Whatever you say."

His gray eyes glittered hot as he seemed to go very still. "Is that an invitation, Emily?"

"Not at all. It's an admission you're right. That I have absolutely no idea what I'm talking about. I've misjudged you, and I apologize. I'm sure the women you seduce are perfectly, ecstatically happy right up until the moment you dump them. So can we please talk about something else now?"

"But I find this conversation so fascinating."

"Of course you do. It's about you." She studied her

newly manicured nails—that was something she had to get used to, since she kept them neat and trimmed and never wore polish. "You are, of course, fascinating and fabulous. But I give in, you are correct in everything you say, and now we can move on."

He leaned toward her then, and it took everything she had not to press herself into the door in an effort to keep distance between them.

"Sassing me isn't working, Emily. If anything, it's having the opposite effect of what you want."

Emily tried to laugh. It didn't come out sounding very much like a laugh, but she decided to pretend it was anyway. "I'm sure I don't know what you mean. I'm not aiming for any particular effect. I just refuse to argue with you another moment."

His gaze slid over her until she tingled as if he'd actually touched her. "Do I need to spell it out for you, *habibti?* Or would you like a demonstration?"

Emily swallowed. "It's all fun and games with you, isn't it?"

He actually looked offended. "You think this is a game?"

Her chest was tight. But that's because Kadir suddenly seemed bigger than life in the small space of the limo. It was like walking into a closet and finding a tiger on a very loose chain.

And this tiger was about to break the chain and pounce.

"What else could it be?" She had to force her voice to work, yet she still sounded wheezy, as if she'd sucked in too much air.

Dangerous. The word whispered through the air around her, caressed her skin, slipped between her ribs and into her chest to grip her heart. Kadir was very dangerous, and not in that usual impersonal way he was when she'd observed him taking down an opponent. This was deeply personal and very intense.

And it was all directed at her. Her tongue grew thick and her breath short.

He reached over and threaded his hand into the hair at her nape, very deliberately, and pulled her gently toward him. "What else indeed?"

CHAPTER SEVEN

"WE HAVE A deal!" Her voice came out as a squeak and Kadir stopped, his gray eyes darkening as he stared down at her. They were inches apart now, and she could feel the heat rolling from his body, the whisper of his breath across her lips.

Her heart slammed against her ribs and she started to see spots.

But Kadir let her go abruptly and she wilted back against the seat, sucking in a deep breath and trying not to shake. When she glanced over at him, he was looking out the window. Oddly, a wave of regret buffeted her.

The tension in his shoulders was evident and she found herself wanting to reach out and soothe him. Which was completely contrary to the way she'd just reacted. What was the matter with her? Why was she so damn hot and cold around him?

Because he was Kadir, that's why. Because she'd watched him seduce women for the past four years. She knew he was good at it—and she knew she couldn't be one of those women. She was afraid she would like it too much. She was afraid of losing control.

"Yes," he said, not turning around, his voice utterly cool. "We have a deal. And I will honor it."

She didn't know how he managed it, but he suddenly

made her feel as if she'd wronged him. Emily put a hand to her head. Everything was wrong. Backward. Upside-down. Why'd Lenore have to be so spectacularly stupid so quickly? If not for that little scene yesterday morn-ing, Emily would be riding along in the other car while Kadir and his new wife sat in this one. It wouldn't be her playing this role and trying so desperately not to get lost in it, but Lenore Bradford, a woman who'd al-ready been sleeping with Kadir and wouldn't act like a timid virgin whenever he made the slightest motion toward her.

And yet the thought of Lenore in Kadir's arms made Emily's stomach twist in a way it had not only yester-day. She didn't like Lenore, certainly. But she didn't care who Kadir slept with. She never had.

Really?

Emily gritted her teeth together. She did *not* care. Everything was backward and confusing, that's all. She did not want him, even though he seemed to have the ability to make her heart pump and her body ache in spite of her belief otherwise.

It was sensual deprivation, nothing more. She hadn't had sex in so long she'd forgotten what it was like.

Emily stared out her window for the remainder of the trip. Soon they were boarding Kadir's jet. It would take roughly six hours to reach Kyr, and Emily did not know what she was going to do with herself for the du-ration of the journey.

Always in the past, she had worked on something for Kadir. And then she ate and slept and worked some more, depending on the length of the flight. This time, she followed Kadir up the jet bridge and onto the plane with nothing more than a chic handbag and a magazine she'd picked up on their trip through the airport.

She felt…useless. Like a decoration instead of a professional career woman. She hated that feeling so much. It was contrary to everything she'd worked so hard for.

She also felt seriously out of place. Kadir's flight attendants—two women on this particular trip—stared at her with jaws hanging open when she walked into the cabin. She'd spent time chatting with them on previous trips, and though they'd treated her with a strange deference from Paris to Milan, this time they openly stared.

Emily felt the heat of a blush as she took her seat beside Kadir. It had been so long since she'd been the center of anyone's attention that it felt odd to be there now. She buckled herself in and closed her eyes. Beside her, she was acutely aware of Kadir as he settled in. The seats were big and roomy, with plenty of space, but she still felt as if she was too close to him. She could feel his heat, smell his scent—French-milled soap and man, no cologne for Kadir—and nothing she did could make it go away.

They were soon airborne, and one of the flight attendants came to serve drinks. Emily asked for mineral water, like always, and stared at the pages of the magazine without really seeing them.

"You haven't turned a page in twenty minutes."

She looked up, found Kadir watching her with those too-knowing eyes. "I'm thinking."

"I can imagine." He didn't sound especially friendly, but he didn't sound angry either. A good sign.

"I don't know what to expect in Kyr. You haven't told me anything."

"I don't know that anything I say can prepare you, Emily. I am a prince, and Kyr is my country. It's not the same as when we travel and I meet with clients. Outside of Kyr, I am a wealthy man with a title. In Kyr, I am royalty, with all the pomp that entails. Does this make sense to you?"

"I think so. You're telling me that the deference you receive outside Kyr is nothing like what you will experience once there."

A ghost of a smile crossed his mouth. *Sensual mouth, kissable mouth.* Emily tightened her grip on the water. She was not going to think of Kadir's mouth.

"I think you mean *we,* Emily. You are my princess."

"I'm beginning to think you've dragged me into something I'm not prepared for."

He inclined his head only slightly. "Perhaps I have. But I have no doubt you can handle it, my love."

She started to protest, to tell him not to say such things to her, but one of the attendants drifted by and she knew he'd used the endearment for her benefit.

She waited until the woman was out of earshot. "I think I need a raise. After, I mean."

"Maybe you do. But let us get through this first. There is still the chance we will fail, and then I will be the king of Kyr."

And she would be out of a job.

He looked at her hard and her pulse thumped. "We have to sell this, Emily. I need you to exude sexiness, and I need you to be passionate for me."

She wanted to fold her arms and glare at him. She settled for lifting her chin. "I'll do the best I can with what I have."

He sighed. "I did not mean to suggest you had to work at being sexy. You clearly do not—which interests me very much, by the way. Why did you hide this side of yourself from me?"

"I wasn't hiding anything. You're just blind unless a woman puts on a tight dress and makeup."

His eyes glittered. "Perhaps I am," he said without apology. "And now that you've got sexy down, I need you to be passionate. For me. Can you do that, Emily?"

Emily felt a rush of heat beneath her skin. "I said I'd try. I assume you don't want me to crawl beneath the table at dinner and minister to your needs?"

He looked shocked. And then he looked intense. She'd thrown it out there because she was irritated, but she now realized it had been the wrong thing to say. It put an image in her head—and most certainly in his—that was incredibly arousing.

"Perhaps you can save that for when we are alone." His voice was a low growl that stroked over her skin.

She waved a hand breezily, though her body sizzled with fresh heat. "I doubt that, but thank you for clearing it up. No public sex then."

"Another time."

He was silent for a long moment but she didn't dare to look at him. She didn't want to see what was going on in those eyes.

"There is something else you need to know," he said. "There will be those who are not happy I've married you, which was of course the goal. But do not be surprised if you are treated less than kindly by some."

Her stomach hollowed. "I should have asked for more money."

"Perhaps you should have. But it is too late now. We have a deal, remember?"

It was night when they arrived in Kyr, but two things struck Emily at once. First, when Kadir emerged from the back of the plane, where he'd gone shortly before they landed, he was wearing the white desert robes of his people and the dark headdress with the golden coils holding it in place. His face was all that was visible in the frame of the headdress, but it had a startling effect on her.

Emily swallowed, her mouth utterly dry. She had never seen Kadir in desert garb. His home base for the last four years had been Chicago, and they'd traveled the globe building his skyscrapers. But they'd never come to Kyr. Indeed, when she thought back on it, the few times he'd come to the Middle East at all had been during her time off. Always a quick trip, never anything he needed her for.

Oh, she'd seen his picture in native clothing before, certainly. She'd recognized that beautiful, aristocratic face and his piercing eyes scrutinizing her from the headdress.

But the real thing was a completely different experience. Kadir was tall and commanding and regal—and the desert robes made him seem even more so.

She felt underdressed and puny next to him. Panic set in. This was not going to work. No one in his or her right mind would believe Kadir had chosen her for his wife—plain Emily Bryant who cleaned up nicely but was nothing compared to the beautiful women he usually dated.

The second thing that struck her—aside from the heat of the night air—was the delegation waiting at the bottom of the stairs. Men garbed in desert robes, waiting as a group. She was accustomed to walking out of airports, discreetly following Kadir, while cameras flashed and popped into the air.

There were no cameras here. Only hard desert nomads. Emily chided herself the instant she thought it. Kyr had industry, and people did not live in tents on the edge of the harshest deserts. Some did, certainly, but most people had houses and apartments in the major cities. These were their traditional robes, but that did not make them nomads.

Kadir stood at the top of the stairs and spread his hands wide. He said something in Arabic to the gathered men. Emily stood off to the side, out of view of the men, but where she could see them from the open door.

Her heart throbbed and her palms were sweaty. Her beautiful plum dress felt like a sack now, and she wished for her comfortable shoes to walk down those stairs in. Her legs were shaking so much she didn't know how she'd manage it in high heels. Her hair was too thick and heavy, and she wished she could pull it up, off her neck and into her familiar ponytail.

She was lost in her thoughts, worrying her lower lip between her teeth, when Kadir stopped speaking. There was silence for a long moment, and then she looked up and realized he held out his hand to her.

"It's time," he said. "Are you ready for this, *habibti?*"

"Do I have a choice?" She'd wanted to sound brave and defiant, but her voice was barely more than a squeak.

The beauty of his smile hit her like a one-two punch. How had she never fully realized the power of Kadir? How had she spent four years with him and never seen *this?*

"It will be fine. You only have to appear to be madly in love with me. Just follow my lead."

Emily took a deep breath and put her hand in his. A current of electricity buzzed up her arm, into her heart, spread through her limbs until she was almost calm.

Appear madly in love with him? How could she do anything else but? How could any woman?

He pulled her to his side and wrapped an arm tight

around her. He was so close, so *right there,* and her pulse was doing crazy things in response. His smile was almost mocking.

He slid his free hand into her hair, cupped her nape like before. And this time, this time when he lowered his head, she did not stop him, though her heart knocked against her chest like a frightened rabbit. His mouth settled over hers and a shock rippled through her body, slid straight into her core and set up a throbbing response that craved his touch.

She made a noise—she knew she did—but what kind of noise she would never know. Because Kadir caressed the skin of her collarbone, glided his fingers up her throat, cupped her chin and tilted her head back.

And then his tongue slipped between her lips, stroked against her own—and she was lost.

He did not mean to kiss her quite like this. It was supposed to be a sweet kiss for the people observing them. A kiss to show he'd brought home a wife of whom he was enamored. To show he was serious.

A sweet kiss for his new wife. Not this incredibly hot, shocking, erotic tangling of tongues that had him ready to devour her. *This is Emily,* he reminded himself. *Emily.*

Yes, yes.

Emily. Something inside him responded as if it recognized her. Recognized the fit and feel of her mouth against his.

She was lush, his PA, and sweeter than he could have imagined possible. Something about her drove him perfectly insane with the kind of need he didn't recall feeling in ages—not since he'd been a young man learning his body and how it responded to a woman's touch.

She made him feel that eager, that green.

But no, that could not be right. He was thirty years old. He'd had his share of lovers over the years, but he was not jaded. Surely someone else had excited him this much. Had made him feel this, well, new.

He just couldn't recall it right this moment. And he had to cease this demonstration, before it turned into something that would embarrass them both. Already, he'd lost control of his ability to regulate his body's response.

Which was going to be quite obvious in another few seconds.

Reluctantly, he dragged his mouth from hers. Heard her intake of breath, her shocked gasp when she realized what had just happened. Her eyes fluttered open and for a moment he saw everything in them.

Lust, confusion, need, pain—so many emotions crossed those lovely eyes before she locked them down tight and pressed her lips together. Her fingers were still clutched in his robes. He thought she might let him go too quickly, might give away the game—but she didn't. Not Emily. No, she let him go softly, smoothed her fingers over his chest, her gaze dropping from his as she did so.

The shy, desperately-in-love bride. By Allah, he was proud of her for it, even if it wasn't quite the response he'd been looking for. He'd wanted her bolder and more passionate, but this first reaction was perfect.

She was amazing, his Emily. And beautiful. That had certainly been a surprise.

Guido's people had not turned her into someone else. They'd simply showcased the beautiful body she already had, highlighted her features—her cat's eyes and her lush chocolate hair. Not to mention those lips he'd just kissed. He'd never seen them in anything but a serious expression—maybe the occasional smile—but like this? Moist and swollen from the pressure of his mouth on hers? So enticing, like the sweetest honey?

How had he managed to ignore her charms for four years?

"Can you walk down the stairs?" he asked, because he had to say something. Something normal, regardless that his heart pounded in his chest and he could still feel the heat of that kiss down to his toes.

She glanced down the steep stairwell. "I'll do my best."

He took her hand in his, gripped it tight. "I'll hold you, Emily. I won't let you fall."

She smiled then, but it wavered at the corners, and he knew she was feeling overwhelmed. Guilt pierced him. He'd dragged her into this out of desperation, and now he wasn't sure it had been the right thing to do. Still, it was done, and he couldn't turn back now.

"I know you won't."

"Do you trust me?" he asked suddenly.

Because, he realized with a start, he wanted *something* about this to be real. He was back in Kyr after a long absence, and the father who'd filled his childhood with such confusing emotion was dying. The metaphorical ground—the ground he'd taken for granted, no doubt—was being ripped out from under him.

And he wanted something—someone—to hold on to. Something in his life that made sense. Just for now. Just this once.

She squeezed his hand. It was a light touch, tentative. But it was something. "I've trusted you for four years, Kadir. I'll trust you awhile longer."

He lifted her hand to his mouth, pressed a kiss to the

back of it without breaking eye contact. He didn't miss the shiver that rippled through her, or the answering shudder deep inside him.

The next few days in Kyr would be interesting indeed.

CHAPTER EIGHT

"THIS CANNOT BE happening," Emily muttered to herself as she turned around in the palatial room she'd been shown to. The floors and ceiling were tiled in the most beautiful gold-and-blue mosaic.

The walls were plain white, but the color wasn't stark in this setting. It was soothing and somewhat necessary after the ornateness of the tile. There was a living room with a sunken area that contained low-slung couches with lots of colorful cushions, and a television glided up from where it was hidden in a cabinet.

The bathroom was larger than her father's house in Chicago. There was a tub recessed into the floor and ringed with marble columns, and a shower tucked into one end of the room. There were also acres of mirrors and a dressing room that contained the clothing Kadir had bought for her in Milan.

But it was not *her* room. It was hers and Kadir's. They were sharing a room. Because that's what a husband and wife did.

How had she not seen this coming? Surely Kadir had known it—and he'd not warned her. Maybe he hadn't wanted her to freak out.

She thought back to that moment on the jet when he'd kissed her in front of everyone, and her body flooded

with a fresh wave of heat. She'd been utterly lost in his
embrace. She'd forgotten her name. Where she was.
What was happening.

She'd forgotten it was *an act*. And that horrified her.
Emily put her hands on her hot cheeks and breathed
deeply.

*He is Prince Kadir al-Hassan. He is a playboy.
You've worked for him for four years, and you've lost
count of the number of women he's woken up with.*

She sucked in another breath.

*No, you have not lost count. You never kept track!
Because you damn well don't care!*

That's right. She didn't care. He was Kadir, her boss,
and all she cared about was her paycheck. Which was
why she was doing this now. After the kiss on the plane,
they'd descended the stairs and stood on the red carpet on the tarmac while Kadir spoke endlessly with the
men waiting there.

They'd come up to him individually, bowed and then
spoke in low tones while he listened and nodded. She'd
felt so out of place, but she'd been unable to do anything
except stand at his side. Under normal circumstances,
she would have her notebook and be awaiting his orders.

But these were not normal circumstances—and her
feet had been beginning to hurt. It was night, thankfully, so at least the desert was not sweltering. After
what seemed to be an hour, they'd finally moved toward the limousine that awaited them. Kadir had set
her inside and then climbed in beside her. A palace official took up residence in the seat across from them,
notebook in hand, and spoke with Kadir all the way to
the royal palace in the center of the city.

At one point during the ride, when Emily was staring out the window at the city and the palm trees, Kadir

took her hand in his. She'd jumped and he'd squeezed lightly, as if warning her. She'd relaxed only a fraction, finally daring a look at his profile as he continued to speak to the man riding with them.

The beauty of Kadir stunned her in ways it had not only a day ago. She thought she'd been accustomed to how utterly stunning he was, inoculated even, but now that he touched her so sensually, she discovered she was not quite as immune as she'd always believed. He was getting under her skin and she did not like it.

For once, she was glad she didn't understand Arabic, because she would have been unable to concentrate on it anyway. Kadir's thumb rolled inside her palm, stroking softly. She felt as if he were stroking other, more sensitive places on her body. Every glide of his thumb set up an answering throb deep in the heart of her, until she was on edge and ready to jerk her hand from his grip regardless of their audience. Because, if she did not, she would melt against him and beg for more.

Thankfully, they'd arrived at the palace then. When they'd gotten out of the car, he'd hugged her close and kissed her forehead before giving her into the care of the servant who'd shown her to this room. She knew he'd only done it for their audience, but the touch of his mouth on her skin was disconcerting nevertheless. She'd been thinking about everything that had happened since she'd signed the marriage documents—and then the baggage had arrived. That was when she realized they were sharing a room.

Her anxiety levels had gone through the roof then.

She was still pacing and wondering how to fix this mistake when Kadir walked into the room. He looked… angry. That was a surprise. She blinked, but before she could say anything he speared her with a stormy look.

"You are upset with the sleeping arrangements, no doubt."

Emily drew in a breath. It suddenly didn't seem like the time. And yet he already knew what was bothering her. She gestured at the bed. "There is only one."

He stalked toward her, his expression not softening in the least. "Yes, because husbands usually sleep with their wives, even in Kyr." His gaze dropped over her body as he came to a halt. Her skin prickled with heat. "Perhaps especially in Kyr."

She tried not to let the sensual tone in his voice get to her.

"This isn't a public place, Kadir."

His eyes glittered hot. "No, it is not. But if I ask for another room, or another bed to be brought into this one, there will be questions. And I am not willing to answer those questions, *habibti*. It defeats the purpose of our agreement."

She turned her head to look at the bed. At least it wasn't small. Maybe if they put pillows down the center, it would work. It would *have* to work.

"Fine. But you stay on your side."

"If you insist."

She lifted her chin at the mocking note in his voice. "I hope you plan to wear more than you usually do."

One dark eyebrow arched. "I don't know, Emily. The desert is very hot. And one does not wear flannel pajamas to bed in Kyr."

Heat flared inside her at the thought of him naked. Beside her.

Oh, dear.

That simply could not happen. She'd seen him without clothing, yes—but not often and only briefly. The barest flash of male flesh before he robed himself.

This, however, was different. She drew herself up.

"Yes, but this is a palace, not the desert. And I saw a thermostat, which tells me there is air-conditioning. Turn it down and put on some clothes before you come to bed."

Kadir laughed, but the sound was low and sensual and her belly tightened into a knot. "I will consider it."

"You need to do more than consider it."

He looked amused, which was a nice change from when he'd entered the room. She wanted to ask him what was wrong, but she felt as if it would be prying to do so. She was still getting accustomed to this shift in their relationship, however temporary, and she didn't want to cross any deeply personal lines.

"Afraid of losing control, sweet Emily?"

"What? No!" She put her hands to her blazing cheeks and shook her head, her heart thumping in response. "You're outrageous, Kadir."

He walked over and took her wrists gently in his, pulled her hands away from her face. She felt as if she was going to hyperventilate, and he stood there so calm and in control that she almost envied him. Yes, damn him, control was precisely what she was afraid of losing.

Control of herself, of her needs and desires, of her reactions. Kadir had a way of making a woman *want* to lose control. She was beginning to realize how very dangerous he was to her sense of well-being.

He frowned down at her. "There is no need to panic. I won't do anything to make you uncomfortable, Emily."

"Then why did you say—"

"I like teasing you," he said softly. "You are quite emotional, as it turns out. I had no idea."

Emily fought her natural inclination to drop her gaze from his. Instead, she pulled in a deep breath and kept her chin up. "I'm sorry, but this is outside my comfort zone. I know what to do when I'm your PA. I don't know what to do as your wife...especially your fake wife."

He put his hands on her shoulders and rubbed. Another jolt of sensation shot from where he touched her straight down to her sex. She wanted to whimper with it. Had she ever reacted this way to another man? Or was she just so deprived of contact lately that her body was starved for it?

"Just follow my lead and it will all work out."

She closed her eyes for a moment. She was in over her head. She should have realized it before. "I don't like deceiving your family. I should have said no."

"Ah, but you want the money."

She bit her lip. She wanted to explain herself, but he wasn't looking for an explanation. He was stating a fact. And mentioning her father's health issues would only distract attention from Kadir's problems right now.

"I do."

His hands dropped away from her shoulders and disappointment bit into her. He turned away and removed the flowing headdress. His dark hair was a sensual shock to her system, though she'd seen it a million times before. But there was something about the *kaffi-yeh* and its removal that set up a drumbeat in her veins.

Kadir was thankfully oblivious as he set the fabric down and then continued into the outer suite where the seating area was. Once there, he collapsed onto one of the sofas and tilted his head back, his eyes closing. He looked troubled now, no longer angry or amused.

Emily's heart went out to him and she berated herself for being so insensitive. Of course he was troubled. His father was dying and she'd been going on about the sleeping arrangements like a timid virgin.

She walked over and perched on a chair nearby. She didn't know what to say, or if he'd even welcome her presence, but she had a need to be near him. His eyes opened again, a question in them.

"I didn't ask about your father," she blurted.

He shrugged, but she didn't miss the tension vibrating from him. "He is dying. He's frail, weak and shockingly wasted away from the man he was the last time I saw him."

"I'm sorry, Kadir."

"This is the way life is, *habibti*."

Yes, she certainly knew that. She thought of her father and the tense months while they'd waited for a donor heart. "Still, it cannot be easy for you."

His eyes glittered hotly. Angrily. "No, it isn't."

She licked her lips and ran her palms over her thighs. She was out of her depth here, trying to be friendly with the boss she'd only ever been professional with. Trying to be his wife and his companion and an understanding ear all at the same time.

All while worrying about her own problems. What was the matter with her? She did not need to burden Kadir with her own fears. He'd hired her for a job, she'd agreed, and she had no right to question the sanity of the arrangement now.

"If you want to talk—"

"I don't." His voice was firm, final.

Emily swallowed. She knew when he was dismissing her. She'd heard it a thousand times before, though it had never seemed so personal as it did right now. She got to her feet because it seemed the only thing she could do. "Well, then, I think I'll get ready for bed."

"Fine."

She started toward the bathroom, her ears burning

hot. How could she let him think she was such a self-ish creature? How could she be so insensitive to his plight? She stopped and spun around again, her pulse beating a hot rhythm in her veins. "I'm sorry for complaining about the sleeping arrangements. I was just surprised by it."

He shrugged. "It is understandable. We did not discuss it prior to arriving."

He was too polite about it.

"But it's hardly something you should be thinking about right now. I should have been more sensitive."

His gaze was so intense she wanted to drop her eyes. She did not. "If you really want to give me something else to think about, invite me into the shower with you."

Emily swallowed hard. And then a thread of anger unwound inside her belly. She tried to be nice and he taunted her. Dismissed her apology as if it were nothing.

Which was his right, she decided. So she bit her tongue and gave him a regretful smile.

"I'm sorry, but I always shower alone. It's a rule of mine."

"Pity," he drawled.

Kadir went outside onto the balcony while Emily was in the shower and stood in the darkness for a long while. He'd gone to see his father, and he could still feel the shock of that moment when he'd beheld the once-strong king reduced to little more than a gaunt skeleton in an oversize bed.

His father had not smiled when he spoke, but then Kadir had not expected him to. King Zaid had never made it a secret that both his sons had become disappointments to him. Kadir less so than Rashid, but a disappointment nevertheless.

"I hear you have brought a woman with you," King Zaid had said, his voice stronger than Kadir would have thought possible.

"I brought my wife."

His father made a dismissive noise. "You have defied me, Kadir."

"I am in love, Father. I cannot live without her." A lie, but a necessary one.

"I see." King Zaid closed his eyes and swallowed. "I never thought you would disrespect my wishes as your brother has so often done. I thought you were the good son."

Kadir wanted to lash out, wanted to tell the old king that both his sons were good sons—but that he was too hard and proud and blind to realize it.

"A man will do things for love that he would not otherwise do." He should feel guilty for lying, but strangely he did not. "Besides, I've told you many times before that I often blamed Rashid for things I had done."

His father waved a weak hand as if annoyed. What Zaid did not want to hear, he did not hear. One of the reasons why his sons had left Kyr long ago.

"The succession is not decided," King Zaid rasped. "There is time for you to renounce this woman and take your place as king."

Kadir felt the chill of that pronouncement like a dip into an arctic pool. "I am not prepared to do so."

"And if I were to order it?"

"Choose Rashid, Father. He is the right man for the job."

His father spat—and then he began to cough. Kadir stepped forward, alarmed, but the nurse who sat nearby was there instead, offering King Zaid a glass of water and straightening his pillows.

"Leave me," his father said when he could speak again. Kadir had stalked out, furious with the stubbornness of his father and brother both. And perhaps even with himself. He should just go to the council and announce he was not going to accept the throne even if the king chose him, but he wanted very much for his father to make a different choice. A conscious choice.

Kadir wanted the king to pick Rashid, which would be the best choice for Kyr, and then he might feel as if he'd finally done something right by his brother. As if he'd righted the wrongs of their childhood in the palace. Perhaps the things he'd done were not so extreme when viewed through the lens of boyhood—but they felt like crimes against his own flesh. In seeking his father's approval, he'd actively encouraged the king's barely suppressed frustration with Rashid.

And Rashid had been too proud to fight back, which only exacerbated the situation.

After the meeting with his father, Kadir had returned to his room and found Emily fretting over the sleeping arrangements. She'd seemed so ordinary and normal that it had been everything he could do not to drag her into his arms and just hold her close. But she would not have understood, so he had not done it.

The night air whipped up from the sea, ruffling his hair, but it was not quite cool enough to dampen his heightened senses. He remembered their arrival on Kyrian soil. He could still feel Emily in his arms, still taste that kiss as they'd stood in the doorway to the plane. He wanted her with a sharpness that was uncharacteristic of him, and he didn't know why.

Kadir swore softly. He should not be thinking about this. How was he going to lie in a bed with her and not touch her? He was growing hard just thinking about it.

He told himself it was the stress of the current situation making him want her. Rewind the clock a day, and she would still be his PA, dressed in her stark suits and ugly shoes, and he would be none the wiser about what kind of woman lay beneath the professional polish.

He stood for a long time in the night air, until he was chilled and tired, and then he turned and went inside. The lights were dim and the room quiet. He shed the *dishdasha* he wore and padded over to the bed in his underwear. Emily lay on her side, as far from his side of the bed as possible. She was a small lump under the covers. Her hair, he was shocked to realize, was braided. He'd pictured it free, streaming over the sheets, but she'd very sensibly confined it.

Of course she had.

She had also lined the center of the bed with pillows. He didn't know whether to laugh or be offended. In the end, he flipped the sheets back and slid into the bed. And then he lay with his arms behind his head, staring up at the ceiling while his body continued to burn with inappropriate thoughts of her.

He did not know how long he'd lain there when she turned over.

"Are you okay?" Her voice was rough with sleep.

"Define *okay*."

"You've had a shock tonight. You must be feeling so many things."

"I am." Because what else could he say?

She sighed. "I know something about how it feels to get devastating news, and I know it can be hard to make sense of it."

"Do you?" He did not think she could possibly understand how he felt right now. Angry, frustrated, guilty, resigned.

"My father had a heart transplant five years ago. We weren't sure he would make it."

Kadir turned toward her. Out of everything he'd imagined her saying, this had not even made the top ten. How had she worked for him all this time and he'd never known this most important of things? She had never once mentioned it.

In fact, she never talked about anything personal. He realized, lying there in bed with her, a pile of pillows between them, that everything he knew about her was from observation and reading her personnel file. She was the person who was the closest to him on a day-to-day basis, who knew all his business secrets, and he didn't know her at all. It was a stunning realization.

"You never told me this before."

He could feel her shrug more than see it. "It was personal. And we don't exactly do personal chitchat, do we?"

"It would seem not. And yet I wish I had known."

"It's not a secret or anything, but it's not the kind of thing you just up and say either. There never was an appropriate moment to mention it before."

"And is he well now?"

"Well enough, yes. But I really wasn't trying to make this about me." She sighed. "I feel like I'm doing everything wrong. I just wanted you to know I understand how difficult this must be for you. I've done a poor job of that so far."

It was difficult, but not for the reasons she might imagine. Of course a part of him was upset that his father was dying. But their relationship had fractured so long ago that his father almost felt like a distant relative to him. He cared, but it wasn't going to devastate him when the inevitable happened.

No, the most difficult part for him now was in making sure he righted the wrongs he'd done to Rashid. Which his father seemed determined not to allow. He could walk away, certainly. But he wanted his father to choose Rashid because it was right.

How could he explain any of that to her? She'd asked him earlier if he wanted to talk. But what would he say? How could he begin to talk about such deeply personal things with anyone?

"You are close to your father?" he asked.

She hesitated for a moment, as if trying to figure out what he wanted from her. Or maybe she was just confused by the randomness of the question. "Yes."

Kadir let out a breath and rolled back until he was looking up at the ceiling again. There was something about lying in the dark with another person that made him want to confess his secrets. Not all of them, of course.

"I am not close to mine." It was a relief to say it, and yet he also felt as if he was admitting what a terrible son he was. She didn't say anything and he felt a coolness sweep over him. Followed by a needle of pain in his chest. This was why he did not engage in personal confessions with anyone. "You are shocked."

"No," she said in a rush. "Just sad for you."

Now he was the one who was shocked. He couldn't recall any of the women of his acquaintance feeling emotional *for* him. Over him, yes. But this was a novelty and he wasn't quite sure how to respond. "I have made my peace with this long ago. Not all relationships are perfect."

"No. In fact, I'd say none are. But some are better than others."

He wondered at the note of sadness in her voice. He

didn't think it was all for him. Still, he felt the need to lighten things up between them. Before he began spilling things he was not willing to share with anyone. Things that would reveal how damaged he truly was. "This is true. Take us, for example."

"Us?" She sounded surprised and he almost laughed.

"Yes, us. As my assistant, you are the perfect combination of competent and familiar."

She huffed. "But as your wife, I suck."

"I would not have put it quite that way. But no, you have not been very good at it thus far. Which I fail to understand. You are so good at being my assistant that I would have thought pretending to be my wife would come easy. Because you already know me."

"Maybe that's the problem," she grumbled. "I know you too well."

"And what does this mean?"

He heard the covers rustling and then she was sitting up, facing him. "Seriously?"

"Yes, seriously."

She made a noise that might have been disbelief. Or frustration. "I've witnessed far too many mornings after with you. I've escorted women to the door while you turn over and go back to sleep. And let's not forget Lenore and the scene with her—when was that? Just two days ago! It's hard to pretend to be the woman besotted with you when I know how that works out for so many of them. You humiliate them, Kadir. And then you forget them as soon as they're gone!"

Her words surprised him. No, he felt nothing for any of them. But he had not set out to hurt anyone. "You think I humiliate them?"

"Maybe you don't mean to," she said, her voice softer now. "But I think so."

He thought he should be offended, but mostly he was just weary. "And I think they know what they're getting with me. I make no secrets about what I want, Emily. I don't pretend to feelings I do not have."

"Then I think they don't hear that part. Or they hope they'll be the one to change your mind. Because they certainly seem shocked when it's over."

"And how is this my fault?"

She picked up one of the pillows and hugged it to her. "I don't know. I just feel badly for them. *Most* of them," she amended. He thought she might have punched the pillow. "Dammit, Kadir, I hate when you make sense. It's because I'm tired. Tomorrow, I'll think up the perfect answer to your question."

"Perhaps you will. But I doubt it. I'm not cruel, Emily. I never make promises. Any woman who gets involved with me knows that a long-term relationship is not on the menu."

He always made that clear, and yet he knew they didn't always believe it.

She lay down again and he heard her yawn. "I'm sure you're right. Poor things."

He wanted to keep talking, but he didn't know what else to say. Soon, her breathing deepened and he knew she was asleep. He was alone, as always, with his thoughts.

Or maybe he was just alone.

CHAPTER NINE

EMILY SLEPT LIKE the dead. And then she awoke as sunlight filtered through the shutters and crept across the bed to caress her face. She was warm and content. And for a moment at least, uncertain where she was. It wasn't unusual to wake up disoriented when working for Prince Kadir al-Hassan. You could be in Paris today, Hong Kong tomorrow and Sydney the next day.

But she knew she wasn't in any of those places. And she knew something was different about this trip. It hit her simultaneously that two things were unusual. First, she was no longer Kadir's PA and she didn't have to leap out of bed and tend to his breakfast before waking him.

Second, there was a warm body pressing into hers and an arm slung over her waist. That was not at all correct. She hadn't been in the same bed with another human being in a very long time—unless she'd gotten drunk last night and picked up a stranger. She turned her head slowly, her heart beginning to pump harder. Because she knew the truth before her gaze landed on the face of the man whose body was curled around hers.

Kadir.

Emily's heart rocketed. She barely managed not to squeal. Her fingers wrapped around his hand and she started to lift it so she could slide out from under his grip. But his eyes snapped open and she found herself staring into his clear gray gaze.

He moved slightly and she felt the hard press of his erection against her bottom. Emily gasped as blood flooded her cheeks. It was followed by an answering wetness in her feminine core that both shocked and dismayed her.

"Salaam, habibti."

"You crossed the line," she accused. "You promised you wouldn't."

One of his eyebrows arched. "Did I?" He lifted his head to peek over her body. And then he lay on the pillow again. "I believe you need to look to your left."

Emily did so—and felt the burn of embarrassment grow even hotter than it already was. The pillow line was still there and she was facing it. Kadir had not crossed her barrier; she had.

"I must have been cold," she sniffed. "You turned the air-conditioning up so high."

"Because you told me to, if you will recall."

She tried to move away, but his arm tightened slightly. "Kadir—"

"You have to admit it feels nice to wake beside someone. Comforting." He put his nose against her neck and breathed.

Her pulse beat hard and fast. Emily closed her eyes and swallowed. "That's beside the point."

"So you admit it feels nice?" His voice was a soft rumble in her ear. And her body was snapping with sparks that scared her.

"I didn't say that." Not precisely, anyway. She moved against him, trying to pull away—and nearly groaned as his erection pressed into her again. What would it be like to just turn around in his arms and...?

No! She couldn't think like that. She could not, for one moment, allow that kind of breach in her personal code to happen. She tugged again...

And this time he let her go. She slipped across the sheets until she was back on her side of the pillows. Her heart thrummed as she sat up and tried to fake nonchalance.

"You do realize that's an effect of morning, yes?"

She turned to look down at him. He lay against the white sheets, his body dark and perfect. The covers were pushed down to his waist and his chest was gloriously bare. All those rock-hard muscles. And that damn arrow of hair dipping beneath his belly button.

She knew what lay down there and she experienced a pang of longing as she thought of him sliding the covers down the rest of the way, of her pressing her mouth to his abdomen and tugging off his briefs...

"What?" she asked after a long second in which she couldn't remember what he'd said.

"The erection. An effect of morning. And your shapely bottom wedged against me, I imagine."

Emily closed her eyes for a second and tried to get her racing heart under control. "You say the most outrageous things."

"Do I?" He wasn't smiling but she got the impression he was grinning at her anyway. "And here I thought I was being honest."

Emily pushed her braid back over her shoulder. "All right, you were being honest. And I'm sorry I crossed the pillows. I can only imagine I got cold. And I'm not used to sleeping with anyone else, so..."

She realized what she was saying—babbling, really—and ran out of words. Kadir's gaze gleamed.

"This is a shame, Emily. A woman as lovely as you shouldn't spend her nights alone."

"You are *such* a player."

He looked at her quizzically. "A player?"

His English was so good that she sometimes forgot he wasn't always conversant with all the idioms. "It means you're good at getting women to slip into bed with you. And that it happens often. Flattery is no doubt one of the tools in your arsenal."

"Ah. But you are already in bed with me. Why would I need to flatter you?"

"Don't be obtuse, Kadir. You know what I mean." Emily folded her arms over her chest, suddenly aware of her nipples pressing against the thin cotton of the tank top she'd worn to bed.

Kadir whipped the sheets back then and stood. Emily's mouth went utterly dry. He was tall, golden and perfectly formed. He was wearing the barest of black briefs—and they were stretched out in the front by an impressive erection. Oh, it was so unfair that he was so beautiful. And that she wanted him.

Emily licked her lips automatically and Kadir's gaze sharpened. She dropped her eyes and pretended to be unaffected. But her pulse was hammering so hard in her throat she was certain he must know.

Dammit. She'd been so careful—so *careful*—to keep Kadir compartmentalized in her head in the category of *boss: off-limits* that to suddenly realize he was no longer there was a shock. He'd moved into another compartment and she couldn't seem to move him back. This one was labeled *sexy male: need immediately*.

Emily closed her eyes and took a deep breath. Okay, this was a setback. But she could deal with it. She *would* deal with it. There was no other choice.

"I do know what you mean, Emily. But I like teasing you." She glanced at him and saw he'd tilted his head to watch her. "Your skin is the most interesting shade of pink right now."

Emily wanted to drag the covers over her head. "It's the sunlight coming into the room. And all this gold on the ceiling."

It was a lousy excuse, but hey, she wasn't going to admit she was thinking about him naked—about her wrapped around him naked—was she? Nooooo, not happening.

"Of course it is," Kadir said. He laughed softly as he went into the bathroom. Naturally, he did not close the door and she could hear the water falling against the tiles as he started the shower. She imagined Kadir sliding those briefs down his thighs and stepping under the spray.

Her sex throbbed with heat and need and she closed her eyes, forcing herself to take slow, deep breaths. It was only the second day of their sham marriage.

And already her purpose grew muddled and her will teetered on shaky ground.

Emily showered and dressed in the least sexy dress she could find in her wardrobe—which, she had to admit, didn't mean much. This dress had a square neck that didn't show any cleavage and a swirly skirt that flared out thanks to a tulle underskirt. But it was still form-fitting through the bosom and it hugged her curves like Kadir had this morning. Emily forced that thought from her mind as she stood in front of the mirror and surveyed the outfit.

The dress was chic and lovely, a vibrant turquoise, and she paired it with the lowest heels she could find in the closet. They were perhaps four inches high and nude. Not much lower, but somewhat easier to walk in than yesterday's snakeskin platforms.

"Not quite as sexy as I'd hoped, but still very unsuitable."

Emily spun to find Kadir in the door to the dressing room. He was dressed in traditional robes—a *dishdasha*—and the dark *kaffiyeh* of Kyr. Golden ropes—the *igal*—held the headdress in place. He looked every inch a sheikh, and so very unlike the boss she was accustomed to. There was something almost primitive about him now, though she chided herself for thinking so. Clothing did not change a man. This was his culture, not a costume donned for effect.

And yet it was having an effect on her.

She smoothed her fingers over the silk of her dress. "I like this dress."

"As do I. You look lovely, though you will certainly elicit disapproval from the old guard for being so vibrantly female."

Her heart skipped a beat. "You said *some* people would not approve of me. I hope you aren't setting me up for a huge breach of decorum so that every single person in Kyr will despise me."

He frowned. "I would do no such thing, Emily. You are still my wife. Your unsuitability rests primarily on your not being Kyrian. But yes, there will be those who are shocked by your clothing, your passion for me and your bright inner fire. They are the ones who will not approve." He came toward her then, and she realized he was holding a velvet box in his hand. "You are missing some things," he told her as he opened the box and set it on the table beside her.

Emily gasped at the sparkling diamonds nestled

against the black velvet. Her gaze lifted to Kadir's. "I can't wear those."

He frowned. "Of course you can. You will wear them." He took the diamond-and-platinum necklace and fitted it around her throat. She turned so he could clasp it, her heart beating wildly in her chest as his fingers skimmed the bare skin of her neck. The necklace fit close to her throat but it was only when she turned around that she realized it was a collar. And it glittered as though someone had turned on Christmas lights.

"This is too much, Kadir."

"Not for my wife it isn't." He ruthlessly went about clasping on a matching bracelet. And then he handed her a pair of diamond drop earrings that she fitted into her ears with shaking hands.

"Won't I look a bit gaudy for daytime?"

His eyes roved over her. "Not at all. You will look amazingly beautiful."

She glanced down at the bracelet—a sizable platinum-and-diamond concoction that caught the light and sparkled as crazily as the necklace—and realized what was missing. A wedding ring. Unless, maybe, they didn't wear them in Kyr?

As if he knew what she was thinking, Kadir produced another box from somewhere. A smaller box. This one he opened away from her. And then he set it aside and lifted her left hand. When he slid the giant diamond on her finger, she actually felt light-headed.

"This is insane. Someone will bash me over the head and take this stuff. And then you'll be right back where you started."

He laughed softly. "You are a princess of Kyr, Emily. No one is going to bash you over the head."

She shivered as she stared at the ring. It was lovely,

but a bit more ostentatious than she was accustomed to. The thought hit her that it was something her mother would have loved. And that was not a pleasant thought.

"I don't like this, Kadir. It feels…wrong somehow."

He took her by the shoulders and held her firmly. His eyes bored into hers. He was so very handsome, so commanding, and she felt herself melting beneath those eyes. "It's just a few days, *habibti*. You can do it. You may even have fun."

His head descended and she closed her eyes. When his mouth brushed over hers, she nearly swayed into him. Instead, she put her hand against his chest, though she wasn't sure whether it was to stop him—or to stop herself from leaning in closer.

The kiss was brief, an intense meeting of tongues that both shocked and aroused her, and then he pulled away and she found herself looking up into glittering eyes that had darkened several degrees. "For luck," he said.

Emily blinked. "We are alone," she answered almost breathlessly.

"I am aware of this."

"You kissed me. That's not part of the agreement."

He lifted an eyebrow imperiously and she realized that while he might not technically be her boss any longer, he was still a sheikh. And a prince. How many people argued with a prince?

His fingers ghosted over her cheek before dropping away. "You still don't quite understand. We are in Kyr, *habibti*. And you are my lawful wife. My property to do with as I wish."

Emily trembled deep inside. Because, for a moment, she wondered what it would be like for him to do whatever he wished. But she couldn't let him think she was growing soft. She drew herself up.

"I very much doubt an unsuitable wife is your property. If she were, she might be more suitable, yes?" Feeling a moment of inspiration, she lifted her hand and ran her fingers along his hard jaw. His eyes darkened and her breath caught in her lungs. "I own *you*, Kadir. This is why you brought me here. I own you, and your father will not approve."

He didn't say anything and her heart pounded while she waited for him to react. She couldn't tell what thoughts were crossing that brilliant mind of his. But then he laughed and relief washed through her.

"Touché, Emily." He took her hand and drew her to his side. "I believe you are ready now."

He led her out of the room and down a long hallway where servants scurried to and fro. He didn't walk too fast, for which she was thankful since he'd stripped her of her sensible shoes, and she found herself peering into ornate room after ornate room as they strode by.

The royal palace of Kyr was filled with priceless objects—marble and gold statues, intricately carved furniture, paintings, tapestries, and the most colorful rugs she'd ever seen. Some of them were huge and must have taken many years to weave. She knew enough about Oriental carpets to know they were not made on machines. Hundreds of women would have labored for many hours a day on the works of art gracing the palace floors.

Outside the soaring windows, the sky was a blazing, clear blue. The horizon shimmered with heat and the brown mountains in the distance appeared to wobble at their bases. Emily could see tall palm trees and a camel train plodding along. It was starkly different from any-where else she'd been with Kadir thus far.

But it had a compelling beauty of its own and she wondered at Kadir's seeming discomfort about re-turning to Kyr. Had his life in the palace been lonely? Harsh? Or maybe it was just boring and he much pre-ferred his life now.

She found herself suddenly wanting to know more about him, about who he'd been as a child and why he seemed so intent on presenting his father and the royal court with a bride of whom they would not approve. Because if she knew anything at all about him, it was that he was brilliant and capable. He would handle in-heriting a throne with the grace and skill with which he handled every business encounter she'd ever seen him in. Kadir was a born leader.

But Kadir wasn't going to give her a chance to ask any questions just now. Instead, he steered her into a giant room filled with milling people—who instantly stopped what they were doing and sank to their knees as a man in a uniform bellowed something. She would have gasped at the sight if not for Kadir giving her a warning look.

It was extraordinary to see so many people drop so quickly, to hear the rustling of their clothing and the hush that spread over the room. Emily's belly clenched tight as Kadir said something in Arabic. A second later, people rose, their gazes landing on her.

"Keep your chin up," Kadir murmured, tucking her arm into his and anchoring her to his side.

"What is this?" she whispered back as panic began to unwind inside her.

"The daily audience. My father cannot attend, of course, and he's asked me to do so in his stead."

"Audience? Does this mean you have to sit somewhere and receive them one by one?"

"No. This is a formality. Their petitions to the throne are filtered through the functionaries and addressed by the king and council in session. Rarely, one of them receives a private audience. This is merely for appearances."

Appearances. Emily gazed out over the crowd and felt her heart thrumming against her chest. Not because she wasn't accustomed to attending large gatherings with Kadir, though she was usually standing behind him with a notebook and pen, but because she was so visible. And garnering more than a few stares.

"I don't think they like me," she muttered.

Kadir smiled. Somehow, it seemed as if it was for her alone. She told herself it was just a part of the mirage.

"That is the plan, is it not?" He squeezed her hand. "Now come, let us mingle. And don't forget to hang on my every word."

"Except I won't understand a thing you say," she grumbled.

He dipped his head toward hers, his breath whispering against her ear. "Then you can gaze at me lovingly instead." His lips skimmed her cheek and sensation streaked down to her sex. It was shocking and alarming at once. If they weren't in public, she would…

Emily blinked. No, she wouldn't. She wouldn't do a damn thing.

She forced herself to smile up at him, aware they were the center of attention. "I'll do my best, Your Highness."

He stopped his forward motion and gazed down at her, his brows drawing together. "Your Highness? I thought we had an understanding."

She stood on tiptoe—odd to have to do that in heels, but there it was—and whispered in his ear. "Just reminding myself what's really happening here. You are the prince. I'm the hoochie mama."

He shook his head. "And here I thought I understood English. What is this hoochie thing, Emily?"

She could almost laugh at his confusion. Except the words hurt. She didn't know why she'd said them in the first place, or why it stung so much—no, that wasn't true. She did know. They made her think of her mother. Of what others had said about her mother when she'd run away with her lover.

Emily gave him a bright smile to hide her discomfort.

His eyes flashed hot. "You are not a hoochie mama. Or a whore, if I understand the meaning correctly."

She could feel tears pricking at the backs of her eyes. She should not be surprised he'd understood. "It was just a joke, Kadir."

His expression was fierce. "I won't allow you to make jokes like that. Not about yourself. Not when it upsets you."

She hadn't expected him to be so perceptive. Her impression of Kadir did not include sensitivity—or a desire to protect her. Once more, she had to revise her opinion of him. Her heart throbbed. "It's nothing. Forget I said it."

He tipped her chin up with a finger. Beyond him, she could see the people milling about almost impatiently. But Kadir didn't seem to care as he focused the power of his gaze upon her. He still looked fierce, and her heart swelled with feeling.

"You are my wife. A princess. You are beautiful and valuable. Don't forget it."

Emily throat was tight. "I won't."

But as Kadir led her into the crowd, his hand tight on hers, all she could think was that this was an act between them. A performance. That was what she couldn't forget. He did not mean to make her heart pound or her emotions roil with his intensity. He simply did it because that's what he always did to women. He conquered with words, with looks, with touches.

She could not allow herself to be conquered.

Emily decided to throw herself into her role as Kadir began to speak with different people. She would not fail him. She stayed by his side, smiling at people and chatting to those who spoke to her in English. Some people seemed uncertain what to think of her, but some of the women were openly curious and made no efforts to hide it.

Emily was relieved she was not the only woman in Western clothing or the only one wearing jewels. Some of the Kyrian women dressed in jeweled *abayas;* some covered their hair, and some did not. They were friendly and polite and she found herself interested in them and they in her. She did not sense that they disapproved of her or despised her. In fact, many of them seemed to enjoy talking with her.

Eventually, however, as the afternoon wore on, she and Kadir were surrounded by several older, serious-looking men who seemed content to pretend she did not exist. Emily frowned and tried not to concentrate on how much her feet were starting to hurt or how much she missed her low heels.

All she wanted was to sit down, but Kadir showed no signs of slowing. The men ignored her completely. After the warmth of the women, it made her feel unwelcome—and uncharitable. When she could take it no more, she put her hand in Kadir's to get his attention.

He stopped speaking instantly and turned to gaze down at her, a question in his eyes. If she were Lenore, she would have pouted and stuck out her lip, but Emily couldn't bring herself to behave that way. She was a good girl, not a self-centered drama queen.

Still, he expected her to be unsuitable. So she would do her best, especially as this small audience seemed tailor-made for such a performance.

"I'm bored, Kadir."

She could feel the men's gazes hardening and she knew they understood English perfectly well. Kadir's dark brows drew down. She wasn't sure if he was amused or irritated at her little outburst.

"And what would you prefer to do, my love?"

Emily's heart throbbed as she stepped closer to him and trailed a finger up his arm. "I think you know, darling."

This time an eyebrow arched. "Do I? Perhaps you should tell me what you want."

She stood on tiptoe and put her lips against his cheek. It was naughty and exhilarating and she liked it far too much. "I suppose I should say I want you desperately, but those awful men can't hear me now so I'll just say that my feet hurt and I'm tired of feeling shut out of this conversation."

He caught her around the waist and dipped his head to her ear. A shiver ran down her spine when his breath caressed the shell of her ear. "I wish you really did want me desperately. Because I'd love to strip you, Emily. Strip you and lick you from head to toe."

She almost backed away from him. Except that would give away the game and she couldn't do it. Not only that, but she didn't *want* to do it. She liked the way it felt to have him so close. Her sex flooded with wetness as a thrill shot through her, filling her with heat.

"You're a bad man, Kadir."

His voice came out as a growl. "You have no idea, Emily. No idea."

"Oh, I think I do. Just not from inside information, so to speak."

He nipped her ear and she gasped. Her body throbbed.

"The moment you want that *inside* information, I'm yours. Now go, before I do something the likes of which will scandalize Kyr for the next fifty years."

Emily backed away slowly as his hands slid from her body. She stood there for a long moment looking at him, and he at her, her body aching in ways she'd forgotten. His eyes blazed and part of her, the part that sparked and burned, suddenly wanted to catch his hand and lead him away with her.

"Emily?"

His voice was filled with promise—and with just enough of a question to break the spell. What was she doing standing here and staring at him as though he was the last glass of water in the desert?

Emily turned and fled. When she reached their room, she went into the bathroom to lean over the sink and splash her face with cold water. If she didn't cool this fire raging inside her, there was no telling what she might do when Kadir turned up again.

CHAPTER TEN

KADIR THREW THE phone down in disgust. He'd called
Rashid again, and again Rashid had not answered. It
was five days since they'd arrived in Kyr, and there was
no sign of his brother. What was Rashid doing? Had he
changed his mind about coming? Was he just going to
let the throne go without a fight, or was he making a
statement by taking his time?

If Rashid did not arrive soon, it would be too late.
Their father was growing weaker by the hour. And more
insistent that Kadir divorce Emily and take the throne.
Kadir was furious and frustrated. But he had to acknowledge that perhaps he was well and truly trapped.
If Rashid no longer wanted to be king, if he'd decided
he was finished with their father, with Kyr and even
with Kadir himself, there was nothing Kadir could do
but accept the responsibility.

His deception had only been meant to steer his father toward Rashid as the logical choice, but if Rashid
did not come, there was no choice. Kyr could not go un-
governed by an al-Hassan. They had been this nation's
leaders for centuries. And Kadir would not allow it to
change, though his life would transform so drastically.
To walk away now would plunge Kyr into chaos because
there was no one else who could lead. No one but the

council, and it would fracture as each member tried to put forth his own candidate for the throne.

No, Kadir would not allow that, though it would mean the end of everything he'd worked for. And the end of his time with Emily.

Emily. Just thinking of her made him as restless as a caged leopard.

Quite simply, Kadir was going mad with desire for his fake wife. He'd spent the last few days getting hard at the sight of her. And many nights going to bed frustrated. After that first night, he'd stuck to his side of the pillow wall and she to hers, but it was sheer torture. He lay there willing her to come across the barrier since he'd sworn he wouldn't do so, but she never did.

His days were so busy now that he hardly saw her, except at functions they attended together. He was beginning to regret the impulse to dress her in beautiful, fitted clothing. It not only made him physically uncomfortable, but it also made him angry as hell when he caught some other man staring at her.

Her clothes were fashionable, not at all trashy or—what had she said?—something a hoochie mama would wear. It shamed him that she had thought he wanted such a thing for even a moment.

The clothing Guido chose for her showcased her figure in ways that had Kadir imagining his hands on her. On the high swells of her breasts, the delicate curve of her waist, the arch of her hips. Hell, even her bare calves, accentuated by the high heels he'd insisted she wear, inflamed him.

What had he been thinking? He shoved a hand through his hair in frustration. Clearly, he had not. Or he'd thought he was made of sterner stuff where she was concerned. Idiot.

Though it had been only a few minutes since he'd tried to call Rashid, Kadir snatched up his phone and checked his messages, the same as he'd been doing all day.

Of course there was nothing. If Rashid wanted to punish him, he'd picked the perfect way to do it.

"Kadir?"

He turned at the sound of Emily's voice. She stood in the door to the private courtyard off their suite of rooms, where he had retreated to call Rashid. His blood beat at the sight of her. She was wearing a body-hugging black dress, her breasts wedged firm and high in the bodice, her dark hair loose, his diamonds sparkling at her throat and ears. He glanced at her hand, felt a current of possessiveness wash through him at the sight of his ring on her finger.

It wasn't real, he reminded himself. And yet it was the most real thing in his life right now. *Emily* was the most real thing in his life.

He tamped down on his wayward desire and leveled her with an even look so she would not sense his turmoil. "Yes, *habibti?*"

She twisted her fingers together in front of her. He was learning that Emily contained depths of emotion he'd never suspected. And part of how she kept it in check was with her nervous fidgeting.

"I was just wondering how you are."

He sat and leaned his head back against the soft cushions of the couch that perched on one side of the courtyard. "Well enough. You?"

She came over and stood nearby, though she did not sit. "I'm all right. The tea with the governing council wives was somewhat awkward."

He felt as if he should apologize. But what would be

the point? They both knew why she was here. If only
Rashid would come, the plan would work perfectly. "I
am certain you managed it with aplomb."

She blew out a breath. "It wasn't that bad, truly. A
couple of them don't seem to care for me, but the others…well, some of them are quite nice. They seem to
understand how strange this must be for me as an out-
sider."

He looked up and met her soft green gaze. He had
asked a lot of her in coming here. And he'd not prepared her nearly well enough. "You must despise me."

"No, of course not."

He sat forward, his eyes searching hers. "It's all right.
You can admit it."

She sighed. "I don't despise you, Kadir. I actually
like some of the people I've met. It hasn't been nearly
as bad as I thought it would be. But I hate deceiving
them. I'll be glad when it's over." As if she realized what
she'd just said, her mouth snapped closed. "I'm sorry,
I didn't mean that. For this to be over, your father—"

He stood and put a finger over her lips, silencing her.
Her mouth was soft but he resisted the urge to slide his
finger along her lips. Somehow, he resisted. "I understand what you mean. And I share the sentiment."

Her eyes were troubled. "I shouldn't have said it."

He tilted his head back and gazed up at the slice of
blue sky visible above the walls and minarets. There
was no point in hiding the truth from her. "I am going
to be king. It's inevitable."

Because Rashid wasn't coming, their father was slipping in and out of consciousness with more regularity,
and the council was growing restless with the uncer-
tainty of the situation. Kadir had to act before the council splintered under the strain.

He heard her pull in a breath. "Oh, Kadir. I tried to be unsuitable, I really did. But sometimes I've just been me, and that clearly hasn't been enough."

Her head was bowed, her hands clenched into fists. He tipped her chin up and forced her to look at him. "You have not failed, Emily. You've done a brilliant job." He ground his teeth in frustration. "It is I who have failed. And it's time to accept my fate and get on with it."

She was looking at him with an admiration he didn't expect. "You'll be an excellent king."

He wanted to laugh. "You have no reason to think so. You are being kind."

Her eyes widened indignantly. "Of course I do! I've never seen anyone talk so many people into doing things his way as you have over the last four years. If that's not a skill a king needs, then I don't know what is. You'll be great at it, because you are great at everything else."

"I am apparently not great at some things." When she frowned at him, he wanted to kiss her. But he did not, because he wasn't certain he could stop at just a kiss. "I am not great at everything, Emily, because you continue to sleep on your side of the bed. If I had my way, you would sleep wrapped around me."

A blush spread across her cheeks. "You already know you're irresistible to women. You don't need me to prove it yet again."

"But I am not irresistible to you."

"You're not my type. Tall, handsome, kingly." She shook her head. "Oh, no, I like my men short and quiet and willing to be bossed around."

"Emily," he growled, the idea of her having a type— especially a type that wasn't him—burning a hole in his gut.

"Stop worrying, Kadir. You're handsome and re-markable and fabulous. And you'll be the best king that Kyr has ever had. I just know it."

She was being prickly with him, but her praise warmed him deep inside. He didn't feel as though he was the best at anything right now. Oh, he could build skyscrapers that no one else could, but that wasn't run-ning a kingdom.

If his skill at personal relationships was any indica-tion, he was doomed to failure. He had a contentious relationship with his father, an apparently nonexistent one with his brother—and then there was Emily. She was the person who'd worked the closest to him for the longest time. Until just a few days ago, he would have said she did not like him much.

And now? Now she felt sorry for him. He could hardly bear it.

"Sit with me," he said, catching her hand and pulling her down with him. It wasn't a big settee and she ended up right beside him, her hip crowding against his. Her eyes were wide as she blinked at him.

He held his arm out, daring her to come into the cir-cle of his embrace. He desperately wanted to be close to someone right now. Close to her. He expected her to trot out their agreement, to shoot up off the settee and stammer about an appointment or something. But she didn't. She folded herself against him as if she al-ways did so, as if it were as natural as breathing, and he closed his eyes on a rough sigh.

"Thank you," he said against her hair, and she wrapped one arm tentatively around his waist. A simple touch, and yet he burned deep inside for more. "When my father dies, you will need to remain for the funeral. After that, I will divorce you and you'll be free to go."

Just saying the words sent a chill washing over him. He wasn't certain if Emily trembled or if it was simply the strength of his emotions making him think so. She'd been a part of his life for long enough that he couldn't quite imagine it without her. But he was resigned to his fate and he had to let her know what came next for her. For them.

He would miss her, but in time it would ease.

"Whatever you think best," she said, her voice muffled against his robes.

"I'll wire the money into your account. And I'll give you references."

Even as he said it, he knew he would give her enough money so she wouldn't have to work again if she did not want to. She could take her father to Florida and live there with him if she chose. It hadn't been a part of the plan, but he couldn't bear to send her back to Chicago with only what they'd agreed upon. He didn't want her to work for anyone else. He wanted her to do whatever she wanted in life.

"Thank you," she said. He thought she sniffed. A moment later, she was pushing herself away from him. Her eyes were watery, though she did not let a single tear fall. "I think I have a headache. I should go inside and rest."

He wanted to reach out and trace her cheek with his finger. And then he wanted to do so much more. He kept his hands to himself. "Yes, perhaps you should."

She stood and smoothed the dress over her body and he found himself aching to span her hips with his hands, to press his mouth right against her belly. To drag it lower until she screamed his name with passion rather than frustration.

But he would do none of these things.

"I'm sorry, Kadir."

He looked up into her soft green eyes and had the strangest sensation when he imagined those eyes gone from his life. It was as if a piece of his soul had withered and died.

"So am I, *habibti*."

Two days later, the king of Kyr died in the middle of the night. His passing was peaceful and quiet, but the aftermath was not. Emily was shaken awake during the dark hours. She was disoriented, groggy, and her eyes felt gritty with the silent tears she'd spilled into her pillow.

"We must leave, Emily," a deep voice said, and a current of alarm prickled inside her as she recognized the urgency in Kadir's tone.

"What's wrong?"

"My father has passed."

She sat up immediately as the last veil of sleep fell away. "Oh, Kadir, I am so sorry."

He stood there, tall and remote, already dressed in his desert robes, and she wondered if he'd even been to bed. The last she recalled, he'd been working on his computer when she'd gone to bed earlier. He'd had trouble sleeping lately and he often stayed up late to work.

She thought that he also spent time trying to track down his brother, hoping that he would get a last-minute reprieve. But now it was too late. Rashid had not come and their father was dead. Kadir was truly the next king of Kyr.

"It's fine," he said coolly. "I'm fine. But we have to journey to the King's Oasis. It is required that I spend the next twenty-four hours there, isolated from the court. You are the only one permitted to go with me."

"Of course," she said, throwing back the covers and

hurrying to get dressed. She didn't think it mattered much now, so she donned jeans and tennis shoes. She grabbed a jacket and put it on over her T-shirt because it was cold in the desert at night.

Within half an hour, they were packed and in a Land Rover. When Kadir said they were going alone, he meant it. There were no servants with them, no caravan of vehicles as they began the journey into the dark desert.

She didn't know what to say, so Emily leaned her head against the window and gazed up at the stars. They were so plentiful out here, away from the city lights. A shooting star blazed across her field of vision and she made a quick wish.

She wished that Kadir would not send her away. A stupid wish, but there it was. She'd realized over the last several days that she cared about him. She couldn't imagine her life without him in it. And yet she had to do just that, because he would be a king and she was not needed. Or wanted.

She gritted her teeth against the fantasy that he might decide to keep her with him. *Oh, for goodness' sake, you're just as bad as all those other women, wanting what he cannot give.*

Not only that, but she knew she would not be welcomed in Kyr as a permanent part of his life—and certainly not as his queen. While there were people who seemed to like her, even welcome her, the governing council did not. They'd frowned at her and ignored her and clearly did not approve of her. Which was precisely as Kadir had wanted it.

Truly, if she'd been swathed head to toe in black robes, she still didn't think they would have liked her. She was too foreign in their eyes, and certainly not good enough for a prince of Kyr. That was the true measure of her unsuitability, not her clothing or her actions or anything else she did or did not do.

Emily closed her eyes and somehow managed to fall asleep against the bouncing of the vehicle. When Kadir awoke her later, the first rays of dawn were beginning to peek over the horizon. They drove into the oasis and she was surprised to find it wasn't empty, as she'd thought it might be, but filled with tents and animals. A couple of dark bodies moved between the animals, feeding them.

Kadir exited the Land Rover and stood beside it. Emily climbed out, her feet landing with a squish in the sand. She walked around to Kadir's side and stood there as a tall, dignified man in dark robes made his way to them. He was worn and weathered, his face brown and wrinkled with sun and wind. His eyes, however, were dark and glittering as he looked at them both.

Kadir spoke to the man, and his old eyes drifted closed. Then he sank to his knees and intoned something in Arabic. Kadir reached out and touched his shoulder and the man stood again. Soon, other men appeared and the contents of the Land Rover were whisked into a tent set aside from the rest.

Kadir turned to her and held out his hand. Emily slipped her hand into his and let him lead her inside the tent. It was opulent, with colorful carpets blanketing the floor and walls. Copper and gold gleamed on tables and in low cabinets. There were cushions spread liberally across the floor for seating, and a separate area that contained a large bed covered in furs.

The oil lamps were lit and the soft scent of incense wafted to her nose. Someone brought a tray with food and coffee and then disappeared. The man who had greeted them was the last to go and Emily found herself blinking at Kadir and wondering what would happen now. Twenty-four hours in the oasis. For what?

She wanted to go to him, wrap her arms around him and hold him tight, but she didn't dare. Because she didn't know if she could stop once she did.

"How are you feeling?" she asked softly.

Kadir spun toward her, his eyes sparking with emotion. "How am I feeling? Trapped."

It wasn't quite what she'd expected. "I don't know what to say to you, other than I'm sorry."

Kadir closed his eyes and tilted his head back. And then he said something she didn't understand. When he shook his fist at the top of the tent, she assumed it was probably something she didn't want to hear anyway. He was angry and emotional and she understood that he needed to vent.

"Do you want to know what the worst part is?" he said suddenly, his gaze hard on hers again. Daring her, maybe.

"What?"

"I think I got what I deserved."

Emily's heart squeezed at the raw pain in his voice. "I'm not sure I understand you."

He shook his head. She didn't think he would speak, but then suddenly the words tumbled from him. "I am a rotten brother, Emily. And when I tried to make it right again, Rashid did not come. I tried to make sure the throne was his, as it should be, but it no longer matters. My father is dead, Rashid is not here and the council will formally choose me before the world—if my father did not leave a will already proclaiming me heir. He claimed he had not chosen, but I believe he did. I think the old bastard was just manipulating us one last time."

Emily tried not to be shocked, but she knew she hadn't succeeded when one corner of his mouth curled in a hard smile.

"I failed to tell you what kind of dysfunctional family I have, didn't I? Well, here it is—my father is dead, and I don't feel much of anything at the moment but anger. And not for the reasons you would suppose." He clenched his hands into fists as his side. "He wasn't a kind man, or a loving man. He was exacting and proud, and though I loved him when I was a child, I grew to fear him. And then I despised him."

She couldn't imagine feeling that way about her father, but her mother was a different story. She'd been angry with her mother for years now.

"If you mean to shock me, you are doing so. But not for the reasons you suppose."

"You aren't horrified to your sweet little core that I couldn't stand the man who left me a crown? That his death doesn't bother me nearly as much as the situation I now find myself in?"

"I didn't live your life, Kadir. It's not my place to decide how you should be feeling right now."

He laughed. It was a bitter, angry sound. And then he ripped his headdress off and tossed it on the cushions. "Damn, Emily, I wish we'd been more honest with each other a long time ago."

Her heart beat hard. "That's not the kind of relationship we had."

He stalked toward her, stopped before he got too close. He vibrated with suppressed energy. "No, it's not. But I wish it had been." His gaze slid down her body, back up again. "I wish I'd noticed what was under those dull suits of yours. I wish I'd taken your hair down years ago and plundered your mouth until you begged me to strip you naked and kiss the rest of you."

Emily's breath shortened. "You don't mean that. You're just angry and upset—"

He moved closer and her voice died in her throat. All he had to do was reach out and touch her. She found herself wishing he would do so. Holding her breath waiting for him to do so.

And wondering how to say no if he did.

"I am angry, but I've wanted you for days now." He picked up the braid she always wore to bed and undid the elastic while her heart pounded hard. Then he started to unbraid her hair, shaking it loose with his fingers until it flowed over her shoulders and down her back. "I think I've wanted you for a very long time."

Emily swallowed. "Don't say that. You didn't look at me twice before Guido—"

"I did look, Emily. I looked a lot. And yes, I brought Lenore home—so many women home—but I looked at you and I wondered what it was about you. Why I was comfortable with you. Why I tried to provoke a reaction out of you. Why it made me happy when you frowned at anyone I was with. Why I looked forward to mornings and you being there—"

Emily cried out as she put a hand over his mouth. She couldn't bear to think of any of it just now. To think of it ending. "Stop! Don't say these things. Don't make me want…"

He took her arm and tugged her closer. His mouth landed on the inside of her wrist, his breath against her skin. A fiery current of need shot down her spine and into her sex as his tongue slid over her.

"Want what, Emily? This?"

He licked her skin again and an answering shudder

rolled through her. She had never, not once in her whole
life, wanted a man as desperately as she wanted this one.
It was crazy but true. She'd had boyfriends, she'd had
sex—though not in a very long time—and she knew
what it felt like to be wanted and to want.

But oh, God, not like *this*. Not as if every nerve ending she possessed was on fire. Not as if she needed this
man to breathe, to survive. Not as if she would never
be happy if she didn't have him.

And yet how could she do this with him and survive
it? Because they were finished and she had to walk
away soon. No, he would *send* her away soon. He had
to. They'd failed and she had to go so he could be king.

"We can't." The words were wrenched from her.

He dragged her into his arms then, dragged her hips
against his body until she felt the strength of his need
for her. His voice was thick. "Why not? Why not just
this once?"

Emily put her forehead against his chest, felt the
quick beat of his heart. There was nothing she could say
except the truth. "Because I'm afraid it will destroy me."

He pushed her back and searched her gaze. She was
too weary to care what he saw there. Did she love him?
Maybe she did. She didn't really know anymore what
this feeling was or why it made her so desperate. She'd
thought she was afraid of herself, afraid of what she
might become if she let her hair down and allowed the
sensual creature inside her to emerge from the shell
again—but maybe she was afraid of him, of what he
could do to her.

To her heart. Oh, she was no match for a man like
Kadir. She'd worn her defenses around her like a shield
for so long and she'd grown weary. Living with him

these last few days had destroyed any pretense she had of not liking him.

He pushed her hair back off her cheeks and cupped her jaw in both his hands. The look he gave her was filled with so many emotions: tenderness, frustration, rage, desire. Finally, he took a deep, shuddering breath before tilting her head down to kiss her on the forehead.

Then he backed away from her and grabbed the head-dress he'd tossed aside before striding from the tent.

CHAPTER ELEVEN

THE SUN SANK below the horizon again before Kadir returned. Emily shot up from the cushions, her heart in her throat. He'd been gone all day and she'd been worried about him. But no one at the oasis understood her queries for his whereabouts. They brought her tea and food, and left her alone for long hours.

"Kadir." She somehow managed to say his name even as tears filled the back of her throat. "I was worried about you."

He looked weary as he waved a hand dismissively. "It is part of the ritual, *habibti*. I have been in prayer from sunup to sundown."

She let out a shaky breath. "I did not know. I thought…" She shook her head. "Never mind. Are you hungry? One of the women has just brought food."

"Yes, most definitely."

"Sit, then. I'll get it for you."

He took a seat on the cushions and she brought the tray with meat and cheese and fruit over to the low table in the center. Then she poured cool water into glasses and handed him one.

He took a long drink and set the glass on the table. She refilled it.

"I apologize for not explaining the ritual to you," he said.

She shrugged and studied the food. What could she say to him? That she'd missed him? That she'd been worried about him? That she'd spent the last several hours filled with regret that she'd pushed him away? "It's fine. I'm just glad you're well."

He reached out and touched her hand and her nerve endings tingled in response, flooding her senses with too much heat, too much emotion. She was such a mess, and all because of him.

"I left rather abruptly. I'm sorry."

"I don't know that I gave you any choice."

"I would never want to cause you pain, Emily."

"I appreciate that."

But she hadn't been able to stop thinking about the things he'd said to her earlier. He'd said he wanted her, that he'd been thinking about her for far longer than she realized. She wanted it to be true, and yet she doubted. But did it honestly matter? Once this was over, once they went back to the palace and he took his place as king, it was the end. She would leave Kyr and probably never see him again.

And that thought nearly doubled her over as fresh pain streaked through her body, curling and writhing in her belly, her limbs. It had been this way each time the thought crossed her mind today. Never see Kadir again? Never hear his voice stroke across the syllables of her name?

It was unbearable. Except that she had to learn to bear it. Somehow.

Emily picked up a handful of grapes. When she plucked one and held it up to Kadir's mouth, she thought she might melt at the heat flaring in his eyes.

"Emily," he said softly. "What is this?"

She looked at her hand. "I believe it's a grape. But don't quote me on that."

He snorted softly. But then he leaned forward and took the grape from her fingers with his mouth, his eyes never leaving hers. She plucked another grape and fed it to him, and then another, her heart skipping wildly in her chest.

The next time she fed him, he gripped her hand and sucked her index finger. Emily gasped as her body became a lightning rod. Sweet sensation streaked from her finger down to her sex and her feminine core grew wet as his tongue swirled and licked.

It was perhaps the most innocuously erotic thing anyone had ever done to her.

"You play with fire, *habibti,*" Kadir murmured when he finally let her go. "My control is not so strong right now."

Her heart raced a little bit faster than before. She could admit the truth, or she could push him away again. "I'm not sure mine is either."

Insane to divulge such a thing. Dangerous. But if she left this oasis without ever knowing what it was like to be Kadir's lover, just for one night, she would never forgive herself.

His eyes glittered in his devastatingly handsome face. "What has changed your mind?"

She dropped her gaze, her pulse throbbing hard. "Regret. I don't want any."

He put a finger under her chin and brought her head up to meet his gaze. "And what if you regret giving yourself to me?"

"I'll find that out in the morning, won't I?" She put her hand on his chest, smoothed his robes against the hard muscles beneath. "Besides, I rather thought we could give ourselves to each other. I didn't exactly intend to be passive."

With a growl, he pushed her back on the cushions until her body was beneath his, until the delicious weight of him pressed her down and made her shiver because she knew what was coming next. He spanned her rib cage with his broad hands. "Emily, I ache for you."

How thrilling it was to hear those words from his mouth. *For her.* "And I for you," she said breathlessly.

His mouth claimed hers in a hot, wet, deep kiss that made her back arch up off the cushions. "There's nothing here I want more than you," he said urgently, kissing her again and again while she moaned and writhed beneath him.

There was nothing—*nothing!*—better than having the full power of Kadir al-Hassan focused on her. Oh, no wonder all those women had lost their minds....

No, she told herself. *You will not think of that, of them. You will think of nothing but him.*

And it wasn't difficult, not really. Not when his mouth performed such magic on her. He kissed her like a man starved, demanding her passion, her soul. Their tongues met, dueled again and again, sucked each other deep and hard. He found the hem of her shirt and tugged it up and over her head. She thought he would move to her breasts, but he kept kissing her while she wriggled beneath him, flexed her hips and found his hardness. His groan was gratifying.

Emily tried to get her hands beneath his robes, but they were too voluminous and she made a choked sound of frustration. Kadir rocked back on his heels and ripped everything over his head until all that was left was a pair of briefs with a mouthwatering bulge....

Oh my...

"There is nothing in this world more exciting than to have a woman look at me as you are doing right this moment."

Emily's gaze flew to his and she realized she'd been staring. Drooling, perhaps.

"You're a beautiful man, Kadir. Any woman would look at you like I am right now."

"Yes, but I find it's more satisfying when it's you."

He crawled over her again, lowered all that glorious flesh down onto hers, and she gasped when his naked torso met her skin. She was still wearing her bra and jeans, but right now she wanted to be free of everything and just feel her naked body against his. She ran her hands up his sides, her heart throbbing at the fact she was finally caressing his skin, his muscles.

Kadir was beautifully formed, and he knew it. Right now, she didn't care that he knew. She only cared that she was finally, finally getting to touch him the way she'd dreamed.

A part of her hated that anyone else had touched him like this. She focused on her hands, on the way her skin was so light against his darkness. He caught one of them and brought it to his lips.

"You are thinking too much, Emily. About other women, other nights. This is about us. There is only you and me here tonight. And there is no one else I'd rather be with."

She ran her fingers over his sensual lips. "I've spent four years escorting women out of your bedroom. You can't expect me to forget that. Or to forget that I'm no different than they are after all. Wanting you. Craving you. Going mad with the thought of having you."

His smile was tender. "You are *very* different." He

dipped his lips to her throat and she arched her neck, moaning softly. "Because I am mad with the thought of having *you*. And that, you may rest assured, is not a common occurrence."

He flexed his hips against her center and she caught her breath at the feelings rolling through her. He made her feel special, though she told herself it was only a line. He was good at this, so good.

"The things I want to do to you, Emily," he said on a groan. "This night is not nearly long enough."

He kissed her again, his mouth taking hers in a hard, deep kiss. Emily arched up to him, wrapped her arms around him until he slipped her bonds and pressed openmouthed kisses to her neck, her collarbone, the valley between her breasts. Her bra had a front clasp and he did away with it handily. A moment later, his hot mouth was on her aching nipple. Emily cried out as she arched her back, thrusting herself greedily into his mouth.

He sucked hard and soft, nibbled and bit until her body was on fire. How could so much pleasure come from such a tiny spot? But he didn't stop there. He did the same to her other nipple until she was writhing on the cushions and panting his name.

When he unzipped her jeans and tugged them down her hips, she had a crazy moment of panic that she was completely naked before him. He knelt and peeled her jeans and panties off and dropped them. His gaze flicked over her and her breath caught in her throat while she waited for him to say something.

"Emily." He caressed her calves, her knees, the insides of her thighs as he moved over her body again. "So lovely. How stupid I have been not to make love to you before now."

"It wouldn't have happened." She sounded breathless. "Not while I worked for you. And if it had, I would have handed in my resignation."

He blinked. But he didn't stop caressing her. "Then perhaps it's good we have waited." He pushed her knees apart, his gaze dropping to the juncture of her thighs. "But we have much to make up for."

He bent and pressed a kiss to the inside of her thigh. Emily's body felt tight, like a rubber band stretched just under the breaking point. Another inch, and she would snap. Her breath came in tight, shallow little gasps and her skin burned with excitement.

Kadir's breath against her thigh was hot and moist—and then his fingers found her, his thumb skimming over her clitoris while she gasped.

"You like that," he murmured.

"Oh. Oh, yes."

He did it once more, and again her body tightened. "And what will you do if I lick you, Emily? Will you come for me?"

She was so aroused it physically hurt. Her body throbbed with pain and need and all she wanted was for him to ease the ache. She nodded, unable to speak.

His grin was wicked—and beautiful. He pushed her thighs farther apart. And then he bent and licked the wet seam of her sex.

Emily's back arched off the cushions as if someone had touched her with a live wire. The sound coming from her throat was high-pitched and desperate.

And she didn't care. She wanted more. She wanted everything.

Kadir tongued her again and again, until she was fisting giant handfuls of cushion and panting his name. She was so, so close, her body wound tighter than any spring ever could be—but Kadir was skilled and he knew how to keep her from soaring over the edge.

"Kadir," she begged. "Please."

He stopped abruptly, getting to his feet while she cried out. She lay there in shock while he walked out of the room. But then he was back, ripping open a condom and shoving his briefs down before rolling it onto his thick length.

Emily's heart beat harder as he stretched out over top of her again, pressing her into the cushions. His hand went between their bodies, stroked the bud of her sex.

"I have to be inside you, Emily. The first time you come with me, I want to feel it happening."

He captured her mouth, his tongue sliding deep. He tasted like her and it made her feel wildly possessive. She kissed him harder and he responded with a surge of passion that left her breathless.

A moment later, she felt the head of his cock and she reached between them, both to touch him and to guide him into her. He stiffened as she wrapped her hand around him, and then he groaned when she pumped her fist over him once, twice.

In response, he hooked an arm behind her knee and spread her wide before plunging into her. Emily tore her mouth from his as a scream erupted from her throat. Her body was so ready for him, so primed and on edge, that she came immediately, shuddering around him while he rocked into her in short, quick strokes that dragged out her release.

"That's it," he said thickly. "Like that. Lose yourself in it, Emily."

It had been so long since she'd had an orgasm that it seemed to last and last and last. But it ended finally and she went limp beneath him. He kissed her cheeks, her nose, her jaw.

"You needed that."

She managed a laugh. "Yes."

He was still deep inside her, his body as hard as stone. "Has it been a long time?"

She moved her hips, surprised when fresh fire streaked through her. "There was no time for dating while working for you."

He spanned her hip with a broad hand and shifted her upward before stroking into her again. She moaned with pleasure.

"I am very glad for this," he said tightly. "I cannot imagine you with anyone but me."

He moved hard inside her then, branding her with the strength of his possession. Emily wrapped her legs high around his back, locking her ankles as he drove into her harder and faster, building the tension all over again. She didn't think her body could respond so quickly to this fresh assault on her senses, but once again she was surprised by how well Kadir seemed to know her.

Their bodies strained together, rising and falling and melting, over and over, until Emily couldn't hold on another moment. She spun out of control with a cry, falling off the edge and into the blackness below. She thought she might have sobbed his name, but she couldn't be sure. Her every sense was suddenly over-whelmed with pleasure—and love so sharp it sliced her to ribbons inside.

"Emily," he said in her ear, his voice urgent and tight. And then it broke as he found his own release, his body shuddering deep inside hers. He said her name again, but it cleaved in half with a groan.

She lay beneath him, stunned with the intensity of

everything she was feeling. She was wrapped in his heat and the scent of sex, her body shuddering, her pulse pounding. All her worst fears had come true, in spite of her caution.

Kadir took everything from her, turned her inside out and shone a light on all the dark corners she'd tried to keep hidden. But she couldn't deny the truth of her feelings anymore.

She'd tried so hard not to fall in love with him. She'd convinced herself for years that she despised him, that he was a playboy with no feelings and no heart and that he was beneath her contempt.

But it wasn't true. He had feelings and he was as lost and alone as anyone, no matter how hard he tried to hide it from the world. If not for that, she could have remained apart. She could have kept her heart intact. But she'd fallen in love with Kadir al-Hassan, and she never wanted to be anywhere but here, lost in this tent in the desert with him.

Sadness overwhelmed her then. She would never have a life with him beyond tonight. There was no future with Kadir. Even if he was not going to be the king of Kyr, there was no future with him.

Because this was what he did—he broke women on the rocks of his passion, made them feel special and wonderful, and then he cut them loose without a backward glance.

Emily closed her eyes and swore she would not cry. She could spin up a fantasy where she spent the next several weeks in Kadir's bed, but she would not lie to herself. For her sanity, she had tonight with him and that was it. And she wasn't going to spend it sobbing or feeling sorry for herself. There was time enough for that when they returned to the palace and he became immersed in duty.

He rolled away from her and rose, disappearing for a few moments before he returned and pulled her up and into his embrace. She didn't know what to say, so she said nothing. He tilted her chin back and kissed her hard, possessively, before hooking his arms behind her and sweeping her up. Then he carried her over to the bed and deposited her on it before climbing in beside her and dragging the covers up and over their naked bodies.

She was wrapped around him and she never wanted to be anywhere else. She closed her eyes and pressed her mouth to his chest, tasting the salt of his sweat against her tongue.

"I hope you don't want to sleep at all tonight," he growled, rolling her beneath him until she could feel the thickness of his cock swelling again. "Because I intend to use every minute we have together."

CHAPTER TWELVE

IN SPITE OF his best intentions, reality intruded and they fell asleep tangled in each other's arms after another hot coupling that left them both breathless and spent. It was sometime around one in the morning when Kadir woke, blinking as he groped for his phone to check the time. Out of habit, he checked for any messages from Rashid. There was nothing. It was truly over.

As if being here at the oasis hadn't already taught him that. He was about to become king, and there was nothing he could do to change it.

Emily lay curled against him, one arm thrown across his waist and a leg propped over his thighs. A current of longing slid into his bones, made his cock start to harden in spite of how many times he'd already come tonight. It would be so easy to turn her over and slide deep inside her again.

Kadir shuddered with the strength of the hunger he felt to do just that. He'd spent much of his life bedding women, but he'd never quite experienced this intensity before. He understood that it had everything to do with the situation he now found himself in. His life was in crisis, caught at a crossroads, and he felt everything strongly.

Emily had said she wanted no regrets, but he had

them. He wished he'd stripped his PA down to her delectable skin and explored her sweetness years ago. She said she would have left him, but he would have found a way to make her stay. He did not doubt his ability to have done so and he cursed himself for being so stubborn and blind when he could have had her like this much sooner than now.

He turned and glided a hand over her hip, cupped her breast. Male satisfaction filled him when her nipple began to harden. He wanted to suck it between his lips, but he didn't really want to wake her when she was sleeping so soundly.

"Kadir," she breathed, and his heart turned over in his chest. So she wasn't sleeping after all. And he was damn glad.

"Yes, *habibti?*"

"What time is it?"

"A few minutes to one."

Her breath came out as a shaky sigh. "We have more time then. I'm so glad."

He spanned her rib cage and bent to tease her nipple. "Me, too."

He was tired, but more than willing. Apparently, so was she. But instead of opening her arms to him, she pushed him until he was on his back and she straddled him.

"My turn."

Kadir lifted an eyebrow. "Your turn?"

"For once in my life, I want the mighty Kadir al-Hassan at *my* command. I want to drive you crazy, Kadir." She bent and pressed an openmouthed kiss to his chest, trailing her tongue over to his nipple and swirling around it while a sensation very like pain shot to his groin. Except it was too pleasurable to be pain. "I want you to remember me."

He fisted a hand in her hair. "I could never forget you, Emily."

How could he? She'd been with him for four long years, and while he'd been an utter fool and not taken full sexual advantage of their time together, he'd never forget the woman who had been his companion day in and day out for all that time. No, they'd not been romantic, but she'd been important to him.

The most important person to him.

He shuddered as her mouth slid down his chest. Yes, she was the most important person in his life. The one he depended on. And he was losing her. Tonight was the last night they would have alone before he had to return to the palace and take up the duties of king while he waited for the coronation.

Selfishly, he thought of keeping her with him, of keeping her in his bed and in his life—but it was impossible. She was his unsuitable bride, not at all the sort of woman the council would approve of as his queen. She'd won over many people in the palace, whether she knew it or not—but not the hardened council, who saw any woman who was not of Arab descent as highly inappropriate. They had the power to make his life—and hers—hell if he did not conform to tradition and take a Kyrian wife. He closed his eyes and cursed Rashid and his father both.

He had no right to keep Emily. She had a father who needed her and a life waiting in the States. Once she was gone, once his life settled into the routines of being king, he would become accustomed to his life without her in it. It wasn't as if they were in love. It was lust and friendship and the pain of losing someone he'd known for so long.

And that was not a reason to ask her to give up everything and remain in Kyr.

Her tongue glided around his belly button—and then her cheek rubbed against his cock and his body stiffened. She laughed softly before taking him in her mouth. Kadir had a sudden need to plunge into her mouth, to make her his this way, too, but he forced himself to remain still and let her torture him.

Her mouth was hot and wet and magical and he gave himself up to the pleasure, his eyes closing and his back arching as the sensations built inside him, propelling him to another orgasm as strong as the last.

But he couldn't bear to come this way when they had no time left. He wanted to be inside her, her body wrapped around his, her eyes glazing and breath panting as he took her over the edge with him.

He reached for her and dragged her up his body, thrusting his tongue in her mouth and kissing her hard. She knew what he wanted and she reached for the strip of condoms beside the bed, tearing one off and then breaking the kiss to roll it on before sinking down on top of him.

She took him deep, until they both groaned with it. His hands spanned her hips, gripping her hard against him, and her palms pressed into his chest as she held herself up.

"You're beautiful, Emily," he said, stunned at the picture she presented with her hair falling over her shoulders to tickle him as she leaned forward. Her breasts were high and round and her eyes glittered with some mysterious emotion as she took his mouth possessively.

She whispered as she leaned back again, "You say that to all the girls—"

But she didn't get to finish the sentence because he yanked her down and kissed her hard. And he didn't stop kissing her, or thrusting up inside her, until she shuddered around him and ripped her mouth free, gasping his name into the darkness of the tent.

He didn't let her recover before he flipped her over and rode her deeply, driving her across the bed, driving his demons before him. Vaguely, he thought he was too rough, too uncontrolled, but she gripped his buttocks and lunged hard against him when he would have slackened his pace.

It was a war, but one that exacted pleasure rather than pain. They finally climaxed together, gasping and groaning and sweating and swearing, before rolling apart and kicking the covers off the bed.

When he could speak again, he turned his head, watched her chest heaving. "I don't," he told her between breaths as anger and confusion swirled inside him.

Her gaze was puzzled. "Don't what?"

He gritted his teeth. She didn't even know. "Say that to all the girls," he ground out. "You keep trying to bring others between us, but there's no one in my head except you. No one else I want."

"I'm sorry," she said, her voice soft. And hovering on the brink of tears, he realized.

He reached for her hand, caught it in his and squeezed. He was angry with her for bringing other women into their bed and yet he'd trained her to think that way. He thought of all the times she'd escorted his dates from his suite and wanted to groan. Damn him for being so thoughtless. So arrogant.

"It's my fault. I know it. I've not behaved well."

She let out a shaky sigh. "You behaved like a rich, entitled, handsome prince. And I have no right to blame you for it. It's who you are."

A wave of anger flooded him again. And frustration. "It's not who I am," he practically shouted. "It's who you want me to be."

He shoved his way off the bed and took care of the condom before yanking on his clothes. She sat up, her eyes wide in the darkened tent.

"What are you doing?" She sounded frightened, but he forced himself to ignore his desire to haul her into his arms and hold her tight.

"I need air," he said, dragging on his boots and standing over the bed, where she sat naked and alone.

"I'm sorry, Kadir," she said, her voice containing a hint of desperation that twisted his heart. "I don't mean to hurt you."

He forced a laugh. "Hurt me? How can you possibly hurt me? I'm arrogant and entitled. And unfeeling. Don't forget unfeeling."

He turned to go but she appeared in front of him. Small, naked and fierce. Her hands fisted into his robes and hurt spiraled deep into his soul. What was wrong with him? He was like a little boy again, trying to get his father's affection and failing miserably at it.

And hurting others to do so.

"You are *not* unfeeling. And neither am I, dammit. But you scare me, Kadir. You scare me to death."

That made him pause. "I scare you? I would never hurt you, Emily. I've told you this."

"You wouldn't do it on purpose. Don't you understand that I have to remind myself of the last four years so that I can—" Here, her voice choked off and she swallowed hard. "So I can leave you, Kadir. So I can bear to go away and never see you again."

He wanted to hold on to his anger and pain and shove her away so he could stride outside and brood over his fate. But he couldn't do it. Instead, he tugged her into his arms and held her close, so close he could feel her heart beating hard and fast. She trembled and he scooped her up and returned her to the bed, dragging the covers from the floor and trying to tuck her under them.

"No, don't leave me. Not tonight. Please, not tonight."

There was a hard lump in his throat. "I won't." He disrobed and climbed under the covers with her again. She wrapped her body around him and held on tight, as if he would disappear if she let go.

He stroked her soft hair, wound his fingers in it, tried to imprint the texture of it on his skin so he would always remember. She was precious to him, and maybe it was more than just the situation that made her so. But he wasn't ever going to find out, because he would send her away tomorrow.

It had to be tomorrow. He'd intended to have her stay through the funeral, but now he couldn't bear to have her near him and not be able to touch her again. Part of him, the selfish part, told him he could have her as often as he wanted right up until the moment he sent her back to Chicago. There was nothing to stop him. They were married, and though he had to divorce her soon, they weren't divorced yet. He could take her back to the palace, spend his nights with her until it was time for the coronation.

Kadir closed his eyes and a wave of pain and loneliness washed over him. He could do that, yes. But he wouldn't. Because it would hurt her. Because she'd told him she was scared of him. He wanted to know precisely what that meant, wanted to hear her say that she cared for him, but he knew he couldn't ask her to explain. There was a veneer over this night that was so thin it hurt, but it was essential for them both if they were going to get on with their separate lives.

Separate lives. Those words were like a dagger plunged into his chest. How would he live without Emily?

He closed his eyes tight against the pain and held her close. He didn't know the answer to that question. But he knew he had to send her away tomorrow if he was going to keep from hurting her any more than he already had.

Emily woke before dawn, exhausted. But that didn't stop her from reaching for Kadir. He came into her eagerly, his body hard and ready. They did not use a condom this time and they both gasped with how perfect it felt to be joined without that barrier. He'd tried to get one, but she'd told him it didn't matter. She was on the pill.

But even if she hadn't been, she would have wanted him inside her. If she could take a piece of Kadir with her forever, she would happily do so. When she'd told him that, he'd closed his eyes on a groan and slid inside her.

His voice had been husky. "The idea of you pregnant with my child makes me happy, regardless of destiny or duty or any other damn thing anyone cares to throw at me."

They made love more gently than the night before, and when he came this time, she felt the hot spurt of his seed inside her. It made her hope, and yet she knew it was a senseless hope.

After they'd washed and dressed and had a meal of baked bread, honey, butter, fruit and coffee, they climbed into the Land Rover to make the journey back to the capital city. They did not speak much, but Kadir reached over and took her hand in his. He held it through the entire trip, until they reached the city and he needed both hands to drive again. The palace knew they were coming and sent out an escort to meet them and clear the way.

They reached the palace sometime before noon and Emily's heart clenched tight at the change in Kadir's face. He'd closed himself off, closed his emotions off, until he was once more the arrogant ruler. She thought of him last night in her arms, thought of his raw confession about his family, and ached for him.

How had she been so cruel to him? How had she accused him of not having feelings? He had them and they ran deep. Yes, she'd insisted on bringing the past into bed with them, but it had been to protect herself.

A futile hope, since she loved him so much it physically hurt. She'd thought to inoculate herself against the pain of losing him by dragging the past into the room with them, but she'd only succeeded in hurting him, too.

And now, when she wanted to reach out and touch him, she couldn't. What they'd shared last night was over. As if to emphasize that fact, he didn't even look at her as they exited the vehicle. A group of men surrounded him, bowing low, before one began to refer to a notebook he held as he spoke to Kadir in Arabic.

His new PA, she decided, her chest squeezing tight as another servant gestured to her to follow the group into the palace. When they stood inside the vaulted chamber where everyone had gathered to watch their new king return from his vigil, Kadir turned, his eyes meeting hers over the lowered heads of the assembly.

The look he gave her was unreadable, but her heart began to beat a little harder. It wasn't the look of a man who had any hope, and that made her want to scream at them all that they couldn't have him, that he was hers and no one else's.

But he wasn't hers. He had never been hers.

Emily kept her gaze on him even as he turned away and began to speak to the crowd. His voice boomed over their heads, echoed off the tiles and bounced to every corner of the giant room. She wished she knew what he said, but no one bothered to translate for her. She was already being marginalized.

When Kadir finished speaking, he did not look at her again. He simply walked away with his attendants at his side. Emily's eyes filled with tears. It felt so final, but she comforted herself that this wasn't quite the end yet. There was still his father's funeral to get through, still a few stolen moments where she would see him.

Her chest ached. Would he come to their room tonight? Or were there more rituals he had to observe? She'd intended last night to be their one and only night together, but now she knew she would sell her soul for another. She tried not to think about what that meant for the person she'd become. She was not following her own pleasure down whatever destructive path it led.

This was different. *Different.*

The pleasure she felt with Kadir was beautiful and right. She wouldn't trade a moment of last night, not even for a heart that was unbroken and whole.

She started to trail after Kadir automatically, like a satellite drawn into his orbit, but a frowning man appeared in her path before she'd taken more than a few steps.

"You must return to your quarters, Your Highness."

Emily wanted to argue with him, wanted to look down her nose and order him to take her to Kadir—what good was being a princess if you couldn't order people around when you desperately needed to?—but she didn't know if Kadir would welcome her right now. He had so much on his mind and she would not distract him from his duty.

Instead, she inclined her head and accepted an escort. But the servant did not show her to the suite of rooms she'd been sharing with Kadir before they'd gone to the oasis. He showed her to a different set of rooms, smaller, and she blinked in confusion.

When she turned around to ask the man why she'd been moved, he was gone. Her breath whooshed into her lungs in shallow pulls as she stood in the room and told herself not to panic. It was a mistake, that was all. She started throwing doors open. When she came to the closet, her clothes were not in it and she let out a shaky breath. She pivoted on her heel and started toward the door to find someone, to inform them of a mistake. The man who'd shown her to this room had clearly been wrong.

But then she ground to a halt at the sight of her suitcases nearby. She'd only traveled with one large suitcase and a carry-on, but there were two more cases sitting with the ones she recognized. She went over and picked one up. It was heavy, but she threw it on the nearest surface and ripped at the zipper.

Inside, the lovely clothes that Guido had dressed her in were packed with tissue. She ripped through the case, finding clothing, shoes and scarves. The next bag was also full, and the next. She tore them apart, sobbing like a maniac, until all the clothes were strewn across the furniture and floor.

Then she sank down on the carpet and beat her fist against the cushion of the nearest chair while she pressed her face into it and cried harder. She cried until her body ached, until her throat was raw, until she wanted to curl into a ball and go to sleep for days.

But then, the longer she sat there, as her tears leaked away, she got angry. Was this what her mother had done? Was this what sex and a dynamic lover had done to Rachel Bryant? Had she been so desperate for pleasure, for her lover's touch, that she'd given up her pride and her dignity and followed him to her doom?

Emily shuddered. She was so close to being that kind of woman right now. She would do anything Kadir asked her. Anything for one more night with him. She sucked in a deep breath, determined to get control of herself. She'd spent years making herself into a serious, professional woman. She would not lose that person simply because Kadir had turned her world so completely upside down.

She got to her feet and went into the bathroom to wash her face. Her eyes were puffy and red and she laughed brokenly at her reflection. So pitiful. But then she stared at herself until her jaw hardened. She was done being pitiful. She'd made her choice and she'd had her blissful night with her former boss.

She would not allow it to break her. She was stronger than that. She'd made the decision and she would deal with the consequences. Life would go on. She'd entered the fire with Kadir and she'd been burned. But she would not let it consume her, because she was made of sterner stuff.

Emily finished washing up, changed into a fresh dress and heels, and then she carefully repacked everything she'd strewn across the room. When it was done, when she believed that she was ready for anything, she sat down to wait for whatever came next.

When a man appeared some time later, holding a sheaf of papers, her heart sped up. But she refused to betray herself. She simply sat and waited. Whatever happened, she could handle it.

But she was not quite as prepared as she'd believed. She'd thought a heart could only break once. She discovered she was tragically mistaken. Apparently, a heart could shatter into a million pieces even after it had already done so.

"The king has signed the divorce decree, madam," the man said, bowing low. "You will be taken to the airport now."

CHAPTER THIRTEEN

KADIR NO LONGER heard what was being said to him. He'd tuned out hours ago. All he could think of was Emily. Last night with her, he'd felt things he'd never felt in his life. He kept telling himself it was the situation, the fact his life was changing so drastically, but hours after he'd signed the divorce decree, he didn't feel any better.

He couldn't stop thinking about what it had felt like to make love to Emily. He never did this. He never spent his day thinking about the woman he'd been with the night before. Sex was like eating—you ate when you were hungry but you did not think about food after you'd had breakfast. You thought about food when it was time for lunch, but not every second in between.

But it was more than sex. He couldn't stop thinking about the way she sighed in his arms, the way she felt curled up against him. He traveled back over the last four years together and realized that he couldn't stop thinking about any of it. Emily had always been there, notebook in hand, ready to organize his life and take care of what needed to be taken care of.

He'd asked a lot of her. Too much sometimes. She'd dealt with his schedule, his romances, his arrogance, and she'd never once failed him. He'd pushed her hard over the years. When she'd finally opened up and pushed back, he'd found himself wishing she'd gone head-to-head with him a long time ago.

He missed her. Dreadfully. She was his best friend and he'd sent her away.

He closed his eyes and rubbed his temples to ward off the headache threatening to crash down on him. Maybe he should have kept her and to hell with the council. She was his wife—*had been* his wife—and he needed a queen. But she hadn't signed on for a permanent job and he had no right to ask her to give up everything to stay in Kyr.

Besides, one blissful night together did not add up to a lifetime commitment. He should know that better than anyone. He wasn't a long-term kind of guy. He never had been.

If only he had more time with her, he would find out what this feeling was that had him turned upside down. He would discover the secret to why he felt so desolate over her absence. And then maybe he could conquer it.

She would be on the plane now. In the sky, flying back to Chicago. Away from him. Kadir clenched a fist as his chest grew unbearably tight.

"Enough," he said, standing abruptly. The functionary who had been speaking stuttered to a halt. And then he dropped to his knees. They all did.

Kadir looked out over the room and gritted his teeth. This was his fate. His destiny. He had no right to walk away from it. He would not walk away from it. But he would walk away right now, because he needed to be alone. That much they could give him.

"We will discuss the coronation later. Surely it can wait a few more hours. King Zaid isn't even buried yet, and I am tired."

He was already moving toward the door when the room murmured agreement. He burst out into the cool, dark hallway and started toward his room. The palace rippled around him like a giant wave, people sinking to their knees as he passed. He did not speak to anyone. When he reached his room, a guard opened the door and Kadir went inside. He didn't even get the satisfaction of slamming it because the guard tugged it closed again.

The room was strangely empty. Lonely. He went to the closet and yanked it open, knowing what he would find. Emily's clothes were gone because Emily was gone. He'd ordered it done because he'd thought it was like ripping off a bandage. Do it quick to minimize the pain.

It was, surprisingly, nothing like ripping off a bandage. It was more like digging a sharp knife into his chest and carving out his heart very, very slowly. She was gone because he'd ordered her gone. And she wasn't coming back.

It was what he deserved. What he had to live with.

He went into the private courtyard and stood gazing up at the slice of sky visible above the rooftop. This was his life now. Gazing at freedom and never having it. Giving up everything he'd ever wanted in order to do what he had to do.

If he'd been a better son, a better brother… *No.* Kadir sucked in a deep breath and told himself to stop. There was nothing he could have done differently to make his father and his brother like each other more. Or like him more.

"*Salaam,* brother."

Kadir whirled to find Rashid standing in the door to the courtyard. It was so unexpected that he did not know what to say at first. But Rashid looked tired and worn, so Kadir held his anger in check.

"I thought you were not coming."

Rashid came forward. He was still wearing western clothing: jeans and a button-down shirt. He looked a little foreign, a little out of place. A little bit lost.

"I wasn't." He shrugged and shoved his hands into his pockets. "Or not right away. I thought he was manipulating us, as usual. And I wasn't going to dance to his tune."

So stubborn, even to the end. Fury roiled inside Kadir's gut. "I tried to call you. If you'd taken the calls, you would have known it was bad."

"I shut off the phone for a few days. I needed to think."

Kadir dragged an irritated breath into his lungs. "And now you've emerged to find our father dead and me preparing for a coronation. If you had only come, Rashid. We could have worked this out."

Rashid's laugh was bitter. "Worked what out? He was always going to choose you. There was never any question. I'm not sure he ever really liked either one of us, but he found you less objectionable than I."

Kadir's jaw was tight. He was furious, but not faultless. "I'm sorry for my part in making that so."

Rashid frowned. "What are you talking about?"

"When we were kids. The horses. The dog. The hawk. All of it. Everything I ever did that you were blamed for. I confessed my crimes long ago. But I waited too late, I suppose. You were grown and gone by then."

Rashid went over and perched on the edge of one of the chairs ringing the courtyard. "Kadir." He shook his head sadly. "You thought you were the reason he disliked me so intensely? All this time, you thought that?"

"I was not a good brother."

"You were," Rashid said fiercely. "You are five years younger and you were much smaller than I was back then—did you really think our father did not know who did which things? He had spies, Kadir. Many of them. He always knew the truth."

Kadir felt as if his legs were suddenly made of concrete. He couldn't move. "Then why...?"

Rashid raked a hand through his hair. He didn't speak for a long moment. But then, when he did, Kadir was stunned.

"My mother. She was promised to another when our father took her to his bed. He married her—but then he married another soon after, and she was furious. When I was born, she swore to him that I was her lover's child." His eyes were piercing as he looked up then. "I am not, by the way. But DNA testing was not something our father would submit to then. When I was old enough, I did it myself."

Kadir could only blink. He'd never imagined... "We have different mothers, but we look alike. We look like him. Surely he could see that."

"Everyone could. But he was stubborn, and my mother was, too. They despised each other. She went to her grave claiming I was another man's son. Though not, of course, to anyone but him. I only knew because I overheard them fighting once when I was twelve."

Kadir swallowed. All this time, he'd thought he was to blame for the rift between his father and Rashid. But how could his childish antics have created a fracture so deep? He'd always wondered, but then he'd reasoned it was not up to him to figure out why. It just was. And he'd felt guilty for it.

But now Rashid was telling him it was never his fault, and he didn't quite know how to process it. "Why did you never tell me?"

"I should have."

"Yes, you should have." Anger bubbled up inside him, a well that was deep and strong and had been capped for far too long. "I've blamed myself for most of our lives. And now, when you should have been here to take your place, to make things right again, you would not come."

Rashid shook his head. "It's not my place, Kadir. It's yours. He wanted you to rule, not me."

Kadir's body was on fire with fury. He'd sacrificed so much just to get to this moment. He'd let Emily go. He'd sent her away, and now when he might have her back again, when he might have his life back, Rashid was determined to play the martyr one more time.

"Yet our father is gone, and the council has the power to decide. We will tell them what we want, and you will take the throne."

Rashid got to his feet. "No, Kadir. I came for the funeral. But you are the king of Kyr."

Bitterness flooded Kadir then, hot and sharp and metallic. "You would deny your heritage simply to win some kind of fight with a dead man? Or are you frightened to take the throne? Scared that everything he thought about you was right? That you will be a poor king after all?"

Rashid's eyes flashed. And then he growled. "If you were not my brother…"

Kadir laughed harshly. "Your brother? What does

that matter? I am your *king,* Rashid al-Hassan. And I command you leave my presence immediately."

Rashid's face turned an interesting shade of red. His mouth worked. But he spun on his heel without saying a word and stalked from the courtyard.

Kadir stayed for a long time, thinking and raging inside while he paced back and forth. He was not to blame for his father and Rashid's relationship. It was a revelation, and yet on some level he had always known he was not at fault. He just hadn't known what *else* could be the problem, so he'd blamed himself.

He'd tried to bring them together at the end, but for selfish reasons. He did not want to be king of Kyr. He did not want his life to change so drastically, nor did he want the guilt of taking Rashid's birthright.

But he was through feeling sorry for himself. Through thinking he was stealing something that did not belong to him. If Rashid wasn't prepared to step up and do his duty, then Kadir would. Emily had told him he would be a good king.

Emily. Thinking her name sent a shard of longing deep into his soul. She made him feel like a normal man, not a prince, not a king, not a playboy. With her, he could be himself. He'd given her plenty of reasons to walk out on him in the past, but she never had. She'd stayed and done her job.

She'd finally left him, but only because he'd sent her away. *He'd sent her away.*

Cold fear washed over Kadir as he stood in the Kyrian heat. Emily was gone and he was truly alone. She was the only person who *knew* him. Without her, he would no longer be a man.

He would be a king. A ruler. A potentate.

He would have to close his feelings up and keep them

locked away. He would have no one to share a laugh with, no one to tease him about his magic mattress or his giant ego. No one to chide him for his arrogance or gaze at him with disapproval when he needed it.

No one to love him.

Kadir's chest hurt so much he had to sit down. He dropped onto the cushions and sat there with his head forward, breathing in against the pain that he thought must surely tear him in two.

It was a physical pain, yes, but it was more than that. It stemmed from the chaos in his head, his heart. His skin felt tight, his brain whirled and a wave of anguish formed into a ball in his gut, pressing hard upward. He held it back as long as he could.

And then it erupted from him in a harsh cry that rang through the courtyard and floated into the sky above.

He was a fool! Such a fool. She loved him and he'd sent her away.

Palace guards burst into the courtyard then and Kadir shot up from his seat.

"Your Majesty," one man said as they all bowed low. "We feared for your safety."

His safety? Kadir feared for his sanity if he did not act now. He snatched up his mobile phone and prayed he was not too late as he punched in the number that would connect him to his plane.

Emily was numb. She'd been numb since the moment the man in palace robes had told her that Kadir signed the divorce decree. And then she remained numb as she was ferried to the airport, as she climbed on board Kadir's private jet and waited to depart. But they didn't depart.

Instead, they deplaned and she had to spend time

in a private lounge while they waited for a sandstorm to pass before the airport could be reopened. Finally, someone came and touched her elbow and she looked up to find one of the flight attendants whom she knew from before she'd married Kadir telling her she could board now. The airport was open and they had clearance to fly.

Emily took her seat and strapped herself in. She shook her head when asked if she wanted a beverage. She slid the window shut so she wouldn't have to look at the harsh desert beauty of Kyr for another minute. So she wouldn't have to remember what it was like to spend the night in a tent with Kadir.

But closing the window didn't do a damn thing to help her forget. She closed her eyes and saw Kadir's naked body again. She thought that if she just reached out, she could touch all that smooth, beautiful skin.

Oh, she was such a fool. She'd agreed to marry him in order to help him out, in order to get the money to pay for her father's hospital bills and move him to a warmer climate. She'd thought it would be so easy. Just wear the clothes and play the part and soon it would be over.

It was not over. It would never be over in her heart. She'd fallen in love with him. Emily dragged in a shaky breath. Dammit. How could she ever forget Kadir al-Hassan? She'd spent four years with him, and though he'd made her so angry for much of that time, she'd realized that she wouldn't have been half so incensed with him if she hadn't cared about him.

The plane began to move and Emily sucked back the tears that threatened to spill free. This was it. She was leaving Kyr forever, leaving Kadir. She would go home to Chicago, sell her father's house and move him to Florida, and then she would find another job. Maybe one day she would find another man.

It hardly seemed possible when her body still ached from Kadir's possession last night. How would she ever be able to let another man touch her? Maybe crashing into a concrete embankment on a dark highway was sometimes a kindness.

Emily gritted her teeth. That was a terrible, terrible thought. Her mother died because she was selfish and uncontrollable, not because it was romantic to die with your lover rather than be parted. And hadn't Emily already decided she was not that weak?

Emily reached over and threw the window up, determined to watch Kyr slide by as the plane began to charge the runway. The palms and desert and sandstone blended together faster and faster until suddenly she could feel the ground drop out from beneath them. The plane soared into the sky and she pressed her face to the window, hoping for a glimpse of the royal palace.

But it didn't happen and she sat back again, her heart hurting with everything she felt. She would survive this, but it would take time. She picked up the remote and turned on the television across from her. She needed something to concentrate on, something to distract her. She found a movie and started it. Not a romantic movie, but a taut suspense thriller about some woman running from an organization that wanted her dead.

She'd barely begun the story when the plane banked. There was nothing unusual in that—except that it kept banking, almost as if they were going in a circle. When the nose tilted down rather than up, Emily's gaze snapped up.

A flight attendant hurried over at the look on her

face. "We are returning to the airport, madam. Everything is fine."

"Justine, please call me Emily. We've known each other too long for all this *madam* stuff."

Justine nodded. "Emily, then. The pilot says he's been ordered to return. I don't know why."

Ordered to return. Emily hugged her arms around herself as the plane descended. Soon they were on the ground and taxiing back to the terminal. Emily wanted to scream. She'd already made it through one departure. She didn't want to endure another one, though it seemed as if she would have no choice.

When the door opened, a man in palace robes entered the plane. "Your Highness," he said, bowing low. "Please come with me."

Emily couldn't move for the longest time as she tried to process this latest development. What was going on? Where were they taking her? Had something happened to Kadir?

It was that last thought that had her fumbling for her seat belt and rising on shaky legs to follow the man off the plane and into the waiting limousine. It was nearly dark now and a bloodred moon hung low over the horizon. The sky was that deep purplish-blue that happened only at dusk.

"Where are we going?" she finally asked when the car started to move.

"To the palace, Your Highness. The king commands it."

She turned her head and leaned against the glass. *Why, Kadir? Why?* Her throat ached with the giant lump forming there. How could he bring her back again after he'd dismissed her so coldly earlier? He'd sent her divorce papers and sent her to the airport. And now this.

They soon arrived at the palace. Emily smoothed her skirt and lifted her head high. And then she followed the man inside. People stopped and stared as she passed. A few whispered loudly to each other.

But then the man halted in front of a door flanked by two tall guards with swords that she was positive weren't just ceremonial. After a quick conversation, her escort turned to her. "Are you prepared, Your Highness?"

Emily blinked. He'd called her that three times now, but she was no longer Kadir's wife. It was a mistake, but one that rattled her. "Prepared for what?"

"To appear before the council."

"The council?"

He didn't answer, just flung the door wide and stood back so Emily could enter. Her legs trembled as she stood in the entry to the grand room, but she told herself it was no worse than attending meetings with Kadir in his other life. She'd often sat off to one side and listened to people fight over business while she took notes. How could this be any worse?

She went into the room and ground to a halt as she realized this wasn't a small meeting. The entire council ringed the room on a dais, their faces stern and unfriendly. Emily swallowed. But then a man stood up at the far end of the room and her eyes flew to him.

Kadir.

He looked magnificent in a black *dishdasha* trimmed in gold. Around his waist was a wide belt with a ceremonial dagger and on his head he wore a white *kaffiyeh* held in place with a golden *igal*. Her heart throbbed with love and relief at the sight of him—and, yes, annoyance. She wanted to go to him, but she knew she could not. She remained where she was and waited for someone to tell her what the hell was going on.

Kadir stepped off the dais and came toward her and the trembling in her legs grew stronger. His face was hard and dark and beloved. He was remote and handsome and she reminded herself that she had faced this situation many times before as his PA. She'd stood beside him and not shown an iota of emotion. She could certainly do so now, even if her heart cried out for him.

"Your Majesty," she said, dropping her chin when he strode up to her. The council could not fail to approve of that, she decided.

"Emily." He reached out, and then he was tilting her chin up until she had to look at him. His eyes were softer than before and she swallowed.

"Why am I here?" Her voice was a whisper because she could not manage anything more.

He took her hand and lifted it to his lips, and her body sizzled with that simple touch. "Because I need you."

CHAPTER FOURTEEN

EMILY SWALLOWED AND warned herself sternly not to read anything into this. Kadir had said he needed her many times over their four years together. Usually he needed her to take notes, make calls, reschedule meetings. Last night he'd needed her in a different way, and while her body melted at the memory of everything they'd done together, she would not allow herself to be weak now when she'd been strong for so long.

"Surely you have people who can take notes for you."

His grin was unexpected and her heart skipped a beat. "This is why I love you, Emily. You say things to me that no one else would. You make me laugh."

Emily's lungs refused to fill for a long moment. "Please don't say those words to me. I'm in no place to take them as a joke right now."

He frowned. "I am doing this badly, then. They were not meant as a joke."

She closed her eyes and forced herself to be calm before she could look into his gray gaze again. "You're seriously telling me right now, right here, in front of a council of Kyrian leaders, that you love me?"

His frown deepened. "Bad timing, yes? I apologize, but I'm desperate."

She let her gaze drift over the gathering. They still

looked stern, but she was fairly certain they couldn't hear what she and Kadir were saying. And then his words sank in and she realized what he was doing. Still playing the game, still trying to prove to these men he wasn't a king.

"I take it your brother has arrived." She said the words dully even as her heart froze solid.

Kadir was looking at her curiously. "Yes. I have summoned him to this meeting as well. He will be here any moment."

"I see." And she did. Kadir was making one last desperate bid for his freedom. Everyone believed he was the next king, but if his brother was here, then he could formally renounce the throne in front of the council and Rashid would take it. She was here to remind them how faulty his judgment could be. Perhaps he'd even decided to insist she be his queen. That would give the old boys a heart attack for sure.

He kissed her hand again and then tucked it into his arm before leading her up to the dais and seating her in one of the chairs placed against the wall. He touched her cheek, his fingers lingering for a long moment. It took everything she had not to lean into his touch. Not to close her eyes and press his palm to her skin.

He needed her to help him once more. To get him out of a predicament. So why did he have to carry the game too far and tell her he loved her? Her soul was already broken and battered because of the last few days with this man. She didn't need to heap a false promise of love on top of the pile of rubble her life had become.

Kadir took his seat again. She tried not to look at him, but she couldn't drag her gaze from his profile. But then the door opened and another man came in. This man looked so much like Kadir that she might have sworn they were twins. Tall, handsome, yet somehow colder and far more remote than Kadir had ever been.

Rashid looked angry, haunted, and yet he also looked as if no man in this room could defeat him. No matter what anyone did to him, his eyes said, he would always win. Because, she realized, he didn't care what happened to him. She could see it in the set of his shoulders, the defiant look in his sharp gaze. He looked like someone who had lost everything and therefore couldn't care about anyone. This was the Lion of Kyr, a fierce, hard, brooding man who would as soon chew his own leg off than be trapped and tamed.

"Welcome, brother," Kadir said in English. The council swung their gazes to him, no doubt surprised that he wasn't speaking Arabic. Kadir stood and walked down the steps to the floor. Then he turned around, his arms wide, and faced the entire council. He said something in Arabic and a man hurried over to the foot of the dais.

"Omar will translate what I say, but I will be speaking in English so that my wife can understand."

Emily's jaw dropped, but Kadir kept speaking. "Yes, you are still my wife, Emily. I have rescinded the divorce decree. We are married, unless you tell me you want it otherwise."

He bowed his head a moment, and then he shook it, muttering to himself. A second later, he was bounding up the stairs and pulling her to her feet. They stood facing one another while the council, Rashid and the translator looked on.

"I will not divorce you, Emily. I love you too much. And if I am to be king of Kyr, you will be queen."

Emily's heart pounded. The words coming from his lips were so beautiful, so amazing, but she told herself not to believe them. It was a performance, and a good one. But oh, how it hurt. How much she wanted it to be real, for this amazing man to truly want her as his wife.

The interpreter finished speaking and the council started to murmur. She couldn't tell if it was an angry murmur or what because her blood hummed too loudly in her ears. She couldn't drag her gaze away from Kadir, though she desperately wanted to. She was just like all those other women, wanting him so much, wanting to believe everything he said, reading more into it than there was.

"There is another solution," Kadir continued, this time turning to face the room. He held her hand tightly in his. "My brother, Rashid, can take the throne. He is the eldest. He has no wife. His business is oil, whereas mine is building skyscrapers. A good skill, but not quite the one Kyr needs."

Rashid stood, tight-lipped and furious, but he did not speak. His arms were folded over his chest and he glared at them both. Emily knew then that this performance was as much for Rashid as for the council.

Kadir led her down the stairs and over to Rashid. His gaze flickered over her but stayed on Kadir.

"I have seen his last decrees, Rashid. He did not name his successor. He was stubborn to the last."

"He wanted us to fight over it, then." Rashid sounded bitter.

"Or maybe he decided to let us choose."

Rashid's snort said he didn't believe it for a moment. "If that gives you comfort, brother."

"It does not. But I know in my heart that you are Kyr's king. And I am your faithful servant."

Rashid's eyes blazed with fresh agony. "Kadir—"

"Take your place, Rashid. Take your nation and be the king you were meant to be."

The two men stared at each other for a long moment. And then Rashid looked over at her and Emily's belly churned.

"You truly love this woman?"

"With every atom of my being."

Emily couldn't stop the sob that choked out of her then. Both men were looking at her. Kadir seemed alarmed.

"Sorry," she said, yanking her hand from his. "I can't—I can't…"

She rushed toward the door and yanked it open and then she was running blindly down the hall in her too-tall shoes. She tripped and stumbled, catching herself against the wall. Then she reached down and ripped off the shoes, tossing them so she could run barefoot through the palace.

"Emily!"

Kadir's voice behind her sounded frantic, but she didn't stop. She couldn't. She kept running, past people who stopped and stared, past servants and delivery-men, past the dignitaries who were gathering in Kyr for the old king's funeral. Tears streaked down her cheeks, blurred her vision, but she kept running until she burst into an outdoor gallery that flanked a giant grassy courtyard ringed by palm trees. Water tinkled in a fountain at the center of the courtyard, an extravagance in the desert.

"Emily."

She spun to find Kadir behind her. The moonlight on his face revealed confusion and apprehension. Or maybe it was just a trick of the light. Maybe it was what she wanted instead of what was.

She backed away, hitting the lip of the fountain. Somehow she managed not to fall in, but what did it matter? Her dignity was already ruined. She'd burst into tears in front of him, in front of them all, and she'd failed in her performance as his wife when he'd needed it most.

"Why did you have to say that?" she demanded. "Why did you have to taunt me that way?"

Kadir came forward, holding out a hand as if trying to gentle a frightened animal. "Say what, Emily? What did I say that upset you so much?"

She couldn't breathe. She pressed her hand to her stomach and tried to concentrate on pulling air into her lungs, but it hurt so badly. "You lied, Kadir. In front of them all. You lied so your brother would take the throne."

"I did not lie." His face was a thundercloud now and she marveled at how he could be so indignant when she was the one who'd been wronged.

"You said you love me." It hurt to repeat the words, but she shook her head and continued. "You said it so the council would think you were a bad choice to rule this nation. I understand why you did it, but it's wrong to say something like that."

He came closer then, his eyes narrowed. "What if I meant it?"

She snorted. "You can't mean it."

"Why not? Because I am a player? Because I tend to pick women based on their bra size rather than their intellect?"

He somehow managed to prick her conscience. Last night he'd grown angry when she'd said something about his smooth talking. And she'd admitted to herself that he was not unfeeling. But that was before he'd used love to get what he wanted.

"I'm just your temporary wife, Kadir. And your former employee. You can't love me after one night of sex."

"No, I don't love you after one night of sex."

Her lungs deflated again. But at least he was being honest.

He grabbed her shoulders and forced her to look up at him. "I love you because I can't live without you. Because you're my best friend in the world, the one person who knows me for who I really am and who loves me in spite of myself."

"I never said I loved you." Her voice was a whisper and her pulse was a hot rush in her veins.

He smiled and there was a world of feeling in that smile. For her. "But you do. I know it, Emily. I know it because I feel exactly as you feel. As if my world would end when you walked out of it."

"That's not love. That's infatuation." She sniffed.

"I don't believe that for a minute."

Panic flooded her as old fears sprang to the fore. "But what if it's true? What if one day one of us wakes up and decides this is no longer enough? What if we want more than the other can give?"

His brows drew down, his eyes searching hers. "Why are you saying these things?"

Emily trembled. "My mother left my father when he got sick. For another man. She claimed to love Dad, but when he needed her, she left." Her throat ached. "If she hadn't left us, she wouldn't have been in the car with that man when he, when he—"

"He what, Emily?"

"He drove into an embankment. They were killed instantly."

He yanked her into his arms and hugged her tight. "I'm sorry, so sorry. But please tell me what this has to do with us."

She clutched his robes and hid her face among the folds. He smelled so good. When she was in his arms like this, she never wanted to leave. But what if she had no choice?

"What if I turn out like her in spite of my best intentions? What if I make a bad decision? What if, six months from now, you decide you've had enough of me? What will I do then? Something stupid?"

He squeezed her against him. "Other than falling in love with me, I am pretty certain you are incapable of stupid things."

"I never said I loved you."

He gently pushed her back and gazed down at her. "No, you didn't. And I want to hear it."

Panic twisted in her belly. "I'm afraid, Kadir."

"So am I. I just gave up a throne for you and maybe it was all for nothing."

She laughed, but it wasn't precisely a happy sound. "You did not give it up for me. You never wanted it in the first place."

"No, this is true. But I would have taken it to save Kyr. And I would have given it up to have you, even if having you meant ruining Kyr."

"Don't say that!" She glanced at the surrounding courtyard, worried that someone would overhear him. Surely he was committing treason to even think such a thing.

"I'm not worried. Besides, Rashid is king now. I can say what I wish."

"He agreed?"

"I didn't give him much choice, I'm afraid." He ran

his hands down her arms and bent to meet her gaze again. "We are not finished yet. I'm waiting for you to admit you love me."

Fear was a palpable thing in her chest. "What happens in six months? A year?"

"I have no idea, but I know that whatever it is, it will happen with you at my side."

He sounded so certain, so confident, but how did he know?

"If I left you now, you'd get over it."

"Eventually." He sighed and took a step back. "Emily, all I want is your happiness. If leaving me is what will make you happy, then I'll grant you the divorce. But I have no fear about the strength of our love, if you will only admit the way you feel."

"You aren't worried I'll leave you in six months? Or twenty years?"

"No." He spread his arms and flourished his palms as if showcasing the merchandise. "Six *days* with all this and you will be incapable of ever looking at another man."

Emily couldn't help but laugh, in spite of the fear still gripping her heart. "You're incorrigible, Kadir."

"I believe *delightful* is the word you are looking for."

Something gave way in her heart then, some last little lock that was holding tight to her fear and pain and binding her in chains of unhappiness. And when it did, when her heart could finally beat again, the feelings swelling inside it were all for this man. Her love was bright and hot and true and she knew it would last.

Just as his would last for her.

"Yes," she said softly, "I think that *is* the word."

Kadir dragged her into his arms and kissed her hard.

"You are mine," he growled when he finally let her breathe again. "Mine forever."

"And you are mine."

"This is a deal I'll happily accept."

They kissed under the moonlight until Kadir swept her into his arms. Emily wrapped her arms around his neck, giddy with love and excitement and sheer joy as her gorgeous sheikh strode into the palace and up to their suite of rooms.

Then he set her down, stripped her slowly and spent the rest of the night showing her just how delightful—and incorrigible—he could be.

* * * * *

MORE PRECIOUS
THAN A CROWN

CAROL MARINELLI

Carol Marinelli is a Taurus, with Taurus rising, yet still thinks she is a secret Gemini. Originally from England she now lives in Australia and is a single mother of three. Apart from her children, writing romance and the friendships forged along the way are her passion. She chooses to believe in a happy ever after for all and strives for that in her writing.

PROLOGUE

'Has anyone seen Trinity?'

Dianne's voice carried through the still night. It had become a familiar cry this past year or so, and one that Sheikh Prince Zahid of Ishla had grown more than a little used to whenever he spent time at the Fosters' residence.

Zahid had been a regular guest to the household since he had been sixteen but now, about to turn twenty-two, he had made the decision that this would be his last time he would stay here. The next time he was invited he would politely decline.

Zahid walked through the woods at the edge of the Foster property. He could hear the sounds of laughter carry across the lake on this clear summer night. Zahid was flying back to Ishla soon and he hoped that his driver would arrive early rather than promptly, for he really would rather not be here. The Fosters were throwing a party to celebrate their son Donald's graduation and, given that they had added the fact that Zahid too was graduating, it would have been rude to decline.

Next time he would.

Zahid did not enjoy their company, he never really had. Gus Foster was a politician and it seemed to Zahid that he never switched off. His wife Dianne's sole purpose in life seemed to be to stand by her man whatever Gus did. Since Zahid had known the family, there had been the humiliation of two very public affairs as well as the scandalous revelations of sleazier encounters and not once had Dianne's plastic smile wavered.

After tonight he would not have to see it again, Zahid thought. Neither would he have to make polite small talk with the obnoxious Gus. He only did it because he was a friend of their son Donald.

Well, as much as Zahid had friends.

Zahid was a lone wolf and very independent. He preferred the company of a beautiful woman on a Saturday night rather than this type of thing, but obligation had brought him here.

When he had been sixteen and a boarder at a top school there had been a random locker inspection and a wad of cash and drugs had been found in Zahid's locker. They had not been Zahid's. It hadn't been the mandatory suspension that had been the problem, though. It had been the deep shame that such a scandal would cause his family.

On hearing the news, Zahid's father, King Fahid, had immediately boarded his jet to fly from Ishla to speak with the headmaster, not to cover things up, for that was not how things worked in Ishla. Instead, Zahid had explained to Donald, the king was on his way to England to apologise and take his disgraced son home. Once in Ishla, Zahid would have to publicly apologise to the people of Ishla.

'Even if you didn't do it?' Donald had asked.

Zahid had nodded.

'It is up to the people if they forgive me.'

Zahid had stepped into the headmaster's office with his back straight and his head held high, ready to meet his fate, only to find out that there had been a misunderstanding.

Donald, the headmaster had informed the prince and king, on hearing about the locker inspection, had panicked and placed the money and drugs in Zahid's. It was Donald who would now be suspended and the school offered its sincere apologies for the disruption the incident had caused the king.

As the king and young prince had stepped out of the headmaster's office, there had stood Donald with his father, Gus.

'Thank you,' King Fahid had said to Donald, 'for being man enough to admit the error of your ways.'

'You miss the point,' Gus had said to the king. 'My son would never do drugs, he did this to help a friend.'

The Fosters had taken it on the chin.

Gus had even given a speech in Parliament, stating that even the most loving, functional families were not exempt from the perils of teenage years.

Functional?

Zahid had frowned at the choice of word then and was frowning now as he walked, recalling that time all those years ago.

The Fosters had appeared on the front pages on the Sunday newspapers. Dianne, smiling her plastic smile for the cameras, Gus with his arm around his suitably sheepish-looking son. The only one who had spoiled the picture-perfect image had been Trinity—she had been dressed in her Sunday best but, rather than smiling, she had scowled at the cameras.

Zahid actually smiled as he recalled the photo from

yesteryear but he wasn't smiling a few seconds later when a streak of blonde caught his eye.

There was Trinity.

She was hiding a bag of clothes beneath a tree and wiping lipstick off, and jumped when she heard Zahid call out and start walking towards her.

'Trinity!' Zahid said. 'Your mother has been calling for you. Where have you been?'

She swung around to face him. 'Please, Zahid, can I say that I've been with you?'

'You know I don't lie.'

'Please,' Trinity said, and then sighed. Zahid was so austere, so formal and so rigid that it was pointless even trying to get him on side. Yet, just as she went to walk off and face the music, he halted her.

'If I am going to cover for you, first I need to know what you have been up to.'

Trinity slowly turned. Even when she had asked Zahid to cover for her, she'd never really expected him to agree, yet it sounded now like he might. 'I was at my friend Suzanne's,' came her cautious reply.

'Doing what?'

'Just…' Trinity shrugged.

'Just what?'

'Dancing.'

'You have been to a party?'

'No! We were just listening to music in her room and dancing.' Trinity almost rolled her eyes as she attempted to explain to his nonplussed expression, because clearly that wasn't the type of behaviour Zahid would understand. 'We were trying on make-up, that sort of thing.'

'Why are you hiding clothes?' Zahid looked at what she was wearing—a long-sleeved top and a pair of jeans—and then he watched as Trinity screwed her blue eyes closed, no doubt to come up with a suitable lie.

Trinity was, Zahid knew, a skilled liar, only what he didn't know was that she wasn't trying to lie now. She simply didn't know, in this, how she could tell the truth, when it was just a feeling she had.

How could she explain that Suzanne had suggested she borrow some clothes because Trinity hadn't liked the way her aunt's new husband had been looking at her in the dress her mother had bought for her? Trinity didn't understand enough herself, let alone know how to explain it to Zahid, just how awkward Clive made her feel.

She refused to call him Uncle.

He was the reason that she'd run off.

It was the reason that Trinity was always running off at family things and, given that Zahid was only ever there on family occasions, he saw this behaviour all too often.

'Last time I was here, I caught you climbing out of your bedroom window,' Zahid said, and watched as Trinity did her very best to keep her face straight. 'It is not a laughing matter.'

No, it wasn't a laughing matter, Trinity thought, but the memory of it made her smile. Zahid had refused to believe she had simply been hungry and, rather than facing all the guests, had simply been trying to sneak into the kitchen. He'd brought her out a plate of food and then watched as she'd climbed back up to her room, using a tree and the trellis. Given her practised movements, it had been a presumably well-worn path for Trinity.

'I haven't done anything wrong,' Trinity said.

'Perhaps not, but on family occasions you should be here.' It was black and white to Zahid yet sometimes with Trinity it blurred to grey. She was so spirited and wilful and just so visibly unimpressed with her family that at times she made Zahid silently cheer, not that he would let her know that. 'You don't just disappear.'

'I know, I know,' Trinity started, but then a mischievous smile prettied her sulky face. 'So, what's your excuse, then?'

'Excuse?'

'What are you doing in the woods?' And then, as realisation hit, she started to laugh. 'Sorry, that was a stupid question.' Zahid's frown only deepened the more she tried to explain. 'Well, I guess you needed to…' Trinity stopped then. There was not a single vulgar thing about Zahid and, no, now that she came to think of it, Trinity could not imagine Zahid popping into the woods to answer the call of nature! 'My mistake.'

'I went for a walk so that I could think.' Zahid looked down at her. Of all the Fosters, Trinity was the only one he would miss. Yes, she made him smile at times, but he wasn't smiling as he saw that since her last escapade Trinity had changed. She had, in fact, grown into a very beautiful young woman. Her hair was blonde and had been cut in a jagged style, her eyes were huge in a too-thin face and they sparkled as she waited for him to speak. 'If you were in Ishla you would be expected to support your parents and mix with the guests…'

'I'm not in Ishla, though.'

As they started to walk back towards the party, Trinity tripped a little.

'Have you been drinking?'

'No.'

'Are you sure?'

'I think I'd remember if I had.'

He turned her to him and took her cheeks in his hands. He saw her dilated pupils and neither quite recognised the lust between them yet. 'Blow.'

'You're breath-testing me?'

'Blow,' Zahid said, and she did, but he could smell no alcohol.

'What are you up to, Trinity?' Zahid asked, except his hands did not leave her face and neither did Trinity want them to. Yes, he was boring, yes, he was yawn-yawn dignified, but sometimes when he smiled, sometimes when his subtle humour went completely over her parents' heads, he made her laugh. She had never understood what women saw in him. Donald was bitterly jealous and complained often to his family that women only went after Zahid for his title.

Tonight Trinity would beg to differ.

Now she understood his attraction, for those black eyes made the skin on her cheeks flare with heat and the height of him, instead of intimidating her, had her wanting to stand on tiptoe and lift her face to his like a flower to the sun.

Now they recognised the lust.

Zahid looked down at her. She was like a little wild kitten that any minute might scratch but right now was temporarily tame, and Zahid was knocked sideways by her appeal.

'Am I to breathe out again…?' Trinity said, and as he went to open his mouth to tell her they should get back, Trinity blew into his open mouth. He captured her breath and then swallowed, and for the first time Zahid wrestled with self-control.

'You need to be more careful,' Zahid warned. 'You should not be walking alone in the woods at night.'

'In case a handsome prince happens to be walking by?'

'I could be anyone,' Zahid pointed out, but his hands were still on her cheeks.

Their lips were almost touching.

'You're you,' Trinity said, 'and I want you to give me my first kiss.'

Her mouth was, to Zahid, perfect and he was, rarely for him, tentative as his lips grazed hers for he was wrestling for control, forcing himself to hold back not just want, for the pulse of her flesh on his lips gave him more than the usual want, it filled him with need, and a man of Zahid's standing must never feel need that wasn't met.

For Trinity to feel him kiss her so tenderly, to feel that sulky mouth now soft against hers, was sublime.

A late developer, for six months now, or perhaps a little more, Trinity had loathed her body. The feel of another's eyes on her had made her feel ill. Family functions had been spent fighting hands that wandered, yet she was not fighting hands now. She loved the feel of Zahid's hands moving from her cheeks and down to her waist, and when her lips parted the slip of tongues was so mutual, so natural that Trinity let out a moan.

Zahid would have loved to linger, she tasted of cinnamon and was so sweet and warm, but the purr of her too-thin body beneath his hands, the sudden tip into sexual hunger from Trinity, the raw need in himself were enough for Zahid to attempt to halt things.

'That was not your first kiss.' His voice was not accusing, he was merely stating a fact, for never had a mouth had such an effect on him before and surely it had been a practised kiss.

'Okay, it was my second,' Trinity admitted. 'Suzanne and I practised a while back so that we'd know what we were doing, but this doesn't feel like practice, though,' she breathed, her mouth searching for his again.

'You need to get back,' Zahid said. His voice was just a touch stern, for he was cross at his own lack of control. His life was ordered, the women he dated were generally a few years older than him, not the other way around, and with reason, for emotion he kept at a distance and love was something to actively avoid.

Sex was the name of the game but it felt like more than that now.

Trinity's hands met at the back of his neck and she looked up at him. His hands were just above her hips and she knew that at any moment they would disengage, that he would take her back, but Trinity didn't want that. She wanted her first proper kiss to go on for longer, she did not want to return to her family and the house, but more than that, she wanted more time with Zahid.

He was far too tall for her mouth to reach his without Zahid lowering his head, so when still he did not, her mouth moved to his neck, and worked upwards, inhaling his lovely scent and feeling his hands digging deeper into her hips.

There was a strange push-pull, for he should push her off, take her hand and walk back, yet Zahid was resisting the urge to pull her into his groin. Trinity's tongue licked up his neck and then one hand did move. Zahid took her chin in his fingers and Trinity blinked up at him. She thought for a moment that she was about to be told off, but instead his mouth came down on hers

and she found out that the first kiss had been but a pre-
cursor to bliss.

Trinity's eyes snapped open at the passion behind his
kiss. She was a little shocked, a little heady and then,
when she saw the usually remote Zahid so consumed,
Trinity's eyes closed again and just revelled in the bliss
of being so thoroughly kissed. One of his hands was
stroking her hip and his tongue was sliding around hers
and there was nothing but pleasure to be had. His other
hand was on her shoulder but almost pushing her back
in an attempt to resist pulling her in, yet it was Trinity who ignored the pressure and moved a delicious bit
closer and discovered her home.

In the circle of his arms, pressed against him, she
found herself.

Trinity loved the feel of his sex against her stomach
and finally the bliss of the pressure of his hand pulling her in as his tongue duelled with hers. Now she
moved up on tiptoe, wanting to feel that delicious hard
length lower yet. Still fighting himself, Zahid pushed
her down. It was like a match to gasoline for Trinity
and she rose to her toes again and then it was she who
pushed down and Zahid wrenched his face back, ending the kiss but not the contact of their groins, his dark
eyes assessing her but with a smile on that stern mouth,
which was shiny from hers.

'Don't stop,' Trinity urged, pressing herself to him,
She was building towards something that felt like a faint
wail of sirens in the vague distance. Her body was on
delicious alert, seeking their direction, as Zahid did his
best to contain her.

'We shall stop,' Zahid said.

'Why?'

'Because…' Zahid did not want to stop, but neither did he want to continue things here. 'Because my driver shall be here soon to take me back to Ishla, and you are too good for the woods.'

'Take me back to your palace.' Trinity smiled but then it disappeared, a note of urgency creeping into her voice. 'I need to get away…'

Zahid frowned. 'When you say—' He never got to finish, Dianne's shrill voice terminating their conversation.

'There you are. What the hell…?'

Zahid dropped contact as soon as he realised that her mother was there but Trinity still hung like a cheeky monkey around his neck.

'Mrs Foster, I apologise. I was—'

'Oh, it's you! It's fine, Zahid.' Dianne was instantly mollified when she saw that it was Zahid who her daughter was with. 'Zahid, your driver is here and, Trinity, you need to come and say goodbye to our guests…' They walked back through the woods and towards the house, Zahid frowning at Dianne's rather inappropriate response—surely she should be furious but she was chatting away as if nothing had happened. 'Clive and Elaine are staying. Trinity, I want you to go and get the guest room ready.'

His driver was waiting and he pulled Zahid aside to tell him that if he wanted to fly tonight, they needed to leave now.

Zahid said swift goodbyes, but Trinity caught his hand and he could see the tears filling her eyes.

'Zahid, what I said about you taking me with you. Do you think maybe—?'

'Trinity.' He could have kicked himself. She was

reading far too much into one kiss and he had never meant to confuse her. He was just glad that Dianne had disturbed them when she had.

'I have to go.' Zahid's words were a touch abrupt but better that than she even glimpse the effect she had had on him.

Her hand gripped his fingers and he felt the brush of her fingertips as he pulled away from her and glanced at his watch.

It was ten minutes after eleven and as he climbed into his car, little did he know that it was a moment in time he would regret for ever.

He looked out of the window and cursed his brief lack of control as the car pulled off.

It was better that he return now to Ishla, Zahid decided, for he did not like her unsettling effect on him.

Yet it was one kiss that he would always remember.

As for Trinity...

She saw his car drive off and on her mother's orders headed back into the house to prepare the guest room.

Trinity too would never forget that night.

But for all the wrong reasons.

CHAPTER ONE

'DECLINE.'

Sheikh Prince Zahid's response was immediate.

The king, his son and Abdul, the king's chief aide, were walking through the second palace of Ishla, discussing the refurbishments that were necessary if it were to be inhabited again. As they walked Abdul discussed the diaries of the royal prince and king and raised the matter of Donald Foster's wedding.

The Fosters had always imbued a certain discomfort in Zahid—loud, brash, their egos and need to further themselves at all costs had not sat comfortably with Zahid. As he had matured he had done his best to politely sever contact but Donald had remained persistent and they still occasionally kept in touch.

'But Donald has asked you to be his best man.'

Zahid's jaw tightened a fraction as Abdul spoke on. Zahid had not told his father that just last week Donald had called, asking him if he would be his best man at his wedding to Yvette. Zahid had said to Donald that, while flattered, he had duties in his homeland at that time and would not be able to attend. He had rather hoped that that would be the end of it, but of course Donald had persisted and it would now appear that a formal invitation had been sent, along with a repeated request that Zahid be Donald's best man. 'I have already explained that I cannot attend his wedding,' Zahid said to Abdul. 'Offer my apologies and arrange a gift…'

'Donald Foster?' The King halted and turned round and Zahid silently cursed Abdul for insisting that they go through the diaries now. He had been hoping that his father would not find out. 'That is the man who saved our family from shame…'

'That was a very long time ago, Father.'

'Our country has a long memory,' the king responded. 'You owe that man…'

'I have more than repaid my debt to him.'

Over and over Zahid had repaid his debt to Donald—he had been his friend when, perhaps, Zahid would rather not have been, he had secured invitations to functions that Donald would never have got into had he not asked Zahid to intervene, and over the years Donald had also borrowed significant amounts of money and made no effort to pay him back.

'Were it not for Donald,' the king pointed out, 'you would have been brought into disrepute. More than that, you would have brought our country into disrepute. When is the wedding?'

'It is in two weeks,' Abdul said, then looked at Zahid. 'We could rearrange your schedule.'

'First a wedding and, given the speed it's been arranged, soon it will be a christening…' Zahid pointed out, and the King tutted.

'I would support a polite declining of your attendance at a christening for a child conceived out of wedlock, as would our people, but the wedding…'

To the king's surprise, Zahid took no more persuading, for he interrupted with a brief nod and then turned to Abdul. 'Very well, arrange my schedule but make it a brief visit, two nights at the most. I will fly out the day after the wedding.'

'If only it were that easy to get you to agree to more pressing matters,' Fahid commented, but Zahid did not respond, for he knew what was coming next—his father had brought him here for a reason, Zahid was sure. 'We need to speak about the renovations that are needed here.'

Memories stirred for both the king and Abdul as they walked through the second jewel of Ishla. The second palace was where Zahid and his sister Layla had been born and raised. Even on their mother's death, when Zahid had been seven, they had lived here. The king had been heartbroken at the death of his wife, Annan, but thanks to the privacy the second palace had afforded them, he had been able to grieve largely in private.

Zahid deliberately kept his face impassive as they discussed the work that needed doing, but he knew that just the fact his father had chosen to speak with him here meant that the reins were tightening.

His father had long since wanted him to choose a suitable bride. So far Zahid had resisted, he liked his freedom far too much, but this was a working royal family and Zahid's skills in engineering were being utilised, his vision for Ishla was taking shape, and more and more his time was spent here.

It was time for Zahid to raise a family.

'There is much work to be done,' Abdul said. 'The chief architect is concerned about some erosion on the cliff face and, as we thought, the great hall and the master suite are in need of structural repair.'

'How long will that take?'

'Six months to a year is his best estimate,' Abdul said, and went into further detail. It wasn't as simple as commencing work—the second palace contained many valuable pieces that would need to be catalogued and stored before work could even begin.

'You do realise, Zahid,' the king said to his eldest son, 'that once it gets out that activity has commenced at the second place, our people will assume that we are preparing the palace for the crown prince and his bride.'

'I do,' Zahid replied.

'And does six months to one year sound like a time-frame you could operate within?'

Black eyes met black eyes and there was a small stand-off. The king had raised a leader, which meant Zahid would not simply be told what he should do.

'I think that at this stage, it would be premature to go ahead with the renovations.' Zahid did not flinch as he defied his father's request that he marry soon.

'Your country wants to know that they have a prince who will—'

'They have a prince,' Zahid calmly interrupted, 'who shall one day rule fairly and wisely. I do not need a bride to assure them of that.'

'You need an heir,' the king said. 'If something should happen to you, they need to know that the line will continue.' He let out an irritated breath. Zahid re-fused to be pushed into anything, which the king grudg-ingly admired, but the people needed reassuring. Time was running out for the king and so he chose now to play the one card he had that just might persuade Zahid to submit to his will. 'Of course, should something happen to you, it would be Layla's son who would be next in line.'

Zahid's jaw gritted because Layla did not have a husband, let alone a son.

'Perhaps,' the king continued, 'if the crown prince chooses not to marry yet, another royal wedding might appease the people.'

'Father…' Zahid addressed him as a father and not a king, trying to reach for his softer side, for the king truly adored his daughter. 'Layla does not like any of her prospective husbands.'

'Layla needs to understand that with privilege comes responsibility. I am thinking of inviting the Fayeds to dine here at the palace next week.'

Zahid thought about Layla, who had kicked, screamed and bitten when her father had once attempted to drag her out to meet suitors.

She was a rebel, a challenge, and reminded him of…

Perhaps it was the wedding invitation but Zahid's mind drifted back in time and he recalled Trinity. Not the kiss but the fire in her eyes and a spirit that would not be crushed. Imagine Trinity being forced to marry. It would never happen.

'You wouldn't do that to Layla,' Zahid said, but the king nodded for Abdul to leave them for a moment and, once alone, he addressed his son.

'Today there are reports in the news that I have lost weight. Last week it was reported that during my last overseas trip I was hospitalised. Soon I will not be well enough to leave Ishla for my treatments and the people will know that I have little time left. They need to know the future is secure.' It was said without emotion and should be accepted the same way. Feelings were frowned upon, especially for a male royal, but Zahid could not allow Layla to be used as a pawn. If he married then he could change things for Layla, who, unlike him, believed in foolish things like a marriage based on love.

It was not just the king that Layla had wrapped around her little finger. History meant that Zahid too, was extremely protective towards his sister. Not that Layla knew why, for the time of the queen's death and its aftermath must never be discussed.

'I want to announce a royal wedding,' the king reiterated. 'I want to hear cheering in the street when you walk onto the balcony with your chosen bride.'

'Chosen?' Zahid's word was tart. For all the dining with families that would take place, for all the pomp and ceremony that went in to choosing a bride, both the king and Zahid knew it was a given. Zahid must choose Princess Sameena of Bishram and right his father's wrongs for Fahid had not chosen wisely.

Instead of choosing Princess Raina of Bishram, a younger Fahid had fallen in love.

Zahid though, would choose wisely. Sameena was his father's first choice, for the long-ago snub to the now Queen Raina still caused problems and both men hoped for friendlier relations between Ishla and Bishram.

Zahid, though, leaned towards Sheikha Kumu.

Her country, though small, was prosperous and had an extremely efficient army.

It was a business decision to Zahid and one he would not take lightly.

'You do not need to ask the Fayeds to dine just yet.' Finally Zahid relented. 'You are right: the people have already waited long enough for their prince to choose his bride. Six months to a year sounds a suitable time frame.'

'I am pleased to hear it,' the king said, and then called his aide to join them again. 'Abdul, do what is necessary for the renovations to commence.' He did little to contain the smile of victory that played on his lips as he continued speaking. 'And send out the invitations for potential brides and their families to dine.'

Zahid walked through to the master suite and on the king's instruction a servant opened the huge shutter and the sun streamed into the room and fell on a large carved wooden bed. Here, Zahid and his bride would first live till, on the king's death, they moved to the first palace to rule the land that he loved.

Zahid did not have six months left to enjoy being single for once his bride was officially chosen his playboy reputation must become a thing of the past.

It was a very sobering thought and one that did not go unnoticed by his sister.

As he prepared to fly to London for Donald's wedding, Layla came to his suite.

'Father says that the renovations are starting.'

'Correct.'

'Do you know who you will choose as your bride?'

Zahid did not answer, not that Layla let that stop the conversation.

'Perhaps Sheikha Kumu?' Layla fished. 'She is well connected and very pretty, or maybe Princess Sameena, she's so beautiful—'

'It is not about looks,' Zahid interrupted. 'I will choose the bride who will best serve our people. One who will understand that my heart belongs to them.'

Layla rolled her eyes. 'Ah, but I bet you take looks into consideration when you are choosing your lovers.'

'Layla!' Zahid warned, but she would not quiet.

'Why don't women get to go overseas? Why were you allowed to leave Ishla for your education?'

'You know why, Layla.'

'Well, it's not fair. At least you have had some fun before you choose your bride. Father is speaking about the Fayeds again. I don't want Hassain to be my first love.' She pulled a face and Zahid suppressed a smile. He wanted to tell his sister that when he was king he would change things, but that conversation was too dangerous to have just yet.

'I want to know what it is to fall in love.' Layla pouted.

Zahid could think of nothing worse than a mind dizzied by emotion. He truly could not stand the thought of a life lived in love.

Yes, there was a year of her life that Layla didn't know about.

The first year.

He looked at his sister who lived with her head in the clouds, yet he cared for her so. He could still remember her screaming in the crib, could still recall their father's repeated rejection of his second born, who he had blamed for his wife's death.

No, Layla must never know.

'Layla, the palace will be busy preparing for my wedding. You do not have to worry for a while.'

'But I do worry,' Layla said. 'Zahid, can I come to England with you? I would love to see the sights, and to go to a real English wedding...'

'Layla, you know that you cannot travel until you are married.'

'No,' Layla corrected him, 'the rule is that I cannot travel unless I am escorted by a family member. If you took me...'

'I am not taking you to England with me,' Zahid said. He would already have his work cut out with the Fosters and their debauched ways, let alone adding Layla to the mix. Zahid rolled his eyes. There was no doubt in his mind that his best-man duties would involve policing Trinity.

Once he had agreed to attend the wedding, Zahid had looked her up and his face had hardened as he had read on and flicked through images. Having completed school, or rather, as Zahid knew from Donald, a stint in rehab, Trinity had, it would seem, jumped straight off the wagon. There were several pieces about how she loved to party, combined with several images of her falling out of nightclubs. Things had gone quiet in recent years, though. She was now living in California and only came home on occasion, such as for the wedding of her brother.

His curiosity about Trinity surprised even Zahid. He could barely remember most of the women he had dated, yet the one kiss that he and Trinity had shared still remained clear in his mind, so much so that it took a moment to drag his mind back to the conversation.

'Can I come on your honeymoon, then?' Layla persisted.

'I will hopefully be busy on my honeymoon,' Zahid said.

'Not the desert part.' Layla laughed. 'After. When you travel overseas, can I at least come with you then?'

It was not such a strange request—sisters often travelled as companionship for the new bride.

'You might not like the bride I choose,' Zahid pointed out.

'*You* might not like the bride you choose.' Layla smiled. 'So I will entertain her so that you do not have to worry about such things as shopping and lunch.'

'We shall see.'

'Promise me that you will take me, Zahid,' Layla said. 'I need something to look forward to.'

'You are up to something?'

'No,' Layla said. 'I am just bored and I want something to dream about, something to look forward to.' She glanced at the clock. 'I need to go and meet my students.'

'Then go,' Zahid said, but Layla would not move till she got her way.

'How can I teach my students about the world when I have never even left Ishla?'

Zahid accepted that she made a good point. 'Very well, you can travel overseas with us when I take my bride on honeymoon.'

It was no big deal to Zahid.

Romance was not part of the equation in any marriage that he had in mind and that was the reason he said yes.

CHAPTER TWO

AN ASH CLOUD, perchance? Trinity's heart lurched in hope when she saw that her flight was delayed.

A really, really big ash cloud that would ground aviation for days.

Or maybe the baggage handlers could go on strike.

LAX had been busy, busy and JFK was much the same. Trinity knew she had been cutting it almost impossibly fine to get back in time for her brother's wedding and now that her flight had been delayed there was a very real prospect that the bridesmaid wouldn't make it to the church on time.

Had she been willing that ash cloud to appear perhaps?

Of course she had.

Just a nice natural disaster where no one got hurt and one where it could be explained in the speeches that, though Trinity had done everything she possibly could to get there...

Boarding.

Trinity watched as the sign flicked over and dragged herself to the back of the line. Even as she took her seat on the aircraft she was hoping for a black miracle.

A flock of seagulls perhaps?

Yes, an aborted take-off seemed preferable to facing her family, or rather her aunt and her husband.

When Donald had called Trinity to tell her that he was marrying Yvette, though she had given her congratulations and said that, of course, she'd be thrilled to be there, inside her stomach had churned.

On concluding the call, Trinity had actually dashed to the toilet to be sick.

She felt sick now.

A harried mother and baby took the seat next to her.

Why, oh, why, hadn't she used the money her father had given her to buy a business-class seat, Trinity thought as the baby told her with his big blue eyes that he was going to do everything in his power to scream all the way to Heathrow.

The take-off was impeccable, not a seagull to be found!

Then the captain came on and said that he would do his level best to make up lost time.

Trinity wished she could do the same—that she could push a few buttons and ride a tail wind if it meant that she could erase lost years. An ancient art history degree that she'd somehow obtained, as she'd struggled merely to operate, lay unused. Clubs, bars, dancing had been but a temporary escape from her pain and grief. California healing had beckoned, but neither reiki, nor chakra cleansing, nor the roar of the vast Pacific could replace what had been lost.

Her latest attempt to cure her repulsion to anything that hinted on sexual had been positive-reinforcement-based training.

Ha-ha.

Two thousand dollars later and several pounds

heavier, Trinity had decided that no amount of chocolate or affirmations were going to cure her particular
problem.

She loved herself?

Most of the time, yes.

She'd just prefer not to be touched.

The meals were served and Trinity just picked at hers
and refused wine. Despite what the newspapers said,
she really only drank at family things.

Which it soon would be.

No.

As the cabin lights were dimmed Trinity tried to
doze but Harry, as it turned out the baby was called,
had decided now that he liked her. He kept patting her
cheeks with his little fat hands.

'Sorry,' his mum kept saying.

'It's not a problem.'

Trinity tried to doze some more.

It didn't work.

The only consolation to attending the wedding was
that she had just found out that, though at first he had
declined, Zahid was going to be the best man.

She hadn't seen him since that night ten years ago
and Trinity wondered what he would be like now, if he
even remembered that kiss in the woods.

If he'd ever given her a thought since then.

Trinity closed her eyes and briefly returned to the
rapture of being in his arms and the bliss of his kiss,
but her eyes suddenly snapped open for she could not
even escape to the sanctuary of them without recalling
what had happened later that night and in the months
that had followed.

There was so much adrenaline in her legs that Trinity

tried walking around the sleepy cabin, dreading what she must face later today. How she'd hoped her mother would tell her that Clive and Elaine hadn't been invited, how she wished her father, or even her brother, would step in.

No one ever had.

Skeletons belonged in the closet. Dirty laundry belonged in a basket.

Clive was more prominent than her father.

Nothing could be gained by speaking out. It was easier to simply smile for the cameras.

It wasn't, though.

All too soon the scent of breakfast came from the galley and, opening the shutter, she saw dawn.

The wedding day was here.

Trinity returned to her seat, where Harry was shrieking. 'Would you mind?' his mum asked. 'I have to go to the restroom.'

'Of course.'

Trinity held Harry, who stood on her thighs with his knees buckling as he screamed and screamed. 'Go, Harry!' Trinity smiled. Wouldn't it be lovely to be as uninhibited as Harry, to simply scream out your pain and not care a jot what others thought?

She didn't get to hold babies much. All her family was in the UK and none of her friends in LA had babies yet.

The sting of tears in her own eyes was terribly unwelcome and Trinity swallowed them back, telling herself she was being ridiculous. There was no comparison, Trinity told herself as she looked at Harry.

He was all big and chunky and wriggling.

Whereas *she* had been so tiny and so very still.

The sob that escaped Trinity's lips came from some-where so deep and buried that even Harry stopped his tirade.

'It's okay.' Trinity fought to quickly compose her-self and smiled into his curious eyes as he patted her cheek. 'I'm fine.'

Trinity had no choice but to be fine.

She just missed her baby so.

Ached for the time that her daughter had never had.

'Thanks so much.' Harry's mum was back and Trin-ity handed him to her but the bubble of panic was rising inside her and Trinity truly did not know if she could get through today.

She pressed her bell.

'Breakfast won't be a moment.' The steward smiled.

'I'd like a bourbon, please,' Trinity said. 'A large one.'

A few minutes later the steward returned with two tiny bottles of bourbon and a pussycat smile that told Trinity she was a lush.

Trinity didn't care.

At least it calmed her enough to get off the plane.

'Where the hell is Trinity?' Donald demanded, as he clicked off his phone. 'Yvette's in tears, there's not a sign of her at the hotel…'

Here we go again! Zahid thought as he felt the pull of the mad Fosters' vortex. A night out last night with Donald and co. and Zahid was remembering all too well why he chose only minimal contact. Gus had kept insisting that Zahid extend his visit, or come and stay later in the year, and Zahid had reluctantly explained that he would be marrying soon and his time was now to be spent in Ishla.

And now, it would seem, Trinity had gone missing in action again.

Nothing changed.

'Why don't I call Dianne and see if there's an update?' Zahid suggested, for it was the best man's duty to keep the groom calm, but he had never seen Donald so tense. He made the call and then gave Donald the news. 'Your mother's at the airport and she says Trinity's plane just landed. As soon as she is through customs, she will take her straight to the hotel and help her to get ready. Call Yvette and tell her that she can stop worrying.'

'You can never stop worrying when Trinity's around!' Donald challenged. 'I just hope she's sober.'

It wasn't Donald's comment that had a certain disquiet stir in Zahid. It was his reaction to the news that Trinity had landed and that soon he would see her again.

Over the years there had been a few near misses. Zahid, when he had heard Trinity's plane was delayed, had assumed that this would be another. But that she was in the same country now brought a strange sense of calm—the planets seemed more neatly aligned, the stars just a little less random. They were in the same country and finally, after all this time, they would see each other again.

He wondered if she would be bringing someone and briefly wrestled with the distaste of that thought but then dismissed its significance. It had nothing to do with feelings, Zahid quickly told himself. After all, it was possibly his last weekend in England as a single man and

certainly there was unfinished business between them.
It was natural to be hoping that she was attending the
wedding alone.

Trinity didn't have to wait for baggage and she raced
out of customs, her heart aflutter. Despite everything,
she was looking forward to seeing her mum. Maybe
things would be different now, Trinity hoped as her
eyes scanned the crowd for Dianne. Maybe her mum
would realise just how difficult today was. Maybe…

Her heart lurched in hope as she saw her mum,
dressed for the wedding, just minus a hat. Trinity raced
over and gave her a hug. 'I'm so sorry.'

'Have you been drinking?' was Dianne's only response to her daughter's kiss.

'I had one bourbon on the plane.'

'It's whisky,' Dianne hissed. 'You're in England now.
Where the hell have you been?'

'The plane was delayed.'

'I don't want to hear your excuses.'

Trinity could feel her mother's fingers digging into
her arms as they raced to get a taxi and Dianne didn't
let up as they sped to the hotel. 'Yvette is in tears.
She wanted her own sister to be bridesmaid and now
you've made us look…' Dianne struggled to contain
her temper. It had taken many, many dinners to convince Yvette's parents to choose Trinity for the role, but
a generous helping hand towards the wedding bill had
given them leverage and the Fosters had insisted that
their voice be heard.

Oh, and so too would Trinity's voice be heard, Dianne remembered. She just had to tell Trinity that! 'I've

told Yvette that you're going to sing near the end of the night.'

'Excuse me.' Trinity's mouth was agape. 'I can't sing.'

'You've got a beautiful voice.'

'Actually, I don't.' Trinity could not believe that they'd ask this of her. 'Mum, please, I don't want to sing, I just want to…'

Hide.

'When do you go back?' Dianne asked.

'Tomorrow afternoon.'

'So it really is a flying visit, then.'

'I've got an interview next week.'

'If you'd let your father help, you wouldn't be out of work.'

'I'm not out of work,' Trinity bristled, because she had a job at the beach bar and she certainly earned her money there, but Dianne pulled a face.

'If anyone asks, say…' Dianne thought for a moment. 'Say you're working in a museum.'

'You want me to lie?'

'Yes, please!' Dianne said. 'We didn't put you through an art history degree to have you working in a bar.'

'Ancient art,' Trinity corrected, and then smirked at her mum. 'What sort of museum exactly?' She watched as her mother's neck went red.

'Okay, a library, then. The reference section. At one of the big colleges.'

Nothing changed.

They got to the hotel and the shoebox of a room that had been booked for Trinity. After a lightning-quick shower she sat as her hair was brushed and coiled and pinned by her tense mother while Trinity quickly did her make-up. Moods weren't improved when her mother unzipped a bag and pulled out the most awful blue dress that Trinity had ever seen.

'You are joking?' Trinity said. 'It's so shiny I'm going to need sunglasses to wear it.'

'Had you bothered to come to any of the fittings then you might have had a say in what you were wearing. As it is…' She lifted up Trinity's arm and attempted to pull up the concealed zip that was located at the side. 'You've put on weight!' Dianne accused.

'No,' Trinity said. 'I gave you my measurements exactly.'

'Then why can't I do it up?'

Because you refused to believe I was ten pounds heavier than your goal weight for me, Trinity thought, but said nothing, just sucked in her stomach and chest as her mother tugged at the stupid zip until finally it was up.

'Is breathing an optional extra?' Trinity quipped.

'Yes,' Dianne snapped back. 'But smiling isn't. This is your brother's day.'

'Oh, funny, that, I thought it was Yvette's.'

'Trinity!' Dianne was struggling to hold onto her temper. 'Don't start.'

'I'm not starting anything, I was just saying…'

'Well, don't!' Dianne warned. 'You've already done your level best to ruin this day. All you have to do now is smile. Can you manage that?''

'Of course, but I'm not singing.'

'And lose the smart mouth.' Dianne secured her hat as she issued instructions. 'Go now and apologise to Yvette. I'm going to make my way to the church. I'll see you there and I'm warning you…'

'Noted.'

'I mean it, Trinity, I don't want a scene from you today.'

She should say nothing, Trinity knew that. She should just nod and reassure her mum that she'd behave, but, hell, she had a voice and as much as her parents loathed that fact, Trinity was determined to find it.

'Then just make sure I'm not put in any position where I might need to make a scene,' Trinity said, and her mother's silk-clad shoulders stiffened and Trinity watched as the feather sticking out of Dianne's hat shivered in anger as Trinity refused to comply with orders.

'Will you just…?' Dianne hissed, and turned around. 'Can you try and remember that this is your brother's wedding and not spoil a family gathering for once.' Her face was right up at Trinity's. 'For once can today not be about you?'

'Of course.' Trinity stared back coolly but her heart was hammering in her chest. 'Just make sure that you keep that sleaze well away from me.'

'Are you still going on about that? It was years ago…' Two champagnes on an empty stomach that was fluttering with mother-of-the-groom nerves and Dianne would not be argued with, and certainly she wanted nothing to spoil what *had* to be a perfect day. 'You will behave, Trinity, you will be polite and you will smile.'

It had been stupid to hope things might be different.

Nothing had changed, Trinity realised.

Nothing ever would.

'What are you doing?' Trinity asked, as she watched her mother's painfully slow attempt to write a text. 'I'll do it.'

'It's done,' Dianne said, as her phone made the small

whooshing sound that meant her text had been sent. 'I was just letting Zahid know that you're on your way to Yvette and that everything's back on schedule.'

As she took the elevator to Yvette's room for the first time that morning Trinity smiled.

As he pulled his phone from his pocket and read the text, so too did Zahid.

CHAPTER THREE

IT WAS NOT the bride who drew Zahid's eye as she entered the church; instead, it was the woman who walked behind her who held his attention.

There was a smile fixed on Trinity's face but her eyes were as wary and as truculent as the teenage Trinity's, but then they met his and Zahid watched as her pale cheeks infused with pink. For both of them there was a moment's return to a wood many years ago and a kiss that both wished had drawn to a more natural conclusion.

Zahid smiled, which he rarely did, and Trinity was so lost for a moment, so taken aback by Zahid's smile that as the bride halted, for a second Trinity didn't. She actually forgot her place, for it was as if she should simply walk on to Zahid—to go now and greet him as her body wanted to and wrap her arms around his neck, but instead, after a brief falter, Trinity halted and took the flowers from Yvette.

Zahid turned his back to her then and the service commenced.

The service was long, not by Zahid's standards, just terribly long to stand there and not turn around when he would have preferred to.

Though Zahid stared ahead, he was looking at her very closely in his mind and re-examining the Trinity he'd seen today.

Her dress was terrible. Like a synthetic sapphire, it lacked depth and mystery and it was far too tight. Her hair was worn up and dotted with violets that matched the dark smudges under her eyes, yet she looked, to Zahid, amazing. Sun-kissed, dirty blonde, fragile and sexy, she was everything he remembered her to be and more.

Trinity stared ahead, loathing that her shoulders were bare and wondering whose eyes were on them. She hated the loud sound of her aunt's husband singing a hymn, as if he meant the words, as if he were a decent man.

So, instead of dwelling on the man behind and to the right, she fixed her gaze ahead and stared at Zahid, a man who did not know the words but neither did Zahid pretend to sing. He stood firm and dignified and she willed him to turn around.

He didn't.

He could have no idea the torture today was for her, for she could tell no one about her past—that had been spelt out to her many years ago. His raven hair was glossy and immaculate, his shoulders wider than before and possibly he was taller. She saw the clenching of his fist in the small of his back and remembered that same hand on her waist when the world had seemed so straightforward. As he handed over the rings she was treated to a glimpse of his strong profile and her ears strained to capture whatever words he murmured to Donald.

Zahid was as conscious of Trinity as she was of him,

so much so that as they all squeezed into the vestry for the signing of the register, despite the chatter from others, he only heard her exhale in brief relief.

'Trinity...' her father warned as she leant against the wall to catch her breath, so relieved was she to be away from Clive.

Donald and Yvette signed the register and Gus added his signature with a flourish. Trinity watched as Zahid added his. *Sheik Prince Zahid Bin Ahmed of Ishla.*

'Leave some space for me.' Trinity smiled and then added her own signature.

Trinity Natalii Foster.

Her hand was shaking, Trinity realised as she put down the pen, only the nerves she had now felt very different to the ones that she'd had before.

As she stepped back from the register she caught the deliciously familiar scent of Zahid and as he lowered his head to her ear the tiny bones all shivered awake to the deep, long-buried thrill of his low, intimate voice.

'Natalii?'

'Born at Christmas,' Trinity said. 'Please never repeat it again, I hate it.'

Of course she had been born at Christmas, Zahid thought, for, unbeknown to Trinity he had returned to the Fosters' in the hope of seeing her in the new year after she would have turned eighteen.

Trinity hadn't been there.

She was here now, though, and Zahid spoke on.

'I thought that it was the bride's prerogative to be late.'

'You know how I loathe tradition.'

'Does that mean we shan't be dancing later?' Zahid

asked, and she turned to his slow smile. 'Given how you loathe tradition.'

Oh!

Trinity blinked for it was as if he didn't know she was dead inside, as if he didn't know that her frigid body no longer worked, yet it felt now as if it did, for a pulse was working high in her neck—Trinity could feel it, and her stomach was fluttering as it had years before on that night.

With Zahid beside her, she could remember the beauty, rather than dwell on the pain.

'I suppose we shall...' Trinity sighed, as if dancing with Zahid would be a huge concession. 'I'd hate to cause trouble.'

'Liar,' Zahid said, and his hand met the small of her back as he guided her out of the vestry.

With one brief exchange, with that small touch, she was back in the woods, innocent and unfurling to his hand, and it was actually dizzying to walk behind Yvette and Donald and through the congregation. More than that, it was exhilarating to step outside into the sun and, on the day Trinity had been dreading, she felt her heart soaring like the bells that rang out around them.

To be, for the first time, at such a function and be just a little bit taken care of, for Zahid's duty now was not just to the groom, was, to Trinity, amazing.

He stood for the wedding photos and even made the unbearable a touch less so as the family all gathered around.

'Smile, Trinity,' he said out of the corner of his mouth, and she forgot the shiver of dread that Clive was near.

'You don't,' she pointed out, and then frowned at her

own words because Zahid smiled so readily when their eyes met and held.

'It is not in my nature to smile.'

For some reason that made her giggle just enough for the photographer to get his shot and then they piled into cars and they met at the hotel.

As the bride and groom entered, one look at her very relaxed brother and Trinity knew that Donald must be on something.

Please, no, Trinity begged in her head.

He had promised her he was over that now.

She and Zahid sat at opposite ends of the top table and though she wished they were sitting next to each other, maybe it was for the best, Trinity thought, for just knowing he was here was distracting enough.

Anyway, they'd no doubt run out of conversation within two minutes, though she was dying to know what he was up to and desperate to know if he was seeing someone.

Surely not, Trinity consoled herself, because back in the vestry Zahid had definitely been flirting.

She struggled through the meal, her reward that awaited her dance with him, and soon enough it was time for the speeches.

To his credit, Zahid did unbend a fraction and asked for some sparkling water for the toasts!

God, he was so controlled, so well behaved, Trinity thought, stretching her legs under the table and slipping off her shoes as the speeches started and doing her best not to yawn, not because she was bored by the speeches but because jet-lag was starting to seriously hit.

Yvette's father went first, thanking everyone and saying how thrilled he was to welcome Donald into the family. Zahid's face was impassive but he privately thought that Yvette's father had the look of a man who had brought home a puppy for the children only to realise it was going to grow into the size of a small horse.

It was the small horse's turn next and Zahid watched as Yvette scratched anxiously at her neck as her very new husband took to his feet.

Donald thanked everyone too, especially his beautiful wife. 'I'd like to thank Zahid for all his help and for travelling so far to be here.' Donald smiled a loaded smile. 'You've been an excellent best man and I hope to return the favour when it is your turn to marry next year.'

Zahid's jaw clamped down as Donald rambled on and he glanced over at Trinity. Her cheeks were red, an angry red, and she was dribbling salt on her sorbet.

He hadn't wanted her to hear his news like that.

As Donald proposed a toast to the bridesmaids, Zahid watched as Trinity raised her glass...

But to a passing waiter.

Oh, Trinity.

He wanted to go over and halt her, to whisk her away, to explain that she had misunderstood.

It was the truth, though.

And this early in the evening the truth hurt them both.

Zahid duly stood and thanked the groom for his words on behalf of the bridesmaids, though privately he'd have liked to knock him out. Then he thanked everyone else that he had to and said all the things that a best man should, but then it came to the part where Donald should star, where this future king should demure and ensure that the groom shone.

'Donald and I...' Zahid glanced at his notes and then faltered, and Trinity looked up at the brief hesitation as Zahid silently recalled a teenage incident and saw it now through the eyes of a man.

They were your drugs.

He could see it so clearly now and yet here he stood, all these years later, paying the price for Donald's supposed valour.

Well, no more.

'Donald and I...' Zahid resumed his speech but he was not looking at his notes now '...attended the same school and later were students at the same university.' Trinity heard her father's cough in an attempt to prompt Zahid, and she looked at her brother's expectant face, but the glory never came. Zahid went on to recall a few antidotes and all in all it was a very nice speech—he just forgot to paint Donald as the hero in Zahid's life.

False duty had been more than repaid.

And so to the dancing.

Zahid stood over Trinity, waiting for her to join him on the floor, but it was a touch more complicated than standing for Trinity, because her already tight shoes refused to go back on, but finally she forced her feet into them. 'The things I do for my family,' Trinity said, as he led her to the floor. 'Not that they appreciate it.'

'I am appreciative...' Zahid said, as he loosely held her and they started to dance and she waited for him to finish his sentence.

He didn't.

'Of what?' Trinity prompted. 'You are appreciative of what?'

'That you are here,' Zahid said. 'That we see each other again after all this time.'

They both knew it was running out for them and there was no tail wind to help them catch up, no buttons to push that could change things.

Except he pushed the right ones.

Zahid was the only man who did.

'I loved your speech,' Trinity said, her words a little stilted, for she was cross with Zahid for flirting when he was about to be wed. Yet she was cross only from the neck up. Her body had seemed to overlook the fact he would soon be marrying the very second that she was in his arms.

'You're the only one who liked it. Your father looks as if he wants to kill me.'

'It's me he's shooting daggers at!' Trinity looked to the right and smiled sweetly at her father. 'I was late, you know?'

'You were.'

'And not looking out for my brother.'

Zahid looked down to those blue eyes again and wondered how much she knew, for he was sure that Donald was high. 'Is it nice to see your brother happy?'

'Donald wouldn't know what happy was if it was hand delivered and he had to sign for it.' She looked over at Donald, who was smiling and laughing to his bride. 'He's loaded,' Trinity said. 'Nothing changes.'

'You?' Zahid said.

'I don't go near anything like that.'

'I meant,' Zahid corrected himself, 'are you happy?'

'Not today,' Trinity said, then it was she who corrected herself. 'Actually, right now I am.'

'Because?'

'Because,' Trinity said, because in his arms she actually was and, no, she should not be flirting, she had been called a tease so very many times when she was unable to follow through, but she just needed one lovely thing to focus on, just the teeniest bit of help to get through the night and, for good or bad, Zahid was it.

'Because?' he said into her ear, and it was then that she succumbed.

'Because my brother has excellent taste in groomsmen.'

'His bride has terrible taste in dresses.'

'She does,' Trinity sighed. 'Though in fairness my mother would have lied about my measurements. She prefers me with an eating disorder, it makes her a more visible martyr...'

Trinity was, Zahid decided, rather wise.

'I'm supposed to be singing later,' Trinity said, and her hands moved up and linked behind his neck and, yes, they were back in the woods again. 'As I said to my mother, my name isn't Trinity Von Trapp.' She went to explain, because he probably had no idea what she was talking about, but then she remembered a long-ago Christmas and Dianne forcing them to watch the *Sound of Music* and Trinity giggling at Zahid's somewhat bemused expression.

More than that, though, somehow he got her—she did not have to explain everything to Zahid.

'Rolfe might join you,' he said into her ear, and though Zahid would no more sing than fly to the moon a smile played on her lips as she pulled her head back, just enough that her back arched in just a little and Zahid's tongue rolled to his cheek as something else stirred to her words.

'I prefer the captain.'

It was a tiny dirty dance, but with words. The heat

from his palms was surely searing her dress and the way
he simply let her be had her breathing freely for the first
time since she could remember. With Zahid her body
seemed to know how to work. He induced only pleasure and made it safe to be a touch wanton.

Then she remembered she was cross with him.

As the music ended, instead of sinking in for another
dance, she pulled back.

'I'd better go and see how Yvette is.'

'I will check on the groom.' He gave a small nod.
'Perhaps later we dance…'

Trinity gave a tight smile as she walked off but she
felt conflicted. No doubt Zahid thought her a party girl,
no doubt he assumed where the night was leading.

He could never guess that she felt ill at the very
thought of sex.

Only she didn't feel ill in his arms.

Trinity wanted to get back to him, only Yvette was
teary and she either had raging cystitis or her bladder
was the size of a thimble or more likely she really was
pregnant, because she wanted to go to the loo on the
hour every hour and Trinity had to help with the dress.

'Your brother…' Yvette was trying to tame her angry
cheeks with Trinity's foundation. 'I just got a call from
the hotel—he hasn't paid the reservation fee…'

'I'm sure it's just a mix-up,' Trinity suitably soothed.

She was quite sure to the contrary, though.

The night wore on and the only time they met was
when Dianne introduced Trinity to a group that Zahid
was in and, of course, one of them had to ask what she
was doing with her degree.

'I'm thinking of moving to France.' Trinity beamed,
deciding that it might not be such a bad idea actually

and feeling her mother's tension beside her, 'but right now I work in a library at a large college—'

'The reference section,' Dianne interrupted, and Zahid watched the daggers that shot from Trinity's eyes.

Dianne was determined that Trinity would sing and trying to escape the inevitable, true to form, Trinity slipped outside for some air.

Zahid wasn't faring much better. All night Donald insisted on introducing him to everyone as his best friend from way back and slapping Zahid on the back as he did so.

It came as no surprise when Donald pulled Zahid aside near the end of the night and asked if he might have a word.

'I know that you're flying back after lunch tomorrow and that we might not get another chance to speak,' Donald said.

'You don't have to entertain me on your wedding night.' Zahid tried to smile, tried to keep things light, tried not to like this man any less than he now did.

'And I know that you've always been a great friend to me, as I hope I have to you.' *They were your drugs,* Zahid said again in his head, but he remained silent as Donald spoke on. 'The thing is, Zahid...' And Zahid listened as, again, Donald asked him to help—that if he could just take care of the honeymoon, then as soon as Donald was back he would repay him.

'I am not paying for your honeymoon.' Zahid interrupted the familiar tirade but with its latest twist. 'What I will pay for is three months of rehabilitation.'

'That's really generous but if I could just get these debts paid then I wouldn't need rehab. All I'm asking—'

'I have told you what I am prepared to do. I have

heard of a good clinic near Texas. A family friend had their son go there…'

'I've just got married I can hardly disappear on Yvette…'

'I would say that you have been absent from your relationship for quite some time,' Zahid said, refusing to be swayed. It was clear from looking at Yvette that Donald would soon be a father—it was time, then, that he grew up. 'If you go to rehab, I will take care of your debts.'

'Zahid, please, can you just—?'

'No.'

Zahid refused to negotiate.

'I will speak with the accounting firm that I use in the UK. The offer is there so long as you are prepared to meet my conditions.'

'You can afford to help me out without blinking.'

'That has nothing to do with it. Even if I had no money but you were determined to change, I would take a loan to pay for your treatment. I will not be used. You can work for a better life, or you can torch what you have. You choose.'

'Some friend!' Donald sneered.

Zahid stepped away from Donald and headed outside just as he heard Dianne start up with the familiar cry. 'Has anyone seen Trinity?'

Zahid was looking at her now.

She was a *bad* bridesmaid, if there was such a thing. The flowers were wilting in her hair as she drained her champagne glass and then muttered something very unladylike under her breath.

'Language, Trinity,' Zahid said, and she rolled her eyes.

'I hate weddings.'

'They are a part of life.'

'Well, if I ever get married it will be on a beach with no guests.' She glanced at him. 'What about you?'

'There will be many guests and it will go for two or three days. It will be a national holiday and the wedding date will be marked each year with the same...'

It sounded so horrific to Trinity that she actually laughed. 'I shouldn't complain really. So—' Trinity tried to keep her voice light '—when is your wedding day?'

'I will marry next year.'

It was ridiculous, Trinity thought, but as she stood there she was filled with a strange ache of sadness.

One kiss might not sound much, but that one kiss was her only pleasant memory even remotely attached to sex.

'You ought to go back inside,' Zahid said. 'Your mother is looking for you.'

'I loathe them,' Trinity said.

'It shows.'

'I love them, though.' He was surprised by her admission, not that she loved her family, more at the hopelessness in her voice. 'Do you get on with your family?'

'I do,' Zahid said. 'Most of the time.'

'Meaning?'

'Meaning most of the time I get on with them.'

'You're terribly straightforward.'

'Meaning?'

'Just that.'

'You should never assume,' Zahid said, for his thoughts were less than straightforward where Trinity was concerned.

'I don't want to go back in,' Trinity admitted. 'Do

you think anyone would really notice if I just disappeared?'

'You know that they would,' Zahid said. 'It will only go for another half-hour or so.'

She let out a breath. Half an hour felt like an eternity right now. 'I don't want to sing.'

'There are many things that I would prefer not to do.'

'But you do them.'

'Some of the time.'

'Would you sing?'

God, but she loved it when he smiled.

'No.'

His smile almost turned to a wince as Dianne's voice invaded them again. 'Trinity?'

He watched her jaw grit as the call continued and her mother's voice started to get near. Zahid took Trinity's arm and led her around the corner to where it was dark, and she could smell the pine from a tree and the thud of music and people in the distance and she wished they were back there in the woods.

'I wish you'd taken me with you that night.'

'I was tempted.'

'It didn't show,' Trinity said, and in sudden defence she mocked him a little. 'Have you been trained to hide your emotions?'

'Who said that I had any?'

She attempted a suitable reply but it dawned then that his hand was on her waist and the other was on her face when normally contact, any contact, was unbearable, just not tonight, and so she answered his question. 'Your kiss told me that you did.'

'Sex is not an emotion,' came his brusque response, but for the first time he lied and she knew it, for nei-

ther could deny what thrummed between them now. It
was more than lust yet it tasted almost the same, it was
more than want yet still he fought not to call it need as
he looked to her lips.

'Where were we?' Zahid asked, but the years could
not disappear. There was so much hurt there that for
Trinity it was not as simple as a kiss. So great was her
fear of contact she was petrified how she might react to
his touch. She knew about his reputation with women
and, of course, he assumed hers, but just as a kiss was
surely inevitable Trinity saw her way out and she leapt
on it and wriggled from his arms. 'I doubt your fiancée
would be very pleased...'

'I have not chosen my bride yet,' Zahid said, and he
took her champagne glass and placed it on a window
ledge then pulled her back to where she had been just
a second or two ago. 'If I had, I would not be about to
kiss you.'

'Oh.'

Well, that settled that, then, Trinity thought. There
was nothing to stop them other than her fear and that
she could not stand being held by a man, except she was
being held now and there was no urge to run, there was
no urge to do anything other than receive the lips softly
descending on hers.

Would he be able to tell from her kiss, her terror?
Trinity wondered.

No, she fast realised, because to his mouth there was
no terror, just the melting of fear and the bliss of his lips
and the stroke of his tongue.

Would he be able to tell from her rigid body that
she did not know how to respond, that her body refused to obey?

No, because she sank into his embrace without thought and the press of his erection against her felt like a reward.

His mouth *did* make the pain disappear; his kiss did, on a night she had been dreading, actually allow her to forget, and Trinity found out something new—it was very hard to kiss and smile at the same time but she was trying.

'What are you doing?' Zahid said, as she paused for a moment and allowed her mouth to stretch into the beam that this moment deserved.

'Smiling,' Trinity said. 'That's better.' For her lips could better relax against his now.

He kissed her deeper, and Trinity felt the weight of his mouth and the hastening of his tongue as he pulled her harder into him, she felt again the press of him on her stomach. The ugliest dress in the world fast became her favourite as his hands roamed the silk and located the not-so-stupid concealed zip and expertly slid it down just enough for his thumb to stroke her aching nipple.

The sirens were back, the sirens she'd heard but once, only they were louder now, closer now, with each and every stroke of his tongue.

Her hands were in his hair, she was back on tip-toe again but with the guide of his hand this time and the sirens neared dangerously close for both of them. She wanted him to lift her, she wanted her legs coiled around his hips. Visions of just that took over as Zahid struggled to halt her ascent, for he wanted to lift her, he wanted to be inside her but he would never compromise her.

'Not here...' Zahid pulled his mouth from her lips but they did not leave her face as she spoke. 'As I said, you deserve better than the woods. Do what you have to and then...'

She shivered at what Zahid left unsaid.

He kissed her ear and then peeled his face from hers and turned her a little. Lifting her arm, he dealt with the zip but did not leave things there. Instead, he kissed the sensitive flesh of her upper arm, and how he found her armpit sexy, she would never know, but clearly he did, because he was deep kissing her there now. Her panties were soaking. Trinity wanted to be back in his arms, but he turned her to face him and straightened her dress and then rearranged a few tendrils of her hair. 'I will be in in a moment,' Zahid said.

'Come in with me.'

'Trinity, go in.' Zahid's smile was wry for there was no way he could go back to the reception just yet. 'I'll be there soon.'

She almost floated in, just on a high from his kiss and the very real promise of tonight. Finally, finally, her body seemed to know how to respond, finally the curse was lifting.

It was possibly the very worst time to come face to face with her mother, closely followed by Clive.

'Everyone's waiting for you, Trinity,' Dianne said.

She just stood there, praying for Zahid to come up behind her, to take her hand, to just walk her away, but instead she faced this man with only the pathetic barrier of her mother between them.

'It's time to sing!' Dianne smiled.

'You want me to sing?' Trinity said, her voice a challenge.

'You know that I do.'

One moment she had been the happiest she'd ever

been, Trinity realised, but now she was suddenly the angriest.

Oh, she'd sing!

Trinity was ready to sing from the treetops now!

She marched into the hall, muttering, and strode up to the microphone.

Yes, she'd sing, Trinity decided, wrenching the microphone from its stand. She'd sing as loudly as she knew how if the microphone would just stop screeching feedback.

Her starting number would be, Trinity decided, 'I Was Seventeen Going on Eighteen', and she'd point to Clive as she sang, as she told the whole world about that night.

The skeletons were coming out to play, the linen basket was going to be emptied too!

Yay!

She felt as angry and as uninhibited as Harry had been on the plane, and there was no need to hide anything, none at all.

Zahid walked into the hall in time to see Trinity stalk to the microphone and start to tap at it, tossing her hair. Her eyes spelt danger and Zahid turned as Dianne came and stood beside him. For once she wasn't wearing that plastic smile and, as everyone had this wedding day, in crisis Dianne turned to Zahid.

'Stop her!' Dianne pleaded.

Zahid wasn't following Dianne's orders as he walked to the stage, it was to get to Trinity, because there was a recklessness to her that troubled him and Zahid would not let her look a fool.

'I'd like to dedicate this number to—' Trinity started,

but Zahid pulled the plug and her arm at the same time and hauled her from the stage.

'Put me down.'

'Not yet.'

'Put me down,' Trinity shouted, as he carried her over his shoulder behind the stage and out through the back exit to the elevators. It all became a little blurry then. She remembered him letting her down and Zahid demanding to know what was going on.

'Nothing!'

Jet-lag, champagne, nerves, fear, want all combined in desperate tears and then she lunged at him, desperate for escape, but Zahid denied her that. She tried to rain kisses on his face but Zahid held her at arm's length as she pecked away like an angry woodpecker who couldn't meet its mark. She wanted the sex he had promised, the bliss of escape with the one man who knew where it resided in her.

She wanted Zahid.

And so she told him.

'I don't reward bad behaviour.'

'You're not training a dolphin!' Trinity shouted, but then she started to laugh. 'I tried that, actually.' She put on an American accent. '"Positive reinforcement-based training"…and it didn't work!'

'If you want sex,' Zahid said, peeling off her dress and offloading her into the bed, 'then you can ask politely in the morning when you are sober.'

'Ask?' Trinity lay on the bed and laughed at his audacity. 'I have to ask?'

'Politely,' Zahid said. 'I want to hear the word "please" when you do,' but as he looked down at her, astonishingly, to Trinity, he smiled. 'You need to learn manners—your behaviour tonight has been shocking.'

'Really?' Trinity said. 'I thought that I'd behaved rather well.'

Zahid didn't have to come up with a suitable answer because less than ten seconds later she was sound asleep.

CHAPTER FOUR

ZAHID SAT WATCHING as Trinity started to stir.

Her bridesmaid's dress was over a chair, her shoes were on the floor, her hair was everywhere and her mascara had escaped her lashes and had moved to the pillow.

Zahid rang for breakfast and saw Trinity's eyes frown at the intrusion when a little while later the doorbell chimed.

'Just leave it there,' Zahid said, as the staff went to set up. 'Could someone draw a bath…?'

She sat up to ask everyone if they could please be quiet and get out of her room but Zahid shot her such a look that she ducked back under the covers and willed the sheikh in her bedroom to disappear.

Actually, Trinity realised, she was in his bedroom, she had to be because this room was massive and the bed seemed even bigger.

Oh, God.

As the maid came out and said that the bath had been run and Zahid said he would call soon to have the room tidied but that was all for now, Trinity had vague memories of kissing him.

Not outside, though. She remembered that that kiss

had been completely lovely. It was the inside attempt to kiss him that had her cringing in recall.

'Does that groaning mean you have a recollection of last night or should I call for a doctor?'

He didn't let her hide; instead, he whipped back the bedding.

'The first one.' Trinity stared up at a very, very beautiful man. His hair was tousled and he was no longer clean-shaven and stood over her in the morning-after version of yesterday's suit.

'How is your hangover?'

'It's not a hangover, it's exhaustion,' Trinity said. 'And forty-eight hours of no sleep, mixed with champagne and my toxic family...' She closed her eyes. 'Did I make a terrible scene?'

'I brought you up here before you could,' Zahid said, 'but, yes, you made quite a scene in the bedroom.' She could hardly breathe but then, when Zahid smiled down at her, so heart stopping was that face there was no 'hardly' about it—her breath was lodged in her lungs and it took a moment for her foggy brain to compute that Zahid wasn't cross. In fact, from the look he was giving her, any moment he'd be stripping the last of her clothing off.

Oh, God!

'Here!' He handed her a large glass of something cold and dark pink. She sat up a touch and when it met her lips, Trinity found out that it was watermelon infused with mint.

'I had no sleep on the flight. There was a baby next to me on the plane...' Trinity explained between draining her drink. 'We don't all have our own private jets to fly us to weddings...'

'You could have put on earphones.' Zahid remained unmoved by her explanations for last night's behaviour.

'You've never flown economy, have you?'

'Your father paid for business class,' Zahid said, because he had overheard Gus telling anyone who cared to listen how much his daughter still cost him, but more than that, Zahid simply would not let her lie.

'And I bought an economy ticket with it,' Trinity whispered conspiratorially. 'It's called ten hours of discomfort for three months' rent.'

'Then you should have taken an earlier flight if you knew that you would be unlikely to get any sleep.'

She lay back on the pillow and stared at him, sulking that he wouldn't give her an out.

Yes, she should have taken an earlier flight, but that would have meant a night in the family home and it had been the last place on earth she'd wanted to be. Economy and a screaming baby had been a far more palatable option.

'Here,' Zahid said. Taking the empty glass from Trinity, he hauled her back up to a sitting position as if she were a hospital patient, and then he sat on the edge of the bed with a plate loaded with tiny sausages and pancakes. He slathered them in maple syrup and, proceeded to cut it all up and then commenced feeding her.

'I was just tired.'

'Of course you were,' Zahid said. 'Eat.'

'You're not cross?'

'No.' He smiled at her but there was concern there. 'What was going on last night?' Zahid asked. 'You were very upset when I got you back to the room.'

Trinity shrugged. 'I'd just had too much to drink.'

'That's not what you said two minutes ago.'

'I just...' Trinity shrugged. She honestly didn't know what to say.

'You can tell me.'

Could she?

He was her brother's best man, a family friend... and, right now, the very best thing in her life, even if just for a little while.

She didn't want to spoil it.

'Things get a bit tense for me when I'm with my family.'

She waited for him to tell her how wonderful her family was and that she should behave better, but Zahid was actually trying to gauge how much he should say. After all, it was her family that he was about to criticise.

He popped a forkful of food into her mouth as he chose to let his ingrained diplomacy leave him a touch, for he wanted her to hear the truth.

'I find the Fosters hard work.' As she opened her mouth to say something he reminded her that it was rude to speak with her mouth full and so Trinity had no choice but to hear him out. 'After last night, I am severing ties with your family.' As she frantically chewed so she could get her words out, Zahid beat her to it. 'When I say the Fosters I don't mean you.' Trinity stopped chewing then as Zahid spoke on—she now wanted to hear what he had to say. 'When I think of you, I do not think of the Fosters, do you understand that?'

'I think so.'

'I need you to understand that when I sever ties with you, it shall be for different reasons entirely. Do you know what they are?'

Trinity gave a tiny shrug.

'If we were to meet in the future, my feelings and

thoughts about you would be very disrespectful to my future wife.' He tried to explain what Trinity could not possibly understand. 'My wife will be chosen with my country in mind.' He saw her frown break into a smile.

'I wasn't expecting her to be me.'

'I know,' Zahid said, smiling at the very thought of Trinity in Ishla. 'I'm sure you could think of nothing worse. I just want to make it very clear that when I sever ties with your family, it has nothing at all to do with how I feel about you.'

'Thank you.'

It was very nice to hear.

'And thanks for saving me from making a complete fool of myself last night,' Trinity said.

'It was no problem.'

'I was just having fun.'

His eyes said that he doubted, again, that he was hearing the truth but Trinity ploughed on regardless. In the sober light of day she certainly wasn't going to reveal the painful past and so she tried to turn the conversation to far lighter matters. 'So what does a sheikh prince do when he lets his hair down?' She stared at him for a long moment. 'I can't imagine you dancing.'

'We danced last night.'

'I mean…' She put her hands above her head and did a little dance in the bed and actually forgot she was only wearing a bra. He made her forget shame, Trinity realised as she put her arms down.

More than that, he erased it.

'I don't dance like that,' Zahid said.

'And we've established that you do sing. You don't drink?'

'No.'

'Because you're not allowed?'

'Because I don't want to.'

'Do you gamble?'

'Never.' He looked at her for a very long moment and then answered her question with one word. 'Sex.'

Trinity blinked.

'It is my vice,' Zahid said. 'We all have them.'

'Is sex a vice?'

'Apparently so.' Zahid gave a brief eye-roll. 'Though that defect will be removed soon.'

'Your wife might be a nymphomaniac,' Trinity said, and she got the lovely reward of his smile.

'We can always hope,' Zahid said, 'though it will not be something that is taken into consideration.'

'Well, it should be.' Trinity yawned.

'I shan't be raising the topic with my father.'

'We have to be down to join the family for breakfast at nine…' Trinity said, glancing at the clock and seeing that it was ten past eight as Zahid dipped the last of the pancake in syrup and offered it to her.

'You make a nice mummy bird,' Trinity said, and then duly opened her mouth, but the fork wavered there, just hovered where she couldn't reach it, and he pulled it back when she stretched her neck.

'Birds feed with their mouths,' Zahid said, and Trinity felt her insides fold in on themselves as he scalded her face with his eyes. Still she did not get that last piece of loaded, sugary pancake and her face turned to fire as he continued to speak. 'Okay,' Zahid said, 'you have two choices—breakfast with your family or we are otherwise engaged.'

'When you say otherwise engaged…'

Did he mean…?

Yes, Trinity realised as he took the last lovely bit of pancake and popped it in his own mouth, he did mean that, for his mouth was pushing her down to the pillow and he was feeding her terribly intimately now. Tongue, pancake and maple syrup were being pushed into her by his tongue and he didn't even let her close her mouth as she struggled to swallow.

It was moreish!

Filthy, messy, sticky and so very, very, nice, but as her mouth emptied and his kiss lingered on she moved her face back. 'I haven't brushed my teeth,' Trinity said, shy all of a sudden, but Zahid seemed more than happy to accept that she might need some space.

'I am going to have a quick shower,' Zahid said, licking the last remnants of maple syrup from her mouth and then releasing her, leaving her more than a bit breathless. 'Then, if you want, you can have your bath.'

It was up to Trinity. Whatever her choice, Zahid would not be joining the Fosters at breakfast.

Duty was done.

He just hoped now that it was time for pleasure.

Zahid stood and started to unbutton his shirt. 'When I come out I will ring for someone to come and sort out the room.'

Trinity nodded, surprised that he clearly expected her to be able to speak at her first sighting of his torso. His coffee-coloured skin gleamed and his dark nipples drew her eyes, but it was the very flat stomach and the snake of dark hair beckoning downwards that had Trinity suddenly look away and start pleating the sheet with her fingers.

'I won't be long,' Zahid said, and headed to the shower as she lay back on the pillows and blew out a breath, trying and failing not to think about him sliding off his trousers and naked on the other side as she heard the taps being turned on.

He was giving her the chance to leave, Trinity realised. The chance to gather her things and go to her own room. To have breakfast with her family safe in the knowledge that this would never be mentioned again.

If she left now, she would never see him again.

Trinity lay on the bed and listened as the taps were turned off and a few moments later he came out, carrying his trousers, which he put over the chair. One white towel was around his hips, the other around his neck.

'Still here?' Zahid smiled and took the towel from his shoulders and started to dry his chest and under his arms.

'Looks like it.'

'I'll get the place sorted.'

'I'll have my bath.'

She climbed out of bed and walked to the bathroom but turned at the last moment, in time to see Zahid take off the towel from his hips. And Trinity got more of a glimpse of what she was letting herself in for. It was darker than he, thick and tumescent, and so incredibly beautiful that rather than wanting to grab her dress and run or head for the other side of the bathroom door, she actually wanted to go back to bed.

'You should call your family,' Zahid said, as if it were completely normal to be chatting to her while naked, as if it was completely normal to want the plates cleared and the place tidied and all distractions put on hold before settling in for a lovely long session.

'Er, after my bath,' Trinity croaked, for she wanted nothing to burst the fragile bubble that she carried into the bathroom with her and only released once she had closed the door. The most fragile bubble she had ever carried, for she actually wanted sex, rather than wanted to want sex.

The lighting had been turned down and the huge sunken bath was filled with warm milky-looking water.

She felt all giddy and disorientated but in the nicest way. She looked in the mirror. Her hair was a disaster, her eyes on fire and her body felt as if it was filled with helium, so floaty and high was she from pancake-laden kisses and the promise of more to come.

There was a little card telling her the infusions that her bath contained—frankincense, neroli and argan oils—and that she was to add the bomb at her leisure.

It was the bomb of bath bombs, Trinity thought as she watched it spinning in the water, tossing out petals and the most heavenly fragrances that lured her to climb in.

She lay there in the just right temperature water, with her stomach pleasantly full and her thirst more than quenched, yet for the first time, the very first time since her very first kiss with Zahid, there was a stir of want for a very different pleasure.

Zahid thought her a party girl—that a morning sex marathon was surely commonplace for her.

He'd fall off his mummy-bird perch if he knew just how limited her experience was.

Yet as she lay there, recalling his kisses and her body's response to them, it dawned on Trinity that after all those years of therapy and Californian healing, which hadn't worked a jot, the answer could well be on the other side of the door.

If Zahid had so much as a clue how messed up she was

sexually then everything they had now would disappear. He'd either do the honourable thing and decline because nothing could ever come of them or, worse, she'd get pity sex, with Zahid being all careful and tender and asking if she was okay every five minutes.

Zahid wanted straightforward sex but there was nothing straightforward about sex for Trinity.

Yet she wanted Zahid to look at her the way he had this morning, she wanted the absence of fear that he brought, not just to her mind but her body too.

Still, if she was going to carry this off, then a confident, assured woman must walk out of this bathroom. Somehow she must present herself as the sexually experienced woman that he assumed she was.

'The maid has been.' Zahid knocked at the door. 'And your phone keeps buzzing. Do you want me to bring it in to you?'

'I'll be out in a minute, Zahid!' Trinity called to the closed bathroom door. 'About what you said last night… well, it would seem that I forgot to say please…' She could almost feel his smile behind the door as he answered her.

'Just remember to say thank you.'

Trinity ducked her head under the water but it didn't wipe the smile from her face. It should worry her really that the rather staid Zahid seemed to be the only person in the world who got her sense of humour. Most people frowned, or she had to explain and by then it wasn't so funny.

She didn't have to explain herself to Zahid.

Trinity looked down and saw her nipples peeking up out of the milky bathwater and she didn't understand why she was terrified but not scared.

This was all so…planned, so clinical.

No, not clinical…

Trinity blinked as she realised she had found the word she was searching for—Zahid put the sensual into consensual.

It was a very nice word to ponder as she climbed out of the bath. There were petals from the bath bomb in her hair and sticking to her skin but Trinity just wrapped herself in a robe and ran his comb through her hair.

What if she couldn't carry it off? Trinity thought. What if she started crying or broke down, or her complete inexperience told him that she hadn't a clue?

You'll *never* get a chance like this again, Trinity warned her reflection.

Kill or cure.

She opened the bathroom door, half expecting the slight chaos of this morning.

Instead, the room was in darkness, broken only by the candles dotted everywhere.

The breakfast things had been taken away, all clothes and things tidied, even the bed had that smooth freshly made look, except for the naked sheikh in it!

Trinity was terrified, of course, but nicely so, as she walked over to the bed.

'Nice bath?'

'Lovely.' She sat on the edge of the bed and wondered if the right thing to do would be to tell him but, no, as he welcomed her to his bed with a kiss, she wanted it just as it was.

His kiss made her shiver, the skill of his mouth told her to leave things to him but, just as she almost forgot to be frightened, the bleeping of her phone made her jump.

'Has anyone seen Trinity?' Zahid said, and actually

made her laugh as she rose from his bed and raked her hands in frustration through wet hair. 'I'll just let them know that I won't be joining them.'

She was *far* from grateful for the reprieve—now she and Zahid would have to start all over again, Trinity thought as she picked up the phone from the bedside and read her mother's text.

'They're about to start breakfast and she wants to know where I am.' Her voice gave a little squeak at the end, because he had rolled to the side of the bed and was fiddling with the belt of her robe,

'Text and say Zahid has taken you riding.'

'Horseriding?'

'Don't lie,' Zahid said, and pulled her hips so she was standing, trying to text, as he stayed very much on his side, leaning on one elbow, one hand on her bottom, guiding her hips to his face.

It was terribly hard to text with a mouth nuzzling your stomach. She could see his glossy black hair and feel his hot mouth and tongue as she tried to work out what to write.

Oh, my, Trinity thought as he continued to kiss her stomach, because she actually wanted to drop the phone and hold his head.

Dry from her bath, she was wet from his mouth.

She wanted him lower, yet she didn't.

She wanted fear, yet it steadfastly refused to arrive.

She wanted to run, yet she wanted to remain.

Somehow she hit 'Send' on her text.

'Now turn it off.' Zahid didn't lift his mouth from her skin as he delivered far from his final instruction. 'I want no distractions.'

CHAPTER FIVE

TRINITY TURNED OFF her phone but it did not make it to the bedside table because his mouth was really working her stomach now and instead she just dropped the phone to the floor.

All phones were off, there was a 'Do not disturb' sign on the door, day had become night and all Zahid wanted to do was enjoy.

The soft skin of her stomach tasted better than even he had imagined. Still warm from the bath, it responded so readily to him. Zahid felt the tension in her stomach shifting, he felt the taut muscles relax and then tighten again, but in pleasure as his mouth moved steadily down.

Zahid was working her quickly but for one reason only—he wanted her to come.

Zahid had considered taking care of things in the shower so that he might take more time, but he had chosen to wait.

He was ruing that decision now as he deep-kissed her stomach and his hands slid up her thighs, for he had wanted Trinity for a lot longer than perhaps he cared to admit.

What to do? Trinity pondered. What should she be doing about now? Her hands moved to his hair, more to steady herself, but Zahid moved his mouth lower, nibbling at golden curls then nudging her clitoris out with his tongue as his fingers slid inside a place that no fingers had ever touched.

It was just her mind that was scared, Trinity realised, not her body, for it responded so readily to him.

She could feel a tremble in her thighs as his fingers and tongue stroked her intimately, a tremble that had her wondering if she could remain standing, but his hands soon answered that though, for he released her sex for a moment and guided her to the bed.

She thought he would kiss her, but Zahid had kissed her mouth last night and again this morning, and the first more intimate taste of her had him yearning for more and so he slid down the bed.

'Zahid…' Trinity attempted to halt him, could barely cope with her inhibition, but then came his voice.

'Do you know how many times I have thought of this?' Zahid revealed.

Why was she smiling when she should be in tears?

She could only do this with him, Trinity thought. It could only be this way, Trinity realised, for if he had seen the look of brief horror on her face at such intimate exposure, Zahid would have surely stopped.

He could not see it, though, he was too focused on her sex and guided her hips so she was kneeling over his face.

As she hovered over him his mouth kissed up her inner thigh till it met its shy mark.

'Za—' His name did role from her tongue, it halted in Trinity's throat as his tongue rolled her somewhere deep. She had meant to tell him to stop, but by the time she got to '*hid*' the world as she knew it was different.

Trinity's expression had changed from horror to a

smile and then to a shocked state of bliss as all those years of frustration were swept aside by the masterful strokes of his tongue.

To him she unfolded and, though together, somehow the moment was private, the awakening exclusive to Trinity, which was how she wanted it to be, how it had to be if she wanted him to be this bold.

'I have a rose petal in my teeth,' Zahid said, though his mouth did not move away.

'They're everywhere,' Trinity breathed.

'Good,' Zahid said, returning to his heated mission. 'I find each one.'

She didn't actually have to *do* anything, Trinity realised, all she had to *do* was hold onto the bedhead and try not to moan as she followed instructions.

'Kneel lower...' Zahid breathed. 'Lower.' And she gasped as his face took more of her weight and, once it did, there was no chance of not moaning.

Unshaven, rough, wet and warm, he was everywhere that was needed, inside and out, as he devoured her with relish and his lack of inhibition gained hers.

Thank you, Trinity wanted to whimper, only not because of their earlier game—she had never been more grateful as he stirred her body beyond a simmer. She had to bite on her lip not to say it as he sucked and licked, and ran his stubbly jaw over her. His focus was so concentrated on her that Trinity didn't have to do anything other than rock to her body's tune and let out words that she would rather have kept in because they sounded so lame.

'That's lovely...' she managed. 'Lovely...' Because it was. It was as it should be and no less than that, just so nice to be lifted a little higher by his hands and his tongue kissed her more lightly, swirling her and then probing her, only pausing to tell her she was something, Trinity had no idea what, in Arabic.

'Fantastic,' Zahid translated between licks.

She felt it.

Those sirens were back and moving closer, but there was no sense of danger. She had never had an orgasm, but twice had glimpsed it with Zahid, yet she was on the very edge of one now.

'Zahid.' She said it in one word this time, for now she did want him to slow down.

'Why do you fight it?'

Because she didn't know what *it* was, till suddenly *it* was there and she rose to boiling. The zap of tension that raced up her spine, the shaking of her thighs almost shot Trinity from the bed. Zahid held her hips hard down and his mouth absorbed the energy that pulsed to his lips and tongue as Trinity sobbed out her pleasure. She released a few long-held fears as Zahid fought his—he wanted more, more of the same, more of everything with her. As he lifted her pink and warm from his lips, his mouth suddenly returned again, softly kissing, for he might never be there again.

Trinity wanted to collapse forward but she was already leaning on her arms as Zahid slid up the bed and let her down so she rested at the top of his thighs.

She looked down where he rose between her legs and just explored him a moment with her fingers. Zahid watched, incredibly turned on by her gentle ministrations, very close to coming for the feel of her on his lips had been incredible and the feel of her hands was sublime.

Trinity stroked what would soon be inside her; she felt the soft drizzle of him moisten her fingers and she was actually excited for the moment ahead. Still breath-less from her first orgasm, she wanted to get back on the merry-go-round, loved it that the more she stroked, somehow he became even harder, and bigger too.

'You know...' Trinity said, and then stopped.

'Not unless you tell me.'

'I could get to liking this.' She smiled.

It was the most honest she had been.

'I could get to liking this too,' Zahid said, his face tense from withholding pleasure.

His words were more honest than he should dare to be, for a morning together was becoming far less than enough.

He could not think of that now. His mind was strug-gling just to remember what had once been routine—he reached to the bedside for a condom. Trinity halted him, for she wanted the softness of his skin to meet hers and she mumbled something about an IUD.

'A coil,' she explained, when he frowned.

She'd had one put in when she'd lost the baby, and had had it changed a couple of years ago, the fear of a random attack almost as petrifying as the fear of get-ting pregnant again.

'You're sure,' Zahid said, trying to cling onto the last shreds of common sense, for he never went with-out. 'Because if you get pregnant...' he made a slitting gesture to his throat '...it will be off with mine.' And Trinity actually laughed.

'Very sure.'

He held the base of his thick cock and Trinity lifted herself and lowered herself, loving the feeling of being on top, the control he gave an unwitting gift perhaps, but it set her free.

He filled her completely, she was sure, but then he pulled her hips right down and she shuddered a sob as she struggled to accommodate the full length of him and rose of her own accord to escape, but nature brought her down again. With Zahid her body did not need instruction, it just followed its own lead, until it was Zahid who slowed her down, but for reasons of his own.

He tried to keep things smooth, and although Trinity did her best to move slowly, all she wanted to do was grind against him. Zahid too gave up fighting it and simply let her be.

Was this what she'd been so scared of? Trinity thought as she looked down at Zahid, yet she knew there was no other she could be more herself with. Whatever colour she wore on the day, Zahid saw the person beneath, whatever lie her lips produced, Zahid seemed to extract her truth.

'I think I'm about to come...' Trinity said, and started to chase the feeling, but to no avail. Just as she thought she might not repeat the magic his mouth had given her, Zahid took over, bucking his hips into her, grinding her down to him, and there was nothing to chase, she was already here. The final swell of him inside and the lift of his hips tipped her over the edge and she came to the delicious sight of a very controlled Zahid momentarily out of it, pulling her down to her side and bucking into her for those last delicious strokes, where they met in a place where logic was left far behind.

It was sex, Zahid said to himself as he kissed her down from her climax. Good-morning sex that had been a long time coming.

It must remain as simple as that.

CHAPTER SIX

IT WAS FAR more complicated, though.

Zahid knew it.

It wasn't just that his people would never accept her as his bride. Or that she might not want to be one.

It went a lot deeper than that.

Zahid rolled away as he did after sex, but then thought twice and rolled back to face her again.

'Penny for them,' Trinity said, and it took a moment for him to register that she was asking his thoughts.

'Oh, it would cost a lot more than that,' Zahid said.

It might cost him his kingdom or, worse, he might lose his head, though not in the way he had joked about before. How could he run a country with Trinity waiting in his bed? How could he focus on his people when his mind would be so consumed by her?

It was no surprise when Trinity turned from his silence and picked up her phone.

Whatever he thought of them, they were her family.

'Eight missed calls,' Trinity said.

'You need to go down?'

'I don't want to,' Trinity admitted, 'but, given that I fly out this afternoon, it would be wrong not to put in an appearance.'

'I know.'

Zahid then made a huge concession. Yes, he had decided to sever ties but for her he would do the right thing. 'Do you want me to come down with you?'

Trinity shook her head and climbed out of bed and started to gather her things.

'What are you doing?' Zahid asked.

'I have to get ready. I need to go to my room.'

'You can get ready here.'

'It's going to be bad enough wearing last night's clothes in the elevator, I'm certainly not going down to face everyone in my bridesmaid's dress.'

'Go and have a shower,' Zahid said. 'I will have your things brought here.'

He took care of all the details so easily, Trinity thought as she quickly had a shower and this time she did make a bit of effort with her hair, blasting it with the hotel hairdryer and doing what she could with Zahid's comb.

Now came the hard bit and for once she didn't mean facing her family or facing her fears.

It was facing the man on the other side of the door and pretending what had just happened had been little more than a very pleasant interlude.

Now she had to give him up.

Maybe she could go to the pharmacist and ask for Zahid patches, like Donald had when he'd tried to give up smoking, Trinity thought, making a little joke to herself, trying to lighten the load on her mind. But no gradually reducing dose was going to wean her off Zahid. Trinity knew that already.

Cold turkey, here I come, she decided, opening the door and wearing a smile.

Zahid lay in bed, watching as she put on some make-up and then tied up her hair.

It was over.

He just didn't want it to be.

Or rather he did, for these feelings that he had for her did not sit right with him, these feelings spelt danger.

His mind flicked to his father, bereft on his mother's death, scarcely able to stand, let alone lead a country.

The same would not happen to him.

The dress she had bought for this morning was colourful and floaty and did not quite match her threatening tears as she took the case to the door.

'I'll drop it in my room on the way down.'

Zahid nodded.

So this was goodbye.

'You look beautiful,' he told her, for it was the truth.

'Thank you.'

She ached, not just from him but for him.

'What time is your flight?' Zahid asked.

Trinity told him.

'That is an hour before I am scheduled to fly,' Zahid said.

Their eyes met as they did the maths in their heads, as their brains raced to mental calculators to tap in more time.

One more kiss, one more taste, one more time.

'I could take you to the airport.'

'So I...'

'Leave your case here.'

She almost ran to him. Maybe she did, for suddenly she was back on the bed and in his arms and responding to the fierce promise of his kiss.

'Take as long as you need with your family,' Zahid

said as she wrenched herself off, 'but not five minutes more.'

They smiled because they both wanted that little sliver of time before they had to leave.

'Are you sure that you don't want me to join you?' Zahid offered again.

'I'd rather go down on my own.'

She looked at Zahid and there was a moment when she truly wanted to tell him the truth but the very fact that she hadn't meant that, no, he could not join her downstairs.

If he did then it would be a huge disservice to Zahid for, yes, he would do the right thing and make polite small talk with her family, even Clive.

She would not put him, even unwittingly, through that.

'Penny for them,' Zahid said, and Trinity just gave a pensive smile.

'They're not even worth that.'

They weren't, Trinity realised.

Not a pennyworth of thoughts did she want to give to a man who had no place in this room.

'Thank you,' Trinity said, and Zahid's eyes narrowed in a slight frown, for it had been a little joke that she might want to thank him but it sounded like she meant it.

'The pleasure was mine.'

One more kiss, and then just one more, before Trinity headed downstairs to where both Donald's and Yvette's families were gathered. Surprisingly it was a lot easier, knowing that if things got too difficult she could go back up to Zahid.

Even not by her side, he gave her a confidence that she had never had.

'I hear you're working in a library,' Yvette's mother said, and she almost went to correct her but for the sake of peace Trinity lied.

'In the reference section.'

She was the *perfect* daughter, circulating nicely, even pretending that she was listening as her mind roamed several floors upwards. Finally, when she glanced at the clock for the fiftieth time, it was time to say goodbye.

'I'm sorry I got so upset yesterday,' Yvette said as Trinity kissed her goodbye and wished her well for the honeymoon. 'I spoke to Donald last night and it was all just a miscommunication with the hotel.'

'That's good.'

They spoke for a suitable time and Trinity was just saying her goodbyes to everyone else, silently congratulating herself on a job well done and about to slip away to spend a final, magical hour with Zahid, when Donald pulled her to one side.

'Can I have a word, Trinity?'

She felt her heart sink and just closed her eyes as history repeated itself.

'You know how I hate to ask,' Donald said.

Except it didn't stop him from doing so!

'The hotel is insisting I pay for it all up front. How can I tell Yvette that I've messed up the honeymoon?'

'I haven't got it to give you.' That wasn't the issue, though and, not for the first time, she did her best to face it. 'Donald, you need help.'

'I need my honeymoon,' Donald said. 'It's just been an expensive few weeks. If I can just get away...'

Trinity was too worried to be cross.

So, instead of heading back to Zahid and the bliss of his arms, after a lengthy discussion she sat in the business centre of the hotel and pulled up her account as her time with Zahid slipped ever further away.

She didn't need to ask for Donald's bank details, she had already used them several times.

Thanks to flying economy and saving what she could, Trinity had just over eight thousand dollars in her account. 'How much do you need?'

'Well, there's the hotel, taxis, going out…'

'How much?' Trinity asked, and she couldn't even manage a shrill edge to her voice.

'Whatever you can manage.'

She left herself one hundred dollars and she was too tired from it all to be angry and too scared for her brother to be cross.

'Please, get help, Donald.' She gave him a hug when she stood.

Trinity truly did not know what to do.

She'd begged and pleaded with him over the years, she'd argued and threatened, had offered him the chance to come and stay at hers and just hang out by the beach, but all to no avail. 'I don't want anything to happen to you. I don't want to be at one of these bloody family things without you.'

'I'm fine,' said Donald, peeling her off, only she didn't want to let go.

'I'm scared I'm going to lose you.'

'Honestly, Trinity, there's nothing to worry about.'

'I love you,' Trinity said, 'and so I do worry.'

'Well, there's no need. Thanks for this.'

By the time she'd calmed down and sorted out her make-up to look as if she hadn't been in tears enough to go back to Zahid's room it was already time for she and Zahid to leave for the airport.

'I'm sorry, I got stuck…'

'It's fine.' Zahid pulled her into his arms as their baggage was placed onto a large gold trolley. It wasn't just sex he wanted from Trinity but this, that moment when he held her in his arms and she almost relaxed to him.

He could feel her heart hammering in her chest and, despite a brilliant make-up job, he knew there had been tears, and from the way she clung to him now he doubted that they had been happy ones. 'How was it?'

'Same old, same old,' Trinity attempted, forcing herself to pull back and smile, but she met very serious eyes. 'It was fine,' she said, adding another log to the fire of lies between them.

The traffic was light and in no time they were at Trinity's terminal. Zahid would go onto the VIP section and so they said their final goodbyes in the back of his car. Zahid raised his hand so that no one opened the door to let her out but her luggage was unloaded and it taunted Trinity from the corner of her eye.

'Take me with you.' Trinity smiled. She was joking, sort of, and then she wasn't. There was the threat of tears in her eyes again as she recalled the first time she'd asked him to take her with him. It was combined with this horrible feeling of impending doom.

Zahid had no idea what had happened that terrible night and rather than him see that, she moved in for a kiss, but Zahid halted her, his hand cupping her chin.

'I would love to take you with me,' Zahid said. 'You would be like a breath of fresh air in the palace…' And so very dangerous to his heart. 'You would be the biggest distraction, though.'

Normally, Zahid had no trouble ending things. It was just proving more than a touch difficult now. He actually wanted to take her hand and tell the pilot that there would be another passenger, to take her home to Ishla with him and to hell with consequences.

That was not him, though.

With Trinity he barely recognised himself.

Trinity too was having a lot of trouble remembering that she was supposed to be at ease with this, that it should be easy to simply kiss him goodbye, especially when Zahid started to make promises he surely would not keep.

'Give me your number and I will call...'

'Don't.' She pressed a finger to his lips. 'Don't say you'll call when you won't.'

He stared into very blue eyes and wished he was not going home to start the process of selecting a bride, wished for just a few more months of freedom...but wishes had to be denied when duty called.

'No doubt I'll see you in a few months at a christening.' Trinity attempted a brave smile but it wavered when Zahid shook his head.

Trinity was a luxury that even a married Zahid would find hard to deny.

'I think that this has to be it.'

'Such a terrible shame,' Trinity said, trying to keep things light, trying to pretend this wasn't breaking her heart. 'You could almost make family functions bearable.'

Zahid was struggling too as he tried to relegate it to a one-night stand, or one-morning stand, instead of lovers who were parting for good.

His goodbye was distant.

CHAPTER SEVEN

The cause of death has not been released and the family have requested privacy at this difficult time.
   A small, intimate funeral is being held today, followed by a private burial.

THEN THERE WAS the small spiel at the end of the report urging readers struggling with personal issues to 'ring this number'.

No doubt it would be engaged.

Trinity folded the newspaper and put it on the table in front of her as the steward came round.

'Can I get you anything before we start our descent?'

Trinity shook her head and got back to staring out of the window as morning continued to arrive.

She had always feared that this day would come but only in her worst nightmare had she thought that less than a month after the wedding she would be flying to the same church to say goodbye to her brother for the last time.

It had been a terrible month.

She had mourned Zahid, had ached to call him, to make contact somehow, though knowing that it was not what they had agreed.

No-strings sex, yet her emotions were more than frayed when she'd found out that ten days into their honeymoon Yvette had walked out on Donald and after that her brother had gone spectacularly off the rails.

It had from then on been a rapid descent into hell and Trinity actually couldn't remember when she'd last slept for more than a couple of hours.

Panic had descended when she had first taken the call and heard that Donald had died but it had been quickly replaced by numbness and she was grateful for that as she made her way through customs.

Her mum's family had naturally descended on the house. Her mother needed her sister but the thought of seeing Clive at this impossible time was more than Trinity could face.

Tonight she would stay at the hotel where the wake was being held before flying back tomorrow.

Yes, another flying visit.

She'd learnt her lesson and so, when her father had transferred money to bring her home for the funeral, she had flown business class this time, but she still hadn't been able to rest.

Heathrow airport saw its share of tears but it didn't glimpse Trinity's today for she held them back, petrified that if one escaped, the floodgates would open.

They nearly did.

As she turned, there was Zahid, the very last person she had been expecting to see, for the funeral was being kept low key. Her mother hadn't mentioned that Zahid would be there when she had spoken to her yesterday.

'You will be okay.'

It was a strange greeting. There was no embrace, just

the guidance of his hand on her arm as his driver took her baggage and they were led to his car.

'I wasn't expecting to see you.' Trinity didn't speak till they were in his car. 'Mum said nothing about you coming.'

'I only just found out. By the time I did you had already left for the airport...' Zahid did not elaborate. Now was not the time to tell her that he had finally caved and, unable to get through to Donald, he had rung Dianne to ask for Trinity's number, only to hear the news.

His plane had touched down twenty minutes before hers.

Trinity looked at Zahid. His lips were pale and his features taut. His thick hair was a touch too long and that tiny detail made her frown, for she had never seen him looking anything other than immaculately groomed.

'Let's first get you home.'

'I'm staying at a hotel,' Trinity said. 'You?'

'No hotel—I fly back this afternoon,' Zahid answered. 'When do you go back?'

'Tomorrow.' Her voice was dull and she went back to staring out of the window.

It was not his place to be angered by her lack of duty today. It was not his place to point out that surely she should be by her parents' side, not just for the funeral but in the days that followed.

It did anger him, though, for it just reinforced the fact that she bucked convention, that she refused to do the right thing, especially on a day like today.

They pulled up at the hotel and as the driver removed her luggage Zahid noted the time as they needed to leave soon for the funeral.

'You check in and change. I will wait in Reception.'

'Why?' Trinity said. 'Or are we pretending today that you've never seen me naked before?'

She was, Zahid decided as they headed to her room, the most volatile that he had ever known her and any doubt that he should be here today was erased from his mind.

She needed him today, Zahid told himself, still fighting that he might need to be with her today too.

'Your mother asked that I deliver the eulogy,' Zahid said, as Trinity tried to plug in her heated rollers then realised that she'd forgotten her adaptor.

'Great!' Trinity hissed, and then turned and gave him a bright smile. 'Great,' she said again.

'In what order?' Zahid asked. 'Is the hiss for the state your hair will be in, or that I have been asked to speak?'

'You choose.'

'Why are you…?' He halted. Now was perhaps not the time to ask why she was so angry at him, now not the time to tell her just the hell this month had been for him too.

'I'm going to have a shower,' Trinity said.

'A quick one,' Zahid warned. 'We have to—'

'I'm not going to be late for my own brother's funeral,' Trinity almost shouted. 'I do know how to tell the time.'

He arched his neck to the side as the bathroom door slammed. Zahid walked on eggshells for no one, yet he could almost feel them crunching beneath his feet as he paced the room.

Leave it for now, he told himself.

Trinity was not his and so he had no right to insist on better behaviour.

She was who she was and in truth he would not change her.

Zahid made a quick phone call and when the adaptor she needed was promptly delivered he sat as she came out from the shower wrapped in a towel and watched her eyes fall on the blinking light of her hair appliance.

Zahid did not expect her to thank him, so her silence came as no surprise.

She flipped open her case and like a depressed magician pulled out black, after black, after black.

Zahid turned his head as she dropped her towel and he heard her snap on her bra, then the sound of her pulling on her panties and then the tear of cellophane as she opened new stockings.

'I'm sorry for the imposition.' Trinity popped the tense silence with the tip of her anger. 'I know that you never wanted to see me again.'

'Of all your lies, and there are many, that is the biggest.' Zahid looked at her now, appalled at how much weight she had lost this past month, how her skin had paled. He silently berated himself about how much he still wanted her. 'How long did it take you to twist my words into my never wanting to see you again?'

'You said—'

'I said that this had to be it. I said my feelings for you would be inappropriate in the future.' He watched as she started to crumple and he knew enough about Trinity to know that any crumpling would be spectacular and so couldn't happen just yet.

To embrace at the airport would have opened the floodgates but his touch might just hold them closed for a little longer now. 'Come here,' Zahid said, and when she did, he pulled her to his lap.

Her skin did not arouse him this grey morning. Instead, he answered the tiny goose-bumps on her arms and her stomach in their plea for strength and warmth and held her tightly to him. 'I'm here to get you through today,' he said. 'Our stuff can wait. I will call you in a few days and then we can speak properly.' Zahid felt her nod on his chest. 'Today you have enough on your mind without being concerned about us.'

So much on her mind.

Not just that Clive would be there today.

It was the first funeral she had been to since her daughter's, which had been the loneliest day of her life.

'I'm here with you,' Zahid said, and he could never know just how much those words helped. 'Now, get ready.'

He did not avert his eyes as she dressed. There was no point—her scent was on him and his mind would caress her intimately later.

Right now, though, there was a funeral to attend.

As they took their places in the church Zahid recalled their last conversation. '*You could almost make family functions bearable.*'

Nothing could make this bearable, though.

As he stood to read the eulogy, she reminded him of a fragile flower blooming in winter surrounded by the ice of grief.

He looked at Donald's wife, Yvette, whose face was etched in bitterness, and wondered about her pain of the last weeks as her handsome groom had faded to the husband from hell.

Speaking at the funeral of a man you did not admire was a hard task but Zahid executed it well. He spoke of better times, of a younger Donald and family gatherings that...

Zahid glanced up from the notes he had written on the plane. Even as he had penned them he had known that the words were inaccurate, though the right ones to utter, yet Zahid never lied. His eyes turned to Trinity, who started down at black-stockinged knees, and there was the reason he had kept going back. Having admitted that to himself, he was able to speak the truth then. 'Family gatherings that I always looked forward to and will remember with deep affection...' He gave a pale smile as Trinity looked up. 'While we remember the good times,' Zahid said, and looked to Trinity, 'we should not ignore the pain left to us now.'

It was the only time Donald's life was painted as anything other than perfect, Zahid realised as the Fosters micro-managed their son's funeral.

The cemetery was awful. Zahid watched as Trinity held back despite her mother urging her to step forward.

Zahid moved and stood beside Trinity.

The light refreshments were downed with whisky back at the swanky hotel, yet when he wanted to be by her side, the Fosters still kept pulling him away, dragging him into other conversations when he so badly needed to be with her.

He saw her glance at the clock, knew that again they were running out of time and Zahid excused himself from second cousins and made his way over to the one who came first to him. 'How are you?'

'Fabulous!' Her smile was as dangerous as her eyes.

'How are you?' Zahid said again.

'I'm going to lose it in about thirty seconds from now.'

'You're not.'

'I might.'

'You won't,' Zahid said.

Zahid watched as she pushed on a smile as someone approached and offered their condolences but soon it was just them and she told him a little of what was on her mind.

'I don't understand how everyone keeps saying he was a wonderful man, how tragic it was and how sudden. I've been saying for months that this would happen.' She could not stand to be here even a moment longer.

'When do you fly?' Trinity asked.

'In a couple of hours.'

'We could go to my room.'

'I think that would be completely inappropriate,' Zahid said.

'Aww…' Trinity smiled that dangerous smile. 'A playboy with a conscience, how sweet!'

Crunch went the eggshells beneath his well-shod feet. 'You know, Trinity, if it wasn't your brother's funeral…' He halted, not just because Dianne had come over but because of the strength of the words he had been about to deliver, because privately he would like to take her aside and rattle her till she behaved, or tip her over his knee and spank her till she conformed.

He was angry, not just at Trinity but at himself for the foolish moment when he had even considered she might belong by his side, for she could barely behave at her own brother's funeral.

'We've decided to have people back to the house after all,' Dianne informed her daughter.

'I thought the whole point of having it at the hotel was that you wouldn't have to ask people to the house.'

'Well, your father thinks we should ask people back so I need you to go and open up and set up the drinks and glasses—'

'I'm not going back to the house.'

'Trinity…' Dianne had this black smile on in an attempt to disguise the venom in her voice. 'Go and open up and you are to greet—'

'I told you earlier,' Trinity said, 'I'd come to the hotel but I am not—'

'Grow up!' Dianne hissed. 'Grow up and show some respect for your brother's memory.' She walked off and left Trinity standing, her cheeks on fire with years of suppressed rage.

'I will take you back to the house,' Zahid said. He knew today must be agony for her, but there was a part of him that was very cross with Trinity. There were things you did, things that simply had to be done.

He took her rigid hand and led her out to his driver.

'In a couple of hours it will all be over.'

'It will never be over.'

He could not abide her melodrama. Zahid loathed raw emotion unless it came with an orgasm attached.

They pulled up at her house and he noticed her cheeks were no longer pink but instead as white as the lilies that had filled the church.

'Let's just set up then I'm going,' Trinity said. She let them in and started to pull out glasses from the dresser as Zahid sorted out the drinks.

Perhaps realising the reception she might get from Trinity, Dianne chose not to ring her daughter when plans changed yet again. Instead, she dialled Zahid. 'Could you ask Trinity to set up the guest room?'

Trinity said nothing at first when Zahid relayed the

message, she just marched angrily up the stairs and started pulling towels out of the airing cupboard. 'She's got a bloody nerve.'

Zahid was fast losing his patience. Yes, the Fosters were hard work but Trinity was behaving like a spoilt brat and, frankly, he expected more from her.

'Can you just, for five minutes in your life, do the right thing?' he said, as Trinity opened the guest-room door. 'Your mother has lost her son.'

She could hear the front door opening and cars pulling up and everyone starting to arrive, and she was past staying quiet, could not hold it in for even a second longer as she stood in the room where so much had been taken from her.

'She's lost more than her son,' Trinity said. 'How dare she pretend that it never happened? How dare she tell me to set up the guest room when she knows full well what went on in here that night?'

'What night?'

'The night *you left me* here!'

Oh, it had been but the tip of her anger back at the hotel, Zahid realised. He knew, with sick dread, the night she was referring to, he knew from the bleached whiteness of her lips and the anguish in her eyes what must have taken place.

He remembered Dianne telling her to set up the guest room for Elaine and Clive and her fingers grasping his as he'd climbed in the car.

Zahid even remembered the time.

Ten minutes after eleven was the moment that now he would regret for ever.

'My aunt's husband...' Trinity gagged. 'After you'd gone, he attacked me.'

CHAPTER EIGHT

ZAHID KNEW THAT how he reacted to this was important to Trinity so he fought for calm as he processed the news, but there was a dangerous instinct kicking in. One that might see him head downstairs this very moment, as the funeral party had now arrived, and for once it would not be their daughter who misbehaved.

'You need to let your parents know,' Zahid said, relieved when he heard his own voice, for it sounded calm, in control, when he felt anything but. 'They need to know what went on that night and why family functions are so hard for you.'

He had always been proud of his self-control but he was in awe of it when she responded to him.

'They know.'

Just two words but they were almost more than he could process. Zahid could hear long breaths coming out of his nostrils as Dianne called up the stairs for Trinity and he struggled to stay calm. 'Oh, Zahid, your driver said you need to leave.'

'You need to get your flight,' Trinity said, feeling guilty and panicked for telling him and seeing him fight for control. 'Please, Zahid, you can't say anything. It's my brother's funeral.'

He didn't care what day it was.

'Please, don't make this worse for me.'

He pulled her away from the room and wrapped his arms around her in the hall as Zahid for once struggled with what to do.

There were so many reasons not to do what he was about to, so very many, but he simply could not leave her here.

'Usually now you ask to come with me.'

'You always say no.'

'Not this time.' He neither knew nor cared what the reaction would be in Ishla, he just shoved away the thought that in a few days he was to dine with Princess Sameena and her family, then Sheikha Kumu three days after that.

He simply could not leave Trinity here and neither could he stay, because it would be impossible for him not to make a scene.

If his gaze fell on Clive, Zahid knew, there was no telling what he might do.

'You will leave with me.'

'I can't just walk out now.' Even if she had been threatening to just a few minutes ago, the reality was she could not simply walk out and leave, but Zahid had decided otherwise.

'Yes, you can,' Zahid said. 'I will sort it all out. You are not staying here to deal with this alone.' He took her hand and they walked down the stairs and headed to where her parents stood.

'I know it is not the best timing,' Zahid said, 'but I am taking Trinity back to Ishla with me.'

'Sorry?' Dianne blinked.

'I would like to have given you more notice but my return flight has already been arranged.'

So that his eyes would not drift around the room, Zahid stared down Trinity's father and almost dared him to protest, but no one would argue with Zahid in this mood. He was nothing but polite yet there was such a black energy inside him that in a matter of moments they were heading to the airport, only stopping at the hotel to collect her small suitcase.

'I only packed for today. All my things are back in America...'

'You don't need to bring anything,' Zahid said.

'What about work?'

'We'll sort that,' Zahid said, as they neared the airport. 'Tell me where you work and I will call someone.'

'The Beach Bar.' Trinity shook her head. 'It doesn't matter, I'm only casual.'

'I thought...' Zahid halted and let out a breath. He'd spent weeks making phone calls and trying to find out what library it was that she worked out.

Another lie.

What did he know about her?

Even as they boarded his jet, Zahid was quite sure that any minute she would change her mind.

'What will your father say?' Trinity asked.

'Don't worry about that now,' Zahid said. Usually he would let the palace know if he was bringing a guest but in this instance Zahid felt it would be better to speak face to face with his father.

As the plane took to the sky the practicalities of whisking her away were starting to make themselves known. Zahid did think of stopping somewhere en route but there was much for him to do back in Ishla.

He just wanted her away and safe.

She sat beside him and as the plane levelled out in the sky still she said nothing.

'Do you want something to eat or drink?' Zahid asked.

'No.'

'Do you want to rest?'

'No,' Trinity said, but she stood and Zahid watched as she walked towards the sleeping area. Her top was already off. 'I want you to make today bearable.'

'Trinity.' He walked in and watched as she stripped off her black clothes. 'What you need to understand is that once in Ishla we cannot—'

'What I *need* is one pleasant thing to focus on.'

'Sex won't make this better.'

'Oh, I think you could be wrong.'

'I'm not wrong,' Zahid said. 'When did you last sleep?'

Trinity couldn't answer that. Even thinking up an answer to the most simple question hurt too much right now.

Zahid pulled back the bedding. 'In.'

'I'm naked, Zahid.'

'If that's a problem for you I can see if the stewardess can find something for you to wear to bed.'

'It isn't a problem for me!' Trinity was so cross that he would not be goaded.

'Well, it's no problem for me either. Get some rest,' Zahid said, closing the door on her and taking a seat. But two minutes later she was out, thankfully wearing a robe and blinking at the bright lights.

'Can I have a drink?'

'Do I look like a flight stewardess?' Zahid said, deliberately turning away. 'Press the bell by the bed.'

'I don't want to press the bell.'

He did not turn round and finally she gave in and went back to bed. He watched as a few moments later the stewardess came and answered her call and returned a few moments later with a tray and a glass of sparkling water.

But trying to keep her in bed was like trying to squeeze a jack-in-the-box back into a box with a broken clasp.

'There's a noise.'

She was back again.

'A rattling noise.'

'Possibly because we are on a plane,' Zahid answered. 'Go to bed.'

'I can't sleep,' Trinity said, but she did as told.

For four minutes and forty-five seconds.

'Shouldn't there be a belt—?'

'I'll give you a belt,' Zahid said, standing, and he practically hauled her into the bedroom and threw her onto the bed.

'A leather one?' Trinity smiled.

'A human one.' He climbed onto the bed but not in it and lay beside her with his arm clamped over her. He turned her round so she was facing away from him but wedged against him.

'Go to sleep,' Zahid said.

'I can't,' Trinity said, 'because if I close my eyes...' So violent was the shudder that racked her, for a moment Zahid wondered if they had hit turbulence, and so loud were the sobs and tears that came then that the stewardess really had no choice but to knock and pop her head into the dark sanctuary in the sky to check if everything was okay.

'She's fine,' Zahid said as the door opened. And the stewardess nodded and closed it as Trinity wailed.

'I don't have tissue.'

'You have a giant one,' Zahid said, placing the sheet in her hand. And not once, as she sobbed, did he tell her to stop or that she should calm down. He just held her facing away from him, clamped down by him, so there was nowhere to hide.

'I gave him money,' Trinity sobbed. 'If I hadn't…'

'I gave him money too,' Zahid said. 'He called me from his honeymoon and said he could not pay the bill. If you want to blame someone, blame me.'

He could take it.

'I paid for his honeymoon,' Trinity said. 'I've lived on noodles for a month.'

'I paid for his honeymoon too, half the wedding party probably paid for his honeymoon,' Zahid said, and his words honed perspective.

He let her cry and then he let her sleep and he should have left then, Zahid knew. He should have climbed from the bed rather than hold her.

Zahid had not slept much in recent weeks either.

With Trinity resting beside him he finally did sleep but a few hours later the first stirring from her had him awake.

'I'm cold,' she moaned to a universe that did not answer.

He pulled the blanket higher on her shoulder then moved her tighter in to his embrace.

'Sleep,' Zahid said. They were five hours into their flight and it was already the most sleep that either had had in a while.

'I'm awake now,' Trinity said. 'Sort of,' she half explained, for she was in that lovely in-between place where things didn't hurt so much, or was it just that Zahid was beside her?

Zahid was beside her and they were on their way to Ishla!

She struggled to duck back into slumber, to not face the problems that surely awaited. He was still on top of the covers and, from the shirtsleeved arm that was over her, still dressed.

And again she was down to her bra and panties and had been put to bed by Zahid.

'Did I demand sex?'

'You did,' Zahid said, and smiled to the back of her hair. Then he remembered the reason she was there and the terrible thing that had happened to her. 'Trinity...'

'I don't want to talk about it.' She had heard the shift in his voice. 'Please.'

'Okay.' That she had told him was huge, Zahid knew.

'Is it going to cause trouble, you bringing me back to Ishla?' Trinity asked.

'Not for you,' Zahid said. 'But...' the ramifications of bringing her home at such a delicate time were starting to hit him. 'It is my birthday in a couple of days...'

'Will there be a party?' she nudged.

'No.' Zahid smiled. 'After that there are dinners to help make the wisest choice when I choose my bride.'

'Choose me,' Trinity said, and put her hand up in the air as if answering a question in class, and they both laughed. 'I've never heard you laugh,' Trinity said, as his hand came up to join hers.

'Neither have I,' Zahid said, capturing her raised hand and holding it there.

'Will you serve me without question?' Zahid said.

'I won't.'

He felt the resistance as she tried to pull her arm down and it was a game but a sad one for possibly the only way they could discuss it was to have a little play. 'Do you promise to remember to do your duty as I serve my country.'

'I don't.'

'And I don't need to ask if you will obey…' He released her hand and she moved it down and turned to face him and stared unblinkingly into his eyes.

'The closer you get,' Trinity said, 'the kinder you look.'

'The closer you get, the less I can see.'

'Can I be your mistress?'

'I would never take a mistress,' Zahid said. 'Which is why I would not have been at any christening.' She worried him so. 'Why would you want to be a mistress?'

'It was a joke, Zahid.' Trinity tried to turn it into that. In fact, she didn't want to be a mistress, just something of his.

'So how will you decide who will be your bride?'

'Alliances.'

She turned onto her back and chose to stare at the ceiling for she did not like his detached answer and it did not sound like him, or rather it did not sound like the Zahid that only she saw. 'So you'll marry for alliances with the hope love will grow?'

'Love is for fools and peasants, not for a future king.'

'Thanks,' Trinity said, and she turned and watched his haughty face twitch into a slight smile. 'Then I'm either a fool or a peasant.'

'I was not talking about you.'

'Of course you are. Just because you are going to be king one day, you think feelings are beneath you...'

'I am telling you how it is in my land,' Zahid said, refusing to be swayed. 'I am telling you my reasoning.' But not all of it. He chose not to tell her about his father's illness and when Layla had been born, for he could not share that with another and remain aloof, could not return to that memory and somehow stay detached, yet he knew to be fair to Trinity he must make things clear. 'I am telling you that in Ishla things will be very different between us.' He went to get up. 'I will have some refreshments brought in to you and then you should get dressed as we need to be out there when the plane starts its descent.'

'I know things will be different but we're not in Ishla yet,' Trinity said, as he rose from the bed and went to the door and she waited, breath held as Zahid halted and went against his own moral code, just for that one last time with her.

She watched as he turned and then undressed and it was Trinity who held the covers open this time. Naked beside him, it felt as if she had been cold for the entire month and had just remembered how it felt to be warm. 'Thank you,' Trinity said.

'I haven't done anything yet.'

'For making me happy. I shouldn't be happy today but I am.'

'You should be happy every day,' Zahid said, for even on the worst days they made the other smile.

His mouth was tender. It was a slow and long kiss for even if they did not have very long he still did not rush her.

Slow was the hand that explored her, that stroked

her breasts and then her hips, and Trinity could feel the building need in him. When she rolled to her back, when he moved deep into her, Zahid took his own weight on his elbows and their kissing stopped and he looked down at Trinity as she looked back at him.

She felt him build, yet she felt him hold back and it was his passion she wanted.

'You don't have to be careful around me.'

She saw the twist of pain on his lips, for the news had devastated him, she knew.

'You don't have to hold back,' Trinity said, because she wanted the Zahid who wanted her as she was, with no thought what had been. And right now she wanted his anger, for she was angry too and had every right to be—this was their last time. 'Please don't hold back on me, Zahid.'

He took her the way he wanted to and drove hard into her, but far from scaring her he drove her fear away, for her hands were pressing him in and her body was arching to his as they both refused to allow anything other than themselves in the bedroom.

It was Zahid who shouted and to feel him unleash just unravelled her more.

Deep, intense, blissful was the orgasm that met his and Trinity did her best not to cry out, but did and then frantically glanced at the door, but he brought her face back with his hand and his mouth took her moans and there was nothing she was scared of with Zahid.

'You were right,' Zahid said, looking down at the woman he would crave for ever. 'My feelings are beneath me.'

It took a moment for Trinity to understand his words.

Yes, his feelings lay beneath him right now, every one of them contained in her.

As a bell warned that they would soon be descending, Zahid knew he must leave feelings here.

He just wasn't sure how.

They quickly washed and dressed but instead of putting on his suit, for the first time she saw him in robes and wearing a *kafiya*.

He saw her startle.

'I…' She didn't know what to say. 'It all seems a bit more real now.'

'I don't know if I am making things worse for you,' Zahid admitted, for it had simply seemed right to bring her when he had found out what had happened. The reality, though, made little sense.

'I don't want to meet the women you'll…'

'I know.'

For the first time jealousy stirred in Trinity and despite herself she wanted to know more.

'Must she be a virgin?'

'Trinity, we need to get back to our seats,' Zahid said, for he did not want to discuss his future wife now.

'So you're not going to answer my question?'

'She must have kept herself only for me.'

He went to open the door but her words halted him. His kiss, his lovemaking, the way he had been with her had changed her world and Zahid deserved to know the gift he had given her. 'I have.'

She saw the line between his eyes deepen as he tried to fathom her words.

'There's been no one but you, apart from…'

'Don't,' Zahid said. 'Don't put the two together, for what that bastard did does not count in any land that

I would rule.' He did not know what to believe. 'Trinity, the woman I took to bed that day was confident...'

'Not at first,' she admitted. 'Zahid, I've had issues since that night, I've tried so many things. I know I flirt, I know I seem bold but that's how I am with you...'

'I should have known!' Zahid said. 'I would have done things differently.'

'Exactly!' Trinity said, as the bell carried on pinging and then there was a knock on the door.

Zahid called out something in Arabic.

'Had I told you the truth, would it have happened?' When Zahid didn't answer, Trinity did for him. 'Of course not.'

'You *should* have told me.'

'No.' Trinity shook her head. 'Because then it would never have happened and I refuse to regret that it did. I know it can't happen again,' she said. 'I get it that it doesn't change things.'

But for Zahid it did.

CHAPTER NINE

TRINITY HAD NEVER really given his land much thought but as they neared she looked down at and knew it was not what she might have expected.

Old married new, for there were ancient villages, yet as they flew along the peninsula she saw too the high glitter of modern architecture, but most beautiful by far was the palace for it gleamed the brightest all.

'It's amazing.' When she got no response she glanced over at Zahid, whose face might have been carved from one of the stone palace walls.

'Zahid….'

There was no chance to talk. The plane was a second from landing and as it hit the palace runway, Zahid was actually grateful for the jolt of landing and the sound of wheels on the tarmac for it gave him two seconds away from his thoughts.

He had been her first.

He needed to process it, they needed to discuss it, but first somehow he had to clear his head.

A car drove them the short distance from the plane and though Zahid's driver did his best to keep his face impassive, Trinity could feel him repeatedly glancing in the rear-view mirror. It was the same when they arrived. The maids gaped in surprise as Prince Zahid arrived with a blonde foreigner dressed only in black and Trinity stood, her face burning, as Zahid spoke to a man in Arabic, who then walked off.

'That is Abdul, my father's chief aide, I have told him to let my father know that I wish to speak with him and to have a suite arranged for you.' He halted and turned as a very beautiful, raven-haired woman walked towards them with a curious expression on her face. 'This is my sister, Layla.'

'And this is?' Layla asked, when for once Zahid forgot his manners.

'Trinity,' Zahid responded, and Trinity watched as Layla raised an eyebrow and waited for her brother to elaborate. 'Trinity Foster.'

'It is lovely to meet you, Trinity,' Layla said.

'I am about to let Father know that I have a guest,' Zahid said. 'Layla, perhaps you could help Trinity to settle in and sort out some clothes and things for her. She came at short notice and so has nothing much with her.'

'Of course.' Layla smiled. 'This way.'

They were all so terribly polite, Trinity thought. Surely Layla must have a thousand questions but instead a maid was called and they drank mint tea as they waited for her room to be readied.

The king, though, did not hold back.

'Zahid,' the king said sharply. 'You said you wanted nothing more to do with that family…'

'I was not referring to Trinity when I said that.' He looked at his father.

'Perhaps,' the king said, 'but here the rules are different.'

'I am aware of that.'

'Here, you are not the man you are overseas.'

'I have brought Trinity here as a friend as, not for anything else.'

'It is not respectful to your future bride to be housing your mistress!'

'She is not my mistress,' Zahid said, for she no longer was. They had said their intimate goodbyes on the plane.

'Then why is she here?'

'For pause,' Zahid said. 'She has just lost her brother and there are family issues.'

'What does that have to do with you?'

When Zahid did not respond the king breathed out loudly. 'You are to say to Abdul that she is here to help Layla with her English.'

'Why lie?'

'It is not a lie,' Fahid said. 'Layla is, after all, helping to teach the girls of Ishla English and, given you have many functions and dinners to attend in the coming days, I assume it will be Layla who entertains her.'

'Yes.'

'And that will help Layla's English.'

'Fine,' Zahid said, and he looked at his father and saw he was visibly worried, for Zahid had never brought any friends from England, let alone a woman, back to the palace. 'It is just for a few days. You will hardly see her…'

'Why would I not greet your guest? Why, if you have nothing to hide, is she to be tucked away?' The king would prefer to confront the enemy, the woman who could seemingly so easily sway his son from the marriage that the king had in mind for Zahid. 'Tonight we will dine, and I would like to meet your guest'

'Trinity is tired from her travels.'

'Then we will dine early. Layla has to teach in the morning anyway.'

'It is nothing to be nervous about,' Layla said after Zahid had told Trinity a little later that she would be dining with the king tonight. 'You won't be expected to say much.'

Trinity smiled at Layla's rather wry comment.

'I talk too much,' Layla said, 'I question things and it itches my father.'

'Irritates,' Trinity corrected her, and Layla frowned. 'It irritates your father.' Trinity explained but she watched as Layla's cheeks turned pink. 'Zahid just said I was to help you with your English.'

'My English is perfect,' Layla said. 'Don't correct me again.'

Whoa!

They were all terribly polite, Trinity amended, *if* you remembered your place.

Yet Layla, in her own, very odd way, was lovely. 'Try this.' She held up a lilac tunic for Trinity but as soon as she tried it on, both women realised it was far too tight. It clung instead of hung and gave her more curves than were polite in Ishla.

'Oh, no.' Layla laughed, making the same cut throat gesture that Zahid once had. 'Try this one instead.' But as she handed her a pale mint one that would hopefully fit better, Trinity suddenly stopped smiling as she stared at her refelction.

Yes, she had lost a lot of weight this past month, just not from her breasts—for once she actually filled her bra.

Layla misread the sudden silence.

'I am sorry you lost your brother. I would die if something happened to Zahid.'

'We weren't very close in the last few years,' Trinity admitted.

'It must hurt.'

'It does,' Trinity said, 'but I am very angry with him at the moment.'

It felt strange to be able to speak with Layla, who she had only just met, more easily than she could with her parents.

'There are other hurts,' Trinity said, glad when Layla did not ask her to elaborate.

Only it wasn't the other hurts that were worrying Trinity now.

As she slipped the tunic over her head, that brief second of privacy had Trinity's face screw up in a frantic, silent panic as she willed her brain to remember her last period, but with all that had happened since that day, the last month was a painful blur.

'That's better.' Layla smiled and helped Trinity arrange the tunic. 'There are some lovely gold slippers that go nicely with it, or these jewelled ones, which I think would go really well.'

'The gold are beautiful…'

'But I prefer the jewelled ones,' Layla said.

She was in Ishla, Trinity reminded herself as she accepted Layla's suggestion, but even a detail like slippers served to remind Trinity that she knew nothing about this strange land.

* * *

Zahid was rather nervous both for Trinity and himself.

He watched as she walked in and after a flurry of introductions took a seat on a low cushion. He was grateful to Layla, who quickly moved Trinity's feet so her soles were facing away from the king.

'My son tells me you live in America?'

'I have for a few years.'

'You studied?'

'Ancient art history.'

'You must take Trinity to the second palace.' The king looked at his son. 'I am sure she would be interested. Perhaps Trinity would like to start the cataloguing.'

'Trinity is not here to work.'

'It wouldn't be work.' Trinity smiled. 'I didn't know there was a second palace. I don't remember seeing it as we came in to land.'

'It is hidden,' the king said. 'I am sure Zahid will be grateful for that in the coming year.'

'Coming year?'

'Once married, Zahid will live there with his bride until it is time for him to be king.'

Trinity reached for her water. Suddenly the thought of going there, seeing first hand where Zahid would live, held little appeal, but taking a cool drink she forced her smile brighter and Zahid could only admire her composure, for he knew his father was goading her for a reaction.

'And then Zahid will rule from here,' the king continued.

'Well, you'll need a lot of baby gates.' Trinity smiled sweetly, looking around at the many treasures.

'The future princes and princesses shall not live here till they come of age.' The king's explanation only added to her confusion. 'There are many treasures at the second palace too but, you are right, it is less formal. A lot of the artefacts at the second palace have significant, personal meaning.'

There were treasures everywhere. Even the plate she was picking up sticky rice from could have held her attention for an hour or more. Gold and blue, the more she ate, the more of the pattern it revealed, and Trinity would have loved to simply clear it and turn it around.

'You should take Trinity over there tomorrow,' the king said to Layla.

'I have a class to teach tomorrow,' Layla said.

'And I would be the worst person to attempt to catalogue a palace.' Trinity smiled. 'It would never get done.' She looked at the plate again and then at the king. 'Among so many beautiful things, do you have favourites?'

Zahid caught Layla's eye, both waiting for the king to silence her, yet the king actually forgot to be cross for a moment and smiled. 'I do, though I have not looked at them in a long time. My wife collected amulets, they are stored in a mandoos, or rather, a wooden chest.'

'In the second palace?'

'No,' the king said. 'I had it moved here, not that I have looked through it in a while.'

They spoke easily through dinner but then the king turned to Layla.

'Perhaps it is time for you to retire,' the king said to his daughter, 'if you want to be alert for your students tomorrow.'

Zahid caught Trinity's eye for a brief second and

again they were back in the woods, Zahid reminding her how much freedom she had, for he could not imagine Trinity at seventeen, let alone Layla's twenty-four, being told, however politely, to go to bed.

After dinner they drank coffee that would surely keep Trinity awake till the small hours but soon the king retired, leaving Zahid to walk Trinity back to her quarters.

'You did well,' Zahid said.

'I wasn't aware it was a test,' Trinity snapped.

'I was just commenting...' Zahid halted. 'You are tired, it has been a long day. Perhaps...'

'Please, don't try to tell me when I need to go to bed again.'

'I wasn't,' Zahid said. 'I was going to suggest we take a walk on the beach. I thought that might relax you.'

'Isn't it forbidden?'

Zahid said nothing and they walked through the moonlit night, past the palace, but as Trinity turned in the direction of what she assumed was the path to the beach, Zahid's hand gripped her arm and halted her.

'It is this way.'

'Oh,' Trinity said, 'so where does that lead?' She saw his face shutter, acknowledged his lack of response to her question and, realising it was the entrance to the second palace, she let out a mirthless laugh.

'Trinity, I am sorry if my father upset you tonight but I have never lied, I have never tried to hide my truth.' His eyes were accusing. 'Unlike you.'

'I've told you why I couldn't tell you.'

'Have you?' Zahid said. 'You tell me only the pieces you want me to know and at a time of your choosing.'

'That's not true.'

'Are you sure?' Zahid asked, for she had lied about her workplace, her sexual history and he knew she had been in rehab too. 'Are you sure you are as honest with me as I am with you?'

Trinity tugged her arm away. She wanted to talk to him, to speak with Zahid, to tell the only person on this earth she could, just how deep her pain went, but for what? At a time of Zahid or the king's choosing she'd be gone. She was scared too to tell him that she was starting to worry about her absent period. She doubted either of them would go unnoticed if they bought a pregnancy test!

'What am I doing here, Zahid?' It was like waking up from a dream. This morning she had been at her brother's funeral, this afternoon she had found herself safe in his arms, and now she was walking deep in the night on a beach in Ishla. Trinity honestly didn't know what part of the day had hurt the most—losing her brother, losing her heart or losing to this strange land. 'Why did you bring me here?'

'Because, given what you told me, I could not leave you with them.'

'I can't hide here for ever.'

'I'm not asking you to hide.'

The beach was as white as powder and the sea the colour of her bridesmaid's dress but with more depth, and Trinity battled the urge to run along the beach and leave footprints or write their names in the sand and watch the ocean take them away.

'It's like paradise,' Trinity sighed, 'but with separate bedrooms.'

They faced each other and it was simply wrong not to be in the other's arms.

'What do you want?' Zahid asked.

'To wake up and not fancy you any more,' Trinity said. 'For even the sound of your voice to annoy me.'

'I hope for the same,' Zahid said. They both smiled reluctantly. 'Nag me.' He smiled again.

'Take up fishing and talk to me endlessly about it.'

They both wanted a kiss, even a touch would do, but it could not happen here.

Ever.

CHAPTER TEN

TRINITY WAS THE perfect guest.

Well, not perfect, for the palace was a little less ordered when she was around.

Zahid woke on the morning of his birthday to a folded piece of paper under his door and he was at first cross when he opened the makeshift card from Trinity, for she should not be wandering at night near his room.

Her words wished him a happy birthday but there was the notable absence of kisses under her name, just a smiley face and two words.

Better not!

And there was a stick figure, Zahid with a fishing rod.

He was no longer cross.

Once he was dressed in full military regalia, Zahid glanced to his bedside where the paper card lay.

Zahid did not keep mementos and he did not know what to do with this, for if he left it in his room, the maids would no doubt think it rubbish. If he put it in his drawer, perhaps it became more than it was.

A memento.

He pulled on long leather boots with a head that was

pounding, for even dressed as heir to the throne, even about to greet his people, Zahid's mind was full of her.

He would decide what to do with the makeshift card later, Zahid decided, folding it and putting it in his pocket for now.

As he walked briskly to his father's study he met Trinity on the way.

'Happy birthday, Captain.' She smiled and though they stood a suitable distance apart as she teased him lightly about his uniform they were back on the dance floor and the dirty dance started again, when it must not.

'Thank you for the card,' Zahid said, 'but it was unwise to come up to my room.'

'Oh, well.' Trinity shrugged.

Zahid gave her a small nod and then walked off but his stride was temporarily broken when she wolf-whistled.

Possibly he blushed.

Possibly not, Zahid quickly decided. Most likely he was cross.

'Where is Layla?' Zahid asked, as he joined his father in his study.

'She is late again,' came the king's curt response.

They did not do 'happy birthdays'.

Layla was happily late. Besotted with Trinity and when she should be meeting with her father and brother, she smiled widely when Trinity knocked and Jamila, Layla's handmaiden let Trinity into her room.

'I got a message that you wanted to speak with me,' Trinity said.

'I want you to join me when I take one of my English classes.'

'I'd be happy to.' Trinity smiled.

'Tomorrow,' Layla said, Jamila finished doing her hair and make-up.

'That would be lovely,' Trinity said, for tomorrow Zahid dined with Princess Sameena and her family and it would be nice to have her mind on other things.

'Walk with me,' Layla said, and Trinity suppressed a smile, for she could not be offended by the way Layla ordered people around, she was completely used to getting anything she asked for. 'We can talk on the way.'

Layla told her about the students she taught and how much she enjoyed the contact, even if it was online. 'It is by video call,' she explained, 'which means I can get to most of the schools. We have a lot of fun and they will be so excited to meet a real English girl.'

'I'm excited to meet them too.'

'They ask so many questions,' Layla sighed. 'Difficult ones.'

'Such as?'

'You'll see,' Layla said. 'I had better hurry. I am already terribly late and my father will be cross that I am not already there.'

He was, especially when a maid informed him that Layla was chatting with Trinity.

'Just how long is your guest here for?' Abdul checked as they went through the briefing for in a few moments they would walk onto the balcony.

'I am not sure,' Zahid said, ignoring Abdul's slight eye rise, but the king spoke on.

'Today there is much celebration in Ishla. Not only does the future king celebrate his birthday but work is to commence on the second palace.' He looked at his son. 'Soon the people will find out who their prince is to marry.'

This time it was Zahid who asked Abdul if he could excuse them.

'I would like the dinners to be postponed,' Zahid said.

'It is far too late for that. Princess Sameena and her family are joining us tomorrow,' the king said. 'And why would you want them postponed?' He dared his son with his eyes to answer him.

Zahid accepted the dare.

'I would like to spend more time with Trinity.'

'Before you make a commitment to marry a suitable bride?' the king checked, and when Zahid did not answer he continued speaking. 'Because you know that Trinity Foster would be a most unsuitable bride and one that the people would never accept.'

'My answer to your question was the correct one. I would like to spend more time with Trinity.' That was all Zahid wanted. Time for Trinity to get used to Ishla and perhaps see its beauty. Time in England as a couple to see if they could work things out.

Time even to find out that they were not suited for each other, Zahid thought, recalling their conversation last night and the card in his pocket with the stick-figure picture on. He did his best not to smile.

Yes, all he wanted was time, and he looked at his father. 'You know I have never made a decision lightly.'

'You understand the offence that would be caused if these dinners were postponed.'

Zahid swallowed, for he did not want to make problems for his country. 'I do.'

'And you know that I want a wedding, so if I postpone these dinners then I shall invite the Fayeds for dinner next Sunday?'

'Father.' Zahid was not interrupting the king for his own benefit. Layla had just walked in unseen by the king and her eyes widened in horror as she heard what was being discussed. 'Hassain too,' the king continued. 'I would like to speak first hand with the man who will soon marry my daughter.'

'No!' Layla screamed, and the king turned as she ran from the room.

'Layla,' Zahid roared as he went to chase his sister, but she had flown straight into a shocked Trinity's arms.

'What's happening?'

'Layla is overreacting,' Zahid said. 'Layla, what you heard was the end of a very difficult conversation...' But Layla would not be consoled. 'You need to calm down so we can go out to the balcony, and then I will explain properly.'

'I'm not going out there,' Layla sobbed.

Abdul approached and told them that the king was making his way to the balcony and it was time for Zahid and Layla to join him.

'No!' Layla wept. 'You can't make me.'

'Layla.' Zahid was stern, for he was used to dealing with his sister's dramas and all too often it fell to him to calm her down, but the reproach in his voice made Trinity shiver. 'First you will do what is right *then* we will talk.'

He ignored Trinity's raised brows and the purse of her lips as Layla joined her brother, but he could not ignore the disquiet of standing, smiling at his people, as his sister stood, not scowling for the camera, as Trinity once had, but meek and fearful for her future, by his side.

'You said I did not have to worry for a while...' Layla said once they were back inside, but her voice trailed off as her father entered the room.

The world, Zahid thought wearily, was far less complicated when it was faced without emotion.

'I need an answer from you, Zahid,' the king warned.

'And I told you I do not make decisions lightly.'

It was an impossibly long day. A formal lunch and then he inspected the army and later a semi-formal dinner that Trinity did attend, but she sat next to a red-eyed Layla. For once it was easy for Trinity to sit quietly, for she had a horrible taste in her mouth. A *familiar,* horrible taste in her mouth, and she took a sip of the fragrant tea at the end of the meal. It tasted like neat perfume.

When would her period come?

After dinner, when Trinity had excused herself to go to her room, Zahid asked to speak with Layla. It was not an easy conversation to have.

'I asked Father if he could postpone the dinners so that I could spend more time with Trinity.'

'You love her?' Layla frowned, for she could not imagine her stern older brother falling in love, as his focus had always been his country.

'You too!' Zahid rolled his eyes. 'I am supposed to give an immediate answer when I am trying to make up my mind what is for the best, not just by my people but by Trinity, by you too...'

'Of course you love her,' Layla challenged, 'or you would not have brought her here and be asking to postpone dinners.'

'Away from here, people date, they get to know each

other, they see if their differences will work better together, or if they should be apart…'

'You think I feel sorry for you?' Layla sneered. 'Well, I don't. You are going to be king, of course you must marry a suitable bride, but at least you have known love in your lifetime, at least you got to be free for a while before you started your family.' Layla started to cry. 'So don't ask me to understand how difficult things are for you when the man I will marry and spend all my life with is Hassain.'

She ran crying to her room and Zahid walked in the grounds, but it did not relax him because the day replayed over in his head.

He turned and looked as a noise disturbed him. He saw shutters open but he looked away when he realised it was Trinity's suite.

Perhaps she couldn't sleep either, Zahid thought; perhaps the air in her room was as stifling as it was out here, for there was no escape from his thoughts.

His eyes moved back to her window and he could only sigh as he watched her peek out and then turn.

One foot, followed by the other.

Zahid walked over quietly as Trinity shimmied down the short drop from her window.

'Are you averse to using doors?'

When she heard Zahid, Trinity jumped.

'I wanted to go for a walk.'

'So why use the window?'

'I didn't know if I could.'

'It is not a prison.'

'You told me this morning that I should not be wandering the palace at night.'

'I meant you should not be near my room.'

'Oh, please…' Trinity started, then halted, for last night the temptation had been great to creep in. Not that she would tell him that. 'There are so many rules, I'm never sure if I'm breaking one or not.'

'Just be yourself.'

'You're not, though,' Trinity pointed out. 'I barely recognised you when you told Layla off this morning.'

'Layla was upset. It was the only way to calm her down.'

'Perhaps, but I don't really know you at all, Zahid.' He didn't respond. 'Does anyone?'

'What do you want to know?'

'You. What you think about things, how you feel, or are you going to tell me again that feelings are beneath you?'

'I have not been fair to you,' Zahid said, and stopped walking. 'Perhaps it was easier to blame your past and your ways on the fact that we cannot have a future but it is more complicated than that.'

'It is,' Trinity said, 'because even if I didn't have a past I'm not sure I'd want…' She gave a shrug and Zahid waited but Trinity didn't say any more. Instead, it was Zahid who spoke on and told her a little of his family's history.

'My father was to choose Raina as his bride, a princess from a neighbouring land who is now Queen. The marriage would have profited our people, ensured swift progress. Instead, progress has been painfully slow.'

'Why didn't he choose her?'

'My father walked into the room and saw my mother. She had been crying because she did not want a loveless marriage and to be chosen by the future king, but then their eyes met and she changed her mind. My father says she smiled at him and in that moment his choice was made.'

'Did it cause problems?'

'Many,' Zahid said. 'It caused division and even today relations are strained. That can be rectified now, though, if I choose Raina's daughter, Sameena.'

'Oh, so you do lie, Zahid!' Trinity said. 'You told me that you hadn't chosen.'

'I haven't,' Zahid said. 'I would prefer not to go with the elders' choice because one of the other potential brides comes from a country with a very organised army—'

'I don't want to hear,' Trinity said, for she did not want to hear about any future wife, but she did want to know about the marriage of his parents and all the trouble that it had caused. 'Were your parents happy?'

'Yes, they were happy, while their people bore the cost of a decision made in a rash moment.' Zahid shrugged. 'And then, when my mother died, their king fell apart. That is what love does to a man. When I saw how my father crumbled on my mother's death I decided I wanted no part in a marriage that made one so weak. My father could barely move from his bed. What if there had been trouble with neighbouring countries, what if there had been an emergency and decisions had been needed to be made? He was incapable.'

'I doubt that could ever happen to you.'

'I never thought it would happen to my father, yet it did,' Zahid said. 'I want no part in a love that renders you incapable.'

It was a very backhanded way of revealing his feelings but Trinity just shrugged and started walking, thinking over his words. They actually made a lot of sense to her.

'So you want your own Dianne?'

'Excuse me?'

'Your own Dianne, standing smiling and plastic by your side and agreeing, without question, to whatever you decide.'

'Do not compare me...' He caught her arm and swung her round. It was rather a difficult conversation because to reveal the absolute insult that was meant that he had to criticise Trinity's parents, but another Dianne was the very last thing he wanted from his wife. 'I do not want that from a wife.'

'You told me so yourself. You want a wife who will obey and serve without question,' Trinity challenged. 'That's what my mother does, she stands idly by.'

'Your father has made many mistakes.'

'Oh, and you're exempt from making them?' Trinity checked. 'I'm sure my father would insist he was only doing the best for his family and constituents, that my mother doesn't understand what it takes to do the job he does. I'm quite sure if he loved her he wouldn't have had those affairs and I'm quite sure he blames her for what happened to me. It was her side of the family after all.'

Zahid stood there a touch breathless, furious at her challenge, reluctantly acknowledging her words.

'I don't want my past pardoned in some grandiose gesture,' Trinity said, 'only to be thrown back at me, and, no, I would never stand with a plastic smile, meekly accepting that you know best.' She gave him a bright smile. 'See, we're completely incompatible, but it works both ways, Zahid. I don't want your idea of a marriage. I want a love that burns and sometimes hurts,

one that challenges me at every turn. I want a father for
my children who does not hold onto his emotions, whatever the cost.' The absence of her period had Trinity for
once thinking ahead and what she saw was not pretty. 'I
don't want a family tucked away in the second palace,
with their father an occasional guest, till they come of
age and can move to the main one…'

'You don't understand.'

'I don't, Zahid.' She smiled a plastic smile that infuriated him. 'But that's okay—clearly, I don't have to. I
just have to agree to your ways.'

'I would always do the right thing by my family but
there are rules in place and those rules mean I must do
the right things by my people.'

'Yes, Zahid.'

'And I would never cheat on my wife.'

'Yes, Zahid.'

'Stop agreeing with me.'

'Oh, sorry, I thought that was what you wanted.'
Then she smiled a very slow smile and his face was
rigid as she made him examine a truth. 'Why did we
have to sever contact?'

'You know why.'

'Are you worried that you couldn't keep your hands
off me, even with a wife by your side?'

'No!'

'Oh, just those pesky inappropriate thoughts, then.'
Trinity winked. 'Well, that's okay, then,' she said, and
ran off towards the palace.

Never, not once, had anyone challenged him so; never
once had he questioned his own integrity so much;
never had he wanted to chase someone so much, to

catch her and turn her round, to press her to the jew-elled palace wall and demand she retract her words.

And Zahid did just that. In a moment he had caught up with her and, yes, he pushed her to the wall but in the way that lovers did and he demanded then that she take back what she'd said.

That she retract.

'Retract what?' Trinity asked.

The truth.

She looked deep into his eyes, could feel his erection pressed into her, and she just stared and challenged him to kiss her, to break the strange rules of this beautiful land. And then she did the unforgivable. She smiled, the plastic smile of her mother, and Zahid pulled back, staring into the tempting pool of her mouth and trying to shift decades of thinking as his mouth moved towards her, but Trinity turned her head.

'I'm going to bed, Zahid, presumably alone.'

'Stay.'

'No!' Trinity said. 'I'm too good for a shag against the palace wall.'

'I would not do that to you.'

'You want to, though.' Her hand reached down and what met her hand did not deny the truth.

But though she returned alone to her room, Trinity did not go to bed.

She couldn't be pregnant, Trinity thought as she lifted her leg on the bed and pushed her fingers inside, feeling for the strings that would tell her the IUD was in place, but was unable to find them. She felt behind her cervix hoping to find them nestling there but, no, they were nowhere to be found.

Trinity undressed and examined her body. Apart

from slightly bigger breasts, there were no changes she could see. She didn't feel sick, she felt exactly as she always had. In fact, better than she always had, for the most part. Here in Ishla she was relaxed.

Not now, though.

She remembered Zahid's slitting gesture to the throat and how she had laughed at the time.

She wasn't laughing now.

CHAPTER ELEVEN

LAYLA WAS NOT quite so gushing with Trinity the next morning.

'Is everything okay?' Trinity checked, as they walked to her study where Layla would take her class.

'If Zahid does not choose his bride, the next bride will be me.'

'That is not what you want?'

Layla's black eyes met Trinity's. 'It would seem that it has nothing to do with what I want.'

'Layla.' Trinity's hand went to her shoulder, but Layla shrugged it off.

'Please, don't,' Layla said. 'I am cross with you even though deep down I know it is not your fault. I will not stay cross for long.'

They were all so honest, Trinity thought, but in the nicest of ways, because where else could you deny a touch because of the mood you were in?

Here they did not pretend.

'Do you want to do the class tomorrow?' Trinity offered.

'No,' Layla said. 'I have promised the girls that you will meet them today, they would be so disappointed if that did not happen. I too have told them that you are here in the palace to help me with my English but you are not to correct me in front of them. It is easier to say that than explain you are here to sabotage my life.' She saw Trinity startle. 'Sorry, was "sabotage" the wrong word?'

'I'm not allowed to correct you,' Trinity pointed out, and Layla narrowed her eyes.

'You can with my permission.'

Trinity thought for a moment. 'Actually sabotage is the perfect word. I'm so sorry, Layla.'

'See! I was right,' Layla said, but then she smiled. 'I know it was unintentional, though,' she said, and gave Trinity a hug.

They were friends again.

English with Princess Layla was far more fun than Trinity remembered her English lessons to be!

Really, it was more an hour of conversation, for Layla did not know how to read or write in English.

Layla did not know how to drive either, Trinity found out as the questions poured in from Layla's students and one of them asked how you would get to school in England if you did not have a driver like Princess Layla.

'You would walk, or get a bus or train,' Trinity said.

'I would take my driver,' Layla said, and they all laughed at the thought of their princess walking, or getting a bus or train, and so too did Layla.

It was fun.

Till the topic turned to weddings.

'Does the bride wear gold in England?' a little girl asked.

'She wears white,' Trinity said, wondering if it might be a touch difficult to explain just how diverse weddings could be. 'Well, traditionally she wears white.'

'We are going to say goodbye to Trinity now,' Layla broke in swiftly, for she knew they would have many questions about weddings and it was something neither woman would, today, choose to discuss.

They all said goodbye and thanked her but still the questions came for Layla.

'My mother says that our prince is going to marry soon,' the same little girl said. 'Princess Layla, will they live at the second palace?'

'That is private,' Layla warned, which went against everything Layla's classes were about, it was why the students loved her so.

'You said, so long as we asked politely and in English, that you would answer our questions.'

Layla closed her eyes for a brief moment. 'Yes,' Layla said. 'Our tradition says that the future king will live at the second palace with his bride until it is time for him to rule.' She looked at Trinity, who had moved away from the camera and had tears streaming down her face.

It was cruel to hear about Zahid's future life and Layla nodded when Trinity stood. 'I'm going to go for a walk.'

'Of course.' Layla nodded. 'Wait one moment,' she said to her students, 'and I will be back.' She joined Trinity at the door. 'I am so sorry.'

'It's not your fault. Of course they have questions.'

'You did not need to hear them, though.'

Trinity walked through the palace grounds, overwhelmed with the impossibility of it all, because even a chance of future happiness for Zahid and herself would come at an appalling price.

As she wandered down towards the beach she saw

the entrance to the second palace that Zahid had steered her away from.

The garden was cool and shaded but as she walked further she saw it had its own private beach.

She thought there would be guards, or workers, but there seemed to be no one and when she turned a handle on a huge carved door, as easily as that she was in.

It was agony.

A huge wooden staircase led upwards but that was not what first caught her eye. Neither were the portraits on the wall, but a glass cabinet that contained framed photos.

This was a home.

Layla was the image of Annan, who'd had smiling black eyes and the same long hair. Even Fahid looked happy but what had Trinity's eyes fill with tears was a younger Zahid.

He had even been a serious baby.

Only then, as she looked through the years, did she realise just how lucky she was to receive that smile so easily, for it would seem he shared it with few.

To torture herself she took the stairs upwards and soon found the wing that contained the master suite.

It had to be it, Trinity decided looking at the opulent bed piled with cushions, the bed where Zahid would sleep with his bride. Yes, it had to be it, Trinity thought as she opened huge shutters and stared out at the ocean, for it was a view fit for a king.

'What are you doing here?' Trinity did not jump at the sound of his voice, she was trying too hard not to turn round and to wipe her eyes without him seeing.

'Layla's taking her class. I just wanted to take a walk.' Trinity chose not to tell Zahid that they had been discussing his wedding. 'I wanted to think. I'm sorry I wandered. I never thought it would be open.'

'You don't need keys here.'

He came over and stood by her side. 'You were crying?'

Trinity nodded.

'About your brother?'

Trinity gave a soft shrug then shook her head.

'No.' She looked out at the ocean again and thought of her brother, for without him she would not be standing here. 'You know, if it weren't for his death, we would never have spoken again.'

'That is not the case,' Zahid admitted. 'I had thought about you a lot in the last month. I told you Donald asked for a loan for his honeymoon. The first time was on the night of his wedding. I refused him and offered to pay for rehab instead. The second time…' Zahid hesitated and then continued. 'It was me who called him. I did not get around to asking for your number, though. He was in a bad way and he said again that he needed a loan. If anyone should have guilt for lending money…'

Trinity turned her head. 'No.'

'I had rung every library in Los Angeles,' Zahid said, and watched as her shoulders moved in a soft laugh. 'One by one I ticked them off and in the end I rang your mother. That is how I found out that he had died.'

'Why were you trying to call me?'

'I think we both know why,' Zahid said, 'even if it must remain unsaid.'

Must it?

'Trinity, since our first kiss you have not left my mind.'

'Oh, please.' There was still anger there. 'You never

gave me a thought. If Donald hadn't got married we'd never have seen each other again. You left me that night and you never looked back.' Tears were streaming down her cheeks but they were silent ones. 'You never came back.'

'I did come back,' Zahid said. 'In the new year, after your birthday. I returned, not because I wanted to spend time with your family but because I wanted to see you, but I was told that you had gone into rehab.'

'Oh, is that what they told you?' Trinity gave a mirthless laugh. 'I always wondered how they managed to explain away six months of my life.'

'Where were you?'

She couldn't discuss it, it hurt too much, but Zahid would not let it rest. 'Why would Donald and your family say you were in rehab…?' His voice trailed off as the truth started to dawn on him.

'Tell me.'

'I can't,' Trinity said.

'You can,' Zahid said. 'When will you learn that you can be honest with me?'

She had never been honest with anyone, though, for she had never been allowed to be.

'There is an Arabic proverb,' Zahid said, '*what is hidden is more than what has been revealed so far.*'

She pondered the words for a moment and they were true, so true.

The loss of her baby was, for Trinity *more* than the event that had led to her conception. She had not had to work to separate the two, for her love for her baby had brought out a fierce protectiveness in her.

'I got pregnant…' Trinity said, and then quickly added, 'Please, don't say sorry. I wanted her so much.'

Zahid said nothing, just let her continue.

'My parents wanted me to have an abortion, I just couldn't. I knew right from the start that it wasn't the baby's fault. I went away to have my baby but I lost her at six months...'

For the first time ever he felt the sting of tears in his eyes. Even on his mother's death he had been aware he must hold things together, that he must not, even once, cry, but hearing the love in her voice, despite the pain, had the emotions Zahid despised so much coursing through him.

'Does she have a name?'

Trinity nodded. 'Amara.'

Eternal.

He did what he must not do in Ishla, he sat on the bed and pulled her into him and held her as she wept and did his best to comfort her, but Trinity was still drowning in fear, not for the baby she had lost but the one she might hold inside her now.

'You can talk to me.'

'How?' Trinity asked. 'When tonight you are dining with your future wife?'

'I will sort something out. I will buy us some time.'

'How?'

'Do you even want to be here?'

She was scared to say yes, scared to admit her truth, scared too, given how terrible it had been for her, that if she did admit her truth, if somehow she could stay, then he would forbid her from seeing her family.

'Trinity?' Zahid demanded, for he would move a mountain if he had to, but he had to know first if she wanted it moved. 'Do you want to be here?'

She stared at a man she trusted more than she had

ever trusted another person, but she could not bring herself to tell him what terrified her now.

She looked into Zahid's eyes.

Her instinct was to tell him, but Trinity had been raised to deny her instincts and she did not know how to trust.

'I want to be *here*,' Trinity said, and her meaning was clear for a second later she met his mouth, her drug of choice, and it was Zahid's too and this time he could not deny her.

Their mouths were on each other's, he could taste her tears and her face was flushed from crying and her lips swollen, and it wasn't even a choice for Zahid as to whether or not he kiss her, he gave in to need.

Desperate urgent kisses that had them tearing at each other's clothes till they were naked and they melted into the other as their skins met again and he pressed her down onto the bed. It was dizzying, it had to be, for thought would have told them it was so very forbidden, a single thought would have warned that they could be caught at any moment, that this was wrong, very wrong. Zahid had always held onto emotion but not for a second did he hold on now.

'Tell me what you want.'

'You!' Trinity replied. It was the only answer she knew. 'This,' she said, half sitting against the cushions as he knelt between her legs. His head lowered and Zahid's mouth, hungry and rough, took her newly sensitive breasts deep, and she loved it that with Zahid pain was a new pleasure.

Then, when her breasts were not enough, when her mouth could not quench days of denial, of fighting not to react to her taunts, ended as he knelt back on his knees and pushed her legs further apart. She briefly looked down as he positioned her and then seared inside. Trinity's head went back and she was drunk on the power of him unleashed and raw as his hands moved her hips to his will.

This was Zahid's will, this was his want and even before Trinity came his decision was made and he started to spill into her.

Trinity could even feel the contractions in her womb as Zahid gave her the most intimate part of himself.

'There,' he said, and she understood his word.

'There,' he said again, as he pulsed in the final precious drops, and she forced herself forward and looked down again and watched the milky white on his length as he slowly pulled out and then drove in to her again.

It was done now.

After, they lay on the marital bed catching their breath, her hair in his mouth, her cheek hot and warm by his, and Zahid closed his eyes, but not in regret.

Tonight he dined with Princess Sameena and her family, next weekend it would be Sheikha Kumu, yet the woman he loved lay in the marital bed with him now.

It was too late to cancel the dinners, it would be considered the height of rudeness as the invitations had already been sent out.

He would get through tonight, Zahid decided but first he would speak with his father.

Foolish or not, sensible or otherwise, Zahid had chosen his bride.

His head had no say in the matter.

'I will sort this.'

Her body was so flushed she shivered as she was suddenly drenched in icy fear.

'Shouldn't I be away from here before you say any-thing?' Trinity was starting to panic.

'I don't want you away from me,' Zahid said. 'It's time to start trusting me, Trinity.'

'Zahid…'

'I will handle this,' Zahid said. 'I am going to make a formal request to speak with the king.'

CHAPTER TWELVE

THE KING LOOKED down from his window and saw Trinity walk out from the entrance to the second palace.

Of course she would be interested in the second palace and want to see it, the king consoled himself. After all, she had a degree in ancient art history and the second palace was rich with treasures.

There was little consolation to be had a few moments later when he watched as his rarely dishevelled son walked out.

She must leave, the king decided.

And she would be leaving tonight.

He wanted Zahid back, the man who thought only of his country, a man, the king privately admitted, who must be spared the pain that he himself had endured, for a heart was only so big.

'Is everything all right, Your Highness?' Abdul enquired an hour or so later, when he walked in on the king, who was still deep in thought.

'It will be,' the king answered. 'What are you here for?'

'Prince Zahid has tendered a formal request to meet with you.'

Fahid's stomach churned for the words they would exchange in a formal meeting must be documented.

'I do not have time. We are to greet guests soon.'

'It is a formal request.'

'Which means I must respond by noon the next day,' the king countered, for he, better than anyone, knew the laws of his land.

'You are to arrange for Ms Foster to come and speak with me now.'

'Of course,' Abdul said obligingly. 'Though, given we are soon to receive Princess Sameena and her family, would tomorrow perhaps be a more convenient time to speak with a guest?'

No, the king thought, for this must be dealt with now and once and for all.

And the king knew how.

Zahid needed to find out just how unsuitable Trinity would be as his wife, he needed to see for himself the trouble she would cause—and tonight he would.

He turned to Abdul. 'Summon her now.'

The giddy high from making love had faded the moment Zahid had told her he would be speaking with the king.

Trinity bathed and as she came out of the bathroom her phone buzzed and Trinity let out a tense breath before answering.

'Hi, Mum,' Trinity answered. 'How are you?'

There was a long stretch of silence and it took a while for it to dawn on Trinity that her mother was crying.

'Your father wants to spread the ashes tomorrow. He wants it done but I wanted you here.'

'Who's going to be there?'

'Just family.'

'I can't, then.'

'Trinity, please…' her mother said, but without anger this time. 'I don't want to lose you.'

She might, though.

Zahid would have no part in the strange charades her family played. Zahid had already told her his thoughts on her family and that he was severing ties with them.

She loved them, though.

'You're not going to lose me but I'm not going to attend any more family functions if Clive is there.'

'Trinity—'

'I mean it.'

Finally, she did.

It was a teary Trinity that answered when Layla knocked at her door.

'I did not know that the children would upset you.'

'It was just children asking questions.' Trinity attempted a smile as she let her in.

'I know, they ask so many. All the difficult ones, of course. I did promise them that so long as they asked in English and it was a polite question, they could ask me anything.'

'Polite?' Trinity checked.

'Well, you know girls can ask difficult things and so I tell them when their question is not polite…' Layla gave an uncomfortable shrug at Trinity's questioning frown and elaborated a touch further. 'Today they ask about marriage but some of the older students ask about wedding nights and I don't think they are suitable questions.' Layla went a little bit pink. 'Or rather I don't know how to answer them.'

'I guess it could be awkward.'

'It is.' Layla admitted.

'It's good they feel they can ask questions, though.'
It was Trinity's cheeks who were a bit pink now as
she probed Layla for information, not that Layla could
know the reason for Trinity's interest. 'I mean, where
would they go here to find out about birth control and
the like?' She saw Layla frown.

'Birth control?'

'If you don't want to get pregnant.'

Layla blinked. 'I thought I was the only woman who
felt like that. I don't want to have Hassain's baby.'

'I meant,' Trinity swallowed as she realised the can of
worms she was opening but Trinity desperately needed
to guage how these issues where handled in Ishla and
so she was more specific. 'What would a young woman
do if she wanted to have sex but wasn't married.'

'It would never happen out of wedlock.' Layla's cheeks
were on fire.

'You mean there are no unplanned babies born in
Ishla?'

'Of course not,' Layla said, and Trinity just stood
there as Layla continued. 'It must not happen, it cannot
happen.' To Layla it was as simple as that.

But despite Layla's absolute assurance that it could
never happen, it very possibly had and to the future
king's potential wife.

Of course there must be unplanned pregnancies in
Ishla, she knew that Layla was being naïve.

So what happened when a pregnancy occurred that
wasn't planned?

Trinity did feel sick then but it was in fear for her
unborn child.

Perhaps they'd insist on an abortion, just as her

mother had. Only when Trinity had begged to keep her baby had she been sent away.

Zahid would do the right thing, of course, but would that be by his country or by her?

'Trinity?' Layla dragged her mind back to the conversation, her black eyes alight with curiosity. 'What is this birth control?'

Trinity was saved from answering when there was a knock at the door. It was Jamila who spoke for a moment to Layla.

'My father has requested to speak with you,' Layla told Trinity.

'It's okay,' Layla said, when Jamila had left and she saw Trinity's pale face. 'He is fierce, yes, but he is fair too, and you have done no wrong.'

But by Ishla's standards Trinity had.

CHAPTER THIRTEEN

TRINITY STEPPED INTO the study and looked to the side as she curtsied, hoping that Zahid would be here, for she did not know how to face the king alone.

'How are things?' the king asked. 'I trust you are being well looked after.'

'I've been looked after beautifully.'

'How are your family?'

'I've just spoken to my mother.'

'How is she?'

'She's a bit upset. My father wants to spread my brother's ashes.' They chatted a little about that and Trinity started to relax.

'It is a difficult time for them.'

'It is.'

'Did you enjoy your time at the second palace this afternoon?' The king saw that he had sideswiped Trinity but he would not hesitate to tackle difficult subjects when the future of his monarchy was at stake. 'Are you going to lie and say you enjoyed looking at the antiques and jewels?'

'No.'

'Is your intention to trap my son?'

Trinity had stood blushing and unable to look at the king but now her eyes did meet his. 'Trap him?'

'It is a commoners trick and you,' the king said, 'are a commoner with a past.'

'I'm not going to stand here and be insulted.'

'Where is the insult? You are a commoner, yes?'

'Yes.'

'And one with a past.'

'The insult was that I might trick your son.'

'I apologise, then,' the king answered. 'I forget that you have ways to defy nature. I would have hoped you would not bring them here but perhaps it is better that you did, for an unplanned pregnancy would bring more shame than I can even dare to imagine. More than a drug scandal.' The king gave a tight smile. 'I apologise, that was not you but your brother.'

'I would prefer, if we must discuss this, for Zahid to be here.'

'When I discuss this with my son, I will be far less polite than I am being now. I am furious with him and for the first time ever I am disappointed in him. A few weeks ago we were discussing bridges, and hospitals and the education of our people. Now he speaks only of wanting time to sort out your differences, time to see if you two might work. That is not how things work here in Ishla.' He looked at Trinity. 'We are a kind and fair country,' the king said. 'Until someone interferes in our ways.'

'You want me to leave?'

'You were always leaving, Trinity.' The king was scathing. 'Now though, it is not a question of if you leave, it is *how* you leave that matters...'

'I don't understand.'

'Then think about it,' the king said. 'I shall arrange for a plane to take you home—is that England or America?'

'I want to speak with Zahid.'

'Of course you can speak with him, you will be joining us tonight for dinner.'

'Please, no,' Trinity begged.

'Oh, yes,' the king said. 'You can meet Princess Sameena, you can face your shame and then perhaps you will understand my rage.'

'I'll go.'

'Yes, you will, straight after dinner. And, Trinity, remember what I said. If you do care for my son, please think about what I said. It is *how* you leave that matters.

'One moment.' He paused as there was an angry knock at the door and Zahid barged in uninvited.

'Why did you summon Trinity without me?' he demanded.

'I wanted to see that she was being properly taken care of,' the king answered calmly. 'And to find out her how family was.'

'Don't!' Zahid stood livid before his father, for he could see the paleness of Trinity's cheeks and knew she was upset. 'You do not have time to respond to a formal request for me to speak with you, yet you summon Trinity in here—'

'She was telling me that she must return to England.'

'No.' Zahid's fists were balled.

'After dinner tonight, she is leaving.'

'Oh, no.' Zahid would not put Trinity through that. He was already dreading facing Princess Sameena and he would not foist the same awkwardness on Trinity.

'If there is an issue, you discuss it with me. Trinity is not leaving tonight—'

'I am.' It was the first time she had spoken since Zahid had stormed in. The king had made it crystal clear the shame it would bring if she were to fall pregnant.

Trinity knew that she already was and she had to get away.

'I was just speaking with your father. My mother called and she's upset...' Trinity hesitated, for she knew Zahid would not let her leave if there was even a chance she might see Clive, so she chose not to tell him about the ashes. 'I think she needs me at home.'

'It isn't about what she needs.' Zahid shook his head. 'First we speak—'

'There is not time to discuss this further now.' The king stood. 'Our guests are due to arrive. I am sure Trinity will want to get ready.'

As she put on her make-up Trinity finally understood the king's wise words. Zahid loved her and he would not simply let her go, but if she stayed...

Her only thought now was for her baby. She had no idea of the rules of this land. Even Zahid had spoken of choosing a bride on the strength of an army.

The king was right. If she wanted to leave then tonight Zahid had to see for himself what an unsuitable bride she would be.

'Perhaps you wear too much...' Layla hesitated, reminding herself that Trinity was a guest but her lips worried her as Trinity put on some dark red lipstick and then added more mascara.

Trinity was wearing the lilac tunic that had been too

tight even on her first day in Ishla. Her breasts seemed bigger than they had then, though Layla assumed that must be from her bra, because she caught a glimpse of it when Trinity bent forward for all the buttons were not done up.

'You missed…' Layla pointed to her own buttons as they went to head down to dinner.

Trinity ignored her.

Zahid's jaw tightened a little when he saw Trinity, not because of the glimpse of cleavage and not even because of her dark red lips. It was the dangerous glint in her eyes that had him on high alert as Trinity took her seat next to Layla.

The king made the introductions. 'This is Miss Trinity Foster, she is here to help Layla with her English. I asked her to join us so that we can say farewell to her, as she is flying back to England late tonight.'

Sameena bowed her head in greeting and Trinity did the same, and the introductions continued.

Zahid sat silent.

Oh, there would be words at the formal meeting for putting Trinity through this.

Many, many words.

He looked at Sameena and saw her downcast eyes and Zahid's shame turned to slight curiosity, for having a sister like Layla and after the time he'd spent with Trinity, he recognised swollen eyelids when he saw them.

Perhaps Sameena did not want to be here either.

The conversation was as sticky as the dates for everyone, given that Queen Raina of Bishram was the 'suitable' bride that Fahid had rejected all those years ago.

Only Layla was oblivious to the tension.

'We were talking in my class about transport today,' Layla said, filling in a gaping hole in the conversation as dessert was served. 'Can I learn to drive, Father?'

'Why would you want to drive when you can be driven?'

'I would like to drive. Do you drive, Sameena?'

'I do.'

'Do you work?'

'Layla,' the king warned, 'it is Zahid and Sameena's time to speak with each other.'

'We must go soon,' Queen Raina said.

'Perhaps Sameena and I could walk in the gardens before you leave,' Zahid offered, and Trinity knocked over her drink.

Better that than throw it in his face, Trinity thought as a maid mopped it up.

'Layla might like to join you.' The king smiled.

'Of course,' Zahid responded, and the Queen and King of Bishram nodded their consent.

'It was a lovely dinner,' Sameena said, as Layla walked behind them.

'It was,' Zahid said. 'Were you looking forward to it?'

There was a slight hesitation before she said yes.

'Is there anything you would like to say?' Zahid carefully offered, and Sameena glanced over her shoulder at Layla.

'She is listening to her music,' Zahid said. 'She has her headphones in.'

Sameena laughed and then she stopped laughing, for it was almost an impossible conversation to have. 'My mother is talking of abdicating,' Sameena said. 'Of course, that is just between us.'

'Of course.'

'Soon I will be Queen of Bishram.'

'What is your hope for your country?'

'I have many,' Sameena said. 'Naturally, I hope that relationships between our countries will improve, whatever choice you make.' Zahid looked at her and saw tears in Sameena's eyes.

'Be honest,' Zahid said, 'because whatever you say, I look forward to better relations between our countries.'

'Even if there is anger between them for a while?' Sameena checked, for her parents would be furious with Ishla if she was not the prince's choice.

'We will work well together,' Zahid said, as they carefully forged an alliance but one that did not involve a marriage.

There was a small chink of hope in his heart as he headed back, and Trinity did not like the edge of a smile on his lips or the look that passed between Sameena and Zahid as the families said their goodbyes. It served only to confuse her.

'I need to get my things ready,' Trinity said. 'My flight is soon.'

'You are not boarding the plane tonight,' Zahid said. 'You are not leaving till I have spoken with my father.' He strode over to the king. 'I would like to speak with you now,' Zahid said to his father.

'Not yet,' Fahid said. 'I would like more coffee.'

They returned to the table and the king smiled like the cat that had got the cream. 'That went very well.'

'Really?' Zahid checked. 'I have never endured a more uncomfortable dinner.'

The king looked at Trinity. 'You have been a wonderful guest. Forgive me for not serving champagne tonight, it would have been offensive to our guests. Of course, we are more relaxed here, and it is right that we wish you farewell with a toast.'

He gestured the waiter and champagne was poured. Trinity took the smallest sip of bubbles, for she did not want them to guess the reason she could not join in with the toast properly.

Zahid didn't even raise his glass of sparkling water, for she was not leaving tonight.

Trinity caught the king's eye and as the bubbles went down she topped up her glass and it was time to ensure that she and her baby left safely tonight.

'Is Queen Raina the one you rejected in favour of your wife?'

'Trinity…' Layla breathed, for there were things that must not be openly discussed.

'I get a bit confused,' Trinity explained.

'You are correct.' The king nodded.

'You must miss your wife,' Trinity said.

'Very much.'

They chatted further and after the king said what a wonderful, dignified woman Annan had been, the tone of the conversation moved down.

'You must get lonely,' Trinity said, and she felt the squeeze of Zahid's angry fingers on her thigh as he attempted to warn her quietly just how inappropriate that line of conversation was.

He looked at his plate and did not see the king give Trinity a small smile and he did not see the tears that flashed in Trinity's eyes. 'You're a good-looking man, Fahid. Surely…' she gave a shrill laugh '…you think about dating.'

'Perhaps I have had my time.'

'Oh, come on,' Trinity said. 'You could have your pick, a handsome man like you…'

She was flirting with his father, she was being inappropriate, and Zahid's rage simmered as again she knocked over her glass and then refilled it.

'How would a king date?' Fahid enquired politely.

'I have no idea,' Trinity admitted. 'Where I work, at the beach bar, we have a night for the over-forties…'

'Trinity,' Zahid warned.

'What?' Trinity turned to Zahid. 'I'm just being friendly.'

'I want to speak to you alone.'

He took her wrist, pulled her away, marched her through the palace and to her room.

She could spill her drink, she could be wild, but he had never thought he'd have to tell Trinity that she could not flirt at the king's table.

He turned her to face him and his eyes were black, not with anger but with disappointment, with pain.

'What on earth was that?'

'I was just having fun.' She gave him a look. 'Oh, sorry, that's not allowed here, is it?'

'Of course it is, but tonight—'

'Oh, am I misbehaving?'

'You know that you are.'

'So I'm just supposed to sit quietly while you go for a walk with your future bride, while you make simpering eyes when you say goodbye to her—'

'Do not even suggest that I flirted with Princess Sameena,' Zahid said. 'Tonight I have done everything I know how to secure us some time together, I have spoken with Sameena, I have asked for a formal meeting with my father and then you sit there, pissed, and you flirt with my father, the king.'

'I had two glasses,' Trinity lied, for she'd had none.

'Is that all it takes for you to act like a tart?' Zahid demanded. 'I don't get you, Trinity.'

'I never asked you to,' Trinity said. 'Am I not being respectful enough for you?'

'No,' Zahid said. 'You are not being respectful to yourself.'

'Don't worry, in an hour or so I won't be your problem any more.'

'Go to bed,' Zahid said.

'What?'

'You heard. Go to bed and I will speak with you tomorrow.'

Even at her supposed worst, he would not let her leave, Trinity realised.

Zahid, her eyes begged, let me go, for she was terrified what would happen if the king found out she was with child, not just for herself but for the shame it would heap on Zahid.

'Bed,' Zahid said.

'My flight—'

'Will be cancelled.'

'I want to go home.'

'You are not leaving now. It will all be sorted tomorrow,' Zahid continued, 'once and for all.'

'What if I don't want it to be sorted?' The grip on her arm loosened. 'What if I don't want to be your chosen bride.'

'I understand that you—'

'You *don't* understand,' Trinity choked, because for

the first time in her life it was almost impossible to lie. 'Because you've never asked.'

'I thought we felt the same.'

'No,' Trinity said. 'We don't. I don't want to be your bride.'

'You're sure?'

'Very sure.'

Zahid gave a curt nod and she watched as the beautiful man she knew literally disappeared before her eyes, for he was back to yawn-yawn dignified in that second.

'I will have a maid come and sort out your things.'

CHAPTER FOURTEEN

IN A LAND where emotions were considered best contained, it was Layla who broke the rules, for she sobbed loudly as the driver arrived to take Trinity the short distance to the royal jet. 'I will come with you to the plane.'

'We'll say goodbye here,' Trinity said, and hugged her hard. She would miss Layla so much.

She gave a small curtsy to the king, who gave her a brief nod in return, and then she stood before Zahid and did not know how to say goodbye.

'I will see you to the plane.'

This time she did not refuse.

It was a very short drive to the runway, but if it had been a hundred miles it would have gone by too fast for she was saying goodbye not just to Zahid but her baby's father too.

'I am sorry for my behaviour tonight.'

'It was funny really.' Zahid gave a pale smile. 'I'm sure my father has not enjoyed himself so much in years.'

'You're not cross?'

'Temporarily,' Zahid said, 'then you make me laugh.' He was not laughing now and he only ever had with her. 'I apologise for assuming,' Zahid said, as the car pulled up at the plane. 'I assumed this madness was mutual.'

'Madness?'

'That's what it feels like,' Zahid said, and then he looked at her. 'I enjoyed being briefly insane.'

'You can go back to normal now.'

'I can.'

She went to embrace him but Zahid pulled back. He was gone from her now. 'You will have a safe flight.'

'Will?'

'You are on my plane. Do you need anything?'

'No.'

'You have not worked, you gave all your money to Donald.'

'I'll be fine.'

Sometimes the apple did fall far from the tree.

'I don't know what to say,' Zahid said. 'I never expected to be saying goodbye.'

Would she call him? Trinity wondered as she looked into his eyes. Would she tell him from the safety of England?

Would it be cruel to do so?

For now she just needed to leave.

'Look after yourself better,' Zahid said. 'You have every right to stay away from that man.'

Trinity blew out a breath.

If her mother had her way, she'd be seeing Clive tomorrow.

No.

'I'm going to go,' Trinity said.

If she didn't she might just tell Zahid how much she loved him.

* * *

The king watched as his son returned to the palace and he felt a rare prick of guilt when he saw the confusion in Zahid's eyes, for he had not seen that look since Zahid had been seven and the king had lain in a stupor.

'Happy now?' Zahid shot at his father, as he headed up the stairs.

'You will be,' Fahid said. 'It hurts to lose someone you care for.'

'Don't you ever try to give me advice on this.'

'Her behaviour tonight was shocking.'

'Not to me.' Zahid halted on his climb up the stairs and turned. 'She pushes boundaries, she tests you at every turn, she wants to prove she is right in that she cannot trust you. If you knew what she had been through…' Zahid shook his head. He had never wanted less to be a future king. 'I'm going to bed.'

'We will speak in the morning.'

'We will speak when I am ready to,' Zahid said, 'and that might take some time.'

'There are dinners…'

'Cancel them.'

'Zahid.' The king attempted reason. 'Trinity needs to be with her family. It is right she be with them now. Tomorrow they spread the ashes…'

The king was not scared of danger, he had an army of his own and he would happily lead them, but as Zahid descended the stairs he caught a glimpse of fear.

'What did you say?'

'Her mother called. She wants her to join her family to spread the ashes.'

No.

A thousand times no.

Whether she wanted his love or not, he wouldn't let that happen.

'Why wouldn't she tell me that?' Zahid asked himself out loud.

A lie by omission, but still a lie.

He could not believe a single word that came from her mouth, Zahid realised, which meant that saying she did not want to be his bride might also be a lie.

Oh, there was unfinished business between them again and he was not going to wait months or years to address it this time—another sun would not set without this being sorted.

'I am going to England.'

The King stared at him. 'I forbid you.'

'Then I defy you,' Zahid said.

'You cannot defy me.' The king stared at his son but could only admire him.

'You raised me to be strong.'

'You turn your back on our people, our traditions...'

'If I have to, yes.' Zahid nodded. 'Right now, there is someone that I need to be with and I refuse to have her face things alone.'

'You select a bride in a few days...'

'Perhaps I already have.'

'She is not suitable.'

'For who?' Zahid said. 'She is more than suitable for me.'

'You know the rules.'

'Change them,' Zahid challenged. 'Is that not the point of being a king?'

'It is not as simple as that...'

'It's very simple for me,' Zahid said.

'Our people would not welcome her.'

'They would if you did.'

'And if she won't live here?'

'That is something Trinity and I will discuss but without an ancient rule book over our heads. I am going to England now.'

'She has your plane.'

'Then I will take a commercial flight.'

'Your judgment is blinded by lust.'

'No,' Zahid said. 'My judgement is *clarified* by love.'

'A king must first love his country.'

'Don't worry, Father. I will not repeat your mistakes.' Zahid stared his father down, and brought up what must never be discussed. 'Love did not weaken you, Father, it was her death that you could not cope with.' Fahid had not struck his son in decades but his hand was raised now. 'You could not cope,' Zahid said, 'but I did.' He looked at his father who stood with his arm raised. 'I was seven and I coped with the death of my mother. I dealt with your daughter who you could not bear to look at, I fed you with a spoon when you had no will to live.' Zahid understood then his father's fear for his children but it made little sense. 'Would you rather not have chosen her?'

'Of course not.'

'Do you regret a single day spent with your wife?'

'Only her last day,' Fahid admitted. 'I did not understand her pain, I thought it was normal for women to scream when giving birth...'

'So did the doctor,' Zahid challenged his father's guilt. 'And the doula too. You lost the woman you loved through no fault of your own. Well, I refuse to play a part in losing the woman that I love.'

Zahid turned from his father and went to walk out

and to summon his driver, but the king called him back. 'You could have the plane turned around.'

'If Trinity returns to Ishla, it will be of her own accord.'

Fahid gave in then and looked at his son with slightly shocked eyes, for the day had come where his son was stronger and more knowing than he, a day that for any parent was a challenge, especially when you were king.

'Zahid.' The king halted him again. 'There is something that perhaps you should know. Tonight, when Trinity was being inappropriate—'

'I will discuss the behaviour with Trinity, I do not have to discuss it with you. She does not know how to behave on occasion but—'

'Trinity knew exactly what she was doing,' the king interrupted, 'because I asked her to misbehave.'

Zahid frowned.

'I encouraged her poor behaviour. I thought it would be easier on you in the end if you saw just how unsuitable she was.'

'When you say you encouraged, did you and Trinity discuss this?'

'We did.'

'Could I remind you that though you are my father and king—'

'And sick,' the king added hastily, for he could see the muscle leaping in Zahid's cheek and that his fist was clenched.

'Lucky for you!' Zahid retorted, but it strangled near the end and the king did not now fear his son, instead he was devastated for him. For the first time there were tears in Zahid's eyes and that was something Fahid had thought he would never see.

'Take my plane,' the king said, and for the first time since before Annan had died he embraced his son. 'Go to her now.'

CHAPTER FIFTEEN

ZAHID HAD BEEN angry about many things involving Trinity, but he had never been truly angry with her.

That changed as his plane streaked through the sky, trying to make up the hours between them.

Over and over he replayed last night.

The snap of jealousy about his walk with Sameena did not equate with a woman who did not want him.

Little liar, Zahid said to himself.

He should have known when his father had produced champagne that something was going on. And, no, she had not had even two glasses, for he had never met anyone more clumsy than Trinity last night and she had knocked over her glass...

Every detail he replayed and, apart from once, that glass had not touched her lips.

He thought of her cleavage and it had either been one helluva push-up bra or Trinity was pregnant.

Was that why she had run?

Was he so formidable that she could not share the truth?

He was formidable now!

Trinity arrived at Heathrow still dressed in the lilac dress and wearing jewelled slippers, and she startled when she caught her reflection in the mirror as she stepped into the VIP lounge, because what had started to feel normal felt very different here.

Assuming she would be heading for a taxi rank, Trinity soon found out that luxury didn't end at the landing of a royal flight.

A driver was waiting and he asked her where she wanted to go. She asked that he take her the short distance to the airport hotel.

As she went to check in, instead of asking for a shoebox, Trinity splurged and asked for a nice suite as she pulled out her credit card.

Well, not splurged.

She was simply tired of scrimping and foreseeing disaster and crisis when, really, the disasters and crises had not been of her own making.

When she should possibly be feeling at her most vulnerable and weakest, Trinity felt the strongest she ever had.

Things changed today.

Trinity stepped into the shower and decided that if her family wanted her there at such things, there were conditions that needed to be met.

And if they weren't met then her family would not be seeing the child she was carrying.

It was suddenly as simple as that.

Her time with Zahid had made her stronger rather than weaker; his absolute honesty made it easier for Trinity to know her truth.

She was too numb to start mourning their relationship, too focused on getting through today to break down.

She put on the hotel robe and tied a towel round her

head and was just sorting out the black clothes to wear for the spreading of the ashes later in the day when there was a knock at the door.

Assuming it was breakfast or someone to come and check the mini-bar before she let loose on the chocolate, Trinity opened the door without thinking and came face to face with a Zahid she had never seen.

Oh, she'd seen him angry on occasion but not once, despite all her shenanigans, despite all she had done, never, Trinity realised, had his anger been aimed at her.

It was now.

'How did you know where I was?'

She stood back as he marched in and tossed down his case and there was the same start of surprise at the sight of him in robes that Trinity had felt when she'd seen her own reflection in the mirror at Heathrow.

In England she'd only ever seen him in a suit and being terribly polite.

'Did you collude with my father?' He towered over her and she tried to stand her ground.

'I think "collude" is a bit of a strong word...' Trinity attempted.

'Did the two of you decide that you thought you knew what was best for me?'

'No,' Trinity said. 'We thought, or rather I knew, you were struggling...'

'Struggling?' Zahid frowned. 'What do you mean, struggling?'

'With the decision—' his temper wasn't improving, she could hear his angry breathing '—as to my suit-ability, so I thought—'

'You thought you'd make it easier for me?'

'Yes.'

'You thought you'd flirt with my father and pretend to be drunk and that that would improve matters?' Zahid said, and Trinity swallowed. 'You thought you that if you misbehaved I'd decide you were too much trouble?'

'I guess.'

'Why don't we stop guessing?'

'Zahid, the sex is amazing and all that but it's not going to carry us—'

'You think you're so good in bed that you defy my logic?'

'No,' Trinity said. 'Maybe.'

'You think my judgement is skewed?'

'A bit!'

'What, because I don't just say to hell with it, just because I don't decide on a whim to discard everything I have ever believed in, without due thought, you assume I am struggling.'

No, but she could not tell him that without revealing her truth.

She just didn't know how to tell him.

'Is there anything else you haven't told me?'

'No.'

'Are you sure about that?'

'Completely.'

Zahid picked up her black clothes. 'Where are you off to today?'

'I haven't made up my mind.'

'Do you want to be my bride?'

'No.'

'I'll take that as a yes,' Zahid said, 'because not one honest word has come from your lips since last night. Do you love me?'

'Is it a yes-or-no answer only?'

'Trinity!'

'Yes.' Trinity smiled. 'Yes, Zahid, I love you, but given I'm clearly a compulsive liar...'

She did the wrong thing. Trinity started to laugh at her own joke. 'Zahid,' she yelped, 'what are you—?'

She never got to finish.

Trinity had been tipped over his shoulder once before but it was different this time, she was being tipped over his knee.

'What I should have done a long time ago,' Zahid said. 'Three times I have come back for you and still you doubt me. I tell you this much! I put up with your drama and your carry-on.' His hand came down on her bottom through the thick dressing gown and Trinity shrieked, her hands moving to cover her bottom, but he brushed them away and gave her another slap.

'You do not make decisions about us without speaking with me.' His hand came down again and the wad of material was a hindrance so he ruched it up and brought his hand down on her bare pink cheeks. It stung, it hurt, but the passion that came with the delivery felt delicious to Trinity as he slapped her again.

'You do not lie to me,' he said, as his hand went to come down again and then stilled. Zahid halted, barely able to breathe as he looked down at her red bottom and realised for the first time he was out of control. 'Trinity...' His hand was in mid-air and he waited for her to shout, to tell him what a sick bastard he was, and then he heard her voice.

'One more, Captain.'

He rarely laughed and he'd never thought he'd be

laughing this morning. He was angry, though, still angry as he tipped her off his knee and onto the bed.

'I nearly came,' Trinity said. She was lying there, smiling up at him, watching as he stripped, and nothing was going to tame her and nothing could in this moment tame him.

'You are impossible,' he said to a very over-excited Trinity.

'You chose impossible,' Trinity said. 'Can we talk about this later?'

It wouldn't be much later for he was over her, and he did not need to part her legs for they wrapped around his hips in glee as his mouth crushed hers.

'The last one was true,' Trinity said, as he bucked inside her.

'I know.'

'How?' she begged as he as he thrust deeper. 'How do you know I love you?'

'Because...' His words halted as the sob from Trinity and the throb of her around him told him she might not hear his words, but he said them anyway. 'Because of this.' His answer released into her and it really was a simple as that, for with no one, ever, could it be so lovely. Only Zahid could right a million wrongs.

'Never leave me,' Trinity said, as he collapsed onto her.

'I never will.'

'I'll get things wrong.'

'Oh, I am sure you will.'

'Your father...'

'I have dealt with him,' Zahid said. 'You did not have to run away. Whatever our problems, we can work them out.'

Her eyes filled with tears because the reason that she had run was coming back to Trinity now; the reason for her terror was a secret she could no longer keep.

'Is there anything you are keeping from me?' Zahid said, only very gently this time.

'Yes.'

Finally, Zahid thought, the truth.

'I know you said it must never happen, I know I promised it wouldn't…' She could barely get the words out. 'I'm pregnant.'

She waited for anger, a slap even, just as her mother had, but instead Zahid pulled her tighter in his arms.

'That is why you left?'

Trinity nodded.

'You felt you could not tell me?' Zahid looked at her and how he rued that stupid slit-throat gesture he had made that day, given all that she had been through, and he answered for her. 'Of course you thought you couldn't.'

'You're not cross.'

'I'm thrilled.'

Trinity wasn't particularly used to anyone she loved being thrilled by her *mistakes*.

'I am sad that you could not come and tell me but I understand why.'

'Your father asked if I was trying to trap you,' Trinity explained. 'He saw us leaving the second palace.'

'You got one of his pep talks!' Zahid rolled his eyes. 'Do I look trapped?'

Trinity shook her head. 'I asked Layla about unplanned pregnancies and she said it could never happen…'

'Layla has never been out of Ishla. Layla believes

everything that is told to her simply because she does not know any different. My father wraps her in cotton wool and terrifies her with tales in the hope she will be too scared to ever make a mistake.' Zahid looked at her. 'How many times do I have to tell you that you can come to me?'

'I know,' Trinity said. 'I was just too scared to in this.'

'Never be scared to come to me.'

She looked at Zahid and knew she would never be scared again.

'I want you as my wife,' Zahid said. 'The decision is actually a very easy one, yet I have forced myself to question it many times. I never wanted love, I thought it had destroyed my father, but I was wrong.' He tried to explain better. 'I love my country, I wanted a clear head to rule it, yet my head has never been clearer than it is now. You distract me in a way that is good. It makes me want change, to tackle issues that are difficult, to rule not just with my head but with my heart.'

'What will the people say about the baby?'

'Most will be thrilled, some will say we bring disgrace, others will know we are not so different from their own families...' He smiled at Trinity. 'Controversy is good,' Zahid said. 'It allows for discussion and I think you are going to be a very controversial queen but a very good one.'

'What will your father say?'

'I have been spending too much time with you because suddenly I have the strange compulsion to lie.' He looked at her. 'Shall we tell him after the wedding? Would that make things easier for you?'

'It would.'

'What else are you scared of? What else do you think you can't discuss with me?'

'Nothing.'

'You're sure?'

Honesty had never been on Trinity's agenda. The way she had been brought up had been about smoothing over the bumps with lies, ignoring problems in the hope they would disappear, not sharing the scary, shameful parts.

It was time to change.

'I love my family.' She didn't know how best to describe it. 'They've lost their son, I don't want them to feel that they've lost their daughter too. I can't turn my back on them and I will go to family events.'

'Of course,' Zahid said, 'so what is worrying you?'

'You,' Trinity admitted. 'That you'll cause a scene, say something…'

'It is beyond unfair of your parents to expect you to see this man.'

Trinity looked at him and, yes, at times she was grateful for his excellent self-control and knew he was exerting it now.

'I'd already decided that,' Trinity admitted. 'I was going to ring them and tell them that if they wanted me there today then he wasn't to be.'

'Was?'

'I think we should just get through today and then I'll…' she screwed her eyes closed. 'I don't know what I want.'

'Maybe you need to tell him face to face that you don't want him around,' Zahid said, for clearly she could not rely on her parents to defend her as parents should.

He looked at her as she spoke.

'I don't ever want to speak to him.'

'Are you sure?' Zahid said, 'because I will deal with it if that is what you want.'

'That's not what I want.' She looked back at a very pensive Zahid and, no, she could not put him through this for the rest of their lives, could not ask him to attend functions and stand idly by.

'You don't have to be drunk to take to the microphone,' Zahid said.

'I wasn't drunk that night.'

He smiled in dispute.

'A bit maybe,' Trinity admitted.

'Well, you don't have to be to say what is on your mind.'

'If I do say something…'

'I'll be there.'

'I'd prefer you wait here at the hotel.'

Zahid shook his head.

'In the car, then.'

'No,' Zahid said. 'You are not facing this without me.'

'So, on top of everything else, I have to worry about you losing your head…'

'I won't lose my head,' Zahid said. 'You have my word.'

If ever she was grateful for Zahid's self-control it was today. It made Trinity strong when she questioned her own, it kept her calm enough to face what she had been unable to before.

Zahid dressed in an immaculate suit and Trinity had on her funeral clothes, but they were facing a difficult day together this time.

Zahid waved away his driver, for he could see she

felt awkward enough, and he drove them himself. As he did, Trinity mind flitted to anything other than what lay ahead.

'Poor Sameena…' She turned in sudden anguish. 'What will happen to the two countries?'

'A war perhaps,' Zahid said, then he stopped teasing her. 'Had you not decided to escape you would have found out that Sameena and I had a very polite conversation.'

'In the garden?'

Zahid nodded. 'Soon Sameena will be Queen and she looks forward to happy relations between our countries, whatever my choice. It was a very discreet conversation but reading between the lines she was asking me not to choose her.'

'She rejected you!' Trinity beamed.

'You're going to get so much mileage out of that,' Zahid sighed.

'I am,' Trinity said, and then stopped smiling, for Zahid was pulling up at the river that had been chosen for the occasion. It was a place the family had gone for drives to at times and where Donald had proposed to Yvette.

'Ready?' Zahid checked, and Trinity nodded.

'You can do this.'

'I don't think Yvette knows…'

'Well, let her find out,' Zahid said. 'Maybe some honesty will allow her to speak more openly about what she has been through. Her baby and ours are going to be cousins. Don't you want them to be close?'

'I do.'

'Lies haven't worked for a long time,' Zahid said. 'Maybe you could try the truth.'

'You promise that you won't—'

'I will not lose my head.'

He took her hand and they walked over to the small gathering, but as he went to give her hand a squeeze to offer support her fingers slipped away from his grasp, just not in the way they had on that awful night all those years ago. Instead of reaching out in fear to Zahid, it was an assertive Trinity who walked towards the small crowd.

'What's he doing here?' Trinity asked, pointing her finger at Clive. 'Why on earth would you ask the man who attacked your seventeen-year-old daughter to be here on this day?'

'Trinity!' Dianne said. 'Not now.'

'When, then?'

'Trinity,' Dianne said in low tones as Gus tried to hush her, but finally Trinity refused to be hushed.

'Why are we whispering?' Trinity said. 'I mean it, I want to remember my brother today. I want to think about Donald instead of remembering what this sleaze did to me that night.' She looked at Clive and she saw not a strong, angry man but the pathetic, weak creep that he was. 'I don't ever want to see you again and if I do, I'll be going to the police. And I don't give a damn what it will do to my family, or to your reputation, because I know what you did to me and I'm more than prepared to say it in court.'

'Come on, Clive.' Elaine started to walk off. 'She was always trouble,' she shouted over her shoulder, 'always making stuff up.'

'For God's sake, Trinity,' Gus boomed, 'it's your brother's…'

'I just want to say one thing.' Zahid's deep voice

was out of place with the shouting but even Trinity shivered at the sinister calm of his voice. 'I promised Trinity that I would not lose my head today and I shall keep my word.' He might be in Western clothes but he was a dangerous desert warrior and had she been on the end of his look that was aimed at Clive, Trinity would have run for her life. 'If my gaze ever falls on you again then know I shall keep my word to Trinity and not lose my head, because I won't need to. I will kill you in cold blood.'

'He doesn't mean it…' Dianne's smile was frantic but Zahid's cool disdain met her now.

'You can test the theory if you choose but, I tell you once, my people would expect nothing less from their future king.'

He watched every step that Clive took as he walked off and it was at the right moment that Trinity took his hand because the master of self-control was waning as Clive took one final look around. Trinity felt the zip of tension in Zahid, knew that at any second he'd change his mind and bolt after him, and perhaps Clive sensed it too for he ran the last of the distance to the car and Zahid turned and looked at Dianne.

'I do mean it.' He put his arm around Trinity and they walked down to the river.

It was nice to be able to focus on her brother today, nice to recall the good times with Zahid by her side, and it was actually, for the first time, nice to step into her home.

'Why has Zahid asked to speak alone with your father?' Dianne asked.

'You'll find out soon.'

'Should I check if there's champagne in the fridge?'

'Zahid doesn't drink,' Trinity said, and then smiled at her mum. 'And there's always champagne in the fridge.'

'I'm sorry, Trinity.'

From out of the blue they came—the words she'd never thought she'd hear.

'Thank you.'

'Can we start again?' Dianne asked.

'I think we have to.'

They did start again, right from square one, because after a quiet celebration where they shared the news that they would be married soon, it was not long before Trinity yawned and said she wanted to go to bed.

'Perhaps set up...' Dianne's voice broke off.

'Zahid will sleep with me,' Trinity said, 'or we can go back to the hotel.'

Zahid did not correct Trinity, for to hell with politeness, he would never set foot in the guest room.

He wished them goodnight and they headed to her single bed.

'What did she say?' Zahid smiled as they huddled in the darkness. 'When you started laughing in the kitchen?'

'It was wrong,' Trinity blushed. 'I can't tell you.'

'You can.'

'Okay.' Trinity took a big breath. 'Mum said that when your father dies, will she have a title?'

'She wants a title?'

'She's wants to be the Queen Mother.'

He laughed.

It was rare, it was deep and it thrilled her right down to her bones, and there would be so much more of it, Trinity would make sure of that.

'How could I have ever thought you boring?' Trinity sighed.

'Another thing you haven't told me,' Zahid said. 'When did you think I was boring?'

'For years,' Trinity said. 'Till you took me in your arms.'

EPILOGUE

'WHERE'S TRINITY?'

Zahid heard the whisper from Dianne as he stood in the palace gardens, waiting for his bride to arrive, and, yes, she was more than fashionably late.

Zahid stared ahead. He was dressed in military ceremonials with a red and white *kafiya* tied with gold braid, which indicated he was the groom. His concern was not that Trinity might have changed her mind, his concern was for all she faced not just today but in the two days preceding the wedding.

He stood with his back rigid, feeling all the eyes of the guests on him. It was forbidden that they see each other in the lead-up to the wedding. Tradition did not take into account that the news of the future princess's pregnancy might have broken forty-eight hours before the wedding service.

Tonight they would be in the desert, Zahid thought.

Tonight, whatever the people's reaction to Trinity, he could put her mind at ease and then, in a week's time, they were heading overseas.

As the guests coughed anxiously Zahid actually managed a smile. He had asked Trinity where she would like to go for her honeymoon and, even though they were getting on much better, her answer had been as far away from her parents as possible, so they were heading for Australia. He simply couldn't wait to get away with his bride. The only teeny fly in the ointment was that he had promised that Layla could join them for a week.

Love had been the furthest thing from his mind when he had agreed to that.

It was the closest thing now.

He had watched his father's skin pale when the scandalous news had first hit and, no, when the king had called for him, Zahid had not denied it.

As strong as he was, guilt had washed over him as he'd seen his father, so old and so thin, struggle to take in the latest change.

'I am sorry if you feel I have let down you and my mother's memory.'

'Your mother was as vague as your sister now is,' the king sighed. 'I went through the mandoos last night and I thought how she would be with the news. I held her favourite amulet and I just knew that she would have been delighted.'

Fahid called in Abdul, who immediately said he would issue the strongest denial.

'You shall neither confirm or deny,' the king said, and Zahid watched as Abdul's face paled when he realised the rumour was true, and then the king said the strangest thing to Zahid.

Words he could not wait to share with Trinity.

Yet he had not been able to get to her yet.

'I am so excited.' Layla's endless chatter did nothing to ease Trinity's nerves. 'You don't mind me coming to Australia with you?'

'Of course not.'

'I'm only there for a week…'

'It will be wonderful,' Trinity said, but she could not focus on Layla's conversation or the maids who were doing her hair. Outside the crowd was building and they stood silent, awaiting the news of the formal union.

Layla's chatter was not selfish. She was trying to take Trinity's mind off her pregnancy being referred to as a scandal in some of the papers and that Ishla was alight not just with wedding preparations but with the news that Zahid's bride might already be with child.

At the time she needed to speak with Zahid most, to finally lean on someone she trusted, it was denied.

'Have you seen your father today?'

'No,' Layla said. 'The men's and women's celebrations are kept separate.'

'You must have heard something.'

Layla went a little bit pink. She still felt guilty and a little embarrassed by her naïve reaction when Trinity had clearly needed her advice. Obviously this birth control thing Trinity had spoke of did not work!

'Only what I told you. Zahid asked one of the maids to pass on that you were not to be concerned, to just enjoy the celebrations and that you would be together soon.'

Trinity knew that Zahid would be there for her and no doubt he would already have discussed the revelation with the king. Zahid's rapid departure from Ishla had been noted and there had been an image of them coming out a famous obstetrician's office. As well as that, despite a hastily arranged wedding, despite the gold gown she was wearing, given that it was her second pregnancy, Trinity was already starting to show.

Only it wasn't the king's reaction that worried her, or the damage to Zahid. It was the how the people would respond that gnawed at Trinity. Their reaction mattered, not because it changed the outcome but because it might change how Trinity felt towards them. She had already had one pregnancy steeped in shame, she refused to let this be another.

'You look beautiful,' Layla said, as Trinity stood to have her headwear arranged.

'Thank you.'

'We need to go,' Layla said. 'You are already late.'

'I'll just be a moment.'

Trinity had been raised to care only what others thought, and what others thought mattered terribly now.

No, it didn't.

Trinity knew that their baby had been conceived in love, knew that Zahid and she were meant to be together. Since that night in the woods their love had waited patiently till the time had been right, and she had to trust the timing of their baby had been chosen too.

Trinity peeked out at the silent crowd, who gave no indication as to their response to her.

She would find that out on the balcony.

Right now she had a wedding to attend and she wanted to be there.

Zahid turned as she arrived and it was not the Trinity he had been expecting. Instead of being wary and truculent, her eyes shone with confidence and as her eyes met his her cheeks infused with pink as they did whenever she saw him.

And, yes, the papers would confirm that the rumours were surely right, for the soft breeze pushed the fabric of her dress and there was the curve of her stomach.

Zahid smiled, and, just as she had been at Donald's wedding, so lost was she that she did as her body instructed and walked to be by his side.

'You look amazing.'

'Thank you.'

He had expected a hurried question, to ask if all was well.

It was.

Whatever the ramifications, they would face them together.

The service was quick, given that it was held in the fierce midday sun, but the part she would always remember best was after Zahid made his vows and then offered her a bracelet that had an Arabic saying engraved in English.

'I mean it,' he said as she read what was inscribed inside.

What is coming is better than what is gone.

With Zahid it was always better, Trinity knew.

There was no kissing his bride. Instead, he took her hand and led her back to the palace.

Trinity smiled at her parents and at Yvette, who was a few months ahead of Trinity in her pregnancy.

They were friends now and, as Zahid had pointed out, their children would be cousins.

She would be taken care of too.

There was Princess Sameena, who curtsied to the new princess as her parents stood severely at her side, and they shared a small smile, for the future of both their countries was so bright.

The rest of the guests followed them and still Trinity did not ask his father's reaction to the news.

'We meet the people now,' Zahid said, and squeezed

her hand. The memory of Trinity scowling at the camera did not make him smile now. He was, not that he could show it, worried by the reception from the people. He did not want their wedding day to be one where he asked her to force a smile. 'It won't take long.' Zahid cleared his throat. 'If they are a little hesitant, know that soon they will take to the news…' He frowned as she simply nodded and Zahid actually wondered if she had been shielded from the scandal that had hit Ishla. 'They may—'

'Zahid,' Trinity said, 'I'm not going to apologise or be ashamed.'

'Good.'

As the balcony doors opened and they went to step out, they were halted, as instead of the happy couple leading the way King Fahid did instead.

Zahid blinked.

His father had at that meeting reminded his son that he was still king and that he would sort it.

Zahid had wondered how.

Now he knew, for Fahid walked out onto the balcony to the surprise of the people and met them with a smile they had not seen on his face since before Princess Layla had been born.

He held out an arm and welcomed the couple.

'He welcomed the news,' Zahid said, and Trinity swallowed.

'Really?'

'It took only an hour for him to say that he could not be happier. He does not have much time and this way he gets to meet our child…'

With the king's clear blessing, as the happy couple stepped onto the balcony they were met with cheers and waves. The silence had been broken for things that had never been discussed in Ishla were being talked about now.

How, Trinity wondered, as Zahid now kissed his bride, could she rue the years that had been wasted?

Time knew best.

They were together now.

* * * * *

MILLS & BOON®

Why shop at millsandboon.co.uk?

Each year, thousands of romance readers
find their perfect read at millsandboon.co.uk.
That's because we're passionate about
bringing you the very best romantic fiction.
Here are some of the advantages of
shopping at www.millsandboon.co.uk:

* **Get new books first**—you'll be able to buy
  your favourite books one month before they
  hit the shops

* **Get exclusive discounts**—you'll also be
  able to buy our specially created monthly
  collections, with up to 50% off the RRP

* **Find your favourite authors**—latest news,
  interviews and new releases for all your
  favourite authors and series on our website,
  plus ideas for what to try next

* **Join in**—once you've bought your favourite
  books, don't forget to register with us to rate,
  review and join in the discussions

Visit **www.millsandboon.co.uk**
for all this and more today!